OUTSTANDING PRAISE FOR
SHERRILYN KENYON AND HER NOVELS

"A perfect ten!"

—*Rendezvous* on *Night Pleasures*

"By turns funny and touching . . . a compelling story that will make you laugh out loud. The gods haven't had this much fun since Xena!"

—Susan Krinard, author of
Secret of the Wolf on *Night Pleasures*

"Sherrilyn Kenyon's imagination is as bright as her future."

—Teresa Medeiros, author of
A Kiss to Remember on *Night Pleasures*

"Fabulous . . . one series that belongs on the keeper shelf."

—readertoreader.com on *Night Pleasures*

"Get out a fan. New Orleans is hot and steamy, so is this story."

—*Old Book Barn Gazette* on *Night Pleasures*

"If you love *Buffy the Vampire Slayer* or *Angel*, this is the book for you! Original . . . the characters are unforgettable and the action thrilling."

—romantictimes.com on *Night Pleasures*

St. Martin's Paperbacks Titles
by Sherrilyn Kenyon

Fantasy Lover

Night Pleasures

Night Embrace

DANCE *with the* *Devil*

Sherrilyn Kenyon

St. Martin's Paperbacks

For all my readers—thank you so much for all the e-mails and wonderful support you have shown me and the series, especially the ladies of RBL, Sanctuary and HunterLegends. To Lo, Nick, Tasha and Brynna who keep me sane and who help run the loops and DH bbs. To Janet for the tremendous support you give and work you do. For my husband and boys who are always the highlight of my day and who remind me that happy-ever-afters really can happen. And especially for Kim and Nancy who not only allow me to explore the outer limits of the DH world, but who have also allowed me to share my universe with all of you. God bless and protect you all. Hugs!!

Prologue

Zarek leaned back in his seat as the helicopter took off. He was going home to Alaska.

No doubt he would die there.

If Artemis didn't kill him, he was sure Dionysus would. The god of wine and excess had been most explicit in his displeasure over Zarek's betrayal and in what he intended to do to Zarek as punishment.

For Sunshine Runningwolf's happiness, Zarek had crossed a god who was sure to make him suffer even worse horrors than those in his human past.

Not that he cared. There wasn't much in life or death that Zarek had ever cared about.

He still didn't know why he'd put his ass on the line for Talon and Sunshine, other than the fact that pissing people off was the only thing that truly gave him pleasure.

His gaze fell to his backpack that rested by his feet.

Before he realized what he was doing, he took out the handmade bowl that Sunshine had given him and held it in his hands.

It was the only time in his life anyone had given him anything he didn't have to pay for.

He ran his hands over the intricate designs that Sunshine had carved. She had probably spent hours on this bowl.

Caressed it with loving hands . . .

"They waste their time over a rag doll and it becomes very important to them; and if anybody takes it away from them, they cry . . ."

The passage from *The Little Prince* ran through his mind. Sunshine had wasted much of her time on this and given him her hard work for no apparent reason. She probably had no idea just how much her simple gift had touched him.

"You really are pathetic," he breathed, clutching the bowl in his hands as he curled his lip in repugnance. "It meant nothing to her, and for a worthless piece of clay you just consigned yourself to eternal death."

Closing his eyes, he swallowed.

It was true.

One more time, he was going to die for nothing.

"So what?"

Let him die. What did it matter?

If they didn't kill him on the trip in, he'd go out with a good fight, and good fights were all too few and too far between in Alaska.

He looked forward to the challenge.

Angry at himself and the world at large, Zarek splintered the bowl with his thoughts, then brushed the dust off his pants.

Pulling out his MP3 player, he scrolled to Nazareth's *Hair of the Dog,* put his headphones on, and waited for Mike to lighten the windows of the helicopter and let the lethal sunlight in on him.

It was, after all, what Dionysus had paid the Squire to do, and if the man had a lick of sense he would obey it because if Mike didn't, he was going to wish he had.

Chapter 1

Acheron Parthenopaeus was a man of many secrets and powers. As the firstborn Dark-Hunter and leader of their kind, he had set himself up over nine thousand years ago to be the buffer between them and Artemis, the goddess of the hunt, who had created them.

It was a job he seldom relished and a position he'd always hated. Like an errant child, Artemis loved nothing more than to push him just to see how far she could go before he called her down.

Theirs was a complicated relationship that hinged on a balance of power. He alone possessed the ability to keep her calm and rational.

At least most of the time.

Meanwhile she held the one source of food that he needed to stay human. Compassionate.

Without her, he would become a soulless killer even worse than the Daimons who preyed on humankind.

Without him, she would have no heart or conscience.

On Mardi Gras night, he'd bargained with her to exchange two weeks of his servitude so that she would release Talon's soul and allow the Dark-Hunter to leave their service and spend his immortality with the woman he loved.

Talon was liberated from hunting vampires and other demonic creatures who stalked the earth looking for hapless victims.

Now Ash was restricted from using most of his powers while he was locked inside Artemis's temple where he had to rely on her whims to keep him informed about the progress of Zarek's hunt.

He knew the betrayal Zarek felt and it gnawed at him. Better than anyone, he understood what it meant to be left completely alone, to survive on instinct and to have only enemies around him.

Ash couldn't stand the thought of one of his men feeling like that.

"I want you to call off Thanatos," Ash said as he sat on the marble floor at Artemis's feet. She lay across her ivory-colored throne that had always reminded him of an over-stuffed chaise lounge. It was decadent and soft, a pure study in hedonistic delight.

Artemis was nothing if not a creature of comfort.

She smiled languidly as she rolled over onto her back. Her white, gauzy peplos displayed more of her body than it covered, and as she moved, her entire lower half was bared to him.

Uninterested, he lifted his gaze to hers.

She trailed a hot, lustful glance over his body, which was bare except for a pair of tight black leather pants. Satisfaction gleamed in her bright green eyes as she toyed with a strand of his long blond hair, which covered the bite wound on his neck.

She was well fed and content to be with him.

He was neither.

"You're still weak, Acheron," she said quietly, "and in no position to make demands on me. Besides, your two weeks with me have only begun. Where is the subjugation you promised?"

Ash rose up slowly to tower over her. He braced his arms

on each side of her and lowered himself until their noses were almost touching. Her eyes widened a degree, just enough to let him know that in spite of her words, she knew which of them was the more powerful, even while weakened. "Call off your pet, Artie. I mean it. I told you long ago that there was no need for a Thanatos to stalk my Hunters and I'm tired of this game you play. I want him caged."

"No," she said in a tone that was almost petulant. "Zarek is to die. End of symphony. The moment his picture became the nightly news event while he was killing Daimons, he exposed all the Dark-Hunters to danger. We can't afford to let the human authorities ever learn about them. If they ever find Zarek—"

"Who's going to find him? He's locked in the middle of nowhere per your cruelty."

"I didn't put him there, *you* did. I wanted him killed and you refused. It's all *your* fault he's banished in Alaska so don't blame me."

Ash curled his lip. "I'm not about to put a man to death because you and your siblings were playing with his life."

He wanted another fate for Zarek. But so far, none of the gods nor Zarek had cooperated.

Damn free will, anyway. It got all of them into more trouble than any of them needed.

She narrowed her eyes at him. "Why do you care so much, Acheron? I'm beginning to feel jealous of this Dark-Hunter and the *love* you have for him."

Ash pushed himself away from her. She made his concern for one of his men sound obscene.

Of course, she was good at that.

What he felt for Zarek was kindred brotherhood. Better than anyone, he understood the man's motivation. Knew why Zarek struck out in anger and frustration.

There were only so many kicks a dog could take before it turned vicious.

He, himself, was so close to turning that he couldn't fault Zarek for the fact he had gone rabid centuries before.

Even so, he couldn't let Zarek die. Not like this. Not over something that hadn't been Zarek's fault. The incident in the New Orleans alley where Zarek had attacked the human cops had been set up by Dionysus for no other reason than to expose Zarek to the humans and to cause Artemis to call out a blood hunt for the man's life.

If Thanatos or the Squires killed Zarek, then Zarek would become a bodiless Shade who was doomed to walk the earth for eternity. Forever hungry and suffering.

Forever in pain.

Ash winced at the memory.

Unable to stand the thought of it, he headed for the door.

"Where are you going?" Artemis asked.

"To find Themis and undo what you've started."

Artemis suddenly appeared in front of him, blocking his way to the door. "You're not going anywhere."

"Then call off your dog."

"No."

"Fine." Ash looked down his right arm at the she-dragon tattoo that ran from his shoulder to his wrist. "Simi," he commanded. "Take human form."

The dragon lifted itself from his skin, shifted its shape into that of a young demonic woman, no taller than three feet. She hovered effortlessly to his right.

In this incarnation, her wings were dark blue and black, even though she usually preferred burgundy for them. The darker color of the wings combined with the color of her eyes told him just how unhappy Simi was to find herself here on Olympus.

Her eyes were white, rimmed in red, and her long yellow-blond hair floated around her. She had black horns that were more beautiful than sinister and long pointed ears. Her flowing red dress wrapped around her lithe, muscular body, which she could mold into any size from one inch to eight feet tall in human form or as large as eighty feet as a dragon.

"No!" Artemis said, trying to use her powers to contain the Charonte demon. It didn't faze Simi, who could only be summoned or controlled by Ash or his mother.

"Whatcha want, *akri*?" Simi asked Ash.

"Kill Thanatos."

Simi flashed her fangs as she rubbed her hands together gleefully and cast an evil smirk at Artemis. "Oh, goodie! I get to make the redheaded goddess mad!"

Artemis looked desperately at Ash. "Put it back on your arm."

"Forget it, Artemis. You're not the only one who can command a killer. Personally, I think it would be interesting to see just how long your Thanatos would last against my Simi."

Artemis's face paled.

"He won't last long, *akri*," Simi said to Ash, using the Atlantean term for "lord and master." Her voice was quiet but powerful and had a singsongy quality that was quite musical in tone. "Thanatos is barbecue." She smiled at Artemis. "And I like my barbecue. Just tell me how you want him, *akri*, normal recipe or extra crispy. I'm partial to extra crispy myself. They crunch louder when deep-fried. Reminds me, I need some bread crumbs."

Artemis swallowed audibly. "You can't send it after him. It's uncontrollable without you."

"She does only what I tell her to do."

"That thing is a menace, with or without you. Zeus forbid it should ever go out into the human world alone."

Ash scoffed at that. "She's less a menace than you are and she goes out all the time on her own."

"I can't believe you'd unleash it so carelessly. What are you thinking?"

While they argued, Simi floated around the room, making

a list in a small leather-bound book. "Ooo, let's see, I need to get my spicy barbecue sauce. Definitely some oven mitts, 'cause he's gonna be hot from being flame-broiled. I need to get a couple of them apple trees to make wood chips so the meat be nice and appley tasting. Give it that extra yummi-ness, 'cause I don't like that Daimon flavor. Ack!"

"What's it doing?" Artemis asked as she realized Simi was talking to herself.

"She's making a list of what she needs to kill Thanatos."

"It sounds like it's going to eat him."

"Probably."

Artemis's eyes narrowed. "It can't eat him. I forbid it."

Ash gave a sinister half-laugh. "She can do as she pleases. I taught her to waste not, want not."

Simi paused and lifted her head up from her list to snort at Artemis. "The Simi is very environmentally sound. Eat every-thing except for hooves. I don't like those, they hurt my teeth." She looked at Ash. "Thanatos don't have hooves, do he?"

"No, Simi, he doesn't."

Simi gave a happy cry. "Ooo, good eating tonight. I get a Daimon for barbecue. Can I go now, *akri*? Can I? Can I? Can I, please?" Simi danced around like a small, happy child at a birthday party.

Ash stared at Artemis. "It's entirely up to you, Artie. He lives or dies by your word."

"No, *akri*!" Simi whined after a brief, stunned pause. She sounded as if she were in pain. "Don't ask her that. She never let me have no fun. She a mean goddess!"

Ash knew how much Artemis hated it when he won an argument with her. Her eyes smoldered with barely leashed fury. "What do you want me to do?"

"You say Zarek is unfit to live, that he poses a threat to others. All I ask is that you have Themis judge him. If her judge finds that Zarek is a danger to those around him, then I will send Simi after him myself to end his life."

Simi bared her fangs at Artemis as they exchanged venomous sneers.

Finally, Artemis looked back at him. "Very well, but I don't trust your demon. I will have Thanatos stand down, but after Zarek is judged guilty, I will send Thanatos in to finish him."

"Simi," Ash said to his Charonte companion. "Return to me."

She looked disgusted by the mere thought. " 'Return to me, Simi,' " Simi mocked as she shifted forms. "Don't go frying the goddess. Don't go frying Thanatos." She made a strange horselike snort. "I am not a yo-yo, *akri*. I am a Simi. I hate it when you get me all excited about going to kill something and then tell me no. I don't like that. It boring. You don't ever let me have any fun anymore."

"Simi," he said, stressing her name.

The demon pouted and then flew to the left side of his body and returned to his arm in the shape of a stylized bird on his biceps.

Ash rubbed his hand over the small burn there that he always felt whenever Simi left or returned to his skin.

Artemis stared with malice at Simi's new form. Then, she stepped around him and leaned against his back as she brushed one hand over Simi's image. "One day I'm going to find a way to rid you of that beast resting on your arm."

"Sure you will," he said, forcing himself to endure Artemis's touch as she breathed across his skin while she leaned against his back. It was something Ash had never been able to tolerate with ease, and it was something she knew he hated.

He looked at her over his shoulder. "And one day I'm going to find a way to rid myself of the beast resting on my back."

Astrid sat alone in her atrium reading her favorite book, *The Little Prince* by Antoine de Saint-Exupéry. No matter how many times she read it, she always found something new in it.

And today she needed to find something good. Something to remind her that there was beauty in the world. Innocence. Joy. Happiness.

Most of all, she wanted to find hope.

A soft gentle breeze floated off the lilac-scented river, through the marble Doric columns and across the white wicker chaise where she sat. Her three sisters had been here for a little while, but she had sent them away.

Not even they could comfort her.

Tired and disillusioned, she had sought solace in her book. In it, she saw goodness, a goodness that was missing in the people she'd known in her life.

Was there no decency? No kindness?

Had humanity finally managed to destroy both?

Her sisters, as much as she loved them, were as ruthless as anyone else. They were completely indifferent to the pleadings and suffering of anyone not related to them.

Nothing touched any of them anymore.

Astrid couldn't remember the last time she had cried. The last time she had laughed.

She was numb now.

Numbness was the curse of her kind. Her sister Atty had warned her long ago that if she chose to be a judge this day would come.

Young, vain, and stupid, Astrid had foolishly ignored the warning, thinking it could never happen to her.

She would never be indifferent to people or their pain.

Yet now it was only her books that brought her the emotions of others. Even though she couldn't really "feel" them, the unreal and muted emotions of the characters comforted her on some level.

And if she were capable of it, that would make her weep.

Astrid heard someone approaching her from behind. Not

wanting anyone to see what she was reading lest they ask her why, and she be forced to admit she'd lost her compassion, Astrid tucked it beneath the chair's cushion. She turned to see her mother crossing the well-manicured lawn where a small group of three dappled fawns grazed.

Her mother wasn't alone.

Artemis and Acheron were with her.

Her mother's long red hair was left to curl becomingly around a face that looked no older than thirty. Themis wore a tailored short-sleeved blue shirt and khaki slacks.

No one would ever take her for the Greek goddess of justice.

Artemis was dressed in a classical Greek peplos while Acheron wore his typical black leather pants and a black T-shirt. His long blond hair was loose around his shoulders.

A chill went down her spine, but then, it always did whenever Acheron came near. There was something about him that was compelling and irresistible.

It was also terrifying.

She'd never known anyone like him. He was alluring in a way that defied her best abilities to explain. It was as if his very presence filled everyone with a desire so potent that it was hard to look at him without wanting to rip his clothes off, throw him to the ground, and make love to him for untold centuries.

But there was more to him than his sexual appeal. There was also something ancient and primal. Something so powerful that even the gods feared him.

You could even see that fear in Artemis's eyes as she walked beside him.

No one knew what the relationship was between the two of them. They never touched each other, seldom did they look at each other. And yet Acheron came often to see Artemis in her temple.

When Astrid had been a child, he used to come and visit

with her, too. Play games with her and teach her how to manage her very limited powers. He'd brought her countless books both from the past and from the future.

In fact, it was Acheron who had given her *The Little Prince*.

Those visits had all but ended the day she hit puberty and had realized just how desirable a man Acheron was. He had pulled away from her then, leaving a tangible wall between them.

"To what do I owe the honor?" Astrid asked as the three of them surrounded her.

"I have a job for you, dearest," her mother said.

Astrid made a pain-filled face. "I thought we agreed that I could take some time off."

"Oh, come on, Astrid," Artemis said. "I need you, little cousin." She cast an evil glare in Acheron's direction. "There's a Dark-Hunter who needs to be put down."

Acheron's face was impassive as he watched Astrid without comment.

Astrid sighed. She didn't want to do this. Too many centuries of judging others had left her emotionally bankrupt. She'd begun to suspect that she was no longer capable of feeling anyone's pain.

Not even her own.

Lack of compassion had ruined her sisters. Now she was afraid it was going to ruin her, as well.

"There are other judges."

Artemis let out a disgusted breath. "I don't trust them. They're bleeding hearts who are just as likely to find him innocent as guilty. I need a hard-nosed, impartial judge who can't be swayed from doing what's right and necessary. I need *you*."

The hairs on the back of her neck rose. Astrid slid her gaze from Artemis to Acheron, who stood with his arms folded over his chest. His gaze unwavering, he watched Astrid with those eerie swirling silver eyes of his.

This wasn't the first time she'd been asked to judge a rogue Dark-Hunter and yet she sensed something different about Acheron today.

"You believe him innocent?" she asked.

Acheron nodded.

"He's not innocent," Artemis sneered. "He'd kill anyone or anything without blinking. He has no morals or concern for anyone other than himself."

Acheron gave Artemis an arch look that said those words reminded him of someone else he knew.

It almost succeeded in bringing a smile to Astrid's lips.

While her mother stayed back a few feet to give them room, Acheron squatted down by Astrid's chaise and met her gaze levelly. "I know you're tired, Astrid. I know you want to quit, but I don't trust anyone else to judge him."

Astrid frowned as he spoke of things she hadn't told anyone else. No one knew she wanted to quit.

Artemis turned a jaundiced gaze to Acheron. "Why are you being so accommodating with my choice of judge? She's never found anyone innocent in all the history of the world."

"I know," he said in that rich, deep voice that was even more seductive than his incredible good looks. "But I trust her to do the right thing."

Artemis narrowed her eyes at him. "What trick have you planned?"

His face was completely impassive as he continued to watch Astrid with an intensity that was unnerving. "Nothing."

Astrid considered taking on the mission only because of Acheron. He'd never asked anything of her before and she remembered well just how many times he had comforted her when she'd been a child. He'd been like a father and a big brother to her.

"How long do I have to stay?" she asked them. "If I go in and the Dark-Hunter is beyond redemption, can I pull out immediately?"

"Yes," Artemis said. "In fact, the sooner you judge him guilty the better for all of us."

Astrid turned to the man beside her. "Acheron?"

He nodded in agreement. "I will abide by what you decide."

Artemis beamed. "We have our pact then, Acheron. I have given you a judge."

A small smile played at the edges of Acheron's lips. "You have, indeed."

Artemis looked suddenly nervous. She glanced from Acheron to Astrid, then back again. "What do you know that I don't?" she asked him.

Those pale, swirling eyes cut through Astrid as Acheron said quietly, "I know that Astrid holds a deep truth inside her."

Artemis put her hands on her hips. "And that is?"

" 'It is only with the heart that one can rightly see. What is essential is invisible to the eye.' "

Another chill went down Astrid's spine as Acheron quoted the exact line from *The Little Prince* that she had been reading as they approached.

How did he know what she'd been reading?

She glanced down to make sure the book was completely hidden from their view.

It was.

Oh, yeah, Acheron Parthenopaeus was one frightening man.

"You have two weeks, daughter," her mother said quietly. "If it takes you less time, so be it. But at the end of a fortnight, one way or another, Zarek's fate will be sealed by your hand."

Chapter 2

Zarek cursed as the batteries died on his MP3 player. Just his luck.

He was still a good hour away from their landing and the last thing he wanted was to listen to Mike in the helicopter's cockpit moan and complain under his breath about having to chauffeur him back to Alaska. Even though a foot of solid black steel separated Zarek's sunless, lightless compartment from Mike, he could hear through the walls as easily as if Mike were sitting next to him.

Worse, Zarek hated being stuck in the small passenger compartment that seemed to be closing in on him. Every time he moved, he bumped an arm or leg into the wall. But since they had been flying through daylight, it was either the cube or death.

For some reason he still wasn't quite sure of, Zarek had chosen the cube.

He removed the headphones and his ears were immediately assaulted by the rhythmic pounding of the chopper's blades, rushing winter winds, and Mike's current conversation over the static-filled radio.

"So, did you do it?"

Zarek arched a brow at the anxious, unfamiliar male voice.

Ah, the beauty of his powers. He had hearing that would make Superman jealous. And he knew the topic of their discussion . . .

Him.

Or rather his demise.

Mike had been offered a fortune to kill him, and since the moment they had left New Orleans about twelve hours ago, Zarek had been waiting for the middle-aged Squire to either open the sealed windows and expose him to the deadly sunlight or to jettison his compartment and drop him over something that was guaranteed to take the immortality right out of him.

Instead, Mike was dicking around with him and had yet to pull the switch. Not that Zarek cared. He had a few more tricks to teach the Squire if Mike tried anything.

"Nah," Mike said as the chopper dipped without warning sharply to the left again and slammed Zarek into the wall of his compartment. He was beginning to suspect the pilot kept doing that just for shits and giggles.

The helicopter tilted again while Zarek braced himself for it.

"I thought about it, real hard, but you know I figure frying this bastard is way too good for him. I'd rather leave him to the Blood Rite Squires and let them take him out slow and painfully. Personally, I'd like to hear the psycho-dick scream for mercy, especially after what he did to those poor, innocent cops."

The muscle in Zarek's jaw started to tic in time to his rapid, angry heartbeat as he listened. Yeah, those cops had been real innocent, all right. If Zarek had been mortal, the beating they gave him would have either killed him or he'd be lying in a coma right now.

The voice spoke over the radio again. "I heard from the Oracles that Artemis will pay double to the Squire who kills him. You put that on top of what Dionysus was going to pay you for killing him and I personally think you're a fool to pass on it."

"No doubt, but I have enough money to pacify me. Besides, I'm the one who's had to tolerate the dick's attitude and sneers. He thinks he's such a badass. I want to see them take him down a notch before they cut his head off."

Zarek rolled his eyes at Mike's words. He didn't give a rat's ass what the man thought of him.

He'd learned a long time ago that there was no use in trying to reach out to people.

All it did was get him slapped.

He tucked his MP3 player back into his black duffel bag and grimaced as his knee connected roughly against the wall. Gods, get him out of this tight, cramped place. It felt like being in a sarcophagus.

"I'm surprised the Council didn't activate Nick's Blood Rite status for this hunt," the other voice said. "Since he spent the last week with Zarek, I would think he would be a natural for it."

Mike snorted. "They tried, but Gautier refused."

"Why?"

"I have no idea. You know how Gautier is. He doesn't take orders very well. Makes me wonder why they ever initiated him into Squirehood to begin with. I can't imagine any Dark-Hunter other than Acheron or Kyrian who could put up with his mouth."

"Yeah, he is a smart-ass. And speaking of, my Dark-Hunter is paging me so I better go to work. You be careful with Zarek and stay out of his way."

"Don't worry. I'm going to dump him out and leave him for the others to track down, then get my butt out of Alaska faster than you can say 'Rumpelstiltskin.'"

The radio clicked off.

Zarek sat perfectly still in the darkness and listened to Mike breathing in the cockpit.

So, the prick had changed his mind about killing him.

Well, bully that. The Squire had finally grown a ball, and half a brain. At some point during the last few hours Mike must have decided that suicide wasn't the answer.

For that, Zarek would let him live.

But he would make him suffer for the privilege.

And may the gods help the rest who were coming for him. On the frozen ground that made up Alaska's interior, Zarek was invincible. Unlike the other Dark-Hunters and Squires, he'd had nine hundred years of arctic survival training. Nine hundred years of just him and the uncharted wilderness.

Sure, Acheron had visited every decade or so just to make certain he was still alive, but no one else had ever come calling.

And people wondered why he was insane.

Up until about ten years ago, he'd had no contact whatsoever with the outside world during the long summer months that forced him to live inside his remote cabin.

No phone, no computer, no television.

Nothing but the quiet solitude of rereading the same stack of books over and over again until he had them memorized. Waiting in eager anticipation for the nights to grow long enough for him to be able to travel from his rural cabin into Fairbanks while the businesses were still open and he could interact with people.

For that matter, it had only been about a century and a half since the area had been sufficiently populated for him to have any human contact at all.

Before that, for untold centuries he had lived up here alone without another human being anywhere near him. He'd only occasionally caught sight of natives who were terrified to find a strange, tall Caucasian man with fangs living in a remote forest. They would take one look at his six-foot-six height and musk-ox parka and then run as fast as they could in the other direction, screaming out that the *Iglaaq* was going to get them. Superstitious to the extreme, they had built up an entire legend based on him.

That left the rare visits of the winter Daimons, who would venture into his woods so that they could say they'd faced down the lunatic Dark-Hunter. Unfortunately, they had been more interested in fighting than conversation and so his association with them had always been brief. A few minutes of combat to alleviate the monotony and then he was alone again with the snow and bears.

And they weren't even were-bears.

The magnetic and electrical charges of the aurora borealis made it almost impossible for any of the Were-Hunters to venture so far north. It also played havoc with his electronics and satellite linkups, blacking out his communications periodically year round so that even in this modern world, he was still painfully alone.

Maybe he should have let them kill him after all.

And yet somehow he always found himself carrying on. One more year, one more summer.

One more communications blackout.

Basic survival was all Zarek had ever known.

He swallowed as he remembered New Orleans.

How he'd loved that city. The vibrancy. The warmth. The mixture of exotic smells, sights, and sounds. He wondered if the people who lived there realized just how good they had it. Just how privileged they were to be blessed with such a great town.

But that was behind him now. He'd screwed up so badly that there was no chance whatsoever of either Artemis or Acheron allowing him back into a populated area where he could interact with large crowds of people.

It was him and Alaska for eternity. All he could really hope for was a massive population explosion, but given the severity of the weather, that was about as likely as his getting stationed in Hawaii.

With that thought in mind, he started pulling his snow gear out of the duffel bag and putting it on. It would be early morning when they arrived and still dark, but the dawn wouldn't be far behind. He'd have to hurry to make it to his cabin before sunup.

By the time he'd rubbed Vaseline on his skin and had changed into his long johns, black turtleneck sweater, and long musk-ox coat and insulated winter boots, he could feel the helicopter descending toward land.

On impulse, Zarek sifted through the weapons in his duffel bag. He'd learned a long time ago to carry a wide assortment of tools. Alaska was a harsh place to be on your own and you never knew when you'd meet something deadly.

Centuries ago, Zarek had made the decision to be the deadliest thing on the tundra.

As soon as they landed, Mike cut the engine and then waited for the blades to stop spinning before he got out, cursed at the subzero temperature, and opened the door to the back. Mike raked a repugnant sneer over him as he stepped back to give Zarek enough room to vacate the chopper.

"Welcome home," Mike said with a note of gleeful venom in his voice. The prick was enjoying the thought of the Squires tracking him down and dismembering him.

Well, so was Zarek.

Mike blew his breath into his gloved hands. "Hope it's all you remembered it as."

It was. Nothing here ever changed.

Zarek flinched at the brightness of the snow even in the darkness of predawn. He pulled his goggles down over his eyes to protect them and climbed out. He grabbed his duffel bag, slung it over his shoulder, then waded through the crunching snow toward the climate-controlled shed where he'd left his custom-built Ski-Doo MX Z Rev the week before.

Oh, yeah, now this was the subfreezing temperature he

remembered, the arctic air that bit so fiercely, every piece of his exposed skin burned. He clenched his teeth to keep them from chattering—something that wasn't pleasant when a man had long, sharp fangs in place of teeth.

Welcome home . . .

Mike was heading back for the cockpit when Zarek turned around to face him.

"Hey, Mike," he called, his voice ringing out through the cold stillness.

Mike paused.

"Rumpelstiltskin," he said before he tossed a live grenade underneath the helicopter.

Mike let out a fetid curse as he loped through the snow as fast as he could, trying to reach shelter.

For the first time in a long while, Zarek smiled at the sight of the irate Squire and the sound of the snow crunching under Mike's harried feet.

The helicopter exploded the same instant Zarek reached his snowmachine. He slung one long, leather-encased leg over the black seat and looked back as pieces of the twenty-three-million-dollar Sikorsky helicopter rained fiery metal over the snow.

Ahh, fireworks. How he loved them. The sight was almost as beautiful as the aurora borealis.

Mike was still cursing and jumping up and down like a small angry child as he watched his custom-built baby go up in flames.

Zarek started his engine and rode over to Mike, but not before he dropped another grenade to detonate the shed, thus preventing the Squire from using it.

As the snowmachine vibrated in idle beneath him, he pulled his scarf down enough so that Mike could understand him when he spoke. "Town is four miles that way," he said, pointing toward the south. He tossed Mike a small tube of Vaseline. "Keep your lips covered so they don't bleed."

"I should have killed you," Mike snarled.

"Yeah, you should have." Zarek covered his face, and revved his engine. "By the way, if you happen upon wolves in the woods, remember, they really are wolves and not Were-Hunters on the prowl. They also travel in packs so if you hear one, there's more behind him. My best advice for that is to climb a tree and hope they get bored before a bear comes along and decides to climb up after you."

Zarek spun his machine around and headed toward the northeast where his cabin waited in the middle of three hundred acres of forest.

He should probably feel guilty over what he'd done to Mike, but he didn't. The Squire had just learned a valuable lesson. Next time Artemis or Dionysus made him an offer, he'd take it.

Zarek rotated his wrist, giving the snowmachine more power as it bucked over the rough, snowy trail. He still had a long way to go to get home and his time was running out.

Daybreak was coming.

Damn. He should have ridden his Mach Z in. It was sleeker and faster than the MX Z Rev that he was on now, but not nearly as much fun.

Zarek was cold, hungry, and tired, and in a weird way all he wanted to do was get back to things that were familiar.

If the other Squires wanted to hunt him down, so be it. At least this way he was forewarned.

And as the helicopter and shed had shown, forearmed.

If they wanted to take him on, then he wished them luck. They were going to need it and a whole lot of reinforcements.

Looking forward to the challenge, he flew his snowmachine over the frozen terrain.

It was just before sunrise when he reached his isolated cabin. More snow had fallen while he was away, blocking his door. He pulled the snowmachine into the small shed that was attached to his cabin and covered it with a tarp. As he started to plug in his warmer for the engine, he realized there was no power in the outlet for either the MX or the Mach that was parked beside it.

He snarled in anger. Damn. No doubt the block for the Mach had been cracked from the subzero temperatures, and if he wasn't careful the MX's engine would crack, too.

Zarek rushed outside to check his generators before the sun rose over the hills, only to find both of them frozen solid and not working.

He snarled again as he struck one with his fist.

Well, so much for comfort. Looked like it was going to be him and the small wood-burning stove today. Not the best source of heat, but it was the best he was going to get.

"Great, just great," he muttered. It wasn't the first time he'd been forced to endure a cold sleep on his cabin floor. No doubt it wouldn't be the last.

It just seemed worse this morning because he'd spent the last week in New Orleans's mild climate. It had been so warm while he was there that he hadn't even needed to use the heat at all.

Man, how he missed that place.

Knowing his time before sunrise was growing critically short, he trudged back to his snowmachine and packed its engine with his parka to help keep as much of the heat around it as he could. Then he retrieved his duffel bag from the seat and went to dig his door out so that he could get inside his cabin.

He ducked as he came through the door and kept his head bent down. The ceiling was low, so low that if he stood up straight the top of his head would brush it, and if he wasn't paying attention, his ceiling fan in the center of the room would decapitate him.

But the low ceiling was necessary. Heat in the heart of winter was a valuable commodity and the last thing anyone wanted was the bulk of it gathered under a ten-foot ceiling. A lower ceiling meant a warmer place.

Not to mention that nine hundred years ago when he'd been banished here, he hadn't had very long to build his shelter. Sleeping in a cave during daylight, he'd worked on the cabin at night until he had finally constructed Home Crappy Home.

Yes, it was good to be back . . .

Zarek dropped his duffel bag beside the wood-burning stove. Then he turned and placed the old-fashioned wooden bolt into its cradle over the door to bar it from the Alaskan wildlife that sometimes ventured too close to his cabin.

Feeling his way along the carved wall with his hand, he found the lantern that hung there and the small box of lucifer matches that was attached to it. Even though his Dark-Hunter eyesight was designed for nighttime, he couldn't see in complete darkness. With the door closed, his cabin was sealed so tightly that no light whatsoever could permeate its thick wooden walls.

Lighting the lantern, he shivered from the cold as he turned around to face the interior of his home. He knew every inch of the place intimately. Every bookshelf that lined the walls, every hand-carved, ornamental notch that decorated it.

He'd never had much in the way of furniture. Two tall cupboards; one for his handful of clothes and one for his food. There was also a stand for his television and his book-shelves, and that was pretty much it. As a former Roman slave, Zarek wasn't used to much.

It was so cold inside that he could see his breath even through the scarf and as he looked around the small space he grimaced at his computer and television—both of which would have to be defrosted before he could use them again.

Provided no moisture had gotten into them.

Unwilling to worry about that, he made his way to his food

pantry in the back where he kept nothing but canned goods. He'd learned a long time ago that if the bears and wolves smelled food, they would quickly pay him an unwanted visit. He had no desire to kill them just because they were hungry and stupid.

Zarek grabbed a can of pork and beans and his can opener and sat down on the floor. Mike had refused to feed him during their thirteen-hour trip from New Orleans to Fairbanks. Mike had claimed that he didn't want to chance exposing Zarek to sunlight to feed him.

In reality, the Squire was a jerk, and starvation was nothing new to Zarek.

"Ah, great," he muttered as he opened the can to find the beans frozen solid inside. He considered pulling out his ice pick, then changed his mind. He wasn't so hungry that a pork and beans popsicle appealed to him.

He sighed in disgust, then opened the door and tossed the can as far into the woods as he could.

Slamming the door shut before he let the dawn light in, Zarek rooted through his duffel bag until he found his cell phone, MP3 player, and laptop. He tucked the phone and player down into his pants so that his body heat would keep them from freezing. Then he set his laptop aside until he could get the wood-burning stove lighted.

He went to the corner across from the stove and grabbed a handful of the carved wooden figurines he had piled there and moved to place them inside the stove.

As soon as he swung open the small iron door, he paused.

There was a tiny mink inside with three newborn kits. The mother, angry at being disturbed, hissed a warning to him as they stared at each other.

Zarek hissed back at her.

"Man, I don't believe this," Zarek mumbled angrily.

The mink must have come down the stovepipe and moved in while he'd been gone. It had probably still been warm when she found it and the stove was an extremely safe place for her den.

"The least you could have done was bring about fifty of your friends with you. I could use a new coat."

She bared her teeth.

Aggravated, Zarek closed the door and returned the kindling to the pile in the corner. He was a dick, but not even he would toss them out. Being immortal, he would survive the cold. The mother and young wouldn't.

He picked up his laptop and zipped it inside his coat to keep it warm and went over to the far corner where his pallet was. As he lay down, he thought about going to sleep underground where it was warmer, but then, why bother?

He'd have to move the stove to reach his hidden basement and that would just upset the mother mink again.

This time of year daylight was short. It would only be a few more hours until sunset, and he was more than used to this frozen wasteland.

As soon as he could, he would go to town for supplies and a new generator. Pulling the quilts and furs over him, he expelled a long, tired breath.

Zarek closed his eyes and let his mind wander over the events of the past week.

"Thank you, Zarek."

He ground his teeth as he recalled Sunshine Runningwolf's face. Her large dark brown eyes were incredibly seductive and she was a far cry from the skinny model types most men favored; she had a lush, round body that had made him hard just to be around her.

Man, he should have taken a bite of her neck when he'd had the chance. He still wasn't sure why he hadn't tasted her blood. No doubt it would have kept him warm even now.

Oh, well. Chalk it up to another regret he had on an infinite list of them.

His thoughts returned to her . . .

Sunshine had shown up unexpectedly at his New Orleans town house while he had been waiting for Nick to take him to the landing site to leave.

Her black hair had been braided and her brown eyes had held a friendship in them that he'd never seen before when someone looked at him.

"I can't stay for long. I don't want Talon to wake up and find me gone, but before you left I had to thank you for what you did for us."

He still didn't know why he'd helped her and Talon. Why he had defied Dionysus and fought against the god while the god had sought to destroy the two of them.

For their happiness, he had consigned himself to death.

But as he had looked at her yesterday, it had seemed somehow worth it.

And as he allowed sleep to overtake him, he wondered if he would still think it was worth it when the Squires found his cabin and burned it to the ground with him inside.

He snorted at the thought. What the hell? At least he'd be warm for a few minutes before he died.

Zarek wasn't sure how long he'd slept. By the time he awoke, it was dark again.

Hopefully, he hadn't slept so long that his snowmachine would have had a chance to freeze. If he had, it would be a long, cold hike into town.

He rolled over and grimaced in pain. He'd been lying on his laptop. Not to mention the phone and MP3 player that were biting into something even more uncomfortable.

Shivering against the frigid cold, he forced himself up and grabbed another parka from his wardrobe. Once he was dressed for the weather, he went outside to his makeshift garage. He put the laptop, phone, and MP3 player into his backpack and slung it over his shoulders, then straddled the snowmachine and unwrapped the engine.

Luckily it started on the first try. Hallelujah! Maybe his luck was turning after all. No one had toasted him while he slept and he actually had enough gas to make it into Fairbanks where he could get some hot food and thaw out for a few minutes.

Grateful for small favors, he headed across his land and turned south for the long, bumpy trip that would take him into civilization.

Not that he minded. He was just too damned grateful there actually was civilization now to head into.

Zarek arrived in town shortly after six.

He parked his snowmachine at Sharon Parker's house, which was walking distance from the town's center. He'd met the ex-waitress about ten years ago when he'd found her inside her broken-down car late at night on the side of a seldom-traveled back road in North Pole.

It'd been close to sixty below and she had been crying, huddled under blankets, afraid that she and her baby would die before help arrived. Her seven-month-old daughter had been sick with asthma and Sharon had been trying to get her to the hospital for a breathing treatment, but they had refused her admittance since she didn't have any insurance and no money to pay.

She had been given directions to a charity clinic and had gotten lost while trying to find it.

Zarek had taken them back to the hospital and paid for the baby's care. While they waited, he'd found out Sharon was being evicted from her apartment and couldn't make ends meet.

So he had offered Sharon a bargain. In exchange for a house, car, and money, she provided him with someone friendly to speak to whenever he came into Fairbanks, and a few home-cooked leftovers or meals—whatever she had lying around.

Best of all, in the summertime when he was completely locked inside his cabin during the twenty-three and a half hours of daylight, she would swing by the post office or store and bring him books and supplies and leave them outside his door.

It had been the best deal he'd ever made.

She'd never asked him anything personal, not even why he didn't leave his cabin in the summer months. No doubt she was just too grateful to have his financial support to care about his eccentric ways.

In return, Zarek had never taken any of her blood or asked her anything personal. They were just employer and employee.

"Zarek?"

He looked up from plugging in his block warmer on the snowmachine to see her sticking her head out of the front door of her ranch-style house. Her dark brown hair was shorter than it had been a month ago when he'd last seen her—she had a blunt cut that swung around her shoulders.

Tall, thin, and extremely attractive, she was dressed in a black sweater and jeans. Most any other guy would have probably made a move on her by now, and one night about four years ago, she had insinuated that if he ever wanted something more intimate from her she would gladly give it, but Zarek had refused.

He didn't like people getting too close to him, and women had a nasty tendency of viewing sex as meaningful.

He didn't. Sex was sex. It was basic and animalistic. Something the body needed like it needed food. But a guy didn't have to promise a steak he was going to date it before he ate it.

So why did women need a testament of affection before they opened their legs?

He didn't get it.

And he would never become involved with Sharon. Sex with her was one complication he didn't need.

"Zarek, is that you?"

He lowered the scarf over his face and shouted back. "Yeah, it's me."

"Are you coming in?"

"I'll be back in a minute. I have to go buy a few things."

She nodded, then went back inside and shut the door.

Zarek made his way to the store down the street from her house. Frank's General Store had some of everything in it. Best of all, it had a wide variety of electronics and generators. Unfortunately, he wouldn't be able to use the shop much longer. He'd been a fairly regular customer for about fifteen years now, and though Frank was a bit dense, he had started noticing the fact that Zarek hadn't aged in all that time.

Sooner or later, Sharon would notice it too and he would have to give up his only contact in the mortal world.

That was the big drawback of immortality. He didn't dare hang around anyone for long or they'd find out who and what he was. And unlike the other Dark-Hunters, every time he had requested a Squire to serve him and protect his identity, the Council had denied it.

It seemed his reputation was such that no one wanted the duty of helping him.

Fine. He'd never needed anyone anyway.

Zarek entered the store and took a minute to pull his goggles and gloves off and unbutton his coat. He heard Frank in the back talking to one of his clerks.

"Now listen up, kid. He's kind of a strange man, but you better be nice to him, you hear me? He spends a ton of money in this store and I don't care how scary he looks, you be nice."

The two of them came out from the back. Frank stopped dead in his tracks to stare at him.

Zarek stared back. Frank was used to seeing him with a goatee or beard, his sword-and-crossbones earring, and the silver claws he wore on his left hand. Three things Acheron had ordered him to abandon in New Orleans.

He knew what he looked like beardless and he hated it. But at least he didn't have to look at himself in a mirror. Dark-Hunters could only cast a reflection when they wanted to.

Zarek had never wanted to.

The elderly man smiled a smile that was more habitual than friendly and ambled toward him. Even though the people of Fairbanks were exceedingly friendly, most of them still tended to cut a wide berth around Zarek.

He had that effect on people.

"What can I get for you today?" Frank asked.

Zarek glanced at the teenager, who was watching him curiously. "I need a new generator."

Frank sucked in his breath between his teeth and Zarek waited for what he knew was coming. "There might be a bit of a problem there."

Frank always said that. No matter what Zarek needed, it was going to be a problem to get it, hence he would have to pay top dollar for it.

Frank scratched the gray whiskers on his bearded face. "I've only got the one left and it's supposed to be delivered to the Wallabys tomorrow."

Yeah, right.

Zarek was too tired to play Frank's haggling game tonight. At this point, he was willing to pay anything to get the electricity back on in his house. "If you'll let me have it, there's an extra six grand in it for you."

Frank scowled and continued to scratch his beard. "Well now, there's another problem. Wallaby be wanting it real bad."

"Ten grand, Frank, and another two if you can get it over to Sharon's house within the hour."

Frank beamed. "Tony, you heard the man, get his generator loaded up." The old man's eyes were light and almost friendly. "You be needing anything else?"

Zarek shook his head and left.

He made his way back toward Sharon's and did his best to ignore the biting winds.

He knocked on her door before he shouldered it open and entered. Oddly enough, the living room was empty. This time of night, Sharon's daughter Trixie was usually running around, playing and screaming like a demon or doing homework under extreme protest. He didn't even hear her in the back rooms.

For a second, he thought maybe the Squires had found him, but that was ridiculous. No one knew about Sharon. Zarek wasn't exactly on speaking terms with the Squires' Council or other Dark-Hunters.

"Hey, Sharon?" he called. "Everything okay?"

She walked slowly down the hall from the direction of the kitchen. "You're back."

A bad feeling settled over him. Something wasn't right. He could sense it. She seemed nervous.

"Yeah. Is something up? I didn't crash a date or anything, did I?"

And then he heard it. It was the sound of a man breathing, of heavy footsteps leaving the kitchen.

The man came down the hall with a slow, methodical walk—like a predator taking its time getting the lay of the landscape while it patiently watched its prey.

Zarek frowned as the man stopped in the hallway behind Sharon. Standing only about an inch shorter than Zarek, he had long dark brown hair pulled back into a ponytail and he wore a Western-style outback duster. There was a deadly quick aura around the man and as soon as their eyes met, Zarek knew he'd been betrayed.

This was another Dark-Hunter.

And there was only one out of the thousands of Dark-Hunters who knew about Sharon and him . . .

Zarek cursed his own stupidity.

The Dark-Hunter inclined his head toward him. "Z," he drawled in a thick Southern accent Zarek knew only too well. "Me and you need to talk."

Zarek couldn't breathe as he stared at Sharon and Sundown together. Sundown was the only person he had ever opened himself up to in his entire two thousand plus years of living.

And he knew why Sundown was here.

Sundown alone knew Zarek. Knew his haunts, his habits. Who better to hunt him down and kill him than his own best friend?

"Talk about what?" he asked gruffly, narrowing his eyes.

Sundown moved to stand in front of Sharon as if to protect her. That he would think for even an instant that Zarek would threaten her hurt most of all. "I think you know why I'm here, Z."

Yeah, he knew all right. He knew exactly what Sundown wanted with him. A nice, quick death so that Sundown could report back to Artemis and Acheron that everything was right again in the world, and then the cowboy would return home to Reno.

But Zarek had gone quietly to his execution once before. This time, he intended to fight for his life, such as it was.

"Forget it, Jess," he said, using Sundown's real name.

He turned and ran for the door.

Zarek made it back into the yard before Sundown caught him and pulled him to a stop. He bared his fangs at him, but Jess didn't seem to notice.

Zarek punched him hard in the stomach. It was a powerful strike that made Jess stagger back and it brought Zarek to his knees. Any time one Dark-Hunter attacked another one, the Dark-Hunter who attacked felt the blow ten times worse than the one who received it. There was only one way to avoid this—for Artemis to lift her ban. He just hoped she hadn't lifted it from Jess.

Zarek struggled to breathe from the pain of it and forced himself to his feet. Unlike Jess, physical pain was something he was used to.

But before he could go far, he saw Mike and three other Squires in the shadows. They were walking toward them with determined strides that said they were armed for Dark-Hunter.

"Leave him to me," Sundown ordered.

They ignored him and kept on coming.

Spinning about, Zarek headed for his snowmachine only to find its engine in pieces. Obviously they had been busy while he was at Frank's.

Damn it. How could he have been so stupid?

They must have destroyed his generators to force him into town. They'd flushed him out of the woods like hunters with a wild animal.

Fine. If they wanted an animal to track, he would be one.

He slung his hand out and used his telekinesis to knock the Squires off their feet.

Unwilling to hurt himself again, Zarek dodged Jess and ran for town.

He didn't make it far before more Squires fell in and opened fire on him.

Bullets tore through his body, shredding his skin. Zarek hissed and staggered from the pain of it.

Still, he kept running.

He had no choice.

If he stayed down, they would dismember him, and though his life seriously sucked, he had no intention of becoming a Shade. Nor would he give them the satisfaction of killing him.

Zarek rounded the side of a building.

Something hard hit his middle.

Agony exploded through him as he was flipped head over heels onto the ground. He came to rest on his back in the snow with the breath knocked completely out of him.

A shadow with cold, merciless eyes moved to stand over him.

At least six eight, the man held an unearthly masculine perfection. He had pale blond hair and dark brown eyes, and when he smiled, he revealed the same pair of fangs as Zarek.

"What are you?" Zarek asked, knowing the stranger wasn't a Daimon or Apollite even though he looked like one.

"I am Thanatos, Dark-Hunter," he said in Classic Greek, using the name that meant "death." "And I'm here to kill you."

He seized Zarek by his coat and threw him against the far building as if he were nothing more than a rag doll.

Zarek hit the wall hard and slid to the street. His body hurt so badly that his limbs shook as he tried to crawl away from the beast.

Zarek stopped. "I won't die like this again," he snarled. Not on his belly like some fearful animal waiting for slaughter.

Like a worthless slave being beaten.

His body fortified by his rage, he forced himself to his feet and swung around to face Thanatos.

The creature smiled. "Backbone. How I love it. But not as much as I love sucking the marrow from it."

Zarek caught his arm as he reached for him. "You know what I love?" Zarek snapped the creature's arm and seized him by his neck. "The sound of a Daimon breathing his last breath."

Thanatos laughed. The sound was evil and cold. "You can't kill me, Dark-Hunter. I'm even more immortal than you are."

Zarek gaped as Thanatos's arm healed instantly.

"What are you?" Zarek asked again.

"I told you. I am Death and no one defeats or escapes Death."

Oh, shit. He was screwed now.

But he was far from defeated. Death might take him, but the bastard was going to have to work for it.

"You know," Zarek said, falling into the surreal calmness that had allowed him as a whipping boy to suffer through untold beatings. "I'll bet most people shit their pants in terror when you hand them that line. But you know what, Mr. I-want-to-be-scary-and-am-failing-miserably? I'm not a person. I'm a Dark-Hunter and in the grand scheme of things you don't mean shit to me."

He concentrated all of his powers into his hand, then delivered a powerful blow straight to Thanatos's solar plexus. The creature stumbled back.

"Now I can sit here and play with you." He delivered another staggering blow to Thanatos. "But I'd rather just put you out of both our miseries."

Before he could strike again, a shotgun blast hit him square in the back. Zarek felt the shrapnel ripping through his body, narrowly missing his heart.

Police sirens sounded in the distance.

Thanatos grabbed him by his throat and lifted him up until he was forced to stand on his tiptoes. "Better yet, why don't I just put you out of yours?"

Struggling to breathe, Zarek smiled grimly as he felt a trail of blood run out from the corner of his lips. The metallic taste of it suffused his mouth. He was hurt, but not daunted.

Smiling snidely at the Daimon, he kneed the bastard in the jewels.

The Daimon crumpled. Zarek took off running again, away from the Daimon, the Squires, and the cops, only he was nowhere near as fast as he'd been.

The pain made his eyesight blurry and the more he ran the more he hurt.

The agony of his body was unbearable.

Not in all his beatings as a child had he hurt this much. He didn't know how he managed to keep going. Only that some part of him refused to lie down and let them have him.

He wasn't sure when he lost them, or maybe they were

right behind him. Zarek couldn't really tell due to the buzzing in his ears.

Disoriented, he slowed, stumbling forward until he couldn't go any farther.

He fell into the snow.

Zarek lay there waiting for the others to grab him. Waiting for Thanatos to finish what they had started, but as the seconds ticked by, he realized he must have escaped them.

Relieved, he tried to rise.

He couldn't. His body just wouldn't cooperate anymore. The best he could manage was to crawl forward three more feet where he caught sight of a large cabin-style house in front of him.

It looked warm and cozy and in the back of his mind was the thought that if he could just make it to the door the person inside might help him.

He laughed bitterly at the thought.

No one had ever helped him.

Not once.

No, this was his fate. There was no use fighting it, and in truth, he was tired of struggling alone in the world.

Closing his eyes, he drew a long, ragged breath and waited for what was inevitable.

Chapter 3

Astrid sat on the edge of the bed as she checked the wounds of her "guest." For four days now, he had lain in her bed unconscious while she watched over him.

The tight muscles under her hands were firm and strong, but she couldn't see them.

She couldn't see *him*.

Her eyesight was always forfeit when she was sent to judge someone. Eyes could deceive. They judged things very differently from the other senses.

Astrid must always be impartial even though at the moment she didn't truly feel that way.

How many times had she gone in with an open heart only to be fooled?

The worst case had been Miles. A rogue Dark-Hunter, he had been charming and amusing. He had dazzled her with his vibrancy and ability to make everything a game. Whenever she had tried to push him to his limits, he had laughed off her tests and shown himself to be a good sport about everything.

He had appeared the perfect, well-balanced man.

For a time, she had even fancied herself in love with him.

In the end, he had tried to kill her. He had been completely amoral and ruthless. Cold. Unfeeling. The only person he had been able to love was himself, and while he was nothing but scum, in his mind, he had been wronged by mankind so it was okay to do whatever he wanted to them.

And that was Astrid's biggest problem with Dark-Hunters. They were humans who were usually recruited from the sewers. Spat upon by others from the cradle to the grave, they were hostile to the world. Artemis never took that into consideration when she converted them. All she wanted was a soldier under Acheron's command. Once they were created, Artemis washed her hands of them and left them for others to monitor and maintain.

At least until they crossed whatever line Artemis had drawn. Then the goddess rushed to have them judged and executed, and though she had no proof, Astrid suspected Artemis only followed that protocol to keep Acheron from being angry at her.

So Astrid had been called multiple times over the centuries to find some reason to allow a Dark-Hunter to live.

She never had. Not once. Every one she had judged had been dangerous and raw. A menace who threatened mankind more than the Daimons they pursued.

Olympian justice didn't operate quite the way human justice did. There was no assumption of innocence. On Olympus, once accused, the defendant must prove himself worthy of mercy.

No one ever had.

The closest Astrid had ever come to clemency had been Miles, and look how that had turned out. It terrified her to think of how close she had come to judging him innocent and then having him set loose on the world again.

That experience had been the last straw for her. Since then, she had pulled herself away from everyone.

She wouldn't let a man's beauty or charm trick her again. Her job now was to get to the heart of this man on her bed.

Artemis had said Zarek had no heart whatsoever. Acheron

had said nothing. He had only given her a piercing look that told her he was depending on her to do the right thing.

But what was right?

"Wake up, Zarek," she whispered. "You only have ten days left to save yourself."

Zarek came awake to a pain that was indescribable, which given his brutal background as a whipping boy and slave was hard to believe. Especially since as a human being, pain had been the only certainty in his life.

His head throbbing, he shifted, expecting to feel cold snow and ground underneath him. Instead, he was struck by how warm he felt.

I'm dead, he thought wryly.

Not even his dreams had ever left him *this* warm.

Yet as he blinked open his eyes to find a fire blazing in a hearth and a mountain of quilts over him, he realized he was very much alive and lying in someone else's bedroom.

He looked around the room, which was decorated in earth tones: pale pinks, tans, browns, and dark green. The log-cabin walls were the upper-crust kind that denoted someone who wanted the look and feel of a rustic cabin, but who had enough money to make sure it was well insulated and cozy, and not drafty and cold.

His bed was an expensive iron reproduction of the large beds from the end of the nineteenth century. To his left stood a small nightstand where an old-fashioned pitcher and wash-bowl rested.

Whoever owned this place was loaded.

Zarek *hated* wealthy people.

"Sasha?"

Zarek frowned at the soft, melodic voice. A woman's voice. She was down the hall in another room, but he couldn't quite pinpoint her location through the pain in his skull.

He heard a soft canine whine.

"Oh, stop that," the woman chided with a gentle tone. "I didn't really hurt your feelings, did I?"

Zarek's frown deepened as he tried to make sense of what had happened to him. Jess and the others were hunting him and he remembered falling down in front of a house.

Someone from the house must have found him and dragged him inside, though why anyone would bother he couldn't imagine.

Not that it mattered. Jess and Thanatos would be after him, and it wouldn't take a rocket scientist to figure out where he was, especially given how much blood he'd been losing as he ran. No doubt, there was a trail that led straight to this cabin's door.

Which meant he had to get out of here ASAP. Jess wouldn't do anything to hurt those who'd helped him, but there was no telling what Thanatos was capable of.

His mind flashed to a burning village. To the horrid sight of people lying dead . . .

Zarek flinched at the memory, wondering why it would haunt him now.

It was a reminder of what *he* was capable of, he decided, and a reminder of why he had to get away from here. He didn't want to hurt someone who had been nice to him.

Not again.

Forcing himself to forget the pain of his body, he sat up slowly.

The dog instantly came running into his room.

Only it wasn't a dog, he realized as it stopped by his bed and growled at him. It was a large, white timber wolf. One that appeared to hate him.

"Back off, Scooby," he snapped. "I've made boots from bigger and badder wolves than you."

The wolf bared more teeth as if it understood his words and was daring him to prove them.

"Sasha?"

Zarek froze as the woman appeared in his doorway.

Damn me . . .

She was incredible. Her long blond hair was the color of honey, and it fell in soft waves around her thin shoulders. Her skin was pale, with rosy cheeks and lips that had obviously been protected very carefully from the harsh Alaskan climate. She stood close to six feet in height and wore a white cable-knit sweater and jeans.

Her eyes were a pale, pale blue. So light that at first glance, they were almost colorless. And as she came into the room with her hands stretched out as she moved slowly and methodically, trying to locate the wolf, he realized she was completely blind.

The wolf barked at him twice, then turned and went to his owner.

"There you are," she whispered, kneeling to pet it. "You shouldn't bark, Sasha. You'll wake our guest."

"I'm awake and I'm sure that's why he's barking."

She turned her head toward him as if she were trying to see him. "I'm sorry. We don't get much company and Sasha tends to be a little antisocial with strangers."

"Believe me, I know the feeling."

She walked toward the bed, again with her hand outstretched. "How do you feel?" she asked, patting his shoulder as she located him.

Zarek cringed at the sensation of her warm hand on his flesh. It was gentle. Searing. And it made a foreign part of him ache. But worst of all, it made his groin hard. Tight.

He'd never been able to stand anyone touching him.

"I'd rather you not do that."

"Do what?" she asked.

"Touch me."

She pulled back slowly and blinked methodically as if it

were more habit than reflex. "I see by touch," she said softly. "If I don't touch you, I'm completely blind."

"Yeah, well, we all have problems." He scooted to the opposite side of the bed and rose to his feet. He was bare except for his leather pants and a few bandages. She must have undressed him and treated his wounds. That thought made him feel rather strange. No one had ever bothered caring for him before when he'd been wounded.

Why would she?

Even Acheron and Nick had left him to his own devices after he'd been hurt in New Orleans. The best they'd offered was a ride home so that he could heal in solitude.

Of course, they might have offered him more had he been a little less hostile toward them, but hostility was what he did best.

Zarek found his clothes folded on a rocking chair by the window. In spite of the painful protests of his muscles, he started pulling them on. His Dark-Hunter powers had allowed him to heal for the most part while he slept, but he wasn't in as good a shape as he would have been had the Dream-Hunters helped him. They often came to injured Dark-Hunters to heal them during their sleep, but not Zarek.

He scared them as much as he scared everyone else.

So, he'd learned to take his hits and deal with the pain. Which was fine by him. He didn't like people, immortal or otherwise, anywhere nearby.

Life was better alone.

He grimaced as he caught sight of the hole in the back of his shirt where the shotgun blast had struck him.

Yup, life was definitely better alone. Unlike his "friend," he couldn't shoot himself in the back even if he wanted to.

"Are you up?" the unknown woman asked, her voice surprised. "Dressing?"

"No," he said irritably. "I'm pissing on your rug. What do you think I'm doing?"

"I'm blind. For all I know you really are peeing on my rug, which is a very nice rug incidentally, so I hope you're kidding."

He felt a strange twinge of amusement at her comeback. She was fast and smart. He liked that.

But he had no time to waste. "Look, lady, I don't know how you got me in here, but I appreciate it. However, I have to get going. Believe me, you'll be very sorry if I don't."

She pushed herself off the bed at his hostile words and it was only then he realized he'd growled them at her.

"There's a bad blizzard outside," she said, her voice less friendly than it had been before. "No one is going to be able to go anywhere for a while."

Zarek didn't believe it until he parted the curtains on her window. The snow was falling so fast and thick that it looked like a dense white wall.

He cursed under his breath. Then louder he asked, "How long has it been doing this?"

"The last few hours."

He ground his teeth as he realized he was stuck here.

With her.

This was really not good, but at least it would keep the others from tracking him. With any luck the snow would disguise his trail and he knew for a fact that Jess hated the cold.

As for Thanatos, well, given his name, language, and looks, Zarek would peg him as an ancient Mediterranean, too, and that meant Zarek still had an advantage over both of them. He'd learned centuries ago how to move quickly over the snow and what dangers to avoid.

Who could have known that nine hundred years in Alaska would actually pay off someday?

"How can you be up and moving?"

Her question startled him. "Excuse me?"

"You were severely injured when I brought you in a few days ago. How can you be moving now?"

"A few days?" he asked, stunned by her words. He ran his hand over his face and felt his thick whiskers. Shit. It *had* been days. "How many?"

"Almost five."

His heart pounded. He'd been here for four days and they hadn't found him? How was that possible?

He frowned. Something about that didn't seem right.

"I thought I felt a gun wound on your back."

Ignoring the gaping hole in the shirt, Zarek pulled his black undershirt on over his head. He was sure it'd been Jess who had shot him. Shotguns were the cowboy's weapon of choice. His only consolation was the thought that Jess was aching from it as much as he was. Unless Artemis had lifted her ban. Then the bastard would feel nothing but satisfaction.

"It wasn't a gun wound," he lied. "I just fell."

"No offense, but you'd have to fall off Mount Everest to have those kinds of wounds."

"Yeah, maybe next time I'll remember to take my climbing gear with me."

She scowled at him. "Are you mocking me?"

"No," he answered honestly. "I just don't want to go into what happened."

Astrid nodded as she tried to discern more about this angry man who couldn't seem to speak without growling at her. Awake, he was far from pleasant.

He'd been near death when Sasha had found him. No one should be so badly beaten and shot, and then left for dead as he had been.

What had the Squires been thinking?

She was amazed the rogue Dark-Hunter could stand at all even after four days of rest.

Such treatment was inhumane and unbecoming of those who had sworn to protect mankind. Had a human found

Zarek, his cover would have been even more blown by their carelessness, and the humans would have learned of his immortality.

It was something she fully intended to report to Archeron.

But that would come later. For now, Zarek was up and moving. His immortal life or death rested completely in her hands and she intended to test him fully to see just what kind of man he was.

Did he have any compassion left inside him or was he just as empty as she was?

Her job was to be the epitome of the things that drove Zarek to anger. She would push him to the heights of his tolerance and beyond to see what he would do.

If he could control himself with her, she would judge him safe and sane.

If he lashed out to hurt her in any way, she would judge him guilty and he would die.

Let the tests begin . . .

She ran through her mind what little she knew about him. Zarek didn't like to talk to people. He didn't like the rich.

Most of all, he hated to be touched or ordered about.

So she decided to press his first button with idle conversation.

"What color is your hair?" she asked. The seemingly innocuous question made her memory flash to the way it had felt under her hand as she had bathed the blood from it.

His hair had been soft, smooth. It had slid sensuously through her fingers, caressing them. From the feel of it, she knew it wasn't too short or too long, but probably fell to his shoulders when styled.

"Excuse me?" He sounded surprised by her question and for once didn't growl the words at her.

He had a beautiful voice. Rich and deep. It resonated with

its Greek accent, and every time he spoke, it sent a strange chill through her. She'd never heard any man who had a voice so innately masculine.

"Your hair," she repeated. "I was wondering what color it is."

"Why do you care?" he asked belligerently.

She shrugged. "Just curious. I spend a lot of time alone and though I don't really remember what colors look like, I try to picture them anyway. My sister Cloie gave me a book once that said every color had a texture and feel. Red, for instance, it said was hot and bumpy."

Zarek frowned at her. This was an odd conversation, but then, he'd spent enough time alone to understand the need to talk about anything to anyone who would stand still long enough to bother. "It's black."

"I thought so."

"Did you?" he asked before he could stop himself.

She nodded as she rounded the bed and came a little too close to him. She stood so close that their bodies almost touched. He felt an odd impulse to touch her. To see if her skin was as soft as it appeared.

Gods, she was beautiful.

Her body was lithe and tall, her breasts a perfect handful. It'd been a long time since he had last screwed a woman. An eternity since he had been this close to one without tasting her blood.

He swore he could taste hers now. Feel her heartbeat pounding against his lips as he drank from her while her emotions and feelings poured into him, filling him with something other than numbness and pain.

Even though drinking human blood was forbidden, it was the only thing that had ever given him pleasure. The only thing that buried the pain inside him and allowed him to experience hopes, dreams.

The only thing that allowed him to feel human.

And he wanted to feel human.

He wanted to feel *her*.

"Your hair was cool and silky," she said softly, "like midnight velvet."

Her words made his cock tighten with need and lust.

Cool and silky.

It made him think of her legs sliding against his. Of the delicate, feminine skin that would cover her buttocks and thighs. The way they would feel against his legs as he pounded himself into her.

His breathing ragged, he imagined what it would be like to peel her tight, faded jeans down her long legs and spread them wide. To run his hand through her short, crisp hairs until he could touch her intimately, stroking her until her sweet juices coated his fingers as she murmured in his ear and rubbed herself against him.

What it would be like to lay her down on the bed behind her and sink himself deep inside her warm, wet heat until they both climaxed.

To feel her mouth on his body.

Her hands groping him.

She reached out to touch him.

Unable to move from the force of his fantasy, Zarek stood perfectly still as she placed her hand on his shoulder. The smell of woman, smoke, and roses permeated him and he felt a desperate need to bend down, bury his face against her creamy skin, and just inhale her sweet scent. To sink his fangs into her soft, tender neck and sample the life force inside her.

Unconsciously, he opened his lips, baring his fangs.

The need for her was almost overwhelming.

But not nearly as demanding as the desire to touch her body.

"You're taller than I thought you'd be." She traced the curve of his upper biceps. Chills rushed over him as he hardened even more.

He wanted her. Badly.

Bite her . . .

Her wolf growled.

Zarek ignored it as he continued to stare at her.

His affairs with women had always been kept brief and hurried. Never once had he allowed a woman to face or touch him while they had sex.

He'd always taken his women on all fours from behind, furious and quick like an animal. He'd never wanted to spend any time with them other than what he needed to sate his body.

Yet he could easily envision taking this stranger into his arms and screwing her, face to face. Of feeling her breath on his skin as he rode her slow and hard all night long and drank from her . . .

He didn't speak as she skimmed her hand down his arm and he couldn't imagine why he didn't shove her away from him.

For some reason, she held him immobile with her touch.

His heavy groin burned with vicious need. If he didn't know better, he'd swear she was turning him on on purpose.

But there was an innocence in her touch that told him she only wanted to "see" him. There was nothing sexual in this.

At least not from her end.

Zarek stepped away from her and put a good four feet of distance between them.

He had to.

One more minute and he would have her naked on that bed and at his mercy . . .

Not that he had any mercy for anyone.

She dropped her hand and stood still as if waiting for him to touch her.

He didn't. One touch and he would be the animal everyone thought he was.

"What's your name?" The question was out before he could stop himself.

She offered him a friendly smile that made his groin jerk. "Astrid. And yours?"

"Zarek."

Her smile widened. "You *are* Greek. I thought so by your accent."

Her wolf circled around her feet and sat down next to her to eyeball him. It flashed its teeth threateningly.

He was really beginning to hate that animal.

"Can I get you anything, Zarek?"

Yes, crawl naked into that bed and let me ravish you until dawn.

He swallowed at the thought and his groin tightened even more at the sound of his name on her lips.

He couldn't have been any harder if she had been stroking him with her hand.

Her mouth . . .

What was wrong with him? He was on the run for his life and all he could think of was sex?

He was being a total idiot.

"No, thank you," he said. "I'm all right."

His stomach rumbled, betraying him.

"You sound hungry to me."

Starving, to be honest, but right then he was craving a taste of her a lot more than he was craving food. "Yeah. I guess I am."

"Here," she said, reaching out for him. "I might be blind, but I can cook. I promise that unless Sasha has moved things around in the kitchen, I haven't poisoned my stew."

Zarek didn't take her hand.

She swallowed as if nervous or awkward, then dropped her hand and headed out of the room.

Sasha growled at him again.

Zarek growled back and stamped his foot at the annoying pooch, who looked like it wanted nothing more than to tear his leg off.

He caught an unfocused look of censure on Astrid's face as she paused in the doorway to turn back toward them. "Are you being mean to Sasha?"

"No. I'm just returning his greeting." The wolf's ears were still laid back as it darted out of the room. "Rin Tin Tin doesn't seem to like me very much."

She shrugged. "He doesn't like anyone much. Sometimes not even me."

Astrid turned and headed down the hallway with Zarek behind her. There was something very ominous about this man. Deadly. And it wasn't just the strength she had felt in his arm as she touched it.

He oozed an unnatural darkness that seemed to warn everyone, even the blind, to stay away from him. That was most likely what Sasha reacted to. It was extremely disconcerting.

Even frightening.

Maybe Artemis was right. Maybe she should judge him guilty and just go on home . . .

But he hadn't attacked her. At least not yet.

Astrid led him to the breakfast counter where she had three bar stools. Her sisters had placed them there earlier when they had come to visit and warn her about her latest assignment.

All three of her sisters had been extremely unhappy that she had decided to judge Zarek for her mother, but in the end, they'd had no choice except to let her do her job.

To their eternal consternation, there were some things not even the Fates could control.

Free will was one of them.

"Do you like beef stew?" she asked Zarek.

"I'm not picky. I'm just grateful to have something warm I didn't have to cook myself."

She noted the bitterness in his voice. "You do that a lot?"

He didn't answer.

Astrid felt her way to the stove.

As she neared the pot, Zarek was suddenly there, grabbing her hand and pulling her back. He'd moved so fast and silently that she gasped in startled alarm.

His speed and strength gave her pause. This man could really hurt her if he chose to, and given what she had in store for him, that was a very sobering realization.

"Let me do that," he said sharply.

She swallowed at the unwarranted anger in his tone. "I'm not helpless. I do this all the time."

He released her. "Fine, burn your hand then, I don't care." He moved away from her.

"Sasha?" she called.

Her wolf came up to her side and leaned against her leg to let her know where he was. Kneeling down, she took his head in her hands and closed her eyes.

Reaching out with her mind, she connected with Sasha's until she could use his eyesight as her own. She saw Zarek as he made his way back to the counter and she had to force herself not to gasp.

Afraid that his looks might sway her opinion about his character before she had a chance to interact with him, she hadn't used Sasha before this to see him.

Now she knew how right she'd been.

Zarek was incredibly handsome. His long, black hair was sleek, hanging just past his wide shoulders. The black turtleneck he wore clung to a body that rippled with finely toned muscles. His face was lean and well sculpted. The planes of it, even while covered in whiskers, were a study in perfect male proportions. Yet he wasn't pretty, he was darkly handsome. Almost sinister looking except for his long black eyelashes and firm lips that softened his face.

And when he took a seat, she got a spectacular view of a well-shaped butt covered by leather.

The man was a god!

But what struck her most as he sat down and stared at the counter was the deep sadness in his midnight eyes. The haunted shadow that hovered there.

He looked tired. Lost.

Most of all, he looked terribly lonely.

He glanced at them and frowned.

Astrid patted Sasha's head and gave him a hug as if nothing unusual had happened. She hoped Zarek wouldn't have any idea what she'd been up to.

Her sisters had warned her that this particular Dark-Hunter would have extreme powers such as telekinesis and refined hearing, but none of them knew if he could sense *her* limited powers.

She was only grateful that he wasn't telepathic. That would have made her job infinitely more complicated.

She stood up and went to the cabinet to get a bowl for Zarek, and very carefully, she ladled the stew into it. Then she took it to the counter, not far from where Zarek had been standing.

He reached out and took the bowl from her. "You live alone?"

"Just me and Sasha." She wondered why he'd asked that.

Her sister Cloie had warned her that Zarek could turn violent with little provocation. That he had been known to attack Acheron and anyone else who came near him.

Dark-Hunter rumor said that his exile in Alaska had been caused by his destroying a village he'd been responsible for. No one knew why. Only that one night he'd gone mad and murdered everyone there, then razed their homes to the ground.

Her sisters had refused to elaborate on what had happened on that night for fear of prejudicing her viewpoint.

For Zarek's crime, Artemis had banished him to the frozen wilderness.

Could Zarek merely be curious about her living

arrangements or was there a more sinister reason for his question?

"Would you like something to drink?" she asked him.

"Sure."

"What do you prefer?"

"I don't care."

She shook her head at his words. "You're not very picky, are you?"

She heard him clear his throat. "No."

"I don't like the way he's looking at you."

She arched a brow at Sasha's angry words in her head. *"You don't like the way any man looks at me."*

The wolf scoffed. *"Still, he hasn't taken his eyes off you, Astrid. He's watching you now. His head is bent down, but there's lust in his eyes as he stares at you. Like he can already feel you under him. I don't trust him or that look. His gaze is too intense. Can I bite him?"*

For some reason, knowing that Zarek was watching her made her hot and shivery. *"No, Sasha. Be nice."*

"I don't want to be nice, Astrid. Every instinct I have tells me to bite him. If you have any respect for my animal abilities, let me put him down now and save us both ten more days in this cold place."

She shook her head at him. *"We just met him, Sasha. What if Lera had deemed you guilty on her first encounter with you all those centuries ago?"*

"So you believe in goodness again?"

Astrid paused. No, she didn't. Most likely Zarek deserved to die, especially if half of what she'd been told was true.

And yet Acheron's quote haunted her.

"I owe Acheron more than ten minutes of my time."

Sasha scoffed.

She poured Zarek a cup of hot tea and took it over to him. "It's rosemary tea, is that okay?"

"Whatever."

When he took it from her hand, she felt the warmth of his fingers brush hers.

An incredible rush went through her. She felt his surprise. His heated need. His unsated hunger.

That truly scared her. This was a man capable of anything. One of almost godlike powers.

He could do anything he wanted to her . . .

She needed to distract him.

And herself.

"So what really happened to you?" she asked, wondering if he would breach his Code of Silence and tell her that he was wanted by the others.

"Nothing."

"Well, I hope I never come across Nothing then if it's capable of putting a hole in my back."

She heard him pick up his tea, but he didn't speak.

"You should be more careful," she said.

"Believe me, I'm not the one who needs to be careful." His voice was sinister as he spoke those words, reinforcing his lethalness.

"Are you threatening me?" she asked.

Again he said nothing. The man was a total wall of silence.

So she pressed him once more. "Do you have anyone we need to call and let them know you're okay?"

"No," he said, his tone hollow.

She nodded as she thought about that. Zarek had never been granted a Squire.

She couldn't imagine being banished the way Zarek had been. At the time of his incarceration, this area of the world had been very sparsely populated.

The climate harsh. Inhospitable. Desolate. Bleak.

She'd only been living here a few days and it had taken some getting used to. But at least she had her mother, sisters, and Sasha to help her adjust.

Zarek had been denied anyone.

While other Dark-Hunters were allowed companions and servants, Zarek had been forced to endure his existence in solitude.

Alone.

She couldn't imagine how he must have suffered over the centuries as he struggled through his days, knowing he would never have a reprieve of any kind.

No wonder he was insane.

Still, it was no excuse for his behavior. As he had said to her earlier, everyone had their problems.

Zarek finished his food and then took the dishes to the sink. Without thinking, he rinsed and cleaned them, then set them to the side.

"You didn't have to do that. I would have cleaned them."

He wiped his hands dry on the dish towel she had on the counter. "Habit."

"You must live alone, too."

"Yeah."

Zarek watched her draw near to him. She moved to his side again, intruding on his personal space. He was torn between wanting to stand beside her and wanting to curse her nearness.

He decided on pulling away. "Look, could you just stay away from me?"

"Does it bother you for me to come near?"

More than she could imagine. When she was near him, it was easy to forget what he was. Easy to pretend he was a human being who could be normal.

But that wasn't him.

That had never been him.

"Yes, it does," he said, his tone low, threatening. "I don't like people to get near me."

"Why?"

"That's none of your damned business, lady," he snapped

at her. "I just don't like people to touch me and I don't like them to come near me. So back off and leave me alone before you get hurt."

The wolf growled at him again, more fiercely this time.

"And you, Kibbles," he snarled at the wolf, "had better lay off me. One more growl and I swear I'm going to geld you with a spoon."

"Sasha, come here."

He watched as the wolf went instantly to her side.

"I'm sorry you find us so bothersome," she said. "But since we seem to be stuck together for a bit, you could try and be a little more sociable. At the very least civil."

Maybe she was right. But the bad thing was, he didn't know how to be sociable, never mind civil. No one had ever wanted to converse with him either in his human life or his Dark-Hunter one.

Even when he'd first signed on to the Dark-Hunter.com Web site to chat ten years ago, the other, older Dark-Hunters had thrown a fit and attacked him.

He was in exile. The rules of his banishment required that none of them speak to him.

He'd been banned from posting on the bulletin boards, the chatrooms, even the private loops.

It had only been by accident that he'd stumbled across Jess, who had been in one of the gaming rooms waiting for his Myst opponent to arrive. Too young in Dark-Hunter years to know he wasn't supposed to talk to Zarek, Jess had greeted him like a friend.

The novelty of it had made Zarek vulnerable and so he'd found himself talking to the cowboy. Before he knew it, they had somehow become friends.

And what had that gotten him?

Nothing but a bullet hole in his back.

Forget it. He didn't need to talk. He didn't need anything. And the last thing he wanted was to be sociable with a human woman who would call the cops if she ever found out who and what he was.

"Look, princess, this isn't a social call. As soon as the weather lets up, I'm out of here. So just leave me alone for the next few hours and pretend I'm not here."

Astrid decided to back off a bit and let him get a little more used to her.

Little did he know, he was going to be trapped here a lot longer than a few hours. That storm wasn't going to abate until she wanted it to.

For now, she would give him time to reflect and regroup.

There were still other tests he would have to pass. Tests that she wouldn't relent on.

But there was time for that later. Right now he was still wounded and betrayed.

"Fine," she said, "I'll be in my bedroom if you need me."

She left Sasha in the kitchen to watch him.

"I don't want to watch him," Sasha snapped.

"Sasha, obey."

"What if he does something disgusting?"

"Sasha!"

The wolf growled. *"Fine. But can I have one small bite of him? Just to give him a healthy respect for me?"*

"No."

"Why?"

She paused at that as she entered her room. *"Because something tells me that if you attacked him, it is you who would get the healthy respect for* his *powers."*

"Yeah, right."

"Sasha! Please."

"Fine, I'm watching him. But if he does anything *disgusting, I'm out of here."*

She sighed at her incorrigible companion and lay down on her bed to try and get a little rest before she began her next battle of wills with Zarek.

Astrid took a deep breath and closed her eyes. She connected again with Sasha so that she could check in on Zarek. He was standing at her front window now, looking out at the snow.

She saw the ragged tear in the back of his shirt. Saw the weariness on his face. He looked daunted and at the same time determined.

There was an agelessness to his features. A wisdom that seemed somehow at odds with his sinister appearance.

"What are you, Zarek?" she wondered silently.

The question was morbidly followed by another. In the next few days, she would know exactly who and what he was. And if Artemis was right and he was truly amoral and lethal, she wouldn't hesitate to let Sasha kill him.

Chapter 4

"Wake up, Astrid. Your psychotic criminal is playing with knives."

Astrid snapped awake immediately to Sasha's voice in her head. "What?" she asked out loud before she'd realized it. She sat up in her bed.

A mental image from Sasha flashed in her mind. She saw Zarek in her kitchen, rummaging through the drawer where all her cutlery was kept.

Zarek pulled out a large butcher knife, then tested the edge with his thumb. She frowned at his actions.

What was he doing?

He set the knife aside and returned to the others in the drawer.

Sasha growled.

"Shut up, Scooby," Zarek snarled. He cast a feral, vicious glare at Sasha that held more venom than a rattlesnake farm. "Did I ever tell you how much I love pooch stew? There's enough meat on you to last me for a week."

Sasha moved forward.

Halt! she snapped mentally at her companion.

C'mon, Astrid. Let me bite him. Just once.

No, Sasha. Stand down.

He did, but he was very grudging about it. He stepped back, his eyes never leaving Zarek, who pulled a small paring knife out. Zarek fingered the blade again, looking at Sasha. She could see the gleam in Zarek's midnight eyes that said he really was considering using the knife on her companion.

Finally, he returned the butcher knife to the drawer, then took the paring knife into the den.

Astrid's frown deepened as Zarek went to her kindling pile by the hearth and pulled out a large piece of wood. He took it over to her couch and sat down.

Ignoring Sasha, who followed him every step of the way and finally ended up sitting near Zarek's feet, Zarek started to whittle the wood.

Astrid was transfixed by his unexpected actions.

He sat there for countless minutes in total silence working on the piece. But what amazed her even more than his patient, silent demeanor was the way the wolf he was carving took form. It went from a piece of a limb to a remarkable likeness of Sasha in very little time.

Even Sasha had cocked his head to watch.

Zarek's hands moved the knife over the wood with an expert grace. He paused only at times when he looked up to compare the piece to Sasha.

The man was an extremely talented artist and his talent seemed completely at odds with what she knew about him.

Intrigued, Astrid found herself getting up and returning to the living room. Her movements broke her mental connection with Sasha. Walking always did. She could only use his sight whenever she was perfectly still.

Zarek looked up as he felt the air behind him stir.

He paused as his gaze fell to Astrid and she took his breath away. Unused to having people in a house with him, he wasn't sure if he should greet her or remain silent.

He opted to just watch her.

She was so feminine and beautiful. Kind of like Sharon,

only there was a sense of vulnerability about her that Sharon lacked. Sharon possessed a smart mouth that could rival his own and her years as a single parent had left her with a very hard edge to her. But not Astrid. She had that gentle kind of softness that would cause some people to take advantage or victimize her.

The thought sent an unexpected jolt of anger through him.

Astrid moved forward into the room and was headed straight for the ottoman he'd moved out of his way earlier.

His first thought was to leave it and let her fall, but he barely moved it out of her way in time. She missed the ottoman, but did, however, stumble into him, causing the knife to slip.

Zarek hissed as the extremely sharp blade cut deeply into his hand.

"Zarek?"

He ignored her as he rushed into the kitchen to tend the throbbing wound before he dripped blood all over her polished hardwood floors and expensive rugs.

Cursing, he dropped the knife into the sink and turned the water on to rinse it.

She followed him into the kitchen. "Zarek? Is something wrong?"

"No," he snapped, washing the blood from his hand. He grimaced as he saw the depth of the injury. If he were human, he'd need stitches for it.

Astrid moved to stand beside him. "I smell blood. Are you hurt?"

Before he realized what she intended, she took his hand into hers and felt it with her hands. Her touch was feather light as she gently touched his wound and yet the sensation of her hand on his floored him. It felt as if someone had hit him in the gut with a sledgehammer.

She was so close to him that all he had to do was lean forward and he could kiss her.

Taste her neck.

Her blood . . .

No woman had ever tempted him like this.

For the first time in his life, he wanted to taste someone's lips. To hold her face in his hands and ravish her mouth with his tongue.

What would it feel like to be held . . . ?

What the hell is wrong with me?

He wasn't the kind of man that anyone held, nor did he want it.

Not really.

He only wanted . . .

"This is deep," she said quietly, her voice enchanting him even more.

He looked down, but instead of his hand, all he could see was the deep valley between her breasts that was bared by the V of her sweater. He would only have to move his hand a few inches to sink it down between the soft mounds. To push her sweater aside a little bit until he could cup her with his hand.

"What happened?" she asked.

Zarek blinked to dispel the image that caused his groin to ache and throb as it demanded satisfaction. "Nothing."

"Is that the only word you know?" She grimaced at him as she held his hand with hers and reached up to pull a bottle of peroxide out of the cabinet over the sink. He was amazed that she knew which container it was, but then, everything in the cabinet appeared to be deliberately and carefully placed.

He hissed again as she poured the liquid over his cut. The coldness of it stung as much as the disinfectant.

Still, he was stunned by her caring actions, by the gentleness of her hand on his.

She patted around with her hand for the dish towel by the sink. Once she found it, she wrapped it around his hand. "Keep it elevated. I'll call a doc—"

"No," he said harshly, interrupting her. "No doctor."

"But you're hurt."

"Believe me, this is nothing."

Astrid noted the catch in his voice as he said that. More than ever before, she wished she could see him as he spoke. "Were you cut because I bumped into you?"

He didn't answer.

Astrid tried to reach out to him with her senses and found nothing. She couldn't tell if he was with her or if she was completely alone.

Her senses had never failed her before.

It was scary to have no ability to "feel" him.

"Zarek?"

"What?"

She actually jumped at the sound of his deep, accented voice so close to her ear. "You didn't answer my question."

"Yeah, so what? It's not like you care how I got hurt anyway."

His voice faded as if he were moving away from her.

"Sasha, where is he?"

"He's headed back toward the den."

She heard Sasha growling in the hallway.

"Back at you," Zarek grumbled.

"You know," he said louder. "I hear dogs live longer when they're neutered. And they're friendlier, too."

"Oh, yeah, let's neuter you and see if it affects you, you—"

"Sasha!"

"What? He's obnoxious. And I am not a dog."

She walked down the hallway to pat Sasha's head. *"I know."*

Zarek ignored the wolf and the woman as he went to the window and pulled the curtains back. It was just after one A.M. and the blizzard was as fierce as it had been earlier.

Damn. He was never going to get out of here. He only hoped the weather broke long enough to allow him to make it back to his woods. No doubt the Squires, Jess, and Thanatos were waiting for him at his cabin, but he had several more "safe" areas none of them knew about. Places where he could get weapons and supplies.

But he had to be on his land to reach it.

"Zarek?"

He expelled an aggravated breath.

"What?" he snapped.

"Don't use that tone with me," she said with a sharp note in her voice that caused him to arch a brow at her audacity. "I like to know where people are in my house. Be nice, or I'll make you wear a cowbell."

He felt a strange urge to laugh. But laughter and he were strangers.

"I'd like to see you try it."

"Are you always this cranky or did you just wake up on the wrong side of the bed?"

"This is it, baby, get used to it."

She came to stand right beside him and he had a feeling that she purposely did it just to irk him. "And if I don't want to get used to it?"

He turned to face her. "Don't push me, princess."

"Oooo," she said in a less than impressed voice. "Next thing you'll be talking like the Incredible Hulk. 'Don't make me angry, you wouldn't like me when I'm angry.' " She cast a haughty look in his general direction. "You're not scary to me, Mr. Zarek. So you can just check the attitude at the door and play nice while you're here."

Disbelief racked him. No one in the past two thousand years had dismissed him so easily and it angered him that she would dare discount him now. It reminded him of too many bad memories of people who saw through him. People who held no regard for him whatsoever.

The first vow he had made to himself as a Dark-Hunter was that he would never again worry about trying to earn other people's respect or kindness.

Fear was a far more powerful tool.

He backed her up against a wall.

Astrid panicked as she felt Zarek pressing in on her while the wall behind her blocked her escape. She had nowhere to go. She couldn't breathe. Couldn't move.

He was so large, so strong.

All she could sense was him. He surrounded her with power and danger. With the promise of lethal reflexes. He was trying to make her fear him, she knew it.

It was working very well.

He didn't touch her, but then, he didn't have to. His presence alone was terrifying.

Dark. Dangerous.

Deadly.

She felt him bend down to speak angrily into her ear. "If you want nice, baby, play with your fucking dog. When you're ready to play with a man, then call me."

Before she could respond, Sasha attacked.

Zarek stumbled away from her with a curse as the air around her stirred viciously with Sasha's frantic movements.

Cringing instinctively, Astrid held her breath as she heard the sound of wolf and man fighting. She strained to see, but she was surrounded solely by darkness and overwhelming angry sounds.

"Sasha!" she shouted, wishing she could see what was happening between them.

All she heard was the mingling of hisses, growls, and curses.

Then something solid hit the wall next to her.

Sasha yelped.

Terrified of what Zarek had done to her companion, Astrid knelt on the floor and felt her way over to where Sasha was lying before the hearth.

"Sasha?" She ran her trembling hand through his fur, seeking wounds.

He didn't move.

Her heart stopped beating as terror filled her. If anything had happened to Sasha, she would kill Zarek herself!

Please, please be all right . . .

"Sasha?" She held him close and reached out with her thoughts to his.

"I'll kill him. So help me, I will."

She shook in relief at Sasha's anger. Thank Zeus he was alive!

Zarek pulled his torn shirt off and used it to contain the blood on his right arm, neck, and shoulder where the pooch had shredded his skin with its claws and teeth.

He barely contained his fury. He hadn't been wounded this many times in a single hour since the day he'd died.

Snarling, he stared at the swollen red flesh. He hated to be wounded.

It was all he could do not to go back to the den and make sure that damned dog never attacked another living thing in its life.

He wanted blood. Wolf blood.

For that matter, he wanted human blood. One quick nip to calm his fury and remind him of what he was.

Just one taste of her . . .

Astrid came inside the bathroom and ran into him.

He growled at the warm sensation of her body slamming into his.

Without comment, she pushed him away from the sink and knelt down to retrieve a first-aid kit.

"You could have said 'Excuse me.' "

"I'm not talking to you," she snapped.

"Love you, too, babe."

She froze at his sarcasm and glared in his general direction. "You really are an animal, aren't you?"

Zarek ground his teeth at her words. It was all anyone had ever seen him as. He was too old now to change his ways. "Woof, woof."

Huffing at him, she started to leave, then stopped. She turned back toward him with a snarl. "You know, I have no idea where you come from and I don't really care. Nothing gives you the right to hurt other people or Sasha. He was only protecting me, while you . . . You're nothing but a bully."

Zarek stood immobile while vicious, horrid images tore through his memory. The sight of his village in flames.

Of bodies lying scattered all around.

The faint sounds of people screaming.

The fury inside his heart that demanded blood . . .

He winced as pain lacerated him. He hated his memories almost as much as he hated himself.

"One day someone needs to teach you some civility." Astrid turned and headed back toward the den.

"Yeah," he said, curling his lip. "Go tend your dog, princess. *He* needs you."

Zarek, on the other hand, didn't need anyone.

He never had.

With that thought in mind, he went to the room where he'd awakened.

Storm or no storm, it was time for him to leave.

He pulled his coat on over his bare chest and buttoned it. It too had been damaged by the gunshot and would leave his healing back exposed to the weather. So be it.

It wasn't as if he could freeze to death anyway. There were some advantages to immortality.

The hole would just make for a nice cool breeze to run down his spine until he could find more clothes.

After he was dressed, he headed for the door and did his best not to notice Astrid, who was on her knees in front of the warm fire, soothing and consoling her pet as she tended him.

The sight made him ache in a way he wouldn't have thought possible.

Yeah, it was time he got the hell out of here.

"He's leaving."

Astrid started at the sound of Sasha in her head. *"What do you mean, he's leaving?"*

"He's behind you right now, dressed and headed outside."

"Zarek?"

She was answered by the slamming of her door.

Chapter 5

Zarek froze outside the door. Literally and figuratively. The bite of the wind was so harsh that it took his breath and sent a fierce shiver down his entire body.

It was so cold outside that he could barely move. The snow was falling fast and furiously, and was so dense that he couldn't see more than about an inch from the tip of his nose. Even his goggles had frozen.

No one sane would be out tonight.

So it was a good thing he was insane.

Grinding his teeth, he headed north. Damn, but it was going to be one long, miserable walk home. He only hoped he could make it to some kind of shelter before dawn.

If not, Artemis and Dionysus were going to be two happy gods in a few hours and old Acheron would have one less headache in his life.

"Zarek?"

He cursed as he heard Astrid's voice over the howling winds.

Don't answer.

Don't look.

But it was compulsory. He glanced back before he could

stop himself and there he saw her leaving the cabin with no coat on.

"Zarek!" She stumbled in the snow and fell.

Leave her. She should have stayed inside where she was safe.

He couldn't.

She was helpless alone and he wouldn't leave her outside to die.

Mumbling a fetid curse that would have made a sailor cringe, he went to her side. He picked her up roughly and pushed her toward her house. "Get inside before you freeze to death."

"What about you?"

"What about me?"

"You can't stay out here, either."

"Believe me, princess, I've slept in worse conditions than this."

"You'll die out here."

"I don't care."

"Well, I do."

Zarek would have been far less stunned had she slapped him. At least *that* he would have expected.

For a full minute he couldn't move as those words rang in his ears. The idea that anyone cared whether or not he lived or died was so alien to him that he wasn't even sure how to respond.

"Get inside," he snarled, shoving her gently back through her door.

The wolf growled at him.

"Shut up, Sasha," she snapped before he had a chance to. "One more sound out of you and I'll make *you* go outside."

The wolf sniffed the air indignantly as if it understood her, then darted to the back of the house.

Zarek shut the door while Astrid trembled from the cold. The falling snow melted, making her instantly wet. He was wet too, not that he cared. He was used to physical discomfort.

She wasn't.

"What were you thinking?" he yelled at her, sitting her down on the couch.

"Don't you dare take that tone of voice with me."

So he growled at her instead and stalked to the bathroom where he could grab a towel from the rack. Then he headed to her bedroom and grabbed a blanket.

He returned to her. "You're soaked."

"I noticed."

Astrid was surprised by the sudden, unexpected warmth of a blanket covering her, especially given his angry, gravelly words that had all but called her an idiot for going after him.

Zarek wrapped her up tightly, then knelt before her. He pulled her fur-lined slippers from her feet and rubbed her frozen toes until she could again feel something other than the painful burn of cold.

She'd never experienced cold like this before and she wondered how many times Zarek must have suffered from it with no one there to warm him.

"That was a stupid thing for you to do," he said harshly.

"Then why did *you* do it?"

He didn't answer. Instead, he dropped her foot and moved around her.

She didn't know what he was going to do until she felt a towel covering her head. Tensing, she expected him to be rough.

He wasn't. In fact, his touch was amazingly gentle as he toweled her hair dry.

How strange was this? Who would have thought he would take such tender care of her?

It was completely unexpected.

Perhaps there was more to him than there appeared . . .

Zarek gnashed his teeth at how soft her damp hair was as it fell against his hands. He tried to keep the towel between it and his skin, but it didn't work. Strands of her hair continually brushed his flesh, making him burn.

What would it be like to kiss a woman?

What would it be like to kiss *her*?

He'd never before had the inclination. Every time a woman had tried, he'd moved his lips away from hers. It was an intimacy he had no wish to experience with anyone.

And yet he felt the yearning for it now. Felt a hunger to sample the moist, rosy lips of Astrid.

What are you? Mental?

Yes, he was.

He had no place in his life for a woman, no place for a friend or companion. He'd learned from the hour of his birth that he had but one destiny.

Isolation.

Even when he tried to belong, it didn't work. He was an outsider. That was all he knew.

He pulled the towel away from her hair and stared at her, wanting to run his hand through those damp strands and comb them. Her skin was still ashen and gray from the cold. But she was no less lovely. No less inviting.

Before he could stop himself, he laid his bare hand against her chilled cheek and let the softness of her skin pierce him.

Gods, but it felt so good just to touch her.

She didn't pull away from his touch or cringe. She sat there and let him touch her like a man.

Like a lover . . .

"Zarek?" Her voice was full of uncertainty.

"You feel like ice," he growled, then left her. He had to get away from her and the strange feelings she stirred inside him. He didn't want to be around her.

He didn't want to be tamed.

Every time he had allowed himself to be tied to another human, he'd been betrayed.

By everyone.

Even Jess, who had seemed safe because he lived so far away.

An echo pain stabbed his back.

Apparently Jess hadn't lived far enough away.

Zarek glanced out the kitchen window where the snow continued to fall. Sooner or later, Astrid would sleep and then he would leave.

Then she couldn't stop him.

Astrid started to go after Zarek, but stopped herself. She wanted to see what he would do. What he intended.

Sasha, what is he doing?

She held herself still and used Sasha's sight. Zarek was unbuttoning his coat. Her breath caught at the sight of his bare chest. Every muscle on his body rippled as he removed the coat and draped it over the back of her ladder-back chair.

The man was simply gorgeous. His tawny, bare back and wide shoulders inviting. Delectable.

But what stunned her was his right arm and shoulder, which were a total mess from Sasha's attack.

Astrid gasped at the sight of what her companion had done. Zarek on the other hand didn't seem to be the least bit bothered by his vicious wounds. He went about his business as if nothing had happened.

"Do I have to look at this?" Sasha whined in her head. *"I'm going to go blind looking at a naked man."*

"You're not going to go blind and he's not naked." Unfortunately.

Astrid was a bit taken aback by that uncharacteristic thought. She'd never ogled a man before, but she found herself transfixed by Zarek.

"Yes I am, and yes he is. Naked enough to make me lose my lunch anyway." Sasha started out of the kitchen.

"Sasha, stay."

"I'm not a dog, Astrid, and I don't care for that commanding tone. I stay with you by my choice, not by yours."

"I know, Sasha. I'm sorry. Please, stay for me."

Growling in a manner very reminiscent of Zarek, Sasha loped back into the kitchen and sat down to watch him.

Zarek paid no attention to Sasha while he moved about the kitchen looking for something.

She frowned at him pulling out a small pan. As he moved toward her fridge, her breath caught at the sight of a stylized dragon tattooed onto the small of his back. And right above it was the fierce-looking wound where someone had shot him.

She cringed in unexpected sympathy. For the first time in a long while she actually felt sorry for someone. It looked vicious and painful.

Zarek moved as if he barely noticed it.

He went to the fridge and pulled out her milk and the big Hershey candy bar she'd bought on impulse. He poured the milk into the saucepan and then added pieces of the chocolate to it.

How strange. He'd bit her head off and intimidated her, then tended her, and now he was making hot chocolate.

"It's not for you," Sasha said to her.

"Hush, Sasha."

"It's not. Wanna bet he tries to poison me with the chocolate?"

"Well, then don't eat it."

Zarek turned around and leveled a sinister sneer at Sasha. "Here, Lassie, want to go find Timmy in the well? C'mon, girl, I'll even open the door for you and toss you a biscuit."

"Here psycho-Hunter, wanna find my teeth in your—"

"Sasha!"

"I can't help it. He bothers me. A lot."

Zarek looked over at the water and food bowls that Astrid had placed on a small tray that was about four inches off the floor for Sasha.

Sasha bared his teeth. *"Not my food, man. You contaminate it and so help me I* will *bite the shit out of you."*

"Sasha, please."

Zarek approached the stainless steel bowls.

"I told you, Astrid, the bastard is going to poison me. He's going to spit in my water or do something worse to it."

Zarek did the most unexpected thing of all. He bent down, picked up the almost empty water bowl, washed it out in the sink and refilled it with water, then carefully returned it to the tray.

Astrid wasn't sure which of them was the most shocked by his actions. Her or Sasha.

Sasha moved to his bowl and sniffed it suspiciously.

Zarek returned to the sink to wash his hands. Once the chocolate milk was warmed up, he poured it into a mug and brought it to her.

"Here," he said, his voice ringing with its usual rude, hostile note. He took her hand and led it to the cup.

"What is it?" she asked.

"Arsenic and vomit."

She screwed her face up in disgust at the thought. "Really? And yet you managed to hack that up so quietly. Who knew? Thanks. I've never had vomit before. I'm sure it's *extra* special."

Well, so much for thinking Zarek had a kinder, gentler side.

"Drink it or don't," he growled. "I don't care."

She heard him leave the room again.

Astrid held the cup. Even though she had watched him make it through Sasha's eyes and knew he hadn't done anything to contaminate it, she was still reluctant to taste it after his off-putting comment.

"He's watching you," Sasha told her.

She cocked her head very slowly. *"How so?"*

"Like he's daring you to taste it."

Astrid held her breath, debating what to do. Was it a test of his own? Was he asking her to trust him?

Taking a deep breath, she drank the chocolate, which was a perfect temperature and very tasty.

Zarek was amazed at her bravery. So, she had called his bluff and trusted him. He would never have drunk anything a stranger handed him and it surprised him that she had.

He felt a grudging respect for her. The woman had a lot of guts, he'd give her that.

But at the end of the day, guts didn't account for much, and all they would do is get her killed if Thanatos found them before he had a chance to leave.

His gaze turned dull as he remembered the demon or Daimon or whatever he was who had been sent to kill him.

All this time, the Dark-Hunters had assumed Acheron was the bloodhound Artemis used to track and kill rogue Dark-Hunters.

All the men who knew the truth were now roaming the earth as Shades. Soulless, bodiless entities who could feel hunger and thirst and yet were never allowed to sate it.

They could feel and sense the world, but no one could feel or sense them.

He understood that existence. For the twenty-six years he had lived as a mortal human, he'd been one himself.

Only then, a world that didn't know he existed would have been preferable. Because when people had realized he was around, they had gone out of their way to increase his pain.

Gone out of their way to hurt and humiliate him.

Rage flooded him as his gaze sharpened once more. He looked around the immaculate cabin where every detail showed Astrid's wealth. In his human existence a woman like her would have spat in his face for no other reason than that he dared to cross her path. He would have been so far beneath her that he would have been beaten for even daring to lift his gaze to her face.

To look her in the eyes would have been his death.

"Is this slave bothering you, mistress?"

He winced as the memory ran through his mind.

At age twelve he had been foolish enough to listen to his brothers as they pointed out a woman who was in the marketplace.

"She's your mother, slave. Didn't you know? Uncle freed her just last year."

"Why not go to her, Zarek? Maybe she'll take pity on you and have you freed, too."

Too young and too stupid to know better, he had stared at the woman they showed him. She had hair as black as his and perfect blue eyes. He'd never seen his mother before. Had never known she was so beautiful.

But in his heart, she had always been more beautiful than Venus. He had envisioned her as a slave like himself who had no choice but to do as her master said. He'd built up a whole dream of how he'd been ripped from her arms after birth. How she had wept for him to be returned to her.

How she had pined every day for her lost son.

Meanwhile, he had been given to his merciless father who had vengefully kept him away from her caring arms.

Zarek was sure she would love him. All mothers loved their children. It was why the other female slaves had no use for him. They were saving all their rations and affections for their own.

But this woman . . . she was his.

And she would love him.

Zarek had run to her and embraced her, telling her who he was and how much he loved her.

But there had been no warm welcome. No motherly affection.

She had looked at him with abject disgust and horror. Her lips had curled cruelly as she hissed to him, *"I paid that whore good money to see you dead."*

His brothers had laughed at him.

Zarek had been too crushed by her rejection to move or breathe. He had been devastated to learn that his mother had bribed another slave to kill him.

When a soldier approached them to ask if he were disturbing her, she had said coldly, *"This worthless slave touched me. I want him beaten for it."*

Even after two thousand years those words resonated through him. As did the pitiless look on her face as she turned and left him to the soldiers, who had gleefully carried out her order . . .

"You are worthless, slave. Good for nothing at all. You're not even worth the scraps it takes to keep you alive. If we're lucky mayhap you'll die and save us the winter rations for a slave who has some value."

Zarek growled as his memories took hold of him. Unable to deal with the pain they caused, he lashed out with his powers. Every lightbulb in the den shattered, the fire roared in the hearth, narrowly missing Sasha, who had been lying before it. Pictures fell from the walls.

All he wanted was for the pain to stop . . .

Astrid screamed as her ears were assailed with foreign sounds. *"Sasha, what's happening?"*

"The bastard tried to kill me."

"How?"

"He shot a fireball from the fireplace into my hindquarters. Man, my fur is singed. He's having a fit of some kind and using his powers."

"Zarek?"

The entire cabin shook with such ferocity that she half-expected it to burst apart.

"Zarek!"

Total silence descended.

All Astrid could hear was her heart pounding.

"What's happening?" she asked Sasha.

"I don't know. The fire went out and I can't see anything. It's totally black. He shattered the lights."

"Zarek?" she tried again.

Again no one answered. Her panic tripled. He could kill her and neither she nor Sasha would see him coming.

He could do anything to her.

"Why did you save me?"

She jumped at the sound of his voice right beside her ear as she sat on the couch. He was so close to her that she could feel his warm breath on her skin.

"You were hurt."

"How did you know I was hurt?"

"I didn't until after I got you inside. I . . . I thought you might be drunk."

"Only an absolute idiot would bring a strange man into her home when she's blind and lives alone. You don't strike me as an idiot."

She swallowed. He was a lot smarter than she had given him credit for.

And a lot scarier.

"Why am I here?" he demanded.

"I told you."

He shoved the couch so hard that it skidded forward several inches. Then he was in front of her, pinning her to the cushions. Making her tremble from his fierce presence. "How did you get me inside?"

"I dragged you."

"Alone?"

"Of course."

"You don't look strong enough."

She gasped in terror. What was he going for? What did he intend to do to her? "I'm stronger than I look."

"Prove it." He grabbed her wrists.

She wrestled with him for several seconds. "Let me go."

"Why? Do I repulse you?"

Sasha growled. Loudly.

She stopped moving and glared at where she hoped his face was.

"Zarek," she said firmly. "You're hurting me. Let me go."

To her shock, he did. He moved back ever so slightly but his angry presence was still tangible. Oppressive. Frightening.

"Do something smart, princess," he growled in her ear. "Stay far away from me."

She heard him walk away from her.

"He's guilty," Sasha snapped. *"Astrid. Judge him."*

She couldn't. Not yet. Even though Zarek scared her. Even though at this moment he did seem unbalanced and terrifying.

He hadn't really hurt her. He'd only frightened her, and that wasn't something anyone should die for.

After this, she could well understand how he could have snapped one night and killed everyone in the village he had been entrusted to guard.

Would he snap like that with her?

Because she was immortal, he couldn't kill her, but he could hurt her.

A lesser judge might go ahead and render verdict based on his actions tonight alone. She was tempted herself, but she wouldn't. Not yet.

"Are you all right?" Sasha asked after she refused to respond to his demand for a verdict.

"Yes."

But she was lying and she had a feeling Sasha knew it. Zarek terrified her in a way no one ever had before.

Over the centuries, she had judged countless men and women. Murderers, traitors, blasphemers. You name it.

But none of them had ever scared her. None of them

had ever made her want to go running to her sisters for protection.

Zarek did.

There was something about him that really wasn't sane. She was used to dealing with people who tried to hide their insanity. Men who could play gallant heroes while inside they were cold and cruel.

Zarek lashed out and yet he hadn't hurt her.

At least not yet.

But his bullying tactics were going to have to go.

She remembered Acheron's words to her: "It is only with the heart that one can see rightly . . ."

What was inside Zarek's heart?

Expelling a long breath, Astrid reached out with her senses and tried to locate Zarek.

As before, she couldn't find him at all. It was as if he were so used to keeping himself hidden that he didn't register on anyone's radar. Not even her heightened one.

"Where is he?" she asked Sasha.

"In his room, I think."

"Where are you?"

Sasha came and sat at her feet. *"Artemis is right. For the sake of mankind, he should be put down. There's something seriously wrong with that man."*

Astrid rubbed his ears as she considered that. *"I don't know. Acheron bartered with Artemis so that I could judge Zarek. He wouldn't have done that for no reason. Only a fool barters with Artemis for anything. And Acheron is far from foolish. There has to be something good in Zarek or else—"*

"Acheron will always sacrifice for his men. It's what he does," Sasha scoffed.

"Perhaps . . ."

But she knew better. Acheron would always do whatever was the greater good for all involved. He had never before interfered when it was time to judge or execute a rogue Dark-Hunter, and yet he had asked her personally to judge this one . . .

He hadn't allowed Zarek to be killed nine hundred years ago for destroying his village and killing innocent humans.

If Zarek truly posed a danger, Acheron would never have bargained with them for a hearing or allowed the Dark-Hunter to live. There had to be more to this.

She had to believe Acheron.

She had to.

Zarek sat alone in his room, watching the snow fall outside through the open curtains. He was seated in the rocking chair, but remained motionless. After his "meltdown," he'd gone through the house replacing bulbs and picking up the broken pictures. Now everything was eerily quiet.

He had to get out of here before he snapped again. Why wouldn't the storm break?

The hall light came on, temporarily blinding him.

He frowned at that. Why did Astrid use lights when she was blind?

He heard her padding down the hallway toward the den. Part of him wanted to join her, to talk to her. But he had never been one for idle conversation.

He didn't know how to make small talk. No one had ever been interested in anything he had to say.

So he kept to himself and that suited him just fine.

"Sasha?"

The sound of her melodic voice went through him like shattered glass.

"Sit here while I make another fire."

He almost got up to help, but forced himself to stay in his chair. His days as a servant to the rich were over. If she wanted a fire, then she was just as able to make one as he was.

Of course he could see to light the kindling and his hands were rough from hard work.

Hers were soft. Delicate.

Fragile hands that could soothe . . .

Before he realized it, he was headed for the den.

He found Astrid kneeling before the hearth, trying to push new logs onto the iron grate. She was struggling with it and doing her best not to get burned in the process.

Without a word, he pulled her back.

She gasped in alarm.

"Move out of my way," he snarled.

"I wasn't in your way. You got into mine."

When she refused to move, he picked her up and dropped her into the dark green armchair.

"What are you doing?" she asked, her expression startled.

"Nothing." He returned to the hearth and made the fire. "I can't believe that with all the money you have, you don't have someone here to help you."

"I don't need anyone to help me."

He paused at her words. "No? How do you get around on your own?"

"I just do. I can't stand for anyone to treat me like I'm helpless. I happen to be just as capable as anyone else."

"Bully for you, princess." But he felt the swell of another wave of respect for her. In the world he'd grown up in, women like her never did anything for themselves. They'd bought people like him to serve their every whim.

"Why do you call me 'princess' all the time?"

"It's what you are, aren't you? Your parents' shining darling."

She frowned. "How do you know that?"

"I can smell it on you. You're one of those people who has never had a moment's worry in your life. Everything you've ever wanted, you've gotten."

"Not everything."

"No? What have you ever lacked?"

"My eyesight."

Zarek fell silent as her words rang in his ears. "Yeah, being blind sucks."

"How would you know?"

"Been there, done that."

Chapter 6

"You were blind?" Astrid asked.

Zarek didn't answer. He couldn't believe he'd allowed that to slip out. It was something he'd never spoken of, not even to Jess.

Only Acheron knew and Acheron had thankfully kept the secret.

Unwilling to visit his past again tonight and the pain that waited there, Zarek left the den and returned to his room where he locked the door so that he could wait out the storm in peace.

At least alone he didn't have to worry about betraying himself or hurting anyone.

But as he sat in his chair, it wasn't images of the past that haunted him.

It was the scent of roses and wood, the clear pale eyes of a woman.

The remembered feel of her soft, cold cheek underneath his fingertips. Her damp tousled hair that framed features which were feminine and inviting.

A woman who didn't flinch from him or cringe.

She was astounding and surprising. If he were someone else, he might even go back to the den where she sat with her wolf and make her laugh. But he didn't know how to make people laugh. He could recognize humor, most especially irony, but he wasn't the kind of man to make jokes or nurture smiles from other people. Especially not a woman.

That fact hadn't bothered him before.

Tonight it did.

"Is he guilty?"

Astrid started at Artemis's voice in her head. Every night since Zarek had been brought into her house, Artemis had bugged her with that one question—over and over again, until she felt like Joan of Arc being tormented by voices.

"Not yet, Artemis. He just woke up."

"Well, what's taking so long? As long as he's living, Acheron is on edge and I positively hate it when he's agitated. Judge him rogue already."

"Why do you want Zarek dead so much?"

Silence descended. At first she thought Artemis had left her, so when the response came, it surprised her. *"Acheron doesn't like to see anyone suffer. Especially not one of his Dark-Hunters. So long as Zarek lives, Acheron hurts, and in spite of what Acheron thinks, I don't like to see him hurting."*

Astrid had never known Artemis to say such a thing. The goddess wasn't exactly known for her kindness or compassion, or for thinking of anyone besides herself.

"Do you love Acheron?"

Artemis's voice was sharp when she answered, *"Acheron is no concern of yours, Astrid. Only Zarek is, and I swear if I lose any more of Acheron's loyalty over this, you will be very sorry for it."*

Astrid stiffened at her hostile tone and threat. It would take more than Artemis to hurt her, and if the goddess wanted a fight, she had better come prepared.

She might not like her job anymore, but Astrid took it

seriously and no one, most especially Artemis, was going to bully her into a premature verdict.

"If I judge Zarek too soon, don't you think Acheron would be angry and demand a rejudging?"

Artemis made a rude noise.

"Besides, you told Acheron that you wouldn't interfere, Artemis. You made him swear that he wouldn't contact me to try to sway my verdict and yet here you are trying to do that. How do you think he'd react if I told him of your actions?"

"Fine," she snapped. *"I won't disturb you again. But get up with it already!"*

Alone finally, Astrid sat in the den, thinking over what she should do next, how she could push Zarek to see if he would break again and turn more violent.

He had attacked her house, but not her. Sasha had attacked him, and though he had hurt the wolf, the wolf had hurt him much more. It had been an honest fight between them and Zarek hadn't tried to kill Sasha for the attack. He'd gotten the wolf off him and then left him alone.

Instead of seeking revenge on Sasha, Zarek had given him water.

Zarek's worst crime so far was belligerency and the fact that he had a truly frightening presence. Yet he did kind things that were at odds with his surliness.

Her common sense said to do as Artemis asked, find him guilty and run.

Her gut instinct told her to wait.

So long as he didn't strike out in anger at her or Sasha, she would follow this through.

But if he ever did strike out at them, then she was out the door and he was toast.

"There is no such thing as an innocent man . . ."

Astrid let out a tired breath. She'd said that to her sister Atty the last time they had spoken to each other. Part of her honestly believed it. Never once in all these centuries had she found someone innocent. Every man she had ever judged had lied to her.

All of them had tried to deceive her.

Some had tried to bribe her.

Some had tried to escape her.

Some had tried to beat her.

And one had tried to kill her.

She wondered which category Zarek would fall into.

Taking a deep breath for fortification, Astrid got up and went to her room to dig around in the clothes Sasha wore when he was in human form.

"What are you doing?" Sasha asked as he joined her.

"Zarek needs clothes," she said out loud without thinking.

Sasha nipped at her hands, and nosed his clothes back into the basket in the bottom of the closet. *"He can get his own. Those are mine."*

Astrid pulled them back out. *"C'mon, Sasha, be nice. He doesn't have any clothes here and the ones he's wearing are ragged."*

"So?"

She sorted through the pants and shirts, wishing she could see them. *"You were the one who was complaining about having to look at a naked man. I thought you'd prefer to see some clothing on him."*

"I also complain about the fact that I have to piss outside and eat out of bowls, but I don't see you letting me use the bathroom or tableware around him."

She shook her head at him. *"Would you stop? You nag like an old woman."* She picked up a heavy sweater.

"No," Sasha snapped. *"Not the burgundy sweater. That's my favorite."*

"Sasha, I swear. You are so spoiled!"

"And that's my sweater. Put it back."

She got up to take it to Zarek.

Sasha followed, complaining the whole way.

"I'll buy you a new one," she promised.

"I don't want a new one. I want that *one."*

"He won't hurt it."

"Yes he will. Look at his clothes. They're ruined. And I don't want his body touching something I wear. He'll contaminate it."

"Oh, good grief, Sasha. Grow up. You're four hundred years old and you're acting like a whelp. It's not like he has cooties or anything."

"Yes he does!"

She glared down her leg where she could feel him. He grabbed the sweater with his teeth and pulled it out of her hands.

"Sasha!" she snapped out loud, running after him. "Give me that sweater or I swear *I* will see you gelded."

The wolf ran through the house.

Astrid went after him as fast as she could. She relied on her memory as to where things should be.

Someone had moved the coffee table. She hissed as her leg collided with the corner of it and she lost her balance. She reached out with her hands to catch herself, only to feel the tabletop tilting. It gave under her weight.

The glass top fell sideways, sending things flying.

Something hit her in the head and something shattered.

Astrid froze, afraid to move.

She didn't know what had broken, but the sound had been unmistakable.

Where was the glass?

Her heart pounding, she cursed her blindness. She didn't dare move for fear of cutting herself.

"Sasha?" she asked.

He didn't answer.

"Don't move." Zarek's deep commanding voice shivered down her spine.

The next thing she knew two strong arms lifted her up from the floor with an ease that was truly terrifying. He cradled her against a body that was rock hard and lean. One that rippled with every move he made as he walked her away from the den.

She put her arms around broad, masculine shoulders that stiffened in reaction to her touch. His breath fell against her face, making her entire body melt.

"Zarek?" she asked tentatively.

"Is there anyone else in this house who can carry you that I need to know about?"

She ignored his sarcasm as he carried her to the kitchen and set her down on a chair.

She missed his heat instantly. It brought an odd ache to her chest that she neither expected nor understood.

"Thank you," she said quietly.

He didn't respond. Instead, she heard him leave the room.

A few minutes later, he returned and dumped something into the trash can.

"I don't know what you did to Scooby," he said, his tone almost normal, "but he's off in a corner lying down on a sweater and growling at me."

She stifled the urge to laugh at that image. "He's being bad."

"Yeah, well, where I come from, we beat things that are bad."

Astrid frowned at his words and the underlying emotion they betrayed. "Sometimes understanding is more important than punishment."

"And sometimes it's not."

"Maybe," she whispered.

Zarek turned on the water in the sink. It sounded as if he were washing his hands again.

Strange, he seemed to do that a lot.

"I got up all the glass I could find," he said over the sound of the rushing water, "but the crystal vase on your table shattered pretty badly. You might want to wear shoes in there for a few days."

Astrid was strangely touched by his actions and his warning. She got up from her chair and crossed the floor to stand next to him. Even though she couldn't see him, she could feel him now. Feel his heat, his strength.

Feel the raw sensuality of the man.

It shivered through her and down her body, enticing her with desire and need.

A foreign part of her ached to reach out and touch the smooth, tawny skin that beckoned her with the promise of primal heat. Even now she remembered the way his skin had looked. The way the light had played on it.

She wanted to pull his lips to hers and see what he tasted like. See if he could be tender.

Or would he be rough and forceful?

Astrid should be shocked by her thoughts. As a judge, she wasn't supposed to have this kind of curiosity, but as a woman, she couldn't help it.

It had been a long, long time since she'd felt desire for a man. Deep down there was even a part of her that yearned to find in him the goodness that Acheron believed in.

That was something she hadn't wanted to do in centuries either.

Zarek's kindness was unwarranted. "How did you know I needed you?"

"I heard the glass break and figured you were trapped."

She smiled. "That was very sweet of you."

She had a feeling he was staring at her. Her flesh warmed considerably at the thought. Her breasts hardened.

"I'm not sweet, princess. Trust me."

No, he wasn't sweet. He was hard. Prickly and strangely fascinating. Like a wild beast that needed to be tamed.

If anyone could ever tame something like him.

"I was attempting to give you some clothes," she said softly, trying to regain control of her body, which didn't seem to want to respond to common sense. "There are more sweaters in the bottom of my closet if you'd like to borrow them."

He scoffed at that as he turned off the water and ripped a paper towel off to dry his hands. "Your clothes won't fit me, princess."

She laughed. "They're not mine. They belong to a male friend."

Zarek couldn't breathe with her so close to him. All he had to do was lean down ever so slightly and he could kiss her slightly parted lips.

Reach out and he would touch her.

What truly scared him was just how much he wanted to touch her. How much he wanted to press his body to hers and feel her soft curves against the hard male lines of his.

He couldn't remember ever wanting anything more.

Closing his eyes, he was seared with an image of the two of them naked. Of him placing her up on the counter in front of him so that he could screw her brains out. Of sliding in and out of her heat until he was too tired to stand.

Too sore to move.

He wanted to feel the warmth of her skin sliding against his. Her breath on his flesh.

Most of all, he wanted her scent on his skin. To know what it felt like to have a woman who didn't show fear or contempt of him.

In all these centuries, he'd never screwed a woman he hadn't paid for. Most of the time he hadn't even had that.

He'd been alone for so long . . .

"Where's this male friend of yours?" he asked, his voice strangely thick as he thought of her with another man. It hurt in a way it shouldn't.

Sasha came into the room to stare at them and bark.

"My friend died," Astrid said without hesitation.

Zarek arched a brow. "Died how?"

"Mmm, he had parvo."

"Isn't that a dog's disease?"

"Yes. It was tragic."

"Hey!" Sasha said to Astrid. *"I resent that."*

"Behave or I will give you parvo."

Zarek stepped away from her. "Do you miss him?"

She glanced in the direction of Sasha's bark. "No, not really. He was a bit of a pain."

"I'll show you pain, nymph. Just you wait."

Astrid bit back a smile. "So are you interested in the clothes?" she asked Zarek.

"Sure."

She led him to her room.

"You are so evil," Sasha snarled. *"Just wait. I will get you back for this. You know that comforter you're so fond of? It's toast. And I wouldn't use my slippers again if I were you."*

She ignored him.

Zarek didn't speak as she took him into her room, which was decorated in soft shades of pink. It was all feminine and soft. But it was the scent in the air that made him ache.

Roses and wood smoke.

It smelled like her.

That scent made him so hard and stiff, he hurt. His cock strained against his rough zipper, begging him to do something other than look at her.

Against his will, his gaze lingered on her bed. He could just imagine her lying there asleep. Her lips parted, her body relaxed and naked . . .

The pale pink covers wrapped around her bare limbs.

"Here you go."

He had to force himself to drag his gaze from the bed to the closet.

She stood back to give him access to the men's clothes

that were folded neatly in a wicker laundry basket. "You can take whatever you want."

Now there was a loaded statement if he ever heard one. The only problem was that what he wanted most was definitely not in that basket.

So Zarek thanked her, then dug out a black sweater and gray turtleneck that shouldn't be too small for him. "I'll go change in my room," he said, wondering why he bothered. She didn't care if he left the room or not. It wasn't as if she could see him or anything.

At home he walked about half-naked most of the time.

But that wasn't civilized, was it?

Since when are you civilized?

Tonight, it appeared.

Sasha barked at him as he left the room, then the wolf ran into the room to bark at Astrid.

"Hush, Sasha," she said. "Or I'll make you go sleep in the garage."

Ignoring them, Zarek made his way to his room to put on the fresh clothes.

He shut the door and set the clothes aside as he stood there feeling very peculiar. It was just clothes she offered him. And shelter.

A bed.

Food.

He looked around the elegant, expensively furnished room. He felt lost here. Unsure of himself. Never in his life had he experienced anything like this.

He felt human in this place.

Most of all, he felt welcome. Something he didn't even feel around Sharon.

Like all the others he had known over the centuries, Sharon did what he paid her to do. Nothing more, nothing less. He always felt as if he were intruding any time he came near her.

Sharon was formal and cool, especially after he had

ignored the pass she made at him. He always sensed there was a part of her that was scared of him. A part of her that would watch him, especially whenever her daughter was around—as if she expected him to go wild on them or something.

It had always insulted him, but then, he was so used to insults that he had shrugged it off.

But he didn't feel that with Astrid.

She treated him as if he were normal. Made it easy for him to forget the fact that he wasn't.

Zarek dressed quickly and went back to the den where Astrid sat sideways on the couch reading a book in braille. Sasha was resting on the couch at her feet. The wolf lifted its head and stared at him with what appeared to be hatred in its wolfish gray eyes.

Zarek, who had retrieved the paring knife from the kitchen, grabbed another piece of wood.

"So how did you end up with a wolf as a pet?" he asked, sitting in the chair nearest the fire so that he could toss the wood shavings into the hearth.

He didn't know why he talked to her. Normally, he wouldn't have bothered, and yet he found himself strangely curious about her life.

Astrid reached down to pet the wolf at her feet. "I'm not really sure. Much like you, I found him lying hurt and I brought him in and nursed him back to health. He's been with me ever since."

"I'm surprised he let you tame him."

She smiled at that. "I am, too. It wasn't easy to get him to trust me."

Zarek thought about that for a minute. " 'You must be very patient. First you will sit down at a little distance from me—like that—in the grass.' "

Astrid's mouth opened in shock as Zarek continued quoting one of her favorite passages. She couldn't have been more stunned had he thrown something at her. "You know *The Little Prince*?"

"I've read it a time or two."

More than that for him to be able to quote it so unerringly. Astrid leaned up again to touch Sasha so that she could look at Zarek.

He sat catty-corner from her while he whittled. The firelight played in his midnight eyes. The black sweater hugged his body, and though black whiskers covered his face, she was again struck by how handsome he was.

There was something almost relaxed about him as he worked. A poetic grace that warred with the hard cynical twist of his mouth. The deadly aura that enveloped him tighter than his black jeans.

"I love that book," she said quietly. "It's always been one of my favorites."

He didn't speak. He just sat there with his piece of wood held carefully in his hand as his long, tapered fingers moved gracefully over it. This was the first time the air around him didn't seem so dark. So dangerous.

She wouldn't call it peaceful exactly, but it wasn't as sinister as it had been before.

"Did you read it as a child?" she asked.

"No," he said quietly.

She cocked her head, watching him as he worked.

He paused, then turned to look at her with a frown.

Astrid let go of Sasha and sat back.

Zarek didn't move as he watched her and her pooch. There was something very strange here: every instinct he had told him so. He stared at Sasha.

If he didn't know better . . .

But why would a werewolf be in Alaska with a blind woman? The magnetic fields here would be hard on either an Arcadian or Katagari male who would have a difficult time maintaining a consistent form while the electrons in the air played havoc with their magic.

No, it wasn't probable.

And yet . . .

He glanced from them to the small anniversary clock on the mantel. It was almost four in the morning. For him it was still early, but not many humans kept his hours. "You always stay up this late, princess?"

"Sometimes."

"Don't you have a job you need to get up for?"

"No. I have family money. What about you, Prince Charming?"

Zarek's hand slipped at her words. Family money. She was even more loaded than he had suspected. "It must be nice not to have to work for a living."

Astrid heard the bitterness in his voice. "You don't like people who have money, do you?"

"I'm not prejudiced against anyone, princess. I hate everyone equally."

She had heard that about him. Heard from Artemis that he was coarse, unrefined, rude, and the most obnoxious jerk Artemis had ever known.

Coming from the Queen of Obnoxious, that was saying something.

"You didn't answer my question, Zarek. What do you do for a living?"

"This and that."

"This and that, huh? Are you a vagrant, then?"

"If I said yes, would you make me leave?"

Though his tone was level and emotionless, she sensed that he waited for her response. That there was a part of him that wanted her to throw him out.

A part of him that expected it.

"No, Zarek. I told you, you're welcome here."

Zarek stopped carving and stared at the fire, her words

made him tremble unexpectedly. But it wasn't the flames he saw, it was her face. Her sweet voice resonated deep inside a heart he thought was long dead.

No one had ever welcomed him anywhere.

"I could kill you and no one would know."

"Are you going to kill me, Zarek?"

Zarek winced as memories tore through him. He saw himself walking among the bodies in his devastated village. The sight of them with their throats bleeding, their homes burning . . .

He was supposed to protect them.

Instead, he had killed them all.

And he didn't even know why. He didn't remember anything except the rage that had possessed him. The need he'd felt for blood and atonement.

"I hope not, princess," he whispered.

Getting up, he returned to his room and locked the door.

He only hoped she would do the same.

Hours later, Astrid listened to Zarek's heavy breathing as he slept fitfully. The house was quiet now, safe from his wrath. The air had lost its evil aura and everything seemed calm, peaceful—except for the man, who seemed to be in the throes of a nightmare.

She was exhausted, but didn't feel like sleeping. She had too many questions on her mind.

How she wished she could talk to Acheron about Zarek and ask him what it was about the man that he thought worth saving. But Artemis had agreed to this trial only if Acheron stayed completely out of it and did nothing to sway the verdict. If Astrid tried to speak to Acheron, Artemis would end the test and kill Zarek immediately.

There had to be some other way to learn about her guest.

She looked at Sasha who was sleeping in wolf form on

her bed. The two of them had known each other for centuries. He had been barely more than a pup when his patria had signed on to fight with the Egyptian goddess Bast against Artemis.

Once the war between the goddesses was over, Artemis had demanded a judging for all of those who had fought against her. Astrid's half-sister Lera had been sent in and she had found all of them guilty, except for Sasha who had been too young to be held accountable for following the leadership of the others.

His own pack had turned on him instantly, thinking he had betrayed them for absolution, even though he'd only been fourteen. In the Katagaria world, animal instincts and rules reigned supreme. The pack was always a unified whole and anyone who threatened the pack was slaughtered, even if it was one of their own.

They had almost killed him. But luckily, Astrid had found him and nursed him back to health, and though he truly hated the Olympian gods, he was usually tolerant, if not fond, of her.

He could leave her at any time, but he had nowhere else to go. The Arcadian Were-Hunters wanted him dead because he had once run with the Katagaria Slayers who had turned against the Olympian gods, and the Slayers wanted him dead because they thought he had betrayed his patria.

His life was precarious at best, even now.

Back then, he'd been feral and terrified of being ripped apart by his people.

So centuries ago, the two of them had formed an alliance that benefited them both. She had kept the others from killing him while he was a pup and he had helped her whenever she was without her eyesight.

Over time, they had become friends and now Sasha stayed out of loyalty to her.

His magical Katagari powers were far stronger than hers and he often used them at her request.

She considered that now.

The Katagaria could travel through time . . .

But only with limitations. No, she needed something guaranteed to have her back here before Zarek woke up.

At times like this, she wished she were a full goddess and not a nymph. The gods had powers that could . . .

She smiled as an idea struck.

"M'Adoc," she said softly, summoning one of the Oneroi. They were the gods of sleep who held dominion over Phantosis, the shadow realm between the conscious and subconscious.

The air around her flickered with invisible, powerful energy she could feel as the Oneroi appeared.

Standing close to seven feet tall, M'Adoc dwarfed her—something she knew from experience. Even though she couldn't see him right now, she knew exactly what he looked like. His long black hair would be so dark it barely reflected light and his eyes were so pale a blue they looked almost colorless and appeared to glow.

Like all of his kind, he was so handsome that for those who could see, it was hard to even look at him.

"Little cousin," he said, his voice electrifying and seductive and yet devoid of emotion—since emotions were banned from the Oneroi. "It's been a while. At least three or four hundred years."

She nodded. "I've been busy."

He reached out to touch her arm so that she would know where he was standing. "What do you need?"

"Do you know anything about the Dark-Hunter Zarek?" The Oneroi were often healers of the Dark-Hunters, both physically and mentally. Since Dark-Hunters were created from people who had been horribly wronged or violated, a Dream-Hunter was often assigned to newly created Dark-Hunters to help heal them mentally so that they could function in the world without hurting others.

Once the Dark-Hunter was well mentally, the Dream-Hunter would then follow them through time and help heal them physically whenever they were wounded. That was why Dark-Hunters felt an unearthly need to sleep whenever they were hurt.

Only in dreams were the Oneroi effective.

"I know *of* him."

She waited for an explanation, but when he didn't elaborate, she asked, "What do you know?"

"That he is so far beyond help that none of my kind will aid him."

She had never heard of such a thing before. "Never?"

"Sometimes a Skotos will go to him while he sleeps, but they only go so that they can take some of his fury for their own. It is so intense that none of them can stand it for long before they have to leave, too."

Astrid was stunned. The Skoti were barely more than demons. Brothers and sisters to the Oneroi, they preyed upon human emotion and used it so that they could feel emotions again. Left unchecked, the Skoti were extremely dangerous and could kill the person they "treated."

Instead of soothing Zarek, a visit from one would only escalate his madness.

"Why is he like this? What fuels his rage?"

"What does it matter?" M'Adoc asked. "I am told he has been marked for death."

"I promised Acheron that I would judge him first. He will only die if I say so."

"Then you should save yourself the trouble and order his death."

Why did everyone want Zarek to die? She couldn't understand such animosity toward him. No wonder the man acted the way he did.

Did anyone even *like* him?

Not once in all eternity had M'Adoc ever spoken so harshly about anyone. "This isn't like you."

She heard him take a deep breath as he tensed the hand on her shoulder. "A rabid dog cannot be saved, Astrid. It is best for everyone, including the dog, for it to be put down."

"Shadedom would be preferable to living? Are *you* insane?"

"In Zarek's case, it would be."

She was aghast. "If that were true, Acheron would be merciful to him and wouldn't have asked me to judge him."

"Acheron doesn't kill him because it would be too much like killing himself."

She thought about that for a minute. "What do you mean? I see nothing similar in them at all."

She had the impression M'Adoc was probing her mind with his. "They have a lot in common, Acheron and Zarek. Things that most people can't see or understand. I think Acheron feels that if Zarek can't be saved, then neither can he."

"Saved from what?"

"Himself. Both men have a tendency to choose their own pain. They just don't choose it wisely."

Astrid felt something odd on hearing those words. A tiny stabbing ache in her stomach. Something she hadn't felt in a long time. She actually hurt for both men.

Most of all, she hurt for Zarek.

"How do they choose their own pain?"

M'Adoc refused to elaborate. But then, he did that a lot. Dealing with the gods of sleep was only one step less frustrating than dealing with an oracle.

"M'Adoc, show me why Zarek has been abandoned by everyone."

"I don't think you want—"

"Show me," she insisted. She had to know, and deep

down she suspected it didn't have as much to do with her job as she wanted to think. Her need to know felt more personal than professional.

His voice was totally emotionless. "It's against the rules."

"Whatever the repercussion, I will bear it. Now show me. Please."

M'Adoc had her sit on the bed.

Astrid lay back and allowed the Dream-Hunter to seduce her to sleep. There were several serums they could use to make someone drowsy or they could use mist from Wink, who was a minor sleep god.

The Oneroi as well as other gods of sleep had long used Wink and his mist to control humans.

No matter what method they chose, the effects of it were almost immediate to whomever they tended.

Astrid wasn't sure which method M'Adoc used on her, but no sooner had she closed her eyes than she found herself floating to the realm of Morpheus.

Here she had her eyesight even while she was judging. It was why she'd always loved to dream during her assignments.

M'Adoc appeared beside her. His masculine beauty was even more striking in this realm. "Are you sure about this?"

She nodded.

M'Adoc led her through a series of doors in the hall of Phantosis. Here a *kallitechnis,* or dream master, could move through anyone's dreams. They could go into the past, the future, or journey to realms beyond human understanding.

M'Adoc reached a door and paused. "He dreams of his past."

"I want to see it."

He hesitated as if debating with himself. Finally, he opened the door.

Astrid led the way in. She and M'Adoc stood back from the scene, far away from any who could see or sense them.

Not that they really needed to, but she wanted to make certain she didn't interfere with Zarek's dream.

People who were dreaming could only see the Oneroi or Skoti in their dreams when the sleep gods allowed them to. She wasn't sure if she, as a nymph, was invisible to Zarek or not.

She looked about in the dream.

What struck her most was how vivid everything was. Most people dreamed in sketchy details. But this, this was crystal clear and as real as the world she had left behind.

She saw three little boys gathered in an ancient Roman atrium.

Ranging in age from what appeared to be four to eight, they held sticks in their hands and were laughing and shouting. "Taste it, taste it, taste it."

A fourth boy around the age of twelve ran past her. His black hair and blue eyes were striking, and he bore a remarkable resemblance to the man she had seen through Sasha's eyes.

"Is that Zarek?"

M'Adoc shook his head. "That is his half-brother, Marius."

Marius ran to the others.

"He won't do it, Marius," another boy said before he struck whatever was on the ground with his stick.

Marius took the stick from his brother's hand and poked at the lump on the ground. "What's the matter, slave? You too good to eat scraps?"

Astrid gasped as she realized it was another child on the ground. One who was dressed in rags that they were trying to force to eat rotten cabbage. The boy was curled into a fetal position, covering his head to the point that he barely looked human.

The ones with sticks kept poking and hitting him. Kicking him when he didn't respond to their blows or insults.

"Who are all these boys?" she asked.

"Zarek's half-brothers." M'Adoc pointed them out. "Marius, you know. Marcus is the one dressed in blue with brown eyes. He is nine, I believe. Lucius is the baby, who just turned five and is dressed in red. The eight-year-old is Aesculus."

"Where is Zarek?"

"He's the one on the ground with his head covered."

She flinched, even though she had suspected as much. To be honest, she couldn't take her gaze off him. He still hadn't moved. No matter how hard they struck him, no matter what they said. He lay there like an unmovable rock.

"Why do they torture him?"

M'Adoc's eyes were sad, letting her know that he was siphoning some of Zarek's emotions as he watched the boys. "Because they can. Their father was Gaius Magnus. He ruled everyone, including his family, with a harsh fist. He was so evil that he killed their mother one night because she dared smile at another man."

Astrid was horrified by the news.

"Magnus used his slaves to help train his sons for cruelty. Zarek had the misfortune of being one of their whipping boys and, unlike the others, he wasn't lucky enough to die."

She could barely understand what M'Adoc was telling her. She had seen plenty of cruelty in her time, but never anything like this.

It was unimaginable that they would be allowed to treat him this way, especially since he was family.

"You said they are Zarek's half-brothers. How is it he is a slave when they are not? Was he related through their dead mother?"

"No. Their father brutally sired Zarek on one of their uncle's Greek slaves. When Zarek was born, his mother bribed one of the servants to take Zarek out and expose him so that he would die. The servant took pity on the infant, and instead of killing him, she made sure the baby went to his father."

Astrid looked back at the boy on the ground. "His father didn't want him, either." It was a statement of fact.

There was no doubt that no one in this place wanted the child.

"No. To him Zarek was tainted. Weaker. Zarek might have his blood in him, but he also bore the blood of a worthless slave. So Gaius turned Zarek over to his slaves, who took their hatred for his father out on him. Every time one of the slaves or servants was angry at Zarek's father or brothers, the boy suffered for it. He grew up as everyone's scapegoat."

She watched as Marius grabbed Zarek by the hair and pulled him up. Her breath caught in her throat as she saw the condition of his beautiful face. No older than ten himself, he was scarred so badly that he barely looked human.

"What's the matter, slave? Not hungry?"

Zarek didn't answer. He pulled at Marius's hand, trying to get away. But he didn't utter a single word of protest. It was as if he either knew better or was so accustomed to the abuse that he didn't bother.

"Let him go!"

She turned to see another boy close to Zarek's age. Like Zarek, he had black hair and blue eyes, and bore a strong resemblance to his brothers.

The newcomer rushed Marius and forced him to release Zarek. He twisted the older boy's hand behind his back.

"That is Valerius," M'Adoc supplied for her. "Another of Zarek's brothers."

"What is the matter with you, Marius?" Valerius demanded. "You shouldn't prey on those weaker. Look at him. He can barely stand."

Marius twisted free, then backhanded Valerius, knocking him to the ground. "You're worthless, Valerius. I can't believe you bear grandfather's name. You do nothing but dishonor him."

Marius sneered as if repulsed by the boy's presence. "You're weak. Cowardly. The world belongs only to those who are strong enough to take it. Yet you would pity those too weak to fight. I can't believe we came from the same womb."

The other boys attacked Valerius while Marius returned to Zarek.

"You're right, slave," he said, grabbing Zarek by his hair. "You're not worth cabbage. Dung is all you deserve for your food."

Marius threw him toward . . .

Astrid pulled out of the dream, unable to bear what she knew was going to happen.

Used to feeling nothing for other people, she was now overwhelmed by her emotions. She actually shook in fury and pain for him.

How could this have been allowed to happen?

How could Zarek have stood living the life he had been given?

In that moment, she hated her sisters for their part in his childhood.

But then, not even the Fates could control everything. She knew that. Still, it didn't ease the ache in her heart for a boy who should have been coddled.

A boy who had grown into an angry, bitter man.

Was it any wonder he was so harsh? How could anyone expect him to be otherwise when all he'd ever been shown was contempt?

"I warned you," M'Adoc said as he rejoined her. "That is why even the Skoti refuse to visit his dreams. All things considered, that is one of his milder memories."

"I don't understand how he survived," she whispered, trying to make sense of it. "Why didn't he kill himself?"

M'Adoc eyed her carefully. "Only Zarek can answer that."

He handed her a small vial.

Astrid stared at the dark red liquid that bore a strong resemblance to blood. *Idios.* It was a rare serum that was made by the Oneroi that could enable them or someone else, for a very short period of time, to become one with a dreamer.

It could be used in dreams to guide and direct, to allow one sleeper to experience another person's life so that he could better understand it.

Only three of the Oneroi possessed it. M'Adoc, M'Ordant, and D'Alerian. They most often used it with humans to dispense understanding and compassion.

One sip and she could become Zarek in his dreams. She would have total understanding of him.

She would be him.

And she would feel all of his emotions . . .

It was a huge step to take. Deep down she knew that if she took it, she would never be the same.

Then again, she might find there was nothing more to Zarek than rage and hatred. He might very well be the animal the others accused him of being.

One sip and she would know the truth . . .

Astrid removed the stopper and drank from the vial.

She didn't know what Zarek was dreaming about now, she only hoped he'd moved forward out of the dream she had just witnessed.

He had.

Zarek was now at the age of fourteen.

At first, Astrid thought her own blindness had returned until she realized that she was "seeing" through Zarek's eyes. Or eye, rather. The entire left side of her face hurt every time she tried to blink. A scar had fused the lid to his cheek, making the muscles in his face ache.

His right eye, while somewhat operable, had a strange haze over it similar to a cataract and it took her several minutes before his memories became hers and she understood what had happened.

He'd been beaten so badly two years before by a soldier in the marketplace that the lining of the cornea of his right eye had been severely damaged. His left eye had been blinded several years before that by another beating at the hands of his brother Valerius.

Zarek wasn't capable of seeing much more than shadows and blurs.

Not that he cared. At least this way, he didn't have to see his own reflection.

Nor was he bothered anymore by people's scornful looks.

Zarek shuffled across an old, crowded street in the marketplace. His right leg was stiff, barely able to bend from all the times it had been broken and not set.

Because of that, it was somewhat shorter than his left leg. His was a jarring gait that caused him to not move as swiftly as most people. His right arm was much the same way. He had little or no movement in it and his right hand was virtually useless.

In his good left hand, he clutched three quadrans. Coins that were worthless to most Romans, but they were precious to him.

Valerius had been angry at Marius and had slung Marius's purse out the window. Marius had forced another slave to pick the coins up, but three quadrans had gone uncollected. The only reason he had known about them was because they had hit him in the back.

Zarek should have surrendered the coins, but had he tried, Marius would have beaten him for it. The eldest of his brothers couldn't stand the sight of him and Zarek had learned long ago to stay as far from Marius as he could.

As for Valerius . . .

Zarek hated him most of all. Unlike the others, Valerius tried to help him but every time Valerius had attempted to do so, they had been caught and Zarek's punishment had escalated.

Like the rest of his family, he hated Valerius's tender heart. Better Valerius should spit on him as did the others. Because in the end, Valerius was forced to hurt him all the more to prove to everyone else that he wasn't weak.

Zarek, following the scent of baking bread, limped his way to the baker's stand. The scent was wonderful. Warm. Sweet. The thought of tasting a piece of it made his heart soar and his mouth water.

He heard people curse him as he drew near. Saw their shadows scurry away from him.

He didn't care. Zarek knew how repulsive he was. He'd been told so since the hour of his birth.

Had he ever been given a choice, he would have left himself, too. But as it was, he was stuck in this lame, scarred body.

He just wished he could go deaf as well as blind. Then he wouldn't have to hear their ringing insults.

Zarek approached what he thought might be a young man, standing over a basket of bread.

"Get away from here!" the young man snarled.

"Please, master," Zarek said, making sure to keep his blurry gaze on the ground. "I've come to buy a slice of bread."

"We have nothing for you, wretch."

Something hard hit him in the head.

Zarek was so accustomed to pain that he didn't even flinch. He tried to hand his coins to the man, but something hit his arm and knocked the precious coins from his grasp.

Desperate for a piece of bread that was fresh, Zarek fell to his knees to collect the money. His heart pounded. He squinted as best he could, trying to find them.

Please! He had to have his coins! No one would ever give him any more and there was no telling if or when Marius and Valerius would fight again.

He searched frantically through the dirt.

Where was his money?

Where?

He'd only found one of the coins when someone hit him across the back with what felt like a broom.

"Get out of here!" a woman snarled. "You're driving off our customers."

Too used to beatings to notice the broom strikes, Zarek searched for his other two coins.

Before he could find them, he was kicked hard in the ribs.

"Are you deaf?" a man asked. "Get out of here, you worthless beggar, or I'll call the soldiers."

That was one threat Zarek took seriously. His last encounter with a soldier had cost him his right eye. He didn't want to lose what little sight he had left.

His heart lurched as he remembered his mother and her scorn.

But more than that, he remembered the way his father had reacted once they had returned him home after the soldiers had finished beating him.

His father's punishment had made theirs seem merciful.

If he were discovered out in the city again, there was no telling what his father would do. He didn't have permission to be outside the grounds of their villa. Let alone the fact that he had three stolen coins.

Well, only one now.

Gripping his coin tightly, he ambled away from the baker as fast as his ravaged body would allow.

As he headed through the crowd, he felt something wet on his cheek. He brushed it away only to discover blood there.

Zarek sighed wearily as he felt his head until he found the wound above his brow. It wasn't too deep. Just enough to hurt.

Resigned to his place in life, he wiped at it.

All he wanted was fresh bread. Just one piece of it. Was that so much to ask?

He looked around, trying to use his blurry eyesight and nose to find another baker.

"Zarek?"

He panicked at the sound of Valerius's voice.

Zarek tried to run through the crowd, back toward their villa, but didn't get far before his brother caught him.

Valerius's strong grip held him immobile.

"What are you doing here?" he demanded, shaking Zarek's bad arm roughly. "Have you any idea what would happen to you if one of the others found you out here?"

Of course he did.

But Zarek was too frightened to answer. His entire body shook from the weight of his terror. All he could do was shield his face from the blows he was sure would start at any moment.

"Zarek," Valerius said, his voice thick with disgust. "Why can't you ever do as you're told? I swear you must enjoy being beaten. Why else would you do the things you do?"

Valerius grabbed him roughly by his damaged shoulder and shoved him toward their villa.

Zarek stumbled and fell.

His last coin rolled from his grasp and tumbled across the street.

"No!" Zarek gasped, crawling after it.

Valerius caught him and hauled him to his feet. "What is wrong with you?"

Zarek watched a blurry child scoop up his coin and run off with it. His stomach clenched from hunger pains; he was completely defeated.

"I just wanted a slice of bread," he said, his heart broken, his lips quivering.

"You have bread at home."

No. Valerius and his brothers had bread. Zarek was fed

the scraps that not even the other slaves or dogs would eat.

Just once in his life, he wanted to eat something that was fresh and untasted by someone else.

Something that no one had spat into.

"What is this?"

Zarek cringed at the booming voice that always went through him like shattered glass. He shrank back, trying to make himself invisible to the commander who sat on horseback, knowing it was impossible.

The man saw everything.

Valerius looked as panicked as Zarek felt. As always when addressing his father, the youth stuttered. "I—I—I w-was . . ."

"What is that slave doing here?"

Zarek took a step back as Valerius's eyes widened and he gulped. It was obvious Valerius was searching for a lie.

"W-w-we were going to the m-m-market," Valerius said quickly.

"You and the slave?" the commander asked incredulously. "For what? Were you hoping to buy a new whip to beat him with?"

Zarek prayed for Valerius not to lie. It was always worse on him when Valerius lied to protect him.

If only he dared to speak the truth, but he had learned long ago that slaves never spoke to their betters.

And he, more than the others, was never allowed to address his father.

"W-w-well . . . I . . ."

His father growled a curse and kicked Valerius in the face. The force of the blow knocked Valerius down where he lay beside Zarek with his nose pouring blood.

"I am sick of the way you coddle him." His father dismounted his horse and stormed toward Zarek, who fell to his knees and covered his head, waiting for the beating that was to come.

His father kicked him in his still-sore ribs. "Get up, dog."

Zarek couldn't breathe from the pain in his side and the terror that consumed him.

His father kicked him again. "Up, damn you."

Zarek forced himself to stand even though all he wanted to do was run. But he'd learned long ago not to. Running only made the punishment worse.

So he stood there, braced for the blows.

His father grabbed him by the neck, then turned to Valerius, who was now on his feet as well. He grabbed Valerius by his clothes and snarled at him. "You disgust me. Your mother was such a whore that it makes me wonder what coward fathered you. I know you didn't come from me."

Zarek saw pain flash in Valerius's eyes, but he quickly masked it. It was a common lie their father uttered whenever he was angry at Valerius. One had only to look at the two of them to know Valerius was as much his son as Zarek was.

His father slung Valerius away from him and hauled Zarek by his hair toward a stall.

Zarek wanted to place his own hand over his father's to keep his hold from hurting so badly, but didn't dare.

His father couldn't stand for him to touch him.

"You're a slaver?" his father asked.

An older man stood before them. "Yes, my lord. Can I interest you in a slave today?"

"No. I want to sell you one."

Zarek gaped as he understood what was happening. The thought of leaving his home terrified him. As bad as things were, he had heard enough stories from other slaves to know that life could get significantly worse for him.

The old slaver looked at Valerius gleefully.

Valerius stepped back, his face pale.

"He's a handsome boy, my lord. I can get a pretty fee for him."

"Not him," the commander snarled. "This one."

He shoved Zarek toward the slaver who curled his lip in disgust. The man covered his nose. "Is this a jest?"

"No."

"Father—"

"Hold your tongue, Valerius, or I'll take him up on his offer for you."

Valerius passed a sympathetic look to Zarek, but wisely stayed silent.

The slaver shook his head. "This one is worthless. What did you use him for?"

"A whipping boy."

"He's too old for that now. My clients want younger, attractive children. This wretch is fit for nothing except begging."

"Take him and I'll give you two denarii."

Zarek gaped at his father's words. He was paying a slaver to take him? Such a thing was unheard of.

"I'll take him for four."

"Three."

The slaver nodded. "For three, then."

Zarek couldn't breathe as their words resonated inside him. He was so worthless that his father had been forced to pay to be rid of him? Even the cheapest of slaves was still worth two thousand denarii.

But not him.

He *was* every bit as worthless as everyone claimed.

No wonder they all hated him.

He watched as his father paid the man. Without another look at him, his father grabbed Valerius by the arm and hauled him away.

A younger version of the slaver came into his blurry sight and expelled a repulsed breath. "What are we to do with him, Father?"

The slaver tested the coins with his teeth. "Send him in to clean out the cesspit for the other slaves. If he dies of disease, who cares? Better he clean it than someone we could actually sell for profit."

The younger man smiled at that.

Using a stick, he prodded Zarek toward the stalls. "Come on, rat. Let me show you to your new duties."

Astrid came awake from the dream with her heart pounding. She lay in her bed, surrounded by the darkness she was used to, as Zarek's pain washed over her.

She'd never felt such despair. Such need.

Such loathing.

Zarek hated everyone, but most of all, he hated himself.

No wonder the man was insane. How could he have lived with such misery?

"M'Adoc?" she whispered.

"Here." He sat beside her.

"Leave some more of the serum for me and Lotus serum, as well."

"Are you sure?"

"Yes."

Chapter 7

Zarek woke up just after noon. He very seldom slept through the day. It was more like napping. In the summertime it was too hot in his cabin for him to sleep comfortably and in winter it was too cold.

But mostly it was because his dreams never allowed him to sleep for long. The past haunted him too much to give him peace, and while unconscious, he couldn't keep those memories away.

But as he opened his eyes and heard the wind rushing outside, he remembered where he was.

Astrid's cabin.

He'd sealed the curtains tight last night so he couldn't tell if it was still snowing outside or not. Not that it mattered. During daylight, he was trapped here.

Trapped with *her*.

He got out of bed and walked down the hallway, toward the kitchen. How he wished he were at home. He really needed a substantial drink. Not that the vodka could really chase away the dreams that lingered in his mind. But the burn of it was a bit distracting.

"Zarek?"

He turned at the soft voice that went down him like a silken caress. His body reacted instantly to it.

All he had to do was think her name and it made him rock-hard and needful.

"What?" He didn't know why he answered her when he normally wouldn't have.

"Are you all right?"

He snorted at that. He'd never once in his life been all right. "Do you have anything to drink in this place?"

"I have juice and tea."

"Liquor, princess. Do you have anything in this place with a bite to it?"

"Only Sasha and of course, you."

Zarek glanced down at the vicious cuts on his arm where her pet had attacked him. If he were any other Dark-Hunter those wounds would be gone now. But lucky him, they would be here for a few days more.

Just like the hole in his back.

Sighing, he reached inside the fridge and pulled out her orange juice. He opened the top and almost had the container to his lips before he remembered that it wasn't his and this wasn't his place.

The vicious side of him told him to go for it and drink it, she'd never know, but he didn't listen to that voice.

He went to the cabinet and pulled out a glass, then poured it full.

Astrid could only hear faint tell-tale signs that Zarek was still in the kitchen. He was so quiet that she had to strain just to make sure.

Walking forward, she headed for the sink. "Are you hungry?"

Out of habit, she reached out—and brushed her hand against a hot, naked hip.

It was smooth, inviting.

Scintillating.

Stunned by the unexpected sensation of her hand on his bare flesh, she lowered her hand down his leg before she realized Zarek didn't have any clothes on.

The man was fully naked in her kitchen.

Her heart hammered.

He moved away from her. "Don't touch me."

She shivered at the anger in his voice. "Where are your clothes?"

"I don't sleep in jeans."

Her hand burned with the memory of his skin under her fingers. "Well, you should have put them on before you came out here."

"Why? You're blind. It's not like you could see me."

True, but if Sasha were awake, he'd been having a fit over this.

"I don't need you to remind me of my shortcomings, Prince Charming. Believe me, I'm well aware of the fact that I can't see you."

"Yeah, well, count your blessings."

"Why?"

"Because I'm not worth looking at."

Her jaw went slack at the sincerity she heard in his voice. The man she had seen through Sasha's eyes had been more than worth looking at. He'd been gorgeous.

As handsome as any man she'd ever seen.

Then she remembered his dream. The way other people had once looked at him.

In his mind, he was still the wounded wretch that other people had beaten and cursed.

And that made her want to cry for him.

"I somehow doubt it," she whispered past the tight lump in her throat.

"Don't."

She heard him walk angrily past her, down the hallway. He slammed his door shut.

Astrid stood in her kitchen, debating what to do.

He was so lost.

She understood that now.

No, she corrected herself. She didn't really understand him at all. How could she?

No one had ever dared treat her the way he'd been treated. Her mother and sisters would have killed anyone who dared look down their noses at her. They'd always protected her from the world, even while she struggled to get away from them.

Zarek had never known a loving touch.

Never known the warmth of a family.

He'd always been alone in a way she couldn't even begin to fathom.

Overwhelmed by her newfound emotions, she wasn't sure what she should do. But she wanted to help him.

She went down the hallway only to discover he'd locked his door. "Zarek?"

He refused to answer her again.

Sighing, she pressed her head against the door and wondered if there was any way she could ever reach him.

Any way to save a man who didn't want to be saved.

Thanatos was furious at the order from Artemis.

"Stand down, my ass." He had no intention of standing down. For nine hundred years he had been waiting for this directive.

Waiting for a chance to level the score against Zarek of Moesia.

No one and most especially not Artemis would stand in his way now.

He would have Zarek or he would die trying.

Thanatos smiled at that. Artemis didn't have as much power as she thought. In the end, it would be his will that won the day.

Not hers.

She was nothing to him. Nothing but a means to an end he was determined to claim.

Vengeance would finally be his.

Thanatos pounded on the door of the remote cabin. On the other side of the door, he could hear low, panicked voices—Apollites rushing to hide their women and children.

Apollites who lived in fear of anyone who came seeking them.

"I am the light of the lyre," Thanatos said, speaking words only an Apollite or Daimon would know. Words that were used whenever a Daimon or Apollite sought another of his or her kind for shelter. The phrase was a reference to their kinship to Apollo, the god of the sun, who had cursed and abandoned them.

"How is it you walk in the daylight?" It was a woman's voice. One filled with fear.

"I'm the Dayslayer. Open the door."

"How do we know that?" This time it was a man who spoke.

Thanatos growled low in his throat.

Why did he want to help these people?

They were worthless.

But then he knew. Once, long ago, he'd been one of them. He too would have been hiding, afraid of the Squires and Dark-Hunters. Afraid of the pitiful humans who came for them in the light of day . . .

How he hated them all.

"I am going to open this door," Thanatos warned them. "The only reason I knocked was so that you could unlock it and then get out of the way of the daylight before I enter. Now either unlock it or I'll kick it down."

He heard the lock click.

Taking a deep, calming breath, he pushed the door open slowly.

As soon as he stepped inside and closed the door, a shovel came at his head.

Thanatos grabbed it and jerked hard, pulling a woman out of the shadows.

"I won't let you hurt my children!"

He took the shovel from her and gave her a peeved glare. "Trust me, if I wanted to hurt them, you couldn't stop me. No one could. But I'm not here for that. I'm here to kill the Dark-Hunter who hunts your kindred."

Relief washed over her beautiful face as she looked up at him as if he were an angel.

"Then you really are the Dayslayer." The voice was masculine.

Thanatos turned his head to see a Daimon male leave the shadows. The Daimon looked no older than his early twenties. Like all of his breed, the Daimon was a paragon of physical perfection. Beautiful in his youthfulness and physical bearing, his long blond hair was braided down his back. His right cheek was marked with three blood-red tears that had been tattooed there.

Thanatos knew his breed instantly.

The Daimon was one of the rare Spathi warriors Thanatos had come seeking.

"Are the tears for your children?"

The Daimon gave a curt nod. "Each was slain by a Dark-Hunter. And I in turn slew the Hunter."

Thanatos ached for the man. The Apollites had no real choice and yet they were punished because they dared to choose life over death. He wondered what the humans and Dark-Hunters would do if they were told they had one of two choices: die painfully in the midst of their youth, or take human souls and live.

As a mere Apollite, Thanatos had been prepared to die. Just like his wife . . .

Zarek had taken even that option away from his family.

Insane, the Dark-Hunter had come through his village, laying waste to everyone in it. The men had barely been able to hide the women and children before Zarek had destroyed them all.

No one who had come into Zarek's path had remained alive.

No one.

Zarek had killed Apollite and Daimon indiscriminately. And for that crime his only punishment had been banishment.

Banished!

Rage suffused him. How dare Zarek remain living in comfort all these centuries while the memory of that night festered eternally in Thanatos's heart.

But he forced that hatred aside. This was no time to let his anger rule him. It was the time to be as cold and calculating as his enemy.

"How old are you, Daimon?" Thanatos asked the Spathi.

"Ninety-four."

Thanatos arched a brow. "You've done well."

"Yes, I have. I grew tired of hiding."

He knew the feeling. There was nothing worse than being forced to live in the dark. Living life confined.

"Have no fear. No Dark-Hunter will be after you. I'm here to make sure of it."

The man smiled. "We thought you were a myth."

"All good myths are rooted in reality and truth. Didn't your mother teach you that?"

The Spathi's eyes turned dark, haunted. "I was only three when she turned twenty-seven. She didn't have time to teach me anything at all."

Thanatos placed a comforting hand on the man's shoulder. "We will take this planet back, my brother. Rest assured, our day has come once more. I will summon the others of your kind and we will unite our armies. The humans have no one who can protect them now."

"What of the Dark-Hunters?" the woman asked.

Thanatos smiled. "They are bound to the night. I'm not. I can stalk them whenever I choose it." He laughed. "I am immune to their wounds. I am Death to them all and I am now home again with my people. Together, we will rule this earth and all who inhabit it."

Zarek woke up to the smell of heaven. He would have thought he was dreaming, but his dreams were never so pleasant.

Lying in bed, he was afraid to move. Afraid the delicious aroma would prove to be a figment of his imagination.

His stomach rumbled.

He heard the wolf bark.

"Hush, Sasha. You'll wake our guest."

Zarek opened his eyes then. Guest. No one but Astrid had ever called him that before.

His thoughts turned to the week he'd spent in New Orleans.

"Am I staying with you and Kyrian or Nick?"

"We thought it best that you have your own place."

Acheron's words had kicked something inside him he didn't even know he had anymore.

No one had ever wanted him near them.

He thought he'd learned to not care.

And yet Astrid's simple words touched the same foreign part of him that Acheron's had.

Getting out of bed, he dressed, then went to find her.

Zarek stood in the doorway, watching her as she made pancakes in the microwave. She was amazingly self-sufficient given her blindness.

The wolf looked at him and growled.

Astrid cocked her head as if listening to see if she could hear him. "Zarek? Are you in the room?"

"Doorway." He didn't know why he told her that. He didn't know why he was still here.

Granted, the storm was still ferocious, but he'd journeyed through many such storms during the centuries when he had lived up here without modern conveniences. There was a time not that long ago when he would have had to scrounge for food in the dead of winter. Melt snow so that he would have something to drink.

"I've made pancakes. I don't know if you like them, but I have blueberry and maple syrup or fresh strawberries if you'd rather."

He went to the counter and reached for a plate.

"Sit, I'll bring it to you."

"No, princess," he said sharply. Having been forced to serve others, he refused to have anyone serve him. "I can fix it myself."

She held her hands up in surrender. "Fine, Prince Charming. If there's anything I can respect, it's those who take care of themselves."

"Why do you keep calling me that? Are you mocking me?"

She shrugged. "You call me 'princess,' I call you 'Prince Charming.' I figure turnabout is fair play."

Giving her a grudging amount of respect, he reached for the bacon that was lying on a saucer by the stove. "How do you fry this when you can't see it?"

"The microwave. I just push the timer for it."

The wolf came over and started sniffing at his leg. It looked up at him as if it were offended and started barking at him.

"Shut up, Benji," he snarled. "I don't want to hear about my hygiene from someone who licks his own balls."

"Zarek!" Astrid gasped. "I can't believe you just said that."

He clenched his teeth. Fine, he wouldn't speak anymore. Silence was what he was best at anyway.

The wolf whined and yapped.

"Shh," she soothed. "If he doesn't want to bathe, it's none of our business."

His appetite gone, Zarek set his plate on the table and returned to his room where he couldn't offend them anymore.

Astrid felt her way to the table, expecting to find Zarek there. All she found was his plate of uneaten food.

"What happened?" she asked Sasha.

"If he had feelings, I would say you hurt them. Like as not, he went back to the room to find a weapon so he can kill us."

"Sasha! Tell me what happened just now."

"Okay, he put the plate down and left."

"What did he look like?"

"Nothing. He didn't show any kind of emotion."

That didn't help her at all.

She went after Zarek.

"Go away," he snapped after she knocked on his door and pushed it open.

Astrid stood in the doorway, wishing she could see him. "What do you want, Zarek?"

"I . . ." his voice trailed off.

"You what?"

Zarek couldn't speak the truth. He wanted to be warm. Just once in his life, he wanted warmth. Not just physical but mental warmth.

"I want to leave."

She sighed at his words. "You'll die if you go out there."

"So what if I do?"

"Does your life truly have no value or meaning to you?"

"No, it doesn't."

"Then why haven't you killed yourself?"

He snorted at that. "Why should I? The only enjoyment I have in my life is knowing I piss off everyone around me. If I were dead, it would make them all happy. God forbid I should ever do that."

To his surprise, she laughed. "I wish I could see your face to know if you were joking or not."

"Trust me, I'm not."

"Then I'm sorry for you. I wish you had something that made you happy."

Zarek looked away from her. Happy. He didn't even understand that word. It was as alien to him as kindness. Compassion.

Love.

Now there was a word that never entered his vocabulary. He couldn't imagine what others must feel.

For love, Talon had almost died so that Sunshine could live. For love, Sunshine had bartered her soul to free Talon.

All he knew was hatred, anger. It was the only thing that kept him warm. The only thing that kept him living.

So long as he hated, he had a reason to live.

"Why do you want to live here in this cabin alone?"

She shrugged. "I like having my own place. My family visits me often, but I'd rather be alone."

"Why?"

"Because I hate to be babied. My mother and sisters act as if I'm helpless. They want to do everything for me."

Astrid waited for him to say something more.

He didn't.

"Would you like to take a bath?" she asked after a brief wait.

"Do I bother you?"

She shook her head. "Not at all. It's entirely up to you."

Zarek had never really had to be concerned with things such as bathing. When he was a slave, no one cared whether or not he was clean, and in truth he'd stayed dirty so that no one would want to approach him any more than was necessary.

As a Dark-Hunter, he'd been completely alone even before his banishment to Alaska. And once here it had been so difficult to do anything as simple as bathe that he had all but forsaken it.

It had only been after Fairbanks had started being settled that he had bought a large tub that he used only when he knew he was going into town.

His brief stay in New Orleans had been a treasured delight of running hot and cold water and showers that could last for an entire hour before the water turned cold on him.

Had Astrid ordered him to bathe, he wouldn't have considered it. Because she had offered him a choice, he headed for the bathroom.

"The towels are in the hall closet."

Zarek paused at the closet right outside the bathroom and opened the door. Like everything in the house, it was well kept. All the towels were folded up neatly. Hell, they were even color coordinated to match the rest of the house.

He grabbed a large fluffy green one and went to bathe.

Astrid heard the water come on. She took a deep, fortifying breath.

Strange, until Sasha had mentioned it, she hadn't realized Zarek hadn't had a bath. He hadn't smelled or anything and he washed his hands so much that she just assumed the rest of him was clean, too.

She returned to the kitchen to find Sasha eating Zarek's pancakes.

"What are you doing?"

"He didn't want them. They were getting cold."

"Sasha!"

"What? It's not nice to waste food."

She shook her head at the wolf as she moved to make

another batch for Zarek. Maybe he would be more sociable when he left the shower.

He wasn't. If anything he was even surlier as he gulped down the pancakes.

"He's disgusting," Sasha said to her. *"He eats like an animal. Be thankful you're blind."*

"Sasha, lay off the man."

"Lay off, my ass. He uses his fork like a shovel and I swear he shoved one entire pancake in his mouth at once."

Astrid would have been disgusted had she not been in his dreams. No one had ever taught him even the most basic form of manners. He had been relegated to a corner on the floor just like the animal Sasha called him.

In his human life, food had been scarce. And on the heels of that thought came another startling realization. Food when he was a Dark-Hunter would have been scarce, as well.

Unlike the others of his kind, Zarek didn't have a Squire to plant and grow his food in the daytime. To tend animals and make his meals. For centuries, he'd lived in Alaska's harsh climate where winter sources of food were seriously limited.

She felt suddenly sick at the thought. No doubt he would have starved to death as a human.

Dark-Hunters couldn't die of malnutrition. But they could suffer from it every bit as much as a human being.

She made another plate of pancakes for him.

"What's this?" he asked as she set it down near him.

"In case you're still hungry."

He didn't say anything, but she listened to him slide the plate across the table an instant before she heard him snap open the lid on the syrup.

"I can't stand watching him make pancake soup with the syrup again," Sasha said. *"I'll be in the den if you need me."*

Astrid ignored him as she listened to Zarek eating. How she wished she could see him.

"No you don't," Sasha said.

She had a feeling Sasha was overreacting. She knew the wolf well enough to know Zarek could have impeccable manners and Sasha would complain.

After Zarek finished eating, he got up from the table and rinsed his plate off.

No, he wasn't a pig. He was a lonely, hurt man who didn't know how to cope in a world that had turned its back on him.

She saw in him what Acheron did and her respect for the Atlantean grew immensely to realize that he could see what no one else did.

Now she just had to find some way to save Zarek from a goddess who was through with him.

If she didn't, Artemis would order him dead.

She listened to him tear a paper towel off the rack.

"I heard on the news that it's still storming. They have no idea when the storm will break. They said it was the worst snowstorm in centuries."

Zarek let out a long tired breath. "I have to leave tonight."

"You can't."

"I have no choice."

"We all have choices."

"No we don't, princess. Only people with money and influence have choices. For the rest of us, basic necessity dictates what we have to do to survive." He crossed the floor. "I have to go."

Astrid panicked. Since he was a Dark-Hunter he really could leave. Unlike the humans she'd judged, Zarek's life wouldn't be endangered if he left the cabin tonight. It would be cold and harsh, but he was used to that.

What was she going to do?

If she followed him, he would figure out very quickly that she was immortal, too.

For a second she considered calling on her sisters, then

stopped herself. If she did that, they'd never let her forget it. She needed to handle this alone.

But what would keep him here when he was so determined to leave?

She turned toward the door and knocked over something on the counter. Picking it up, she felt a small bottle of spice that reminded her of the serums M'Adoc had given her.

A large enough dose of Lotus serum would keep Zarek unconscious for a few days . . .

But then he would be trapped in his nightmares with no way to wake up.

Such a thing could cause him to go insane.

Or she could direct his dreams like a Skoti might.

Dare she try it?

Before she could reconsider, she went to her room to get the bottle she had hidden in her nightstand.

Now she just had to find some way to get the serum into Zarek.

Chapter 8

Zarek was headed out into the storm. He lifted the hood of his coat and started down the hallway.

Astrid met him halfway to the door. He paused at the sight of her waiting there for him. Desire rushed through him, making him hard and aching. Her face looked sad and the novelty of that stunned him most of all.

Gods, she was so beautiful. For a moment, he actually wished he could stay here with her. That he could be as lucky as the wolf she had dragged in from the wild and tamed.

He wished he dared to reach out for a star.

Do it!

Zarek balled his hands into fists before he could yield to that burning desire. Slaves didn't have wishes or dreams.

They didn't lust after women who were too good for them.

He shouldn't even be looking at her, let alone be hard from wanting to touch her.

No matter how much he fought against it, no matter how many times he railed against Acheron and Artemis, he knew the truth. Two thousand years later, he was still a slave. One owned by a Greek goddess who wanted him dead.

He could deny his destiny all he wanted to, but in the end, he knew his place in this world.

Women like Astrid weren't meant for men like him. They were meant for decent, civilized men. Men who knew the meaning of such simple words as "kindness," "warmth," "compassion," "friendship."

Love.

He started past her.

"Here," she said, holding out a cup of hot tea.

The aroma was sweet, pleasant, but it didn't heat him half as much as the sight of the slight blush in her cheeks. "What's this?"

"I would say arsenic and vomit, but you trust me so little anyway, I don't dare. It's hot rosemary tea with a bit of honey. I want you to drink it before you leave. It'll help keep you warm on your journey."

Somewhat amused by her reiteration of his rudeness, Zarek at first wanted to toss it. But he couldn't quite do it. It was too thoughtful a gift and thoughtful gifts were an extreme rarity in his experience.

He hated to admit just how deeply this simple act touched him.

He hardened even more with the thought.

Thanking her, he drank it down, staring at her the whole time over the rim of the cup. Gods, how he was going to miss her; but that made even less sense than anything else.

As he drank the tea, his eyes drank in the sight of her.

Her jeans hugged long, shapely legs that a man couldn't help but dream of having wrapped around his waist.

His shoulders.

But it was her butt that he wanted most. It begged to be cupped by his hands while he pressed her softness to his groin so that she could feel just how much he burned for her.

Against his will, he imagined her naked in his arms. Her

lips on his, her breasts in his hands, while he lost himself inside her hot, wet body.

I have got to get out of here.

Zarek downed the last of the tea, then handed the empty cup back to her.

She took a step away from him, clutching the cup in her hands, her face even sadder than before. "I wish you would stay, Zarek."

He savored the sound of those rare words. Even if she didn't mean them, they still made him ache. "Sure you do, princess."

"I do." The sincerity on her face burned through him.

But it was anger he felt most from her comment. "Don't lie to me. I can't stand lies."

He pushed past her, intent on the door, but as he reached it, his head began to fog.

His eyesight dimmed.

Zarek paused as he tried to focus his gaze. His limbs felt heavy all of a sudden. Leaden. It was a struggle just to breathe.

What was this?

He reached for the door only to find his knees buckling. Then everything went black.

Astrid cringed at the sound of Zarek hitting the floor. How she wished she could have caught him before he fell. But without her eyesight, there was nothing she could do.

Going over to him, she checked to make certain he was all right.

Thankfully, he appeared to be none the worse for her deception.

"Sasha?" she called, needing his help to get Zarek off the floor.

"What happened?" Sasha asked as he came to stand beside her.

"I drugged him."

She felt Sasha flash to human form.

She knew from experience that her companion would be naked now—he always was when he changed forms.

She'd only seen him flash on rare occasions. As a Katagari Lykos, his natural and preferred state was that of the wolf, but his inherent magical abilities allowed him to take human form from time to time, as needed or wanted. His powers and strength were weaker in human form than wolf form, which was why he preferred his animal body.

Still, there were certain things his kindred preferred to do as humans.

Things such as mating and eating.

As a human, Sasha had long blond hair so pale that it was virtually as white as his wolf's fur. His eyes were a deep electric blue that were piercing in either incarnation. And his face . . .

Captivating and chiseled. The planes of his face were perfect and hard. Masculine.

It was a pity she had never been sexually attracted to him, because he had a body that was every bit as fit and well muscled as Zarek's.

But Sasha for all his beauty and charm was only a friend to her. One who often acted like an overprotective big brother.

"What were you thinking?" he asked in a deep baritone that carried the weight of his sorcerer's power. It was said the Katagaria could seduce any woman alive just by saying her name.

Their sexual prowess and stamina were the stuff of legend, even among the gods.

And yet all she could do was appreciate the seductive appeal of Sasha. Not once had she ever succumbed to it.

"He can't leave this cabin until the test is over, you know that."

Sasha let out an irritated breath. "What did you use to drug him with?"

"Lotus serum."

"Astrid, have you any idea how dangerous that is? It has killed countless mortals. One sip and they can go insane from it. Or worse, become so addicted to it that they refuse to wake up from their dreams."

"Zarek isn't mortal."

Sasha sighed. "No, he isn't."

She sat back on her heels. "Take him to his bed, Sasha."

The air around him sizzled with ire. "Where's my 'please'?"

She turned to the right and hoped that she was glaring at him. "Why are you being so impossible lately?"

"Why are you being so bossy? I think this man is affecting you and I don't like it." He paused before he spoke again. "Never forget, Astrid, that I am here by choice. The only thing that keeps me by your side is that I don't want to see you hurt."

She reached out and placed her hand on his arm. "I know, Sasha. Thank you."

He covered her hand with his and gave a light squeeze. "Don't let him inside you, nymph. There is so much in him that is dark that it could completely obliterate all the goodness you have."

She thought about that for a minute. She hadn't considered herself good for a long time now. Numbness had ruled her for too many centuries. "There are people who would say the same of you."

"They don't know me."

"And we don't know Zarek."

"I know his kind a lot better than you do, nymph. I've spent my life fighting men such as this. Ones who see the world as an enemy and who hate everyone around them."

Sasha let go of her and huffed as he lifted Zarek up from the floor. "Guard your heart, Astrid. I don't want to see you hurt again."

Astrid sat on the floor as he took Zarek back to his bed, and thought about Sasha's warning. He was right. She had been so beguiled by Miles that, even blind, she had failed to see him for what he really was.

But then, Miles had been an arrogant man. A vain one.

Zarek was neither.

Miles had pretended to care for others while he cared for no one but himself.

Zarek cared for no one, least of all himself.

But there was only one way to find out for sure.

Getting up, she poured Sasha a glass of juice.

"What are you going to do with him now?" Sasha asked a few minutes later when he rejoined her.

"I'll let him sleep for a bit," she said evasively.

If Sasha knew what she had in mind, he'd have a fit and she was in no mood to deal with an irate wolf-man.

She handed him the glass, which he took without comment. She listened to him open the fridge and then moved to wait by the counter while he scrounged for food.

While Sasha had been taking care of Zarek, she had placed a small dab of Lotus serum into Sasha's drink.

It took a little longer for the serum to work on him. Because of their metabolism, Were-Hunters were always harder to drug than humans.

"Astrid, tell me you didn't do this?" Sasha said a short time later as the drug started to take effect. She heard the faint electrical crackle that heralded a change in his form.

Astrid felt her way over to him. He was already a wolf again and was sound asleep.

Alone now, she walked through her house making sure the lights and stove were turned off and the heat was set to a comfortable level.

She went to her room and pulled out the *Idios* serum. Holding it in her hand, she went to Zarek's room.

She took a sip, then snuggled down to sleep by his side, to learn more about this man and what secrets his heart harbored . . .

Zarek was in New Orleans. Distant music filtered out through the cool night air while he paused near the Old Ursuline Convent in the French Quarter.

A group of tourists were gathered around a tour guide who was dressed much like Anne Rice's Lestat, while a second "vampire" dressed in a long black cape and fake fangs stood back, watching him.

The tourists were listening intently as the guide recounted a famous murder in the city. Two bodies had been found on the front steps of the convent, completely drained of blood. The old legends said that the convent was believed to have once housed vampires who came out at night to prey on the city.

Zarek snorted at the absurdity.

The guide, who claimed to be a three-hundred-year-old vampire named Andre, looked over at him.

"Hey," Andre said to his group as he pointed to Zarek. "There's a real vampire, right there."

The group turned as one to look at Zarek who stared evilly at them.

Before he could think better of it, Zarek bared his fangs at them and hissed.

The tourists shrieked and ran.

So did the tour guides.

Had Zarek laughed, he would have laughed at the sight of them tearing down the street as fast as they could run. As it was, he could only appreciate the mayhem he'd caused with a cynical twisting of his lips.

"I can't believe you just did that."

He looked over his shoulder to see Acheron standing in the shadows like a dark specter, dressed in black and sporting long purple hair.

Zarek shrugged. "Whenever they stop running and reflect on it, they'll think it was part of the show."

"The tour guide won't."

"He'll think it was a prank. Humans always explain us away."

Acheron sighed heavily. "I swear, Z. I was hoping you'd use this time here to show Artemis that you can mingle with people again."

He looked at Acheron drolly. "Sure you were. Why don't you cover me in shit and tell me it's mud while you're at it?"

He started to walk off.

"Don't walk away from me, Z."

He didn't stop.

Acheron used his powers to pin him to the side of the stone wall. Zarek had to give the head Dark-Hunter credit. At least Acheron knew better than to touch him. Not once in two thousand years had Acheron laid a physical hand on him. It was as if the Atlantean understood how much mental anguish such contact caused.

In a weird way, he felt as though Acheron respected it.

Acheron met his gaze and held it. "The past is dead, Z. Tomorrow will become whatever decision you make here this week. It has taken me five hundred years of negotiating with Artemis to get you this chance to prove to her that you can behave. For the sake of your sanity and your life, don't blow it."

Acheron released him and headed off after the tourists.

Zarek didn't move until he was alone again. He let Acheron's words wash over him as he stood silently contemplating things.

He didn't want to leave this city. From the moment he'd arrived to see the crowd gathered at Jackson Square, he'd been enchanted with New Orleans.

Most of all, he'd been warm.

No, he wouldn't blow this. He would do his duty and protect the humans who lived here.

No matter what it took, he would do what he needed to get Artemis to let him stay.

He would never kill another human . . .

Zarek had started on his way down the street when a group of four men caught his eye. By their extreme height, blond hair, and good looks, he pegged them for Daimons.

They were whispering among themselves, but even so he could hear them plainly.

"Bossman said she lives above Club Runningwolf's in a loft."

One of the Daimons laughed. "A Dark-Hunter with a girl-friend. I didn't think such a thing existed."

"Oh, yeah. Paybacks will be hell. Imagine how he'll feel when he finds her drained, naked body lying in her bed waiting for him."

Zarek started to attack them right then, but paused as a group of humans stumbled out of a bar, into the street. Intent on their target, the Daimons didn't even look at them.

The tourists stayed on the street, laughing and joking, never knowing that if not for a previous engagement, the Daimons would be headed straight for them.

Life was a very fragile thing.

Grinding his teeth, Zarek knew he'd have to wait until he could corner the Daimons in an alley where they wouldn't be seen.

He dropped back into the shadows where he could still watch and hear them, and followed them toward Sunshine's loft . . .

Astrid's head ached as she followed Zarek through his

dreams and let his anger and pain infiltrate her. She was with him in the alley where he'd fought the Daimons and was then assaulted by the cops.

And she was with him on the rooftop when he called Talon to warn him to watch after Sunshine. She felt Zarek's rage. His desire to help people who could only scorn and berate him.

Wrongfully judge him.

He didn't understand how to reach out to them.

So he attacked them instead. Lashed out at them before they could lash out at him.

In the end, it was too much for her to handle. She had to pull herself away from him or she might find herself driven insane by the raw intensity of his emotions.

It was a struggle to separate herself from him. The binding serum was strong and it wanted to keep them united, but as a nymph, she was stronger.

Summoning all her powers, she ripped her geist from his until she was no longer part of Zarek and his memories.

Now she was only a dream observer, so she could watch, yet not feel his emotions.

But she could feel her own and she ached for this man in a way she had never thought possible. The rawness of her recovered emotions overwhelmed her. His past and his scars tore through her, blasting away the numb cocoon that had encased her for so long.

For the first time in centuries, she felt someone else's agony. More than that, she wanted to soothe it. To hold this man who couldn't escape from what he was.

As she watched, Zarek's dream darkened. She saw him struggle through a fierce blizzard. He was dressed only in a pair of black leather pants with no shirt or shoes. His arms wrapped around him, he shook from the cold and trudged forward, cursing at the howling winds as he stumbled and fell in the ice-cold waist-deep snow.

Every time he fell, he pushed himself up and kept going. His strength amazed her.

The winds whipped at his broad, tawny shoulders, blowing his long black hair around his clean-shaven face. He squinted as if trying to see through the storm.

But there was nothing around them. Nothing but white, barren landscape.

Numb to the cold that plagued him, Astrid followed him.

"I won't die," Zarek snarled, gaining speed as he walked. He looked up at the starless, black sky. "Do you hear me, Artemis? Acheron? I won't give either of you the satisfaction."

He started running then, trudging through the crunching snow like a child running after a toy. His feet were red from the cold, his bare skin mottled.

Astrid struggled to keep up.

Until he fell.

Zarek lay quietly in the snow, facedown with one arm above his head and one out before him, panting from his run. She stared at the tattoo at the base of his spine that moved with his breaths.

Rolling over onto his back, he looked up at the black sky as the snowflakes fell on his naked upper body and leather pants. His wet black hair was plastered to his head. He continued to breathe heavily while his teeth chattered from the cold.

Still he didn't move.

"I just want to be warm," he whispered. "Just once let me be warm. Is there no star capable of sharing its fire with me?"

She frowned at his odd question, but then, in dreams bizarre phrases and events were commonplace.

Zarek rolled over again and pushed himself up, then continued through the blizzard.

He led her toward a small, isolated cabin in the middle of the woods. There was only one window, but the light inside was a bright beacon in the cold desolation of the arctic storm.

It looked so inviting.

Astrid heard laughter and conversations coming from inside.

Zarek stumbled toward the solitary side window. Breathing heavily, he splayed his hand against the frosty glass pane as he stared inside like a small, hungry child standing outside a fancy restaurant where he knew he would never be welcomed.

She came up behind him so that she could see inside, too.

The cabin was filled with Dark-Hunters. They were celebrating something while a blazing fire roared in the fireplace. There was food and drink aplenty while they laughed, drank, and spoke to each other like brothers and sisters. A family.

Astrid didn't recognize any of them, except for Acheron. But it was obvious Zarek knew them all.

Clenching his fist, he pushed himself away from the window and headed to the front door of the cabin.

Zarek pounded fiercely on it. "Let me in," he demanded.

A tall blond man opened the door. He wore a black leather motorcycle jacket with red Celtic scrollwork on it and a pair of black leather pants. His dark brown eyes were scornful and held an extremely distasteful look on his handsome face. "No one wants you here, Zarek."

The blond tried to close the door.

Zarek braced one hand against the doorframe and the other against the door so that he could keep the man from shutting him out. "Damn you, Celt. Let me in."

The Celt stepped back as Acheron came forward to block Zarek's way. "What do you want, Z?"

Zarek's face was anguished as he met Acheron's gaze. "I want to come in." He hesitated and when he spoke his next words, his eyes were bright with humiliation and need. "Please, Acheron. Please let me in."

There were no emotions on Acheron's face. Not one.

"You're not welcome here, Z. You'll never be welcome among us."

He closed the door.

Zarek pounded against the wood and cursed. "Damn you, Acheron! Damn all of you!" Then he kicked the door and tried the knob again. "Why won't you just kill me, you bastard! Why?"

This time when Zarek spoke, the anger was gone from his voice. It was hollow and needful, aching, and it affected her even more than when he'd asked to die. "Let me in, Ash, I swear I'll behave. I swear it. Please don't leave me out here alone. I don't want to be cold anymore. Please!"

Tears fell down Astrid's face as she watched Zarek beating against the door, demanding they open it.

No one came.

The laughter continued inside as if he didn't exist.

In that moment, Astrid fully understood the desolate isolation he felt. The loneliness and abandonment.

"Fuck all of you!" Zarek roared. "I don't need any of you. I don't need anything."

Finally, Zarek threw his back against the door and then slid down to kneel in the midst of the cold, swirling winds. His hair and eyelashes were white and frozen from the snow, his exposed skin red.

He closed his eyes as if the sound of their merriment was more than he could take. "I don't need anything or anyone," he whispered.

And then everything in the dream changed. The cabin shifted form until it became her temporary house in Alaska.

There were no more Dark-Hunters in his dream. No more storm. It was a perfect, peaceful night.

"Astrid." He breathed her name like a gentle prayer. "I wish I could be with you."

She couldn't move as she heard those softly spoken words.

He'd never said her name before and the sound of it on his lips was like a melodic song.

He looked up at the dark sky where a million stars twinkled through the clouds. " 'I wonder,' " he said quietly, quoting again from *The Little Prince,* " 'whether the stars are set alight in heaven so that one day each one of us may find his own.' "

Zarek swallowed and folded his muscular arms around his legs as he continued to watch the heavens. "I have found my star. She is beauty and grace. Elegance and goodness. My laughter in winter. She is courageous and strong. Bold and tempting. Unlike any other in all the universe, and I cannot touch her. I dare not even try."

Astrid couldn't breathe as he spoke so poetically. She'd never really thought about the fact that her name meant "star" in Greek.

But Zarek had.

Surely no killer could have such beauty inside him?

"Astrid or Aphrodite," he said softly, "she is my Circe. Only instead of changing a man into an animal she has made the animal human."

Then anger descended on him and he kicked at the snow before him. He laughed bitterly. "I am such a fucking idiot, wanting a star I can't have."

He looked up wistfully. "But then, all stars are beyond human reach and I'm not even human."

Zarek buried his head against his arms and wept.

Astrid couldn't stand it anymore. She wanted out of this dream, but without M'Adoc's help, she couldn't rouse herself from sleep.

All she could do was watch Zarek. Watch his anguish and grief that cut through her like glycerin on glass.

He was so strong in life. An iron forge that could withstand any blow. One who lashed out at other people to keep them away from him.

It was only in his dreams that she saw what was inside him. The vulnerability.

Only here that she truly understood the man he dared not show to anyone.

The tender heart that was hurt by their scorn.

Astrid wanted to ease his suffering. She wanted to take him by the hand and show him a world where he wasn't locked outside. Show him what it was like to reach out to someone and not be knocked away.

Not once in all the centuries she had judged had Astrid felt this way about anyone. Zarek touched a part of her that she didn't even know existed.

Most of all, he touched her heart. A heart she had feared was no longer functioning.

But it beat for him.

She couldn't just stand here, watching him ache in his solitude.

Before she could think better of it, she flashed herself into her empty cabin and opened the door . . .

Zarek's heart stopped beating as he looked up and saw the face of heaven. No, she wasn't heaven.

She was better. So much better.

Never in this dream had anyone opened the door once he'd been shut out.

But Astrid had.

She stood in the doorway, her face gentle. Her pale blue eyes were no longer blind. They were hot and welcoming. "Come inside, Zarek. Let me warm you."

Before he could stop himself, he stood up and took her outstretched hand. It was something he would never have done in real life. Only in a dream would he have dared to touch her.

Her skin was so warm that it burned him.

She pulled him into her arms and held him close. Zarek shook at the novelty of a hug, at the sensation of her breasts against his chest. Her breath on his frozen skin.

So this is what a hug felt like. Hot. Soothing. Miraculous.

His human contact had been so limited in his lifetime that all he could do was close his eyes and just feel the warmth of her body surrounding his.

The softness of her.

He inhaled her warm, sweet scent and reveled in the new-found emotions that tore through him.

Was this acceptance?

Was this nirvana?

He didn't know for sure. But for once, he didn't want to wake up from this dream.

Suddenly a warm blanket was wrapped around his shoulders. Her arms still held him tight.

Zarek cupped her face in his hand and pressed his cheek to hers. Oh, the feeling of her flesh touching his . . .

She was so soft.

He'd never imagined anyone being soft like this. So tender and inviting.

The warmth of her cheek on his took the stinging burn of the cold away. It crept through his body until he thawed completely out. Even his heart that had been encased by ice for centuries.

Astrid trembled at the sensation of Zarek's prickly cheek against hers. Of his breath falling gently against her skin.

His unexpected tenderness tore through her.

She'd seen enough of his life to know gentleness was not something he had experience with and yet he held her so carefully.

"You're so warm," he breathed in her ear. His hot breath tickled her neck, and sent chills all over her.

He pulled back and stared at her as if she were unspeakably precious to him. He brushed the back of his knuckles against her jaw. His eyes were so dark and tormented while he stared at her, as if unable to believe she was with him.

His gaze uncertain, he touched her lips with the tip of his forefinger. "I've never kissed anyone before."

His confession stunned her. How could a man so handsome have never kissed?

Fire sparked in his eyes. "I want to taste you, Astrid. I want to feel you hot and wet under me. To look into your eyes while I fuck you."

She shivered at his crudeness. It was what she expected from the conscious Zarek, but she refused to take that from this one.

She knew him better than that.

What he suggested now was forbidden. She wasn't allowed to ever cross the physical line with her charges.

The only one who had ever tempted her to break that rule had been Miles. But she had met that temptation and wisely kept herself away from him.

With Zarek it wasn't so easy. Something about this man touched her in a way that nothing had before.

Looking up into his tormented black eyes, she saw his wounded heart . . .

He'd never known kindness.

Never known the warmth of a loving touch.

She couldn't explain it, but she wanted to be his first and she wanted him to be hers. She wanted to hold him and show him what it was like to be welcomed by someone.

If you do this you could lose your job as a judge.

It was all she'd ever wanted to be.

If she didn't do this, Zarek could lose his life. If she reached out to him now, maybe she could teach him that it was okay to trust someone.

Maybe she could touch the poet inside him and show him a world where he would be free to allow other people to see his gentler side. Show him that it was okay to befriend others.

She finally understood what Acheron had meant.

But how could she save Zarek? He had turned on the people whom he'd been sent to protect and had killed them.

She needed proof that he would never do that again.

Could she find it?

She had to. There was no choice. The last thing she wanted was to see him hurt anymore.

She would defend this man no matter what.

"I won't fuck you, Zarek," she whispered. "Ever. But I will make love with you."

He looked puzzled and unsure. "I've never made love to anyone."

She lifted his cold hand up to her lips and kissed his fingers. "If you want to learn, come with me."

Zarek couldn't breathe as she withdrew from him. His head spun with strange, alien feelings and emotions. He was afraid of what she offered him.

If she touched him, would it change him?

He didn't expect kindness from her or anyone. A pitiful and horrifyingly scarred slave, he'd died a virgin and as a Dark-Hunter had only screwed women on rare occasions. Not once in two thousand years had he ever stared into a lover's eyes while he took her. Never had he allowed one to hold or even touch him.

Should he follow Astrid, all that would change.

In his dream, she had her eyesight and could see him . . .

He would be tamed. For the first time in his life, he would have a tie to someone. Physical. Emotional.

Even though this was a dream, it would change him toward her forever because this was what he wanted deep down inside, buried in a place where he dared not look. Buried in a heart that had been crushed by cruelty.

"Zarek?"

He looked up to see her standing in the doorway of her bedroom. Her long blond hair fanned out around her shoulders and she wore nothing except a thin cotton button-down shirt. Her long legs were bare, inviting.

The light behind her showed through the thin fabric, outlining every precious curve of her body . . .

Zarek swallowed. If he did this, Astrid alone would be unique to him in all the world. She would be his.

He would be hers.

He would be tamed.

It's only a dream . . .

But even in his dreams no one had ever tamed him.

Until now.

His heart hammering, he went to her and scooped her up in his arms. No, he wouldn't be tamed. Not by this and not by her. But she would be his in this dream.

All his.

Astrid trembled at the fierce, determined look on Zarek's face as he carried her to the bed. Hunger blazed in his obsidian eyes. She had a strange feeling that Zarek might be right after all.

A man this wild would never make love to a woman.

The saner part of her told her to pull away from him. To stop this before it was too late.

But another part of her refused. This would tell her the true mettle of the man.

He laid her down on the bed and brushed her lips with his fingertips as if he were memorizing them. Savoring them. Then he gently parted her lips and covered them with his.

Astrid was completely unprepared for the passion of his kiss. The ferocity of it. It was both rough and tender. Demanding. Hot. Sweet. He growled fiercely as his tongue brushed against hers, tasting her before he explored every inch of her mouth.

For a man who had never kissed before, he was incredible. She shivered as he tasted her palate, as his tongue swept through her with spears of pleasure.

She buried her hands in his soft hair and moaned as he licked and nibbled until she was nearly unconscious from the ecstasy of it. She'd never known anything like this.

Anything like Zarek.

It had been a long time since she'd kissed a man, and never had any man tasted better than him. She was scared now. Not just of him, but of herself.

No man had ever touched her. She'd never breached her oath to not touch her charge.

Zarek's touch could cost her everything and yet she couldn't find it within herself to push him away.

For once in her life, she wanted something for herself. She wanted to touch the unreachable. To give Zarek something special. A rare moment of peace with someone who wanted to be with him.

No one else would appreciate this as much as he would.

Only he would understand . . .

Zarek pulled back from her to unbutton her shirt. But what he wanted to do was rip it from her. He wanted to lose himself inside her, crush her to him as he possessed her with all the furious passion he felt.

But even in his dream, he wouldn't treat her that way.

For some strange reason he wanted to be tender with her. He wanted to have sex with her like a man, not a wild animal.

He didn't want to pound himself furiously against her, seeking a passing moment of pleasure. He wanted this night to last. Wanted to spend the whole of it holding her.

For once in his life, he wanted someone to treat him as if he mattered. As if she cared for him.

Not once had he allowed his fantasies or dreams to take him here.

Tonight he did.

She cupped his face in her hands and tilted his head until he could see into her pale eyes that looked at him as if he were human. Eyes that saw something good in him.

"You're so handsome, Zarek."

Her calm, sweet words tore through him. There was nothing about him attractive. There never had been.

He was nothing.

But as he stared into her precious face, there for an instant he felt as if he were something more.

Surely a woman like this wouldn't touch him if he were truly nothing.

Not even in his dreams . . .

He pulled her shirt open so that he could stare down at her body. Her breasts were of medium size, the rosy nipples hard and swollen, just begging him for a taste. Her belly was rounded ever so slightly, her skin pale and inviting. But what made his breath catch was the sight of her legs slightly parted. The sight of the damp dark blond curls between her legs that held the promise of true paradise. Or at least as close to it as a man like him could ever hope to get.

Astrid held her breath as she watched Zarek's feral gaze search her body. It was so searing that she felt it like a real touch.

He moved from the bed to remove his pants.

She swallowed as she saw him swollen and hard for her. His tawny skin was dusted with black hairs and was the most incredibly masculine sight she'd ever beheld. He was beautiful. Her dark warrior. Unlike him, she knew this night was real. Knew that she shouldn't be doing this when they would both remember it on their waking.

Her job was to remain impartial. But she wasn't impartial to this man, or to his pain.

She wanted to soothe him any way she could.

No one deserved the life he'd had to endure. The degradations and hostility.

He laid his body across hers and gathered her into his arms. His weight was delectable. She closed her eyes and just let the power and strength of him wash over her as she felt his hard, masculine body with every inch of her own.

Zarek struggled to breathe. The feel of her warm body against his was the most incredible sensation he'd ever known.

Her hands roamed his bare back as he stared down into eyes that warmed him.

There was no scorn. No anger.

They were beautiful eyes.

He kissed her gently, taking her upper lip and sucking it tenderly as he tasted the honey of her mouth.

In his human lifetime, women had cringed anytime he drew near them. They had shrieked and thrown things at him.

He'd lain awake many nights trying to imagine what it would be like to touch one. Trying to imagine the feel of their arms wrapped around him.

The reality of it was so much greater than anything his mind had ever conjured.

Before this dream ended, he intended to claim her over and over again until they were both begging for mercy.

Astrid moaned as Zarek broke from his kiss and trailed his lips and tongue down her throat to her breast. She felt his hard erection and soft sac against her thigh, searing and intimate, and it made her quiver.

He cupped her breast gently in his hand as he rolled his tongue around her swollen nipple, gently sucking and nipping her.

She cradled his head in her hands and watched him as he groaned with bliss. He looked as if her body were ambrosia to him. He took his time tasting her. Every inch of her skin was licked and teased. Tasted and sated. It was as if he couldn't get enough of her.

No man had ever been allowed to do this to her and she was terrified of what was to come. Even though she knew what sex was, the sensation of it was alien to her.

But then, so were the feelings Zarek stirred.

All the nymphs of justice were supposed to be virginal and chaste.

No man was ever to lay a hand on them.

Astrid no longer cared. Surely her mother would understand her passion. After all, Themis had had numerous children. Astrid's father had been a mortal man her mother refused to speak of, and no one had ever known the name or station of the Fates' father.

Surely her mother would forgive her this one transgression.

Was one night too much to ask?

And yet as she thought that, she wondered if one night with him would ever be enough.

Zarek's head swam from the sweet scent and feel of Astrid in his arms. He growled as he licked and nibbled every inch of delectable flesh and listened to her murmurs of pleasure. She was the sustenance he needed to live.

He had to have more of her.

Astrid yelped in ecstasy as Zarek spread her thighs and took her into his mouth.

She couldn't speak or breathe as supreme pleasure racked the whole of her body. Every lick, every gentle suck, sent a wave of fierce ecstasy through her.

Such a thing was unimaginable to her.

She should be mortified at what they were doing.

She wasn't. In fact, she wanted more of this.

More of him.

Her heart racing, she looked down to see him there between her thighs. He held his eyes closed and his face looked as if he took as much pleasure from his tasting as she did from being tasted.

She opened her legs more, giving him access to her as she buried her hand in his silken hair. Zarek laughed darkly against her, sending another pleasurable thrill through her, then he rubbed his stubbly whiskers against her cleft.

She groaned deep in her throat.

He slid his fingers inside her, circling the place where she throbbed in aching need of him.

He took his time with her, and all the while her body burned with tremors of pleasure.

Who knew anyone could feel like this?

The ecstasy built and built until she couldn't stand it anymore. His name was torn from her lips as she came for the very first time.

Still he didn't relent. He only growled at the sound of her pleasure and kept tormenting her until she begged him to stop.

"Please, Zarek. Please have mercy on me."

He pulled back to stare up at her. His eyes burned into her as one corner of his mouth quirked up. "Mercy, princess? I've barely started."

He crawled up her body like some giant, fierce beast, licking and nibbling his way as he went until his body was flush with hers.

He cupped her face in his hand and then kissed her deeply. Passionately.

Astrid moaned as he placed his knee between her thighs. The crisp hairs caressed her skin, making her tremble in expectation.

Zarek's head buzzed with the scent and taste of Astrid. The softness of her silken limbs caressing his. Nothing could ever feel better than her hands gliding down his back to cup his ass and press it closer to her.

Nothing sounded better than his name on her lips as she came for him again.

For the first time in two thousand years, he felt human.

Most of all, he felt wanted.

He pulled back slightly so that he could stare down at her as he spread her thighs wider.

This was what he wanted. Her, wild and wet underneath him. To feel her creaminess coating him until he was blind from the ecstasy of it.

He wanted to see her face when he entered her. Wanted to see if she regretted what she was allowing him to do to her.

Bracing himself for the worst, he held her gaze with his and slid himself deep into the velvety heat of her body.

His head reeled from the pleasure of it. From the pleasure of her.

She hissed, arching her back as her grip tightened on his shoulders.

But there was no scorn; no regret.

Her eyes were alight with needful passion and with other tender emotions he couldn't even begin to comprehend.

He smiled in spite of himself, reveling at the miracle of this woman and what she had just given him.

Astrid couldn't breathe as she felt him hard and throbbing inside her. She'd tried to imagine what it would be like to have a man inside her countless times, but nothing had prepared her for this reality. For the sensation of Zarek's hardness.

He rode her slow and easy as if he wanted this moment to last, as if just being inside her was enough for him. She wrapped her legs around his hips and gazed up at him as he looked down at her.

It was so incredible, this feeling of him being inside and on top of her. She loved the pleasure of his weight. The look on his face as he watched her.

"Hi," she said, feeling suddenly awkward to see him there while they were so intimately joined.

His face was a cross between puzzled and amused. "Hi, princess."

She reached up to cup his cheeks in her hands as he stroked her hard and deep, over and over again. Oh, the feel of him there. He was so deep inside that she could almost swear the tip of him was rubbing the inside of her navel.

Zarek closed his eyes as he savored the feel of her under him while her hands touched his face.

No wonder men killed for women. He understood that now. Knew why Talon had been willing to die for Sunshine.

Astrid touched parts of him he'd never known existed. His heart. His soul. She took him to heights unimaginable.

Here in her arms, for the first time, he felt peace.

There was a part of him so calm now, so tranquil, and another part of him that was on fire, dying to touch her.

Zarek lowered himself down on top of her so that he could nibble the tender flesh of her neck. Her ear. He felt the chills run down her body.

He scraped her skin with his fangs, tempted to sink them in.

What would she taste like?

What more emotions would she make him feel?

"Are you going to bite me, Zarek?" she asked, making her throat vibrate under his lips.

He ran his tongue over the vein that throbbed on her neck. "Do you want me to?"

"No. I'm afraid of it. I don't want to be like other women to you."

"Princess, you could never be that. You are unique to me."

"Am I your rose?"

He gave a short laugh as he thought of the little prince's lesson. "Yes, you are my rose. There is only one of you in all the millions of planets and stars."

She answered him with a hug.

That hug pierced him in a way nothing had before. Something inside him seemed to snap and burst, overwhelming him with tenderness and warmth.

He buried himself deep inside her as he came for her.

Astrid bit her lip as she felt his climax. He shuddered in her arms. She smiled as she held him close and kissed his shoulder.

He was so still. So quiet.

Who would have thought that he would be capable of such a thing? He was always so fierce and forceful.

His mere presence made the air around him snap and sizzle.

But not now. Now there was only silence.

Zarek lay on top of her, weak and spent, his body still joined to hers. He didn't want to move.

He couldn't.

Her touch was sublime. But more than that, he felt connected to her. And he had never felt that before.

Was this really a dream? Please gods, no. Please let this be real.

He needed it to be real, desperately.

Astrid closed her eyes as Zarek nuzzled her neck again. For some reason she felt as if she had just tamed some wild, uncontrollable beast.

She ran her legs up and down his, cradling him with her body as she brushed her hand through his ebony hair. He pulled back slightly to stare at her in wonderment.

She was so glad she had done this tonight.

He dipped his head down to kiss her again.

She inhaled his scent, drank from the tenderness of his lips. "Oh, Zarek," she breathed.

Zarek clenched his eyes closed at the sound of his name on her lips. It was such fierce, bittersweet pain and it tore through him.

He nibbled at the delicate skin on her neck, letting his fangs graze her flesh. In real life, he would have bitten her by now.

He would never have taken her body with his.

He would have shared her emotions as he drank from her and he wondered what she would taste like in his dream . . .

Opening his lips, he felt the pulsing of her blood in her veins against his tongue.

She would be sweet, that much he knew.

"Zarek?"

Her throat vibrated with her words. "Yes?"

"I like you best when you're tender like this."

He pulled away from her and frowned as something tickled his gut.

"Is something wrong?"

Everything. This wasn't his dream. This was a surreal moment. His dreams were never pleasant. Not once had he ever had a lover in them.

No one had ever spoken to him the way she did.

No one had ever opened the door and let him inside the cabin once Acheron had banished him.

He got out of bed and pulled his pants on. He had to get away. Something was wrong. He knew it deep down inside. This was not where he should be.

He had no business with her.

Not even in his dreams.

Astrid watched panic flicker across Zarek's face as he dressed. She wrapped the blanket around her and went to him. "You don't have to run from me."

"I'm not running from you," he snarled. "I run from no one."

Astrid agreed. No, he didn't. He was stronger than any man had a right to be. He took hits and blows no one should have to bear.

"Stay with me, Zarek."

"Why? I'm nothing to you."

She touched his arm. "You don't have to push everyone away."

Snarling, he shrugged her touch away. "You don't know what you're talking about."

"I do, Zarek," she said, wishing there was some way to make him see that she wanted to show him. "I do. I understand wanting to hurt other people before they hurt you."

"Sure you do, princess. When have you ever hurt anyone? When has anyone ever hurt you?"

"Show me the goodness inside you, Zarek. I know it's there. I know that somewhere underneath all the pain and hurt there is someone inside who knows how to love. Someone who knows how to nurture and protect."

He raked her with a cold sneer as he buttoned his pants. "You don't know jack shit." He cast a feral snarl at her and headed for the door.

Astrid started to follow him, then thought better of it.

She didn't know what to do. How to reach him.

She'd meant her words to comfort, not anger him. But Zarek never reacted to her the way she expected.

Frustrated, she dressed and went after him.

Apparently, niceness wouldn't work with Zarek.

So she opted for a different route.

She brushed past him in the hallway, and opened the front door for him.

Zarek paused; it was daylight outside the door and he hadn't burst into flames.

Maybe this was a dream.

It had to be and yet . . .

"What are you doing?" he asked her.

"Opening the door so it doesn't hit you in the butt as you go through it."

"Why?"

"You said you want to leave. So go. Get out. I don't want to keep you here when it's obvious that I repulse you."

Her logic baffled him. "What are you talking about?"

"What do you mean, what am I talking about? Isn't it obvious? I sleep with you and you can't leave me fast enough. Sorry I wasn't good enough for you. I at least tried."

Not good enough for him? Was she joking?

He stared at her in disbelief. Torn between wanting to curse her for the stupidity and wanting to comfort her.

His anger won out. "You're worthless? Then what am I? Do you realize before I died, I was below even a pity fuck? No one would touch me with any part of their bodies. I was lucky if they even used a stick to knock me out of the way. So don't stand there and act all hurt and talk to me about being worthless. No one has ever had to pay someone else just to get you out of their sight."

Zarek froze as he realized what he had just said to her. Those were things he'd kept hidden deep inside himself for centuries. Things he had never spoken of with anyone.

Painful truths that had languished in his heart, eating at him century after century.

No one had ever wanted him near them.

Not until Astrid.

It was why he couldn't stay. She made him warm, and it terrified him because he knew it couldn't be real.

This was another cruel torment fate had inflicted on him.

When he woke up, he would be with her and she would have no use for him. He didn't belong with the real Astrid.

He never would.

"Then they were blind if they couldn't see what you are, Zarek. They are the losers, not you."

Gods, how he wanted to believe her.

How he *needed* to believe her.

"Why are you being so nice to me?"

"I told you, Zarek. I like you."

"Why? No one else ever has."

"That's not true. You've had friends all along, but you've never allowed them to help you."

"Acheron," he said, whispering the word. "Jess." He curled his lip at the thought of Sundown.

"You have to learn to reach out to people."

"Why? So they can shoot me in the back?"

"No, so they can love you."

"Love?" He laughed at the thought. "Who the hell needs

that? I've lived my entire life without it. I don't need it and I damn sure don't want it from anyone."

She stood strong before him. Unyielding. "You can lie to yourself all you want to, but I know the truth." She held her hand out to him. "You have to learn to trust someone, Zarek. You've been brave your whole life. Now show me that courage. Take my hand. Trust me and I swear I won't betray you."

He stood there indecisively, his heart pounding. He'd never been more terrified.

Not even the day they'd killed him.

"Trust me, please. I will never hurt you."

He stared at her hand. It was long, graceful. Delicate. A tiny hand.

A lover's hand.

He wanted to run.

Instead, he found himself lifting his hand and lacing his fingers with hers.

Chapter 9

Tears fell down Astrid's cheeks as she felt the warm strength of his hand on hers; as she saw his long, tapered fingers twined with hers.

His hand was large, masculine and it enveloped hers with power.

Those hands had killed, but they had also protected. They had cared for her and pleasured her.

By this simple action, she knew she had finally made contact with him.

She had just reached the unreachable.

Then the contact was lost.

Zarek's face hardened as he jerked his hand away from hers. "I don't want to be changed. Not by you. Not by anyone."

Snarling in anger, he pushed past her and marched out the door.

Astrid did something she had never done before.

She cursed.

Damn him for not staying. Damn him for being so stupid.

"I told you, he's a hard-ass."

She turned to see M'Adoc standing behind her, staring out the door after Zarek who was trudging shirtless through the snow.

"How long have you been eavesdropping?" she asked the Oneroi.

"Not that long. I know when not to intrude on a dream."

She narrowed her eyes meaningfully at him. "You better."

Disregarding her and her unspoken threat, he moved to watch Zarek make his way across the snow.

"So what are you going to do now?" he asked.

"Beat him with a stick until he listens to reason."

"You wouldn't be the first one to try that," M'Adoc said dryly. "The thing is, he's immune to it."

She let out a long, weary breath. It was true.

"I don't know what to do," she confessed. "I feel so helpless where he's concerned."

Something sagelike flickered behind M'Adoc's pale glowing eyes. "You shouldn't have trapped him here or yourself for that matter. It's dangerous to stay in this realm too long."

"I know, but what else could I have done? He won't stay put and was determined to leave my cabin. You know I couldn't allow that." She paused and gave the Dream-Hunter a pleading look. "I need guidance, M'Adoc. I wish I could talk to Acheron. He's the only one I know who could tell me about Zarek."

"No. Zarek could tell you."

"But he won't."

He met her gaze. "So you're giving up, then?"

"Never."

He gave her a rare smile that let her know he was siphoning off her emotions. "I figured as much. Glad to know you're no longer daunted."

"But how do I reach him? I'm open to any and all ideas and suggestions at this point."

M'Adoc held his hand out and a small, dark blue book appeared in his palm. He gave it to her.

Astrid looked at the copy of *The Little Prince* in her hands.

"It's Zarek's favorite book, too," M'Adoc said.

No wonder Zarek had been able to quote it to her.

M'Adoc stepped back. "It's a book of heartbreak and survival. A book of magic, hope, and promise. Strange that it would speak to him, isn't it?"

M'Adoc flashed out of the dream then and left her flipping through the book. She saw that M'Adoc had marked certain passages and paragraphs.

Astrid closed the door and took it to the comfortable recliner that had suddenly appeared in the cabin.

She smiled. All the gods of sleep liked to speak in riddles and metaphors. They seldom said anything outright, but made people work for their answers.

M'Adoc, the head of the Oneroi, had left her clues in this book.

If this could give her any insight into Zarek at all, she would read what he had marked.

Maybe then she might have a hope of saving Zarek.

Jess ducked into the small convenience store and shook himself like a wet dog coming in from the rain. It was so damn cold up here that he couldn't stand it.

How had Zarek survived in Alaska before central heating? He had to give his friend credit. A man had to be hard and dangerous to make his home here without any help from friends or Squires.

Personally, he'd rather be pistol whipped and thrown naked into a nest of rattlers.

There was an elderly gentleman behind the counter who gave him a knowing smile as if he understood why Jess had cursed as soon as he entered. The man had a thick head of gray hair and a salt-and-pepper-colored beard. His old green sweater had snags, but it looked good and warm. "Can I help you?"

Jess lowered the muffler from his face and gave a curt, friendly nod to the man. Manners dictated he remove his black Stetson while indoors, but damned if he'd do that and let even an ounce of his body heat escape.

He needed ever bit of it.

"Howdy, sir," he drawled all polite like. "I'm searching for some black coffee or anything else you've got that's hot. *Real* hot."

The man laughed and pointed to a coffeepot in the back. "You must not be from around here."

Jess headed for the coffee. "No, sir, and thank God for that."

The old man laughed again. "Ahh, stay up here for a little while and your blood will thicken up enough to where you don't even notice it."

He doubted that. His blood would have to be petrified not to feel *this* cold.

He wanted to get his butt back to Reno before he became the first Dark-Hunter in history to freeze to death.

Jess poured an extra large Styrofoam cup full and headed for the counter. He set it down and dug through the five million layers of coat, flannel shirt, sweater, and long johns to pull his wallet out of his back pocket to pay. His gaze fell to a small glass case where someone had placed a hand-carved statue of a cowboy on a bucking bronco.

Jess frowned as he recognized the horse, then the man.

It was him.

He'd e-mailed a picture to Zarek last summer of him saddle-breaking his latest stallion. Damned if that wasn't an exact copy of the photo.

"Hey," the old gentleman said as he noticed it, too. "You look just like my statue."

"Yes, sir, I noticed that. Where did you get it?"

The man looked back and forth from him to the statue as he compared their likenesses. "The annual Christmas auction we had last November."

Jess scowled at that. "Christmas auction?"

"Every year the Polar Bear Club gets together to raise money for the poor and sick. We have an annual auction, and for the last, oh I don't know, twenty years or so, Santa has been leaving a couple of huge bags of these one-of-a-kind hand-carved statues and figurines that we sell. We figure he must be a local artist or something who doesn't want to let anyone know where he lives. Every month a big money order comes anonymously to our post office box, too. Most of us figure it's the same guy doing it all."

"Santa, as in Claus?"

The man nodded. "I know it's a stupid name, but we don't know what else to call him. It's just some guy who comes around in winter and does good deeds. The police have seen him a time or two carrying the bags up to our center, but they leave him alone. He shovels driveways for the elderly and carves a lot of those elaborate ice sculptures you've probably seen around town."

Jess felt his jaw go slack, then he quickly snapped it shut before he exposed his fangs to the gentleman. Yeah. He had seen those sculptures.

But *Zarek*?

It hardly seemed like something the ex-slave would do. His friend was crusty at best and downright ornery at worst.

But then, Zarek had never told him what he did up here to pass the time. Never said much of nothing to Jess really.

Jess paid for the coffee, then headed back out to the street.

He walked to the end of it, where one of the ice sculptures rested at an intersection. A rendition of a moose, it stood almost eight feet tall. The moonlight glistened off the surface that was so intricately carved that it looked like the moose was ready to break loose and run for home.

Zarek's work?

It just didn't seem right.

Jess went to take another drink of his coffee only to realize it had already chilled.

"I hate Alaska," he mumbled, tossing the coffee to the ground and then wadding up the cup.

Before he could find a trash can, his cell phone rang.

He checked the caller ID to see that it was Justin Carmichael, one of the Blood Rites Squires who was up here hunting for Zarek. It seemed once the Oracles got wind that Artemis and Dionysus wanted Zarek dead, they had immediately notified the Council, who in turn had sent out the orneriest bunch of Blood Rite Squires to hunt and kill the rogue Dark-Hunter.

Jess was all that stood between them and Zarek.

Born and raised in New York City, Justin was a younger man, about twenty-four, with a nasty attitude Jess didn't care for much.

He answered the call. "Yeah, Carmichael, whatcha need?"

"We have a problem."

"And that would be?"

"You know the woman who was helping Zarek? Sharon?"

"What about her?"

"We just found her. She was beaten up pretty bad and her house has been burned to the ground. My money says it's Zarek bent on revenge."

Jess's blood went cold. "Bullshit. Did you talk to her?"

"Trust me, she wasn't in any condition to talk when we found her. She's with the doctors right now and we're headed back to Zarek's cabin to see if we can find that bastard and make him pay for this before he hurts anyone else."

"What about Sharon's daughter?"

"She was staying at a neighbor's house when it happened. Thank God. I've got Mike watching over her in case Zarek comes calling again."

Jess couldn't breathe and it wasn't from the frozen bite in the air. How could this have happened? Unlike the Squires, he knew Zarek didn't have any part in this.

He alone knew where Zarek really was.

Ash had trusted him with the truth of what was going on and had charged him with making sure no one fubarred it until Zarek's test was over.

Well, things just went further south than a herd of geese in the fall.

"Don't move until I get there," he told the Squire. "I want to go to his cabin with you."

"Why? You planning on getting in our way again when we take him down?"

Those words rubbed him like a herd of porcupines. "Boy, you better take that tone and flush it. I'm not a Squire you're talking to; I happen to be one of the guys you answer to. It ain't none of your damned business why I'm going. You just don't move until I tell you to or I'm going to show you how I once made Wyatt Earp piss his drawers."

Carmichael hesitated before he spoke again. When he did, his voice was nice and cool. "Yes, sir. We're at the hotel and are waiting for you."

Jess hung up the phone and returned it to his pocket.

He felt awful about Sharon. She shouldn't have been in any danger at all. None of the Squires would have dared hurt her.

And in spite of what the others thought, he knew Zarek wouldn't have done it even if he'd been able to.

Zarek just didn't strike him as the type to go after those weaker than him.

But then, who else would have dared?

Astrid found Zarek alone in the center of a burned-down medieval village.

There were bodies, burned and unburned, scattered

everywhere. Male and female. Every age. Most of them had torn throats as if a Daimon or some similar creature had fed off them.

Zarek walked among them, his face grim. His eyes tormented.

He had his arms wrapped around himself as if to protect him from the horror he was witnessing.

"Where are we?" she asked.

To her shock, he answered "Taberleigh."

"Taberleigh?"

"My village," he whispered, his voice angst-ridden and tight. "I lived here for three hundred years. There was this one old crone who saw me once when she was a young girl. She used to leave me things from time to time. A leg of dried mutton, a wineskin of ale. Sometimes nothing more than a note to say thank you for watching over them." He looked at Astrid, his face haunted. "I was supposed to protect them."

Before she could ask him what had happened to the village, she heard the muffled cries of an old woman.

Zarek bolted toward her.

The woman lay on the ground wrapped in torn clothes, her old body broken. She was covered in blood and bruises.

Astrid could tell by Zarek's expression that this was the woman he had spoken of.

Zarek fell to his knees beside her and wiped the blood from her lips as she struggled to breathe.

The woman's old gray eyes were piercing with accusation as they focused on him. "How could you?"

The life faded from the crone's eyes, turning them dull, glazed.

She went limp in his arms.

Zarek bellowed with rage. He released the woman and pushed himself to his feet. He paced a wide circle, raking his hands angrily through his hair.

Panting, he looked every bit as insane as everyone claimed.

Astrid hurt for him. She didn't understand what this was about. What he was reliving.

She followed him. "Zarek, what happened here?"

His face anguished, he turned around to confront her. Hatred and guilt burned in the midnight depths of his eyes.

He swept his arm out to indicate the bodies around them. "I killed them. All of them." The words came out as if torn from his throat. "I don't know why I did this. I just remember the rage, the craving for blood. I don't even remember killing them. Just flashes of people dying as they came near me."

His face was bleak. His eyes filled with self-loathing. "I am a monster. Do you see now why I can't have you? Why I can't stay with you? What if one day I killed you, too?"

Her chest constricted at his words as true panic and fear engulfed her.

Had she misjudged him?

"All men are guilty." It was her sister Atty's favorite saying. *"The only honest men are those infants who haven't yet learned to speak lies."*

Horrified, Astrid looked around at the dead bodies . . .

Could he really have been capable of something like this?

She didn't know what to think now. Whoever was responsible for this slaughter did deserve to die. It more than explained why Artemis wouldn't want him around people.

Astrid paused at that thought.

Wait a minute . . .

Something was wrong.

Dead wrong.

Astrid looked at the bodies around them. *Human* bodies. Some of them children, most of them women.

Had Zarek done this, Acheron would have killed him instantly. Acheron refused to tolerate anyone who preyed on the weak and defenseless. And especially anyone who harmed a child.

There was no way Acheron would suffer a Dark-Hunter to live who could destroy and kill the people he'd been sent to protect. She knew that with every molecule of her body.

"Are you sure *you* did this?" she asked.

He looked aghast at her question. "Who else would have done it? There was no one else here. Do you see anyone other than me with fangs?"

"Maybe an animal—"

"*I* was the animal, Astrid. There was no one else capable of this."

She still didn't believe it. There had to be some other explanation. "You said you don't remember killing them. Maybe you didn't."

Rage and pain flared in his eyes. "I remember enough. I know I did this. Everyone knows. It's why the other Dark-Hunters fear me. Why they won't speak to me. Why I was banished to a place where there were no people to protect. Why I wake up every night afraid Artemis is going to move me away from Fairbanks into an area where there are even fewer people."

Part of her feared that he was telling the truth, but she discounted it.

In her heart she knew that the tormented man who could speak poetically and make beautiful pieces of art with his hands, who could care for an animal that had wounded him, would never, ever do this.

But she would need proof.

Gut instinct wouldn't be enough evidence to offer to her mother or to Artemis. They would demand proof of his innocence.

Proof that he wasn't capable of killing humans.

"I just wish I knew *why* I did this," Zarek growled. "What

made me go so crazy that I could kill them and not even remember it."

He looked at her, his eyes bleak. "I am a monster. Artemis is right. I don't belong around normal people."

Tears welled in her eyes at his words. "You're not a monster, Zarek."

She refused to believe it.

Astrid pulled him into her arms, offering him comfort she wasn't sure he would take.

At first he stiffened as if he were about to push her away, then he relaxed. She let out a slow breath, grateful he'd accepted her hug.

His taut, strong arms held her against a lean body that rippled with muscles. She'd never felt anything like it. He was so steely and tender at the same time. Her cheek was pressed against his firm pectorals, her breasts against his ridged abs.

She ran her hand down his back, making him shiver in her arms.

Astrid smiled at this newfound power she had over him. Because she was a justice nymph, her femininity had had to take a back seat. There was no time to feel womanly or sensual.

But she felt that now.

Because of him. She was aware of her body for the first time in her life. Aware of the way her heart beat in time to his. The way her blood simmered from the sensation of his arms wrapped around her.

In that instant, she wanted to do something for him.

She wanted to make him smile.

Reluctantly, she pulled back from him and held her hand out. "Come with me."

"Where?"

"Someplace warm."

Zarek hesitated. He only trusted people to hurt him. And they had never disappointed him in that respect.

Trusting someone to *not* hurt him was another thing entirely.

Deep inside, he wanted to trust her.

No, he *needed* to trust her.

Just once.

Taking a deep breath, he placed his reluctant hand into hers.

She flashed him away from the village to a bright seaside beach. Zarek blinked and squinted against the unfamiliar brightness of the light.

He held his hand up, to cut the glare of the foreign sun he had all but forgotten.

He'd never been to the beach before. He'd only seen pictures in magazines and on TV.

And it had been centuries since he'd seen daylight. *Real* daylight.

The sun shone down on his skin, hot. Tingly.

He let the heat soak into his frozen body. Let the sun caress his skin and melt away the centuries of misery and loneliness.

Dressed only in black leather pants, Zarek walked over the sandy beach, looking at everything and focusing on nothing in particular.

This was even better than his stay in New Orleans. The surf roared around them as it pounded against the beach, the wind whipped at his hair. The sand was warm and clung to his feet.

Astrid ran past him, to the edge of the water.

He watched as she peeled her clothes from her body down to a small blue bikini.

She gave him an impish, hot once-over that made him shiver in spite of the heat. "Would you like to join me?"

"I think I'd look strange in a bikini."

She laughed at him. "Was that a joke? Can it be you made a real joke?"

"Yeah, I must be possessed or something."

Beguiled actually. By a sea nymph.

She came toward him with a determined walk.

Zarek waited, unable to breathe. To move. It was as if he lived or died by the sassy sway of her hips.

She stopped before him and unbuttoned his pants. The sensation of her fingers brushing against the thin patch of hair that ran from his navel to his groin rocked him. He hardened instantly, wanting to taste her again.

She slowly unzipped his pants as she stared up at him from underneath her lashes.

One small millimeter before she freed his erection, she seemed to lose her nerve. Biting her lip, she trailed her hands in the reverse direction, up toward his chest.

Zarek still couldn't breathe as she splayed her hands on his bare chest.

"Why do you touch me when no one else does?" he asked.

"Because you let me. I like touching you."

He closed his eyes as her tender caress seared him. How could something so simple feel so incredible?

She stepped into his arms and he instinctively embraced her. Her breasts brushed against his abs, making him even harder, making him ache.

"Have you ever made love on the beach?"

His breath caught at her words. "I've only made love to you, princess."

She rose up on her tiptoes so that she could capture his lips for a sweet, tormenting kiss.

Pulling back, she smiled up at him as she unzipped the last little bit of his fly and took him into her hand. "Well then, Frosty the Snow-Zarek, you're about to."

Ash sat alone in Artemis's temple, just outside her throne room on the terrace where he could look out onto the beautiful, multicolored waterfall. His golden-blond hair pulled back into a ponytail, he sat on top of a marble banister with his bare back against a ridged column.

Wildlife, safe from hunters and all other danger because of Artemis's protection, grazed in a yard where the ground was made of clouds. The only sound came from the rushing water and the occasional cry of a wild bird.

It should be peaceful here and yet for all his serene composure Ash was agitated.

Artemis and her attendants had left him to go to the Theocropolis where Zeus held court over all the Olympian gods. She would be gone for hours.

Not even that could please him.

He wanted to know what was happening with Zarek's test. Something was going wrong, he knew it. He could feel it, but he dared not use his powers to investigate.

He could take Artemis's wrath, but he would never unleash that onto Astrid or Zarek.

So here he sat, his powers restricted, his anger and frustration leashed.

"Akri, can I come off your arm for a little while?"

Simi's voice took some of the edge off his raw emotions. Whenever she was part of him, she couldn't see or hear anything unless he spoke her name and gave her an order. She was even immune to his thoughts.

She could only feel his emotions. Something that allowed her to know whenever he was in danger, the only time she was allowed to leave him without his permission.

"Yes, Simi. You may take human form."

She pulled herself off and manifested beside him. Her long blond hair was braided. Her eyes were a stormy gray and her wings pale blue.

"Why are you so sad, *akri*?"

"I'm not sad, Simi."

"Yes you are. I know you, *akri,* you gots that pain in your heart like the Simi gets whenever she cries."

"I never cry, Sim."

"I know." She moved closer to him so that she could rest her head on his shoulder. One of her black horns scraped against his cheek, but Ash didn't mind. She draped her arms around him and held him close.

Closing his eyes, he embraced her tightly, cupping her small head in one of his hands. Her hug went a long way toward easing his troubled spirit. Only Simi could do that. She alone touched him without making physical demands on him.

She never wanted anything but to be his "baby."

Childlike and innocent, she was the balm he needed.

"So, can I eat the redheaded goddess now?"

He smiled at her most-often-asked question. "No, Simi."

She lifted her head and stuck her tongue out at him, then flounced over to sit on the railing by his bare feet. "I want to eat her, *akri*. She a mean person."

"Most gods are."

"No they're not. Some, true, but I rather like the Atlanteans. They were very nice. Most of them. You never met Archon, did you?"

"No."

"Now, he could be mean. He was blond, like you, tall like you, well, taller than you, and good-looking like you, but not quite as good-looking as you. I don't think anyone is as good-looking as you are. Not even them gods. You are definitely one of a kind when it comes to looks . . . Oh—" She started as she remembered his twin. "Well . . . you're not really one of a kind, are you? But you cuter than that other one. He a bad copy of you. He only wishes he was as cute as you are."

His smile widened.

She placed her finger against her chin and stopped for a

minute as if trying to gather her thoughts. "Now where was I going with that? Oh, I remember now. Archon didn't like a lot of people, unlike you. You know that thing you do whenever you get really, really mad? The one where you can blow stuff up and make it all fiery and chunky and messy and all? He could do that too only not with as much finesse as you. You got a lot of finesse, *akri*. More than most.

"But I digress. Archon liked me. He said, 'Simi, you a quality demon.' Have you ever seen a non-quality demon, though? That's what I wanna know."

Amused, Ash listened as she rambled on about gods and goddesses worshiped in his mortal lifetime. Gods and goddesses long dead now. He loved to listen to her nonlinear tales and logic.

It was like watching a small child as it tried to sort out the world and remember something. There was no telling from one minute to the next what would come out of her mouth. She saw things clearly, like a child.

If you had a problem, you killed it.

End of problem.

Subtleties and politics were beyond her.

Simi just was. She wasn't amoral or vicious, she was just an extremely young demon with godlike powers who had no comprehension of deceit or treachery.

How he envied her that. It was why he shielded her so carefully. He didn't want her to learn the hard lessons that had been dealt to him.

She deserved to have the childhood he had never known. One that was sheltered and protected. One in which no one was allowed to hurt her.

He didn't know what he would do without her.

She'd been nothing more than an infant when she'd been given to him. Barely twenty-one himself, the two of them had pretty much raised each other. They were both the last of their kind on this earth.

For more than eleven thousand years it had been just the two of them.

She was as much a part of him as any vital organ.

Without her, he would die.

The door of the temple opened. Simi hissed, baring her fangs, letting him know Artemis had returned early.

Ash turned his head for confirmation. Sure enough, the goddess was striding toward him.

He let out a tired breath.

Artemis pulled up short as she saw Simi sitting at his feet. "What is it doing off your arm?"

"Talking to me, Artie."

"Make it go away."

Simi huffed. "I don't have to do nothing you say, you old heifer cow. And you are old. Really, really old. And a cow, too."

"Simi," Ash said, stressing her name. "Please return to me."

Simi cast an evil glare at Artemis, then became a dark, amorphous shadow. She moved over to him and laid herself over his chest to become a huge dragon on his torso with fiery spirals that wrapped around and down both of his arms.

Ash laughed darkly at the sight. It was Simi's way of hugging him and tweaking Artemis at the same time. Artemis thoroughly hated it whenever Simi covered so much of his body.

Artemis let out a disgusted sound. "Make it move."

He crossed his arms over his chest. "Why are you back so early?"

She instantly became nervous.

His bad feeling tripled. "What happened?"

Artemis walked to the column at his feet, wrapped her arm around it and leaned against the marble. She played with the gilded edge of her peplos as she worried her lip.

Ash sat up straight, his stomach knotted. If she was this

evasive something had gone mind-blowingly wrong. "Tell me, Artemis."

She looked exasperated and angry. "Why should I tell you? You'll just get angry at me and you practically stay that way anyway. I tell you, then you'll want to leave and you can't leave and then you'll yell at me."

The knot in his gut tightened. "You have three seconds to talk or I'm forgetting about your fear that one of your family members will discover I'm living in your temple. I will use my powers and I will find out what has happened on my own."

"No!" she snapped, turning to look at him. "You can't do that."

A tic started in his jaw.

She moved back, putting the column between them. She took a deep breath as if for strength, then spoke in the voice of a small, frightened child. "Thanatos is loose."

"What!" he roared, lowering his legs to the floor and coming to his feet.

"See! You're yelling."

"Oh, trust me," he said between clenched teeth, "this isn't yelling. I haven't even come close to it yet." Ash pushed himself away from the banister and paced angrily around the long balcony. It took all his strength not to lash out at her. "You promised me you would recall him."

"I tried, but he got away."

"How?"

"I don't know. I wasn't there and now he refuses to heel."

Ash glared at her.

Thanatos was on the loose and the only one who could stop him was under house arrest in Artemis's temple.

Damn her for her tricks and promises. There was no way he could leave here. Unlike the Olympians, once he gave his word, he was bound by it.

It would kill him to break his oath. Literally.

Anger roiled through him. Had she listened to him the first time, they wouldn't be reliving this nightmare. "You swore to me nine hundred years ago when I killed the last one that you wouldn't re-create Thanatos. How many people did that one kill? How many Dark-Hunters? Do you even remember?"

She stiffened and returned his glare. "I told you, we needed someone to corral your people. You won't do it. You won't even control your demon. It was the only reason I made another one. I need someone who can execute them when they misbehave. You, you just make excuses for them. 'You don't understand, Artemis. Waa, waa, waa.' I understand, all right. You prefer to tend to anyone but me so I created someone who listens when I speak." She glared meaningfully at him. "Someone who actually obeys *me*."

Ash counted to ten three times while he clenched and unclenched his fists. She had a way of making him want to lash out and hurt her that came dangerously close to breaching all of his control.

"Don't get me started on that one, Artie. It seems to me 'obey' isn't a word that belongs in the same sentence as your executioner."

Driven mad by his confinement and thirst for vengeance, the last Thanatos had ripped through England with such force that Ash had had to fabricate stories of a "plague" to keep the humans and Dark-Hunters from learning the truth of what had actually destroyed forty percent of the country's population.

Ash raked his hands over his face at the thought of what Artemis had unleashed onto the world again. He should have known when he asked her to recall it that it was too late for her to do so.

But like a fool, he had counted on her to do as she promised.

He should have known better.

"Damn you, Artemis. Thanatos has the powers to gather

Daimons and make them do his bidding. He can call them from hundreds of miles away. Unlike my Hunters, he walks in the daylight and is impossible to kill. The only vulnerability he has is unknown to them."

She scoffed at him. "Well, that's your own fault. You should have told them about him."

"Told them what, Artemis? Behave or the bitch-goddess will unleash her insane killer on you?"

"I am not a bitch!"

He moved to stand before her, pressing her back against the column. "You have no idea what you have created, do you?"

"He's nothing more than a servant. I *can* recall him."

He looked at her trembling hands and the beads of perspiration on her forehead.

"Then why are you shaking?" he asked. "Tell me how he got loose."

She swallowed. But wisely gave him the information he sought. "Dion did it. He was bragging in the hall about it right before I came to tell you."

"Dionysus?"

She nodded.

Ash cursed himself this time. He shouldn't have removed the god's memory of their fight in New Orleans. He should have let the idiot know exactly what he was dealing with. Left Dionysus so scared of him that the Olympian god would never again dare to confront him or any of his men.

But no, he'd sought to protect Artemis. She didn't want her family to know who and what he was.

To them he was only her pet. A human curiosity, easily discarded and dismissed.

If they only knew . . .

He'd removed enough of everyone's memory of that night so they would only recall that a fight had happened and who the winners were.

Not even Artemis remembered everything.

Artemis had promised him Dionysus wouldn't go after Zarek for retribution. But then Artemis had thought to kill Zarek herself.

When would he learn?

She could never be trusted.

Ash moved away from her. "You have no idea what it does to someone to lock them away. To place them in a hole where they're forgotten."

"And you do?"

Ash fell silent as suppressed memories flooded him. Painful, bitter memories that haunted him whenever he dared to think of the past.

"You'd best pray that you never learn what it feels like. The madness, the thirst. The anger. You've created a monster, Artemis, and I'm the only one who can kill it."

"Then we're in for a bit of a problem, aren't we? You can't leave."

He narrowed his eyes.

She stepped back again. "I told you, I will contact the Oracles and have them bring him home again."

"You better, Artemis. Because if you don't get him under control, the world is going to become the very thing that makes you wake up screaming at night."

Zarek lay on the beach, still inside Astrid, as the waves ran over their bodies. This dream was so real and intense that he never wanted to wake from it.

What would it be like to have her for real?

But even as he thought about that, he knew the truth. A woman like Astrid had no use or need for a man like him.

It was only in his dreams that he could be wanted. Needed. Human.

He moved to her side so that he could watch the water run

over her naked body. Her hair was wet, plastered to her skin. She looked like a sea nymph that had just swum ashore to bask in the warm sunlight and seduce him with her curves and silken skin.

She looked up at him with a sweet smile that made his heart pound as she ran her hand over his arms and chest.

Astrid lay in silence, watching him, too. Zarek looked so lost now, as if their lovemaking had left him confused.

She wondered what it would take to tame this man, just a little. Only enough so that other people could see what she saw.

At least now he let her touch him without cursing or withdrawing from her.

It was a start.

She trailed her hand lower over the hard planes of his chest, down the perfect definitions of his abdomen. Hunger ignited in his eyes as she moved her hand lower.

Astrid licked her lips, wondering if she dared be even more bold with him. She still wasn't sure how he would react to anything.

She played with the small, crisp hairs that ran downward from his navel, raking her fingers through them. He was already starting to harden . . .

Zarek held his breath as he watched her. Her hand felt wonderful on his body as she drew circles around his navel and trailed her fingernail down the short, light dusting of hair on his stomach.

Already he was craving her again.

Then she moved her hand lower.

He growled as she cupped his sac in her palm. Her warm hand enclosed him, squeezing him exquisitely.

His groin jerked, and all the blood rushed back into the region, making him hard and aching for her.

She ran her finger down his shaft to the tip, where she toyed with him. "I think you like it when I do that."

He answered her with a kiss.

Astrid moaned at the passion he showed. He throbbed in her hand while his tongue danced with hers, exciting her to the highest level of need.

She pulled away reluctantly, desperate to give him what was unknown to him.

Kindness.

Acceptance.

Love.

The word caught in her mind. She knew she didn't love him. She barely knew him, and yet . . .

He made her feel again. Touched the emotions she had feared were forever lost. She owed him much for that.

Kissing his lips lightly, she scooted down his body.

Zarek frowned at her actions. He didn't know what she had planned until she laid herself over his stomach. Her bare back was exposed to him as she continued to stroke him with her hand.

He ran his hand through her long, wet blond hair, trailing it over her bare back while her breath tickled his hip. Her skin was so soft, so tender. There wasn't a blemish anywhere on it.

She moved lower.

Zarek gasped as she took the tip of his shaft slowly into her warm mouth.

He was frozen by pleasure. The feel of her lips and tongue caressing him was unlike anything he'd experienced before. No woman but Astrid had ever touched him there. He'd never allowed it.

But he doubted he could deny her anything after this. She had laid claim to him in a way no one ever had.

Astrid moaned at the salty taste of him. When her sisters had told her about this, she had always considered it obscene and nasty. At the time and for centuries afterward, she couldn't imagine herself ever doing something like this with a man.

But she did it for Zarek; there was nothing obscene about

the feelings inside her. Nothing obscene about the way he tasted.

She was giving him a rare moment of pleasure, and strange as it seemed, she enjoyed it, too.

He gripped her shoulders and groaned in response to every lick, nibble, and suckle she gave him. His warm response urged her on. She really wanted to please him. To give him all the things he deserved.

Zarek arched his back, letting her have her way with him. It amazed him that he allowed her to do this. Never before had he trusted a lover with his body. He'd always been in complete control.

The woman didn't touch him. Ever.

She didn't caress or kiss him.

He bent her over, did his business, and walked off.

But with Astrid it was different. He felt as if he were sharing himself with her. As if she were sharing herself with him.

It was mutual and wonderful.

Astrid started as she felt Zarek's fingers slide down her cleft. Opening her legs for him, she gave him access as she continued to pleasure him with her mouth.

Zarek turned more to his side all the while his fingers stroked and delved.

She shivered at the warmth of his touch as the cool surf rushed around them. The heat of the sun on her skin was nothing compared to the heat his touch provided.

He made her burn.

He nudged her legs farther apart.

Astrid moaned as his mouth covered her.

Her head swam in pleasure as he ran his tongue over the center of her body where she craved more of his touch. His tongue flicked across her, spearing her. Enticing her.

His hands gripped her hips as he pressed her pelvis closer to him so that he could torture her with more wicked delights.

Zarek shook at the sensation of tasting her while she tasted him. This was so much more than sex they shared.

She was right, they were making love to each other.

And it shook him all the way to his missing soul.

They took their time with each other, stroking, caressing, making sure that they were both sated. They came together in one pure burst of emotion.

Astrid pulled back as Zarek continued to tease her.

So intent on her, Zarek wasn't paying attention to the water. Not until a large wave rolled over them.

He sputtered as he swallowed a large amount of water.

The wave rolled back, leaving both of them choking and gasping.

Astrid laughed, the sound dulcet and vibrant. "Now that was interesting."

He kissed his way up her body so that he could smile down at her. "More aggravating, in my opinion."

She reached her hand up to touch his cheeks. "Prince Charming has dimples."

He stopped smiling instantly and looked away.

She turned his head back toward her. "Don't stop smiling, Zarek. I like this side of you."

His eyes flared angrily. "Meaning you don't like the other side of me?"

She made a disgusted sound at him. "You are so surly." She ran her hand down his back until she could cup his naked butt in her hands. "After today, haven't you realized I'm rather fond of all sides of you? Even though some are more prickly than others." She ran her hand over his whisker-covered cheek to emphasize her point.

He relaxed a degree. "I shouldn't be with you."

"And I shouldn't be with you. Yet here we are and I am very happy about it." She wiggled her bottom against him, making him groan in response.

He looked at her as if he couldn't believe she was real, and in his mind she wasn't. She was only a dream.

Astrid wondered how he would react when he woke up. Would any of this help or would he withdraw further from her?

She wished she could strip his bad memories from him. Give him a happy childhood filled with love and tenderness.

A life of joy and friendship.

He laid his head down between her breasts and stayed there quietly as if content to feel nothing more than her under him while the sun warmed them both.

"Tell me of a happy memory, Zarek. One thing in your life that was good."

He hesitated for so long that she didn't think he would answer. When he spoke, his voice was so soft that it made her ache. "You."

Tears gathered in her eyes. She hugged him with her body, cradling him, hoping that in some way she soothed his troubled, restless spirit.

Astrid knew then that she would fight for this man, and in the back of her mind came a frightening realization.

She was falling in love with him.

For a moment, she couldn't breathe as the notion hung in her thoughts like a frightening specter.

But there was no denying what she felt for him, the lengths she would go to see him safe and happy.

His breath teased her nipple while his heart thudded against her stomach.

No one had touched her the way he did and it wasn't just the sex. He made her feel soft and womanly. Desirable.

He didn't baby her and yet he did such kind things to take care of her.

Closing her eyes, she let his weight and the water soak into her. Let his slick, cool skin soothe her.

What was she going to do? Zarek wasn't the kind of man to let anyone love him.

Especially not a woman who had been sent to pass judgment on him.

If he ever learned what she was, he would hate her.

That knowledge ripped through her, stealing the happiness of the day.

But eventually, she would have to tell him.

Jess left the black Ford Bronco and slid his sawed-off shotgun out from under the seat.

Just in case.

The night winds were frigid, the moonlight bright and eerie as it reflected off the snow. He adjusted his sunglasses, not that they made much difference.

The Alaskan climate was hard on a Dark-Hunter's sensitive eyes.

Zarek's house was dark and empty, but a bright red snowmachine was parked in front of it. Jess's Squire, Andy Simms, who had come up here with him from Reno, ambled out of the Bronco and eyed the snowmachine suspiciously.

Barely six feet in height with black hair and brown eyes, Andy had just turned twenty-one. He'd only worked for Jess a few months and had come in after Andy's father retired last spring.

Jess had known the pup since the day he was born, and tended to look on him like a little brother.

Pesky and all.

"Is that another Squire?" Andy asked, indicating the snowmachine with a nod.

Jess shook his head. The Squires were in the two SUVs pulling up behind them.

They made more noise than a herd of nervous cattle as they left their four-wheel-drives and gathered round him.

There were twelve of the Squires altogether, but Jess only knew a couple of them.

Otto Carvalletti was the tallest of the group. Standing a cool six feet five inches, he had jet-black hair that was a bit long, but well styled, as if the man spent a lot of time on it.

He glared penetratingly at all times, and Jess figured if the man ever did manage to smile, it would crack his face.

One half of Otto's family was Italian Mafia while the other half was one of the oldest Squire families known. A real blue blood, Otto's grandfather had once headed up the Squires' Council.

Tyler Winstead came to them from Milwaukee. Barely five feet seven, the blond man was wholesome looking until you caught sight of his eyes. There was nothing wholesome in his gaze. Only intensity.

That left Allen Kirby. Another multi-generational Squire, Allen had been called out from Toronto for this hunt. Since Otto never spoke two words, Allen was the smart-ass of the herd.

But, something told Jess, Otto could easily outdo Allen's biting comments if he chose to do so.

"I knew he'd be here," Allen said as he eyed the snowmachine with pert malice.

Jess passed a bored stare at him. "It's not Zarek. Believe me, red isn't his color."

But he suspected the snowmachine did belong to a Dark-Hunter. He could feel the drain on his powers already.

"How do you know it's not him?" Tyler asked.

Jess rested the shotgun on his shoulder. "I just do."

He ordered the Squires to stay put and ambled up the driveway toward the snowmachine. Using his teeth, he pulled the glove off his left hand and placed it on the engine.

It was cold but that meant nothing in this subzero temp, he realized all of a sudden, and he felt like a jackass for even bothering. The snowmachine could have been here five minutes or five hours. In this kind of cold, even a raging fire would be chilled within minutes of going out.

So who did it belong to?

He looked left and right and saw no sign of anyone.

Until he heard a soft thud to his left. He barely had time to pull his gun off his shoulder before four Daimons broke through the foliage.

They paused at the sight of him, then put their heads down and ran headlong toward him.

Jess caught one with a shotgun blast to the chest, then flipped a second one up and over using the stock of his gun.

A crossbow bolt shot past his face, narrowly missing him and striking one Daimon as Jess killed the one at his feet. The last one attacked, but didn't get more than a step before another bolt landed square in his chest and he burst into powdered dust.

"Nasty bloodsucking rats."

He arched a brow at the soft, feminine voice that preceded the appearance of a tall, well-built woman.

Her long, black hair was braided down her back and she wore a tight black leather pantsuit that reminded him a bit of Emma Peel from *The Avengers*. Only it was much more devastating on the woman approaching him.

A second Dark-Hunter came out of the woods behind her. He was a good four inches taller than Jess with white-blond hair and a predator's lope that said "mess with me and get hurt." He was dressed in a long fur coat and he seemed extremely comfortable in the arctic chill.

The woman paused by Jess's side and offered him her hand. "Syra of Antikabe."

Jess inclined his head and took her hand. "Jess Brady, ma'am, pleased to meet you."

"Sundown," the other Dark-Hunter said as he joined them. He kept his hands in his pockets. "I've heard a lot about you. You're a long way from home."

Jess eyed him suspiciously. "And you are?"

"Bjorn Thorssen."

He inclined his head in turn to the Viking warrior. Rumor had it Bjorn had been one of the original Norsemen who had invaded Dark Age Normandy.

"I've heard of you," he said to Bjorn, then he turned to look at Syra. "But no offense, ma'am, you I don't know."

"Sure you do. The assholes on the loop call me Yukon Jane."

He smiled at that. Yukon Jane was an Amazon warrior from the third or fourth century B.C. She was rumored to be almost as ill-tempered as Zarek. She loved to hunt and kill, and was stationed in the Yukon because she'd once maimed a king who annoyed her.

"Well, now," Jess drawled with a wicked grin as he gave her elegant pose an appreciative once over, "all I can say is none of them that insult you have ever had the pleasure of your company, Miss Syra. Otherwise, they'd be calling you Queen Jane."

She smiled warmly at that. "You are a charmer and polite, too. Zoe was right."

Jess's grin widened.

Allen cleared his throat. "Well, Lord Debonair and Lady Lethal, if we can have a minute of your time, we do have a psycho to hunt."

Jess glared over his shoulder at Allen, but before he could comment, Syra shot another bolt from her crossbow.

Allen went flying and landed flat on his back in the snow.

Syra walked over to him and stared down. "I don't particularly like Squires and I really hate the Blood Rites. So save yourself some pain and don't speak to me again. Or next time I'll use a Daimon bolt on you."

She reached down and picked up the flathead bolt she'd used.

Jess laughed. He liked a woman with gumption.

And a deadly aim.

"So," she said, turning around and eyeballing the lot of them. "I've been chasing a group of Daimons for the last four days as they headed toward Fairbanks. Bjorn followed a tribe of them up from Anchorage. That explains why we're here. What about the rest of you? Jess, did you trail Daimons from Reno to Alaska?"

Otto moved out of the group of Squires and paused in front of Syra. "We've come to kill Zarek of Moesia, and if you get in our way, little girl, we're going to kill *you.*"

"I'll be damned," Jess said, pulling his sunglasses down low on the bridge of his nose to stare at Otto. "He speaks. Or rather growls."

"But not for long if he doesn't watch his mouth." Syra gave Otto a mean and lethal glare. "For the record, Squire, it would take more man than you to even scratch me."

Otto returned her glare with a flirtatious smile. "I live for a woman who scratches. Just make sure you keep it on the back, baby. I don't like scars."

Otto brushed past her.

"I really hate Squires," Syra snarled. She pulled another flat bolt out and loaded it, then shot it at Otto.

Moving so fast he could hardly be seen, the Squire turned around and caught it without flinching. He held the bolt up to his nose and inhaled it lovingly. "Mmm," he said. "Rose. My favorite."

Jess exchanged a knowing look with Andy. "Perhaps we should leave you two alone."

"Yeah," Allen said with a short laugh, "this does remind me a bit of the mating rites of the mean and the surly. All we need now is Nick Gautier."

Otto slung the bolt at Allen who grunted as it made contact with his stomach.

Syra's face was beet red as she glared at Otto, who ignored her and sauntered toward the cabin.

"Do you have a Squire, Jess?" she asked as she and Bjorn walked beside him.

He nodded toward Andy. "Raised that one from a whelp."

"Does he listen?"

"Most days."

"You're lucky. I shot my last three." As she headed toward the cabin, Syra added, "And it wasn't with the flat bolt."

Well, at least things were a mite more amusing with the two new additions to their crew.

But as Jess entered Zarek's cabin behind Bjorn, Syra, and three of the Squires, his humor died.

The rest of the group had to wait outside since no one else would fit in the small square space.

This wasn't a case of the cabin being bigger inside than it looked outside. It was just the reverse.

Inside, the place was well kept, but cramped and dismal.

The Squires held halogen lanterns up, illuminating the stark interior. There was a pallet on the floor with an old, worn-out pillow and a few threadbare blankets and furs. The television was set on the floor and the walls were lined with bookshelves. The only pieces of furniture in the house were two cupboards.

"Good Lord," Allen said. "He lives like an animal."

"No," Syra said as she walked over to the bookshelves to skim the titles. "He lives like a slave. For him, this would be a step up from what he was used to."

She met Jess's gaze. "You know the man?"

"Yeah and you're right." Jess had to duck out of the ceiling fan's way as he moved around the room. He remembered that Zarek was a full two inches taller than him.

"Damn," he said as he turned the fan blade with his finger and remembered another thing Zarek had once told him.

"What?" Bjorn asked.

Jess looked back at the Alaskan Hunter who was inspecting Zarek's pantry, which contained only a few cans of food and a ton of unopened vodka bottles. "How hot does it get up here in the summertime?"

Bjorn shrugged. "In the heart of the summer it can get in the high eighties and nineties. Why?"

Jess cursed again. "I remember talking to Zarek once. I asked him how he was doing. He said, 'Baking.' " Jess nodded at the small ceiling fan. "I just now realized what he meant. Can you imagine being trapped in this place in the dead of summer with no windows and no air-conditioning?"

Syra let out a low whistle. "We have round-the-clock sunshine. You're lucky if you can leave for more than ten minutes a day."

"What does he do for a bathroom?" Allen asked.

Syra indicated a small chamber pot in the left corner.

"How long has he been here?" she asked Jess. "Eight, nine hundred years?"

Jess nodded.

She let out a low whistle. "No wonder he's insane."

Allen scoffed. "With the money he gets paid, the idiot could have built himself a mansion."

"No," Jess said. "It's not his way. Trust me, when you're used to nothing, you expect nothing."

Syra walked over to the corner where a mountain of carved figurines were piled. "What are these?"

Jess frowned as he noticed the walls of the cabin and realized every single inch of them was covered with intricate carvings that matched the figurines.

Suddenly he recalled the wood sculptures he'd seen in the convenience store.

The ice sculptures he'd seen in town.

Poor Zarek must have gone loco time and again from boredom during the months he was confined to this tiny shed.

Hell, Jess had a bigger garage at home. "I would say it's Zarek's attempt to maintain a shred of sanity while he's locked away up here."

Bjorn picked up a painted figurine that looked like a polar bear with its cubs. "These are incredible."

Syra nodded. "I've never seen anything like them. It hardly seems right that we kill someone who's had to live like this all these centuries."

Allen snorted. "It hardly seems right that he was allowed to live after he murdered everyone in the village he was charged with watching."

Otto passed an interesting look to the Squire. If Jess didn't know better, he'd suspect the man had second thoughts about killing Zarek.

Their gazes locked.

Nope, no doubt. In fact, he suspected Otto might have been sent along for other reasons . . . as he had been.

"Well, guys, it's been fun," Bjorn said. "But my powers are waning from Jess and Syra and we still have a small matter of the Daimon migration to sort out. Anyone have any ideas why they would do this?"

They all looked to Syra who was the oldest.

"What?" she asked.

"Have you ever seen or heard of anything like this?"

She shook her head. "I've heard of Daimons teaming up. Back in the centuries before you guys were born, they used to have warrior Daimons. But no one has seen a Spathi in at least a millennium. All this beats me. It's a pity we can't reach Acheron. He might have more information."

Bjorn headed out of the cabin.

Jess pulled up the rear and looked back inside the shack one more time.

Damn. He felt real sorry for his friend and the life Zarek had been given.

He couldn't imagine being stuck out in the woods all alone in temperatures that ranged from forty below to ninety.

No wonder Ash took such pity on Zarek.

Six of the squires went to the SUVs and unloaded gasoline containers.

"What are you doing?" Jess asked suspiciously.

"Burning him out," a redheaded Squire said. "You want to hunt, you—"

"Like hell!" Jess grabbed the container from the man's hand and slung it toward the woods. "This is all he has in the world. No way I'm going to let you take it from him."

Allen sneered at him. "He beat up that woman."

Jess narrowed his gaze. "You have yet to prove it to me."

Allen rolled his eyes, as if unable to understand how he could defend his friend. "If Zarek didn't do it? Who did?"

"I did."

Chapter 10

Jess looked up to see the biggest herd of Daimons he'd ever beheld in his life. There had to be at least forty head of them, but it was hard to count—especially since he didn't think they were all visible. His Dark-Hunter sense told him more were still in the woods, acting as standbys.

Some wore leather, some fur coats. Some were male and others female. But they had a few things in common. Blond hair, fangs, and that unnatural attractiveness that was ingrained in their species.

Even so, one glance was enough to identify their leader. It was a Daimon he'd met already while he'd been after Zarek. But instead of fleeing from him like most Daimons did, this one had run *after* Zarek.

Pursuing Zarek even while they did.

The leader stood a head taller than the others and slightly ahead of them. Unlike the ones behind him, there was no fear in his gaze.

Only a raw, tangible determination. And a meanness that ran soul deep.

Syra let out a sound that was a cross between disbelief and humor. "What the hell is that?"

The Daimon leader smiled. "I would say 'Your worst nightmare,' but I hate clichés."

"*Marone,* you're real."

Everyone on the "good" side turned to look at Otto, who stared at the leader as if he were looking at a visitation from the Devil himself.

"You know this guy, Carvalleti?" Jess asked.

"I know *of* him, anyway," he said, his tone deep and heavy. "My father used to tell me about the Daimon called Thanatos when I was a kid. We always thought he was making it up."

"Making up what?" Bjorn asked as he looked back in Thanatos's direction.

"Tales of a Dark-Hunter executioner called the Dayslayer. It's a story that's been handed down through my family for generations. Squire to Squire."

"And you're telling me this asshole is him?" Bjorn asked at the same time Syra said, "Dark-Hunter executioner?"

Otto nodded. "Supposedly Artemis once set up a slayer for you guys in the event you turned rogue. He can walk in daylight and doesn't need blood to live. Legend has it that he's invincible."

Thanatos applauded sarcastically. "Very good, little Squire. I'm impressed."

Otto's eyes turned glacial. "My father said Acheron killed Thanatos about a thousand years ago."

"Not to be a smart-ass," Bjorn said, "but he doesn't look dead to me."

Thanatos laughed. "I'm not. At least no more so than you are."

Thanatos approached them slowly, methodically.

Jess tensed, ready for battle.

Thanatos folded his hands behind his back and offered Otto a wry smile. "Question, human, did your father ever tell you of the Spathi Daimons?"

Thanatos looked at the Dark-Hunters. "Surely you older Hunters remember them?" He sighed nostalgically. "Ah, those were the days . . . The Dark-Hunters hunted us, we slaughtered them. We made our homes in underground catacombs and crypts where the Hunters couldn't go without getting possessed. It was an interesting time to be Apollite or Daimon."

He looked over his shoulder at the herd of Daimons who eyed them nervously for the most part. There were one or two who had no fear and those were the ones Jess paid closest attention to.

He didn't know anything about warrior Daimons, but he did know how to execute any and all who wanted a taste of a human soul.

When Thanatos spoke again, his voice was dark, sinister. "But that was before we discovered civilization and modern conveniences. Before the human world developed enough to where we could exist at night under the pretense of being one of them. Apollites owning businesses and houses. Daimons playing Nintendo. What is this world coming to?"

Thanatos moved so fast that no one had time to blink. He shot a blast from his hands, knocking all the Squires off their feet.

He surveyed his chaos with a pleased look on his face. "Now before I allow my people to feed on all of you and I kill the Dark-Hunters, perhaps we should talk a bit, hmm . . . ? Or do you Hunters really want to battle me while you weaken each other?"

"Talk about what?" Jess asked, moving closer to Syra. Even though he knew she could take care of herself, it was just ingrained habit for him to protect a woman.

"Where Zarek is," Thanatos said between clenched teeth.

"We don't know," Syra said.

"Wrong answer."

One of the unknown Squires let out a howl. Jess watched

in horror as the man's arm was snapped in half by nothing at all.

Holy *Madre de Dios,* he'd never seen anything like that.

Bjorn attacked.

Thanatos caught him, and flipped him to the ground. He ripped open Bjorn's shirt to expose the bow-and-arrow mark of Artemis on Bjorn's shoulder.

Thanatos stabbed Bjorn's brand with an ornate gold dagger.

Bjorn disintegrated like a Daimon.

None of them moved.

Jess could barely breathe as rage suffused him. That had been way too easy for the Daimon. Up until now, the Dark-Hunters had been told that they could only die three ways. Total dismemberment, sunlight, or beheading.

Apparently, Acheron had left out one crucial, and extremely quick, way to die.

This wasn't good, and right now he was pissed that no one had warned them.

But that would have to wait. There were innocent people here and if he fought Thanatos in the presence of Syra, they would both be fighting with their hands tied behind their backs, while Thanatos would be fighting full strength.

"You want Zarek?" Jess asked.

Thanatos rose slowly to his feet. "That's why I'm here."

Jess was shaken by what he'd seen, and though he hadn't known Bjorn long, the man had seemed decent enough. It was a damn shame to lose a comrade, especially to Thanatos.

He'd grieve later; right now he wanted to make sure the Squires survived.

Jess slid his gaze to Syra and sent a mental projection to her. *"Save the Squires. I'm taking Asshole for a run."*

Aloud, he said, "Then follow me and bring all you've got. Zarek's going to enjoy slaying you."

Jess ran for his Bronco.

. . .

Zarek still lay naked in the surf, cradling Astrid against him. He couldn't count how many times they had made love in the last few hours. It had been so many times that he wondered idly if he'd be sore when he woke up.

Surely no one could be this acrobatic, even in dreams, and not have some physical damage to show for it.

He was exhausted from their lovemaking and yet he felt a peace the likes of which he'd never known.

Was this what other people felt?

Astrid leaned up. "When was the last time you had cotton candy?"

He frowned at her unexpected question. "What's cotton candy?"

She gaped in shock. "You don't even know what cotton candy is?"

He shook his head.

Smiling, she stood up and pulled him to his feet. "We're going to the boardwalk."

Okay, she really had lost her mind. "There's not a boardwalk."

"Oh, yes there is, just on the other side of those rocks."

Zarek looked over to see a pier that hadn't been there earlier.

How weird that it had popped into his dream at her bidding and not his. He eyed her suspiciously. "Are you a Dream-Hunter Skotos pretending to be Astrid?"

"No," she said, smiling. "I'm not trying to take anything from you, Zarek. I'm only trying to give you a pleasant memory."

"Why?"

Astrid sighed at the look on his face. Kindness was so far beyond his comprehension that he couldn't even understand why she wanted to make him smile.

"Because you deserve one."

"For what? I haven't done anything."

"You live, Zarek," she said, stressing the words, trying to make him understand. "For that alone, you deserve some happiness."

The doubt in his eyes stung her.

Determined to reach him, she "conjured" herself a pair of white shorts and a blue tank top, then helped dress him in a pair of black jeans and a T-shirt.

She led him toward the "dream" crowd.

Zarek was silent as they walked up the stairs that led to the old-fashioned boardwalk. He tensed visibly as people brushed too close to him. She had the distinct feeling he was one step away from uttering a vicious putdown.

"It's okay, Zarek."

He sneered at a man who came too close. "I don't like for anyone to touch me."

And yet he didn't say anything about the fact that she had her arm hooked in his.

It made her melt.

Smiling to herself, she took him to a small stand where a lady was selling hot dogs and cotton candy. She bought an extra large bag and dug out a handful of the light, fluffy pink sugar, then offered it to him.

"Here you go. One bite and you'll know what ambrosia tastes like."

Zarek reached for it, but she moved her hand out of his way. "I want to feed this to you."

Fury snapped in his eyes. "I'm not an animal to eat from your hand."

Her face fell at his words and her good humor was instantly dampened. "No, Zarek. You're not an animal. You're my lover and I want to care for you."

Zarek froze at her words as he stared at her lovely, sincere face.

Care for him?

A part of him snarled in anger at the idea, but another, alien part of himself jerked awake at her words.

It was a hungry part of him.

A yearning part. Needful.

A piece of him that he had sealed off and abandoned so long ago that he only vaguely recalled it.

Pull away.

He didn't.

Instead, he forced himself to lean down and open his lips.

She smiled a smile that burned him even as the strange sugar evaporated inside his mouth.

She placed her hand against his cheek. "You see, it doesn't hurt."

No, it didn't. It felt warm and wonderful. Joyful, even.

But it was a dream.

He would wake up in a short while and he'd be cold again. Alone.

The real Astrid wouldn't offer him cotton candy and she wouldn't hold him in the surf.

She would look at him with fear and suspicion on her precious face. She would be protected by a white wolf that hated him as much as he hated himself.

The real Astrid would never spend the time it took to tame him.

Not that it mattered. He had a death warrant out on him. He didn't have time for the real Astrid.

Didn't have time for anything other than basic survival. Which was why this dream meant so much to him.

For once in his life, he'd had a good day. He only hoped that when he woke up, he'd remember it.

Astrid led him around the arcade, playing games and eating junk food Zarek told her he'd only read about online. Even though he never smiled, he was like a child in his curiosity.

"Try this one," she said, handing him a candy apple.

Astrid quickly learned eating candy apples with fangs wasn't an easy thing to do.

When he finally managed a bite of it, she looked up expectantly. "Well?"

He swallowed it before he answered. "It's good, but I don't think I'm willing to repeat that experience. Not good enough to make up for all the work it takes to get to it."

She laughed as he tossed the apple into a large white garbage can.

She took him inside the arcade so that she could teach him to play Skee-Ball, one of her favorites. He was amazingly good at it.

"Where did you learn to throw like that?"

"I live in Alaska, princess, land of ice and snow. There's not much difference between this and tossing a snowball."

She was surprised at that. She had a funny image in her mind of him playing in the snow, which would be completely out of character. "Who do you throw snowballs with?"

He rolled another ball up the ramp and into the center circle. "No one. I used to toss them at the bears so that they would get mad and come close enough for me to kill them."

"You killed little bears?"

He gave her a droll look. "They weren't little, princess, I promise you. And unlike rabbits, you can make more than one meal off them and it doesn't take as many hides to make a coat or blanket. In the dead of winter, there's not a lot to eat. Most times before there were grocery stores it was either bear meat or starve."

Astrid's chest tightened at his words. She'd known it wouldn't be easy for him to survive, but what he described made her want to reach out and hold him close. "How did you kill them?"

"With my silver claws."

She was aghast. "You killed bears with a claw? Please tell me there are easier ways to do that. Spear, bow and arrow, gun?"

"It was long before guns, and besides, it wouldn't have been fair to the bear. He couldn't attack me from a distance. I figured he had claws and I had claws. Winner take all."

She shook her head in disbelief.

She had to give him credit, at least Zarek was sporting about it. "Didn't you get hurt?"

He shrugged nonchalantly, then tossed another ball. "Better than starving. Besides, I'm used to being cut up." He gave her a mischievous look. "Want a bearskin rug, princess? I have quite a collection."

She didn't find any humor in his question.

Her throat tight, Astrid wanted to weep from what he was telling her. Images went through her mind of him all alone, wounded, dragging a bear that outweighed him by at least ten times through the arctic snow just so that he could eat.

And getting the bear home was just the beginning of it. He'd have to skin and butcher it before the other animals smelled his kill or their blood.

Then cook it.

No one to help him and no choice except to do that or starve.

She wondered how many days he'd spent with no food at all . . .

"What about food in the summertime when you have twenty-two hours or more of daylight? I mean, you couldn't preserve the meat for long and it wouldn't give you enough time to plant or harvest anything. What did you do then?"

"I starved, princess, and prayed for winter."

Tears welled in her eyes. "I'm so sorry, Zarek."

His jaw flexed. He refused to look at her. "Don't be, it's not your fault. Besides, the hunger wasn't as bad as the thirst. Thank the gods for bottled water. Before that there always were a few days when I couldn't make it to the well even though it's just a short walk outside my door."

He reached for another ball.

Astrid placed her hand on his to stop him.

He turned to face her, his lips slightly parted. She pulled him into her arms and kissed him, wanting to give him some comfort, some degree of solace.

Zarek crushed her to him. She opened her mouth to taste him fully and to let his strength wash over her.

He pulled back with a groan. "Why are you here?"

"I'm here for you, Prince Charming."

"I don't believe you. Why are you really here? What do you want from me?"

She sighed. "You are amazingly suspicious."

"No, I'm realistic and dreams like this don't happen to me."

She arched a brow at him. "Never?"

"Not in the last two thousand years, anyway."

She smoothed the line on his brow with her fingertip and smiled up at him. "Well, things they are a-changing."

Zarek cocked his head at that, not believing it for a minute.

Some things never changed.

Never.

"Zarek!"

He felt an odd tugging at his chest.

But it wasn't Astrid doing it.

"Is something wrong?" Astrid asked.

"Zarek!"

It was a man's voice calling to him. One that seemed to come from miles away.

"I feel suddenly strange."

"Strange how?" she asked.

"Zarek!"

The clear boardwalk turned dark. His sight began to dim, his head to spin.

Zarek felt himself drifting away from Astrid. He fought with all his strength to remain with her.

To remain with his dream.

He didn't want it to end. Didn't want to wake up in a world where no one wanted him.

He had to get back to her.

Please, just one more minute . . .

"Zarek! Damn it, boy, don't make me have to slap you. The last thing I need right now is a concussion. Now get up!"

Zarek came awake to find Jess leaning over him, shaking him hard.

Cursing, he kicked the cowboy back, into the wall.

Jess's foul oath matched his own as Jess rebounded off the wood. Zarek's back and arm throbbed in response to Jess's injuries.

But he didn't care. He intended to add so many more injuries to the cowboy that neither one of them would be able to walk without limping.

He owed the bastard for the shot in his back.

And he always paid his debts in full, with interest.

Zarek came out of the bed snarling, ready for battle.

"Whoa, Z!" Jess said, ducking the punch Zarek swung at him. "Calm down."

Zarek stalked him like a lion eyeing an injured gazelle. One that intended to make the gazelle its dinner . . .

"Calm down? You shot me in the back, you son of a bitch."

Jess's face turned to stone and he gave him a cold, chilling stare. "Boy, don't you dare insult my mama, and you better stop and think about that one for a minute. I was a paid killer since I was old enough to hold a gun. Had I shot your dumb ass, you wouldn't have a head right now. Having been shot in the back by a friend, I sure wouldn't want to return that favor to anyone. Not even an ornery cuss like you. And why the hell would I hurt myself just to get to you anyway? Lord, boy, use your head."

Zarek still wasn't ready to believe him. Though mostly healed, his back was a sore reminder that someone had tried their damnedest to kill him. "Then who shot me?"

"One of them idiot Squires. Hell if I know which one. They all kind of look alike when they're not yours."

Zarek hesitated as he tried to sort out everything that had happened over the last few days.

Everything was a bit fuzzy in his mind. The last thing he really remembered was trying to leave Astrid's cabin . . .

He frowned as he looked around, realizing he was still here.

Jess had awakened him while he was lying fully dressed in a bed he didn't remember climbing into.

He frowned as he saw Astrid lying in that bed, too.

The dreams he'd had . . .

What the hell?

Jess reloaded his shotgun. "Look, I don't have time for this. Do you know who Thanatos is?"

"Yeah, we met."

"Good, 'cause he's already killed one Dark-Hunter tonight and he's right behind me. I need you up and running. Fast."

Zarek's stomach went south at his words. "What?"

Jess's face was grim and lethal. "He took out a Dark-Hunter without breaking a sweat. I've never seen anything like it in my life. Now Thanatos is coming for you, Z. It's time to make like a fox and get the hell out of Dallas."

What did that mean? If Zarek's head hurt before, it was nothing compared to the ache he felt trying to decipher that last bit of cowboy colloquialism.

"Whatever you do," Jess said, his voice deep and thick with warning, "don't let Thanatos near your bow-and-arrow mark. Apparently it works like the Daimons' ink blot in the center of their chests. One tiny stab and we're dust."

Zarek scowled at his words. "What bow-and-arrow mark? I don't have one."

Jess scoffed. "Of course you do. We all have one."

"No I don't."

Jess looked up from his gun, his face completely unamused. "Maybe it's in a spot you don't look at. Like your butt or something. I know you got one. It's where Artemis touched you when she captured your soul."

Zarek shook his head at him. "Artemis never touched me. She couldn't get near me without cringing so she used a stick to make me a Dark-Hunter. I swear to you, there's no mark on me."

Jess's jaw dropped in disbelief. "Wait, wait, wait. Are you telling me they stick you out here where there are no Daimons and you don't have a weak spot? What kind of shit is that? I live in Daimon Central with one hell of an Achilles' heel that no one ever bothered to mention, and you live where there's no danger to you and yet you don't have one?"

Jess paced the floor. It was a habit Zarek had learned about during one of their late-night phone conversations. Once Jess started on a rant, it was hard to get him off it.

"What's not fair with this picture?" Jess railed. "And then Ash asks me to come up here to save your ass and here we are dropping like flies while you're Teflon.

"No, I have a problem with this. I love you, man, but dayam. This just ain't right. I'm up here freezing my balls off, and you, you don't need protection. Meanwhile I have a bull's-eye on my arm that says, 'Hey, Daimon on steroids, kill me right here.'"

Still Jess rambled. "Do you realize, I put my keys in my mouth to pull out my wallet to pay for gas and they froze there? The last thing I want to do is die up here in this godforsaken place at the hands of some freaked-out something no one has ever heard of before except for Guido the

Killer Squire from Jersey? I swear I want someone's ass for this."

Jess took a breath but before he could start ranting again, the front door to the cabin burst open.

The entire house shook from the force of it.

Zarek felt a cold, familiar shiver up his spine.

A faint trace of a memory flashed through his mind. It was vague and disconcerting.

He'd felt this before . . .

With no time to contemplate, he used his telekinesis to slam and lock the bedroom door.

He shoved Jess toward the window. "She has a wolf somewhere in the house. Find him and get him out."

Something struck the door forcefully.

"Come out, Zarek," Thanatos growled. "I thought you liked to play with Daimons."

"Yeah, I'll play with you, you bastard." Zarek blew out the window with his telekinesis and pushed Jess through it while Thanatos continued to assault the door.

Crossing the room, Zarek grabbed Astrid, who was still sound asleep on the bed, and handed her out the window to Jess. "Get her out of here."

Jess had barely taken Astrid from him before the door blew apart.

Zarek turned around slowly. "Didn't your mother ever teach you it's not nice to intrude?"

Thanatos narrowed a cold, harsh glare at him. "My mother disintegrated when I was only a year old. She didn't have time to teach me anything. But you, on the other hand, taught me well how to hunt and kill my enemies."

Zarek was so shocked by the words that it left him open to the first attack.

Thanatos caught him with a blast straight to his chest.

Zarek rolled with it, taking strength from the pain.

He was good at that.

As he braced himself to attack, a gunshot rang out twice. Thanatos staggered forward, then turned around with a snarl.

Zarek's eyes widened as he caught sight of two bullet holes in the back of the Daimon's skull. Bullet holes that healed instantly.

Jess cursed from the hallway. "What are you?"

"Jess," Zarek snapped. "Get out. I can handle this."

As Thanatos went for Jess, Zarek ran at his back and knocked him into the doorframe.

"Go!" he shouted at Jess. "I can't fight him with you here. I need all my powers."

Jess nodded and ran for the front door. Zarek heard him pause long enough to get the wolf out.

"Alone at last." He laughed as Thanatos shoved him back against the far wall. "Oh, the pleasure of the pain."

Thanatos raked him with a disgusted sneer. "You really do suffer from insanity, don't you?"

"Hardly. I have to say I enjoy every minute of it." Zarek let his powers surge through him until his hands burned from the heat of them. He channeled the ions in the air and charged them full, then directed them at Thanatos.

The blast knocked him halfway down the hall.

Gathering more power, Zarek knocked him back again, into the den. He kept hitting Thanatos until the man landed on the floor by the hearth.

If Zarek were smart, he'd take advantage and run.

But he wasn't that smart. Besides, Thanatos would just come after him and he was too old and too damned pissed to run.

Thanatos regained his feet.

Zarek blasted him again, knocking him over the sofa where he landed in a heap.

He shook his head at the Daimon, who was no longer moving. "Tell you what, why don't you look me up when you're ready to play with the big boys?"

Zarek walked out of the house and summoned his powers to lock the door behind him. He could hear Thanatos pounding on the door, trying to break out.

Without a backward glance, Zarek walked to the snowmachine that must belong to Thanatos. He opened the gas tank and made sure there was plenty of gas in it.

He snapped a hose from the engine, then used it to siphon the gas into his mouth.

Walking back to the cabin, he pulled his lighter out of his back pocket.

He lit the lighter, then spewed gas at the house and watched as the door caught fire.

After several more trips, he stood back and surveyed the flames that were quickly consuming Astrid's house.

It was a good thing she was rich.

Looked like she was going to need a new place to live after this.

Zarek pulled a cigarette out of his coat pocket and smiled. Underneath his breath, he sang the Talking Heads' classic song, " 'Three hundred sixty-five degrees . . . burning down the house.' "

Astrid came awake to a roar. Her lack of eyesight momentarily stunned her until she realized she'd been pulled from her drugged sleep.

But how?

Both she and Zarek should sleep for at least another day.

She could tell by the sounds and upright position of her body that she was no longer in her bed.

It felt like someone's car.

"Zarek?" she asked hesitantly.

"No, ma'am," a deep voice drawled in a thick Southern accent. "Name's Sundown."

Her heart pounded. "Where's Zarek? Sasha!"

A hand touched her arm comfortingly. "Easy now, darling. Everything's going to be all right."

"Where's my wolf?"

By the way the air in front of her face stirred, she could tell Sundown was waving his hand about an inch from the tip of her nose.

"Yes, I'm blind," she said irritably. "Tell me where Sasha is."

"He's the furry thing at your feet."

She let out a small breath of relief, but that was only half her concern. "And Zarek?"

"We left him behind."

"No," she said, her heart hammering once more. "I'm not supposed to leave him."

"We didn't have any—"

Astrid didn't hear the rest of his statement. She was too busy trying to open the car door.

A strong hand pulled her back. "Whoa, little lady, what I'm doing here is dangerous. I've got to get you as far away from the cabin as I can. Trust me, if anyone can handle this, Zarek can."

"No he can't," she said, trying to stand up. "I have to go back to him. If anyone finds out that I'm not with him, he's dead. Do you understand?"

"Lady—"

She brushed away his hand. "Thanatos will be sent for him. I have to go back."

"*You* know about Thanatos?"

Astrid reached out, trying to find Sundown's mouth to feel for fangs.

He dodged her hand.

"Do you work for Acheron?" she asked.

"Do you?"

"Answer me. Are you one of his . . . men?"

He hesitated before he answered. "Yes."

She breathed a sigh of relief. Thank Zeus for small favors. "I'm Zarek's judge. If I leave him unchaperoned, Artemis will call out Thanatos to kill him."

"I hate to break it to you. She already did. I just left the two of them at your place to have it out."

Astrid's head spun. How could this be?

"You're sure it was Thanatos?"

"That's what he said and after the way he tore through us Hunters, I tend to believe him."

Astrid felt ill at the news. This couldn't be happening.

Why would Artemis breach their agreement?

She knew Artemis had been anxious for a verdict, but still . . .

"You've got to get me back. Zarek can't kill him. None of you can."

"What do you mean?"

"Only Acheron has the power to kill Thanatos. *Only* Acheron. None of you stand a chance against him."

Sundown cursed. "All right. Hold tight and I pray God you're wrong, lady."

Astrid felt Sasha stirring as Jess turned the car around in a move that reminded her of a carnival ride.

"Shhh, Sasha," she said, reaching down to touch and soothe him.

"Where are we? What happened?"

She felt him shifting slightly to look up at Sundown. He let out a low growl.

"And who the hell is this refugee from A Fistful of Dollars*?"*

"He's a friend. So be nice."

"Nice? Fine. I won't bite him. Just yet." Sasha settled back a bit. *"Why am I in a truck? How did I get here? And why does my head feel like it's about to explode?"*

"I drugged you."

She had a distinct feeling Sasha had his eyes narrowed at her and his teeth bared. *"You what?"*

She flinched at the anger in his voice. *"I had no choice. But yell at me later. We have a problem right now."*

"And that is?"

"Thanatos is loose. And he's already after Zarek."

"Good, the Dayslayer has taste."

"Sasha!"

"I can't help it. You know I don't like the psycho-beast."

Sighing, she buried her hand in Sasha's fur and used his eyes as her own. He climbed into her lap so that he could look out the window for her.

After a few miles, she recognized the scenery as they neared her cabin.

But what scared her was the sight of a huge fire off in the distance.

Sundown cursed and accelerated.

As they came closer, she saw her cabin burning. There was a lone shadow in front of it, but she couldn't tell if it was Zarek or Thanatos.

Terrified, she held her breath, hoping it was Zarek who was still alive.

It wasn't until Sundown pulled to a stop that she could tell for sure.

She went weak with relief. It was Zarek silhouetted by the fire. Letting go of Sasha, she opened the door and ran toward where she had seen him.

Astrid had no idea how he had survived Thanatos or where the Executioner was. All that mattered was getting to Zarek.

She wanted to touch him, to make sure he wasn't hurt.

Halfway there, a fearful, masculine scream rent the air.

Astrid slid to a stop as she tried to pinpoint where it came from.

She heard the snow crunching to the side of her and she assumed that was Sundown, heading for Zarek. Sasha came up from behind and nosed her hand with his muzzle.

It didn't seem to have come from any of them.

Then all of a sudden, an explosion sounded.

She dropped to her knees and used Sasha to see what was happening.

Her house had blown apart. Fire and debris shot high into the air, blending ominously with the aurora borealis.

Out of the midst of the fiery remains came Thanatos. Unmarred and undamaged.

Not even his hair was singed.

It was a horrifying sight.

Zarek cursed. "Don't you ever die?"

Thanatos didn't answer. Instead, he moved to slug Zarek who ducked the blow and delivered a staggering one back.

Sundown moved toward her. "I've got to get you—"

She took off running before Sundown could finish the sentence.

"Sasha," she called. "Attack."

"Like hell!" Sasha snapped. *"I may be your guardian but that is Artemis's pet. I can't kill it. I'll be lucky to even faze him. And you know what people do to injured wolves . . . They shoot them."*

Astrid panicked. She couldn't see. She could only hear the grunts of the men fighting, the sound of flesh striking flesh.

Someone grabbed her and threw her to the ground, then covered her body with theirs.

She screamed.

"Stop it!" Zarek snapped.

He rolled with her, then pulled her up and pushed her forward.

"What's going on?" she asked as he kept moving her forward.

"Not much," he said in a bored yet breathless tone. "Some invincible asshole is trying to kill me. And you're not supposed to be here." He let go of her. "Get her out of here, Jess."

"I can't."

Zarek curled his lip. Had he been able to afford the drain to his powers, he would have slugged Jess for that.

Instead, all he could do was whirl around to face Thanatos who was stalking him relentlessly.

"What's the matter, Zarek? You afraid to die?"

He snorted as he pushed Astrid toward Jess. "Dying's easy. It's living that's hard."

Thanatos paused as if the words caught him off guard.

It gave Zarek just what he needed. Pulling the Daimon dagger from its concealed sheath inside his boot, he rushed forward and embedded it in Thanatos's chest where a stain that looked like an ink blot should have been. Normally the strike would release the human souls trapped inside a Daimon's body. The force of their exit was usually enough to blow the Daimon apart, causing instant decomposition.

This time, it didn't work.

Thanatos pulled the dagger out and reached for him. "I'm not a Daimon, Dark-Hunter. Don't you remember? I was an Apollite until I met you."

Zarek frowned.

Thanatos grabbed him by his collar and held him tight. "Do you remember my wife you killed? My village you destroyed?"

Memories flashed through his mind. Zarek saw nothing but his own village.

No, wait. He remembered something . . .

A flash of an invincible Daimon, but not the man he faced.

This one had red, glowing eyes.

No, that had been someone else.

His thoughts turned to New Orleans.

To . . .

Why couldn't he remember?

He recalled Sunshine Runningwolf in the warehouse room with him as he told Dionysus and Camulus to shove their orders up their sphincter, and then the next thing he remembered was leaving Acheron on the crowded street.

A flash of lightning went through his head.

He saw something . . .

Was it Acheron?

Was it himself he saw?

Zarek struggled to put the memories straight.

Ah, screw it. The only memory he needed was this one.

He kneed Thanatos in the groin.

The Daimon doubled over.

"Dead or alive, the balls still hurt when kicked, huh?"

The Daimon hissed and cursed in response.

Zarek slammed his combined fists down across Thanatos's back. "If anyone has any suggestion on how to kill this guy, I'm open to it."

Jess shook his head. "I'm out of dynamite. You got any grenades?"

"Not on me."

Thanatos righted himself. "Say die, Dark-Hunter."

"Fine. Die, why don't you?" Zarek lowered his head and charged him. They locked arms and hit the ground.

Thanatos rose up from him and ripped open his shirt. From the way he moved his hands, Zarek could tell he was looking for the bow-and-arrow mark Jess had mentioned.

"Surprise, dickhead, Mama forgot to tell you a few things about me."

In the distance, Zarek heard the approach of an engine. He heard its drone over the sound of Jess urging Astrid to leave and Astrid's refusal while Sasha barked and pushed at her.

Suddenly, a snowmachine came flying up at the same time Zarek broke from Thanatos.

"Duck!"

Zarek didn't recognize the voice, and ordinarily, he wouldn't have obeyed, but what the hell? He was tired of getting his butt kicked by this Daimon.

He hit the ground and rolled out of the way while the dark green snowmachine flew over him. The man on it was dressed all in black with a black helmet. The newcomer skidded to a stop and pulled out a gun.

A bright flash of light cut through the darkness. The flare hit Thanatos in the center of his chest and knocked the Daimon flying.

Thanatos roared. "How dare you betray me! You're one of us."

The man slung a long leg over the snowmachine and reloaded his flare gun as he headed over to where Zarek was still lying on the ground.

"Yeah," he said bitterly. "You should have thought of that before you took out Bjorn." The newcomer fired his gun and knocked Thanatos back. "He was the only one of them I could ever stand."

The stranger reached down and helped Zarek to his feet. He pulled his helmet off and gave it to Zarek. "Get the woman and get out. Hurry."

The minute Zarek met the stranger's eyes, he knew him.

This was the only Dark-Hunter he'd ever known who was even more hated than he was. "Spawn?"

The blond Apollite Dark-Hunter nodded. "Go," he said, reloading. "I'm the only one who can hold him off, but I can't kill him. For Apollo's sake, someone get a hold of Acheron and tell him the Dayslayer is out."

Zarek ran for Astrid.

"No!" Thanatos roared.

Zarek saw the blast before it left Thanatos's hand. Acting on instinct, he cut back toward Spawn. The blast missed him, but hit Astrid's wolf.

The animal yelped, then changed from wolf to man, back to wolf.

Zarek drew up short as he realized Astrid's pet was a Katagari Were-Hunter.

Now why would a blind woman with a Katagari companion take in a rogue Dark-Hunter?

"Sasha?" Astrid called.

Jess ran to the Katagari to keep him covered while Zarek went to Astrid.

"Your were-buddy got zapped, princess."

Fear lined her brow. "Is he okay?"

He picked her up, and brought her over to Jess, then cursed as he realized Jess couldn't get both her and the wolf to safety. After an energy blast, the Katagaria tended to flash in and out of their forms for a while.

Jess struggled to get the wolf-man to the safety of his Bronco. As soon as he could, Jess left.

Zarek put the helmet on Astrid's head. "Looks like it's just you and me, princess. No doubt you're going to wish I'd left you here with the Daimon."

Astrid hesitated at the anger and hatred she heard in Zarek's tone of voice. "I trust you, Zarek."

"Then you're a fool."

He took her arm and led her away so she couldn't hear Spawn and Thanatos.

Roughly, he helped her onto a snowmachine.

She expected him to lead her away from the sound of fighting. Instead, they headed toward it.

She covered her face instinctively as something crashed close to them.

"Get on," Zarek snapped. "Hurry."

She felt the seat dip, then they were rushing away from all the noise. Astrid's heart pounded as she waited for something else to happen.

After what seemed like hours, but was probably only a few minutes, Zarek stopped the snowmachine.

Again she felt motion on the seat as someone got off. Since Zarek's arms were still around her, she assumed it must be Spawn.

"Thanks," Spawn said. "I never expected Zarek of Moesia to come to my rescue."

"Ditto, Spawn. Since when do Daimons fight their own kind?"

Spawn's voice dripped with venom. "I was never a Daimon, Roman."

"And I was never a fucking Roman."

Spawn gave a short, bitter laugh. "Truce, then?"

She felt Zarek shift behind her.

"Truce." Zarek seemed to turn around and look in the direction they had come from. "You have any idea what that thing after me is?"

"Think Terminator. The only difference is that he has the sanction of Artemis."

"What do you mean?"

"My people have a legend of the Dayslayer. It says that Artemis chose one of our own to be her personal guard. More beloved than any of her people, the Dayslayer has no known vulnerability. Once he's unleashed, his goal is to destroy Dark-Hunters."

"So you're telling me he's the Bogeyman?"

"You doubt me?"

"No. Not after what I've seen."

She heard Spawn let out a long breath. "I heard that Artemis had called out a blood hunt for you. I figured it would be Acheron who killed you."

"Yeah, well, trust me, I'm not executed yet. It'll take more than that thing to expire me." Zarek paused. "Just out of curiosity, what are all of you doing up here anyway? Did Acheron call for a reunion and not invite me?"

"Bjorn came because he was chasing a group of Daimons. I came because I felt the Summoning."

"The Summoning?" Astrid asked. In all honesty, she knew very little about the Apollites and Daimons. That was the domain of Apollo and Artemis.

"It's like a homing beacon," Spawn explained, "and it's irresistible to anyone with Apollite blood. I can feel Thanatos even now calling out to me. I think the only reason I can resist it is because I'm a Dark-Hunter. If I weren't . . . Let's just say you're in for one hell of a scary time."

Zarek snorted. "Doubtful. So how do I kill him?"

"You don't. Artemis made him so that he could track and kill us. He has no known vulnerability. Not even daylight. Worse, he will destroy anyone who tries to shelter you."

Shelter you . . .

Again, Zarek's mind flashed to his village.

To the old woman who'd died in his arms . . .

What was his brain trying to tell him?

"Has Thanatos ever come after me before?" he asked Spawn.

Spawn scoffed. "You're still living so obviously the answer is no."

Still . . .

Zarek got off the snowmachine. "Here, take Astrid and—"

"Did you not hear me, Zarek? I can't take her. Thanatos will kill her for sheltering you. She's dead if you leave her."

"She's dead if she stays with me."

"We all got problems and she happens to be yours. Not mine."

Astrid had the distinct feeling Zarek was flipping Spawn off.

"Not on your best day, Greek," Spawn said, confirming her suspicion.

Zarek sat back down on the snowmachine.

"Hey, Zarek?" Spawn asked. "Do you have a cell phone with you?"

"No, it went down with her house."

She heard Spawn's footsteps crunching in the snow as he returned to them. "Take this and call Acheron when you're safe. Maybe he can help you with the woman."

"Thanks." The word was more inflected with belligerence than gratitude. "But what are you going to do without a phone or the snowmachine?"

"Freeze my ass off." There was a small pause. "Don't worry about me. I assure you, I'll be fine."

Zarek's arms surrounded her again. She heard him turn the snowmachine back on.

"Where are we going?" she asked him.

"Up Shit Creek sans the paddles."

Chapter 11

"Well," Astrid said, her tone every bit as sarcastic as his, "I hope you have a map. I've never been there before."

"Trust me, I know it like the back of my hand. Been living there most of my life."

Unsure if she should laugh or groan, Astrid held fast to the tank before her as Zarek pushed the snowmachine to the limits. It vibrated so badly that she half-expected it to disintegrate underneath them.

"Cap'n," she said in her best Scotty accent. "I don't think she'll hold. The warp engines can't take any more. It's going to blow apart."

If she didn't know better, she'd swear she actually heard a rumble of laughter from Zarek.

"She'll hold," he said, his deep, penetrating voice in her right ear. It gave her chills that had nothing to do with the freezing temperature.

"I think I may be grateful for my blindness, after all," she said. "Something tells me that if I could see the reckless speed you're driving at, I would probably have a stroke."

"No doubt."

She rolled her eyes at his ready agreement. "You have no idea how to comfort anyone, do you?"

"In case you haven't noticed, princess, social skills aren't my forte. Hell, you're lucky I'm housebroke."

Oh, he was an evil one.

But there was something almost charming about his caustic retorts. They were angry and biting, but seldom mean-spirited, and now that she had seen the real Zarek, the one he kept hidden from everyone, she knew those barbs for what they were.

Armor.

They were sent out to keep everyone away from him. If you let no one into your heart, then you never had to be hurt by betrayal.

She didn't know how he stood living like that. In constant pain and loneliness. Letting hatred guide everything he did or said.

Zarek was a harsh man filled with more venom than the nine-headed Hydra. But even the Hydra had eventually met its match.

Tonight, Zarek had met his and it wasn't Thanatos.

Astrid wasn't going to give up on him.

They rode until her ears buzzed and her body was cold all the way to her bones. She wondered if she'd ever again be able to thaw out.

Zarek, who seemed oblivious to the freezing weather, continually zigzagged their course, as if trying to keep Thanatos from following them.

Just when she was sure that the concept that immortals couldn't die of frostbite was a myth, Zarek finally stopped.

He turned off the engine.

The sudden silence was deafening. Oppressive.

She waited for Zarek to get up and help her off the snow-machine, but all he did was tug the helmet off her head. He pitched it away with a curse.

She heard it hit the ground, then silence returned and was broken only by their breathing.

Zarek's rage reached out to her like a tangible menace. It was vibrant and frightening.

Part of him wanted to hurt her, she could sense it, but underneath that she felt his pain.

"Who are you?" Zarek's voice was demanding and every bit as cold as the arctic winter. He kept his arms around her and his voice was right in her ear.

"I told you."

"You lied to me, princess," he growled. "I might not be able to read minds, but I know you're not what you appear. Human women don't have Katagaria companions. I want to know who you really are and why you were dicking around in my dreams."

She was shaking from nervousness. What would he do with her now?

Would he leave her for Thanatos?

She was scared to tell him the truth, and yet lies weren't something she practiced unless she had to.

He had a right to be angry at her. Not that she had lied to him; she'd only neglected to tell him a few things. Things such as her real purpose, why she had helped him, and the fact that the wolf he hated could become a man . . .

Well, she had lied about Sasha being dead, but Sasha had deserved it.

And she had drugged him.

Yeah, okay, so she wasn't up for Miss Congeniality this year, but then, neither was Zarek.

Especially not in his current mood.

Zarek's warm breath fell against her exposed cheek. "What are you?" he repeated.

Astrid decided the time for deceit was over. He deserved to know the truth, and since Artemis had already broken the agreement and sent in Thanatos, what was the point of shielding the goddess any further?

"I'm a nymph."

"I hope you just left an important syllable off that word, princess."

"Excuse me?" It took a second for her to understand what he meant. When she did her face flamed. "I am not a nympho! I'm a nymph. *Nymph*. No *o*!"

He didn't move or speak for several minutes.

Zarek let out his breath slowly as he considered the woman in front of him and tried for once to rein in his fury.

A friggin' nymph. He should have known it was something like that.

Oh, yeah, right. Like the idea of a Greek nymph in Alaska was something that should have occurred to him. Her kind usually hung around beaches, oceans, and forests or stayed on Olympus.

They didn't pop in during a blizzard and drag a wounded Dark-Hunter into their homes.

His stomach shrank as the reason for her presence slammed into him.

Someone had sent her here.

For him.

He gripped the handlebars fiercely, unwilling to let go for fear of what he might do to her. "What kind of nymph are you, princess?"

"Justice," she said quietly. "I serve Themis and I was sent here to judge you."

"Judge *me*?" He let out an extremely disgusted sound. "Oh, you're un-friggin-believable."

Zarek had never wanted to hurt anyone so much in his life. Getting up from the snowmachine before he yielded to his temper, he put space between them.

Was this his luck or what?

He'd finally found someone whom he thought didn't judge him and she really *was* a judge whose sole purpose was to pass judgment on him and the way he lived.

Oh, yeah, he really knew how to pick them.

The gods were still laughing at him. Mocking him.

All of them.

Enraged, he paced around the snowmachine so that he could watch her sitting on the seat, looking all prim and proper with her hands folded in her lap and her head down.

All ladylike.

How dare she screw with him like this! Who did she think she was?

He was tired of people messing with him. Tired of games and of lies.

A judge. Acheron had sent in a judge before they killed him. Ooo, Zarek was just tickled pink by the consideration.

Maybe he should be flattered that they even gave him a pretense of impartiality. It was a hell of a lot more than he'd gotten as an accused slave.

"This was all just a game to you, wasn't it, princess? 'Come, Zarek, sit on my lap. Tell me why you won't behave.'" His vision turned dark. Deadly. "Fuck you, lady, and fuck them."

Her head snapped up. "Zarek, please!"

"So what, you decided Acheron was right? I'm psychotic, so send in your dogs to kill me?"

She got up and turned to where she heard his voice coming from. "No. Thanatos wasn't supposed to be sent in after you. As for Acheron, he would never convict you. If not for him, you'd be dead now. He bartered who knows what with Artemis so that I could come to you and find a way to save your life."

He snorted. "Yeah, right."

"It's the truth, Zarek," she said, her voice sincere. "Deny it all you want to, but it doesn't change the fact that we are on your side."

He raked her with a repugnant glare he only wished she could see to appreciate. "I ought to leave you here to freeze to death. Oh, wait, you're an immortal nymph. You can't die."

She lifted her chin and stood as if braced to take on his worst. "You can leave me if you want to. But the man I have come to know isn't so callous or cruel. He would never leave someone to die."

He ground his teeth. "You know nothing about me."

Astrid left the snowmachine. Walking slowly, she reached out with her hand, wanting physical contact with him. She needed it, and something told her he did, too. "I've been inside you, Zarek. I know what no one else does."

"So what? Is that supposed to make me all warm and cuddly for you? Look, the little princess stole into my dreams to save me. Ooo, I'm so touched. Should I cry now?"

She grabbed his arm.

His muscles, like him, were tense and hard. Fierce. "Stop it!"

She reached up to touch his ice-cold cheeks with both of her hands. They were chafed from the ride, and yet they still managed to warm her icy fingers.

Half-expecting him to pull away, she was amazed when he didn't. He stood there like a statue. Unmoving. Cold. Inflexible.

Astrid swallowed, wishing for a way to make him understand. Wishing for a way she could reach him so that he would stop being so self-destructive.

Why wouldn't he see the truth?

Zarek couldn't breathe as she cupped his face in her warm hands. She was so beautiful, with tiny sparkling snowflakes on her eyelashes and blonde hair. He saw the pain on her face, the softness.

She seemed to want to help him and yet he couldn't make himself believe that.

People were always self-serving. All of them.

She was no exception.

And yet, he wanted to believe in her.

He did want to cry.

What had she done to him?

For a brief time in his dreams he had begun to think that maybe he wasn't so bad. That he deserved some kind of happiness.

Gods, he was such a fool.

How could he have been so stupid and trusting? He knew better.

Trust was only a weapon that was used to kill people.

It had no place in his world.

Astrid stroked his cheeks with her thumbs. "I don't want you to die, Zarek."

"Here's the kicker, princess. I do."

Tears filled her eyes and melted the snowflakes on her lashes. "I don't believe you. Thanatos would have gladly given you that wish and yet you fought him. Why?"

"Habit."

She closed her eyes as if frustrated with him. Her grip tightened on his face, then to his complete shock, she burst out laughing. "You really can't help it, can you?"

He was completely baffled by her reaction. "Help what?"

"Being an asshole," she said, her voice broken by laughter.

As she continued to laugh, he stared at her in disbelief. No one had dared laugh at him before. At least not since the day he'd died.

Then she did the most unexpected thing of all. She walked into his arms and hugged him. Her laughter brought her body into contact with his, setting fire to him.

It reminded him so much of his dream . . .

She wrapped her arms around his neck and held him close.

No one had ever held him like this. He didn't know if he should embrace her or shove her away.

In the end, he found himself placing his arms awkwardly around her. She felt just as she had in his dream. Every bit as wonderful.

He hated that most of all.

She gave him a tight squeeze. "I'm so glad Acheron sent me to you."

"Why?"

"Because I like you, Zarek, and I think anyone other than me would have killed you by now."

Even more suspicious of her than before, he released her and stepped back. "Why do you care what happens to me? You've been inside me; tell me honestly I didn't scare you."

She sighed. "Honestly, yes. You do scare me, but by the same token, I've seen goodness in you, too."

"And the village I showed you in my dreams? The one I destroyed."

She furrowed her brow. "It was broken and fragmented. It didn't feel like a memory to me, it felt like something else."

"What?"

"I don't know. I think there's more to what happened than you recall."

He shook his head. How could she have faith in him when he didn't have any in himself? "You really are blind, aren't you?"

"No. I see you, Zarek. In a way I think no one ever has before."

"I assure you, princess, if you saw the real me, you'd run for cover," he scoffed.

"Only if I knew you'd be waiting under that cover for me."

He was floored by what she said.

She didn't mean it.

It was another game. Another test.

No one had ever wanted him. Not his mother, not his father. Not his owners. He didn't even want to be with himself.

So how could she?

Zarek paused as he felt a psychic tremor run through him. "Thanatos is coming."

Her eyes widened in fear. "Are you sure?"

"Yes."

He pulled her toward the snowmachine. It would be dawn before long.

He would be trapped, but Thanatos . . .

The Daimon would be able to walk in daylight.

Zarek wrapped his arms around Astrid. He should leave her here for what she'd done to him, hand her over to Thanatos to see if she would buy him more time to escape. Yet he had this crazy idea of protecting her.

No, it wasn't an idea. It was a yearning he had to keep her safe.

Resigned to his stupidity, he started the snowmachine and headed it toward his property.

Astrid took a deep breath as they resumed their trip. She had violated more rules than she cared to think about.

And yet as she felt Zarek surrounding her, she knew it was worth it. She had to save him.

No matter what it took.

She'd never felt so determined. Or more sure of herself. He gave her a confidence and strength she had never known.

He needed her. In spite of what he said or even thought. He needed her in a way that was painful.

The man had no one else in the world. And for some reason she couldn't understand, she wanted to be the one person he relied on. The one person who could tame him.

He drove them for almost an hour before they stopped again.

"Where are we?" she asked as he climbed off the snowmachine.

"My cabin."

"Is it safe?"

"Not a bit. And it looks like all hell broke loose here."

Zarek stood in stunned disbelief as he looked around. There was still blood on the snow, but from whom, he couldn't tell.

The sight tore through him as reality came crashing home. A Dark-Hunter had died here.

His kind didn't die often and he felt a peculiar ache for the man who had died tonight. It wasn't right.

It wasn't fair.

If anyone should have paid that price, it should have been him. He should have been here to confront Thanatos.

The thought of an innocent man being turned into a Shade made him want Artemis's blood.

And where the hell was Acheron? For someone who was supposedly willing to put his ass on the line for the Dark-Hunters, the Atlantean was amazingly absent.

Curling his lip, he went back to the snowmachine.

"C'mon," he said. "We have a lot to do."

He walked off and left her to find her own way.

"I need your help, Zarek. I need you to tell me where things are so I don't walk into anything."

It was on the tip of his tongue to remind her of the fact that she'd claimed she could watch after herself. Then his memories surged and he remembered what it was like to only see shadows.

To walk into things because he couldn't see them.

He didn't want to touch her anymore.

He hated the very thought of it because every time he felt her, he craved more of her.

Against his will, he found himself taking her hand into his. "C'mon, princess."

Astrid bit back her smile. His tone was harsh and yet she felt a small victory inside her heart. Not to mention the fact that he had stopped using "princess" as an insult. She didn't think he even realized that now when he called her that, his voice softened ever so slightly.

Sometime during their dreams, the insult he'd used to keep her at a distance had become an endearment.

Zarek led her into his cabin.

"Stand here," he said, placing her to the left just inside the doorway.

She heard him rustling around to her right. While he was busy, she brushed her hand against the wall to feel her way over to him. What she found there surprised her.

Frowning, she ran her hand over the deep dips and planes of the wall. It was an incredible tactile sensation. Intricate. Complex. But what she touched was so large that she couldn't quite understand what it represented.

As she followed the design with her hand she realized it covered the entire wall.

"What is this?" she asked.

"A beach scene," he said distractedly.

She arched a brow. "A beach scene is carved into your wall?"

"I get bored, okay?" he snapped. "So I carve things. Sometimes in the summer, I run out of wood and I carve the walls and shelves."

Just like the wolf he'd sculpted in her house.

Astrid stumbled over something as she reached for the next wall. Several things fell, scattering over her feet.

Zarek cursed. "I thought I told you to stay put."

"I'm sorry." She bent down to pick the things up to find that they were carved wooden animals.

There seemed to be dozens of them.

She was stunned by the intricacy of each piece as she ran her fingers over them, picking them up from the floor. "Did you do all these?"

He didn't answer as he snatched them up and piled them back.

"Zarek," she said, her tone stern, "talk to me."

"And say what? Yes, I carved the damned things. I usually do three or four of them a night. So what?"

"Then there should be more of them. Where are the others?"

"I don't know," he said, his voice a little less hostile. "I take some into town and give them away and the rest I burn whenever the generators go out."

"Don't they mean anything to you?"

"No. Nothing means shit to me."

"Nothing?"

Zarek paused as he looked at her kneeling beside him. Her cheeks were chafed, the skin no longer soft and protected as it had been when he first awoke in her cabin. She stared over his shoulder, but he knew it was because she wasn't quite sure where he was.

Her lips were slightly parted, her hair mussed.

In his mind he could see her in his arms, feel her skin sliding against his. And in that moment, he made a startling discovery.

He did care about something.

Her.

Even though she had lied to him and tricked him, he didn't want her hurt. He didn't want to see her delicate skin damaged by the extreme weather.

She should be sheltered from such harshness.

How he hated himself for that weakness.

"No, princess," he whispered, the lie catching in his throat. "I don't care about anything."

She reached out then so that she could touch his face. "Is that lie for your benefit or mine?"

"Who says it's a lie?"

"I do, Zarek. For a man who doesn't care, you've made a great effort to make sure I'm safe." She smiled at him. "I do know you, Prince Charming. I really do see what's inside you."

"You're blind."

She shook her head. "I'm not nearly as blind as you are."

Then she did the most unexpected thing of all. She leaned forward and captured his lips with hers.

Something inside him shattered at the contact, at the sensation of her moist, sweet lips. Of her tongue sweeping against his.

This wasn't a dream.

This was real.

And it was wonderful. As good as she had tasted before, it was so much better now.

He crushed her to him, taking control of the kiss. He wanted to devour her. To take her right now on the floor until his hard-on was spent and sated.

But if his dreams were any indication, it would take more than a single act of sex to ease the fire in his groin.

He could love this woman all night long and still be begging for more when the morning came.

Astrid couldn't breathe from the fierceness of his kiss. The heat of his body set fire to her own.

He was truly wild, her warrior.

He slid his cool hand under her shirt until he could cup her breast. She shivered as his fingers pushed the lace of her bra aside so that he could run his palm against her swollen nipple.

She'd never allowed anyone to handle her like this. But then, she'd done a lot of things with him that she had never done before.

All her life, she'd been circumspect and proper. The kind of woman who lived by the rules and who never sought to break or even bend them.

Zarek freed something within her. Something wild and wonderful.

Something unexpected.

He pulled back from her lips as his hand moved lower, over her belly, down toward her waistband.

She trembled as he unbuttoned her pants, then slid her zipper down. In their dream, there was still some protection of it not being real. Of everything being a dream.

Tonight that barrier was gone. Once he touched her in this realm, there was no going back.

What the heck? There was no going back for her anyway. She would never be the same.

"Would you let me screw you on my floor, princess?" he asked, his voice ragged and deep with hunger.

"No, Zarek," she breathed. "But you can make love to me anywhere you want to."

She took his hand in hers and slid it down her pants, into her cotton panties.

Zarek's breathing was ragged as she opened her legs in invitation. He stared at her lying on his floor. Her crumpled shirt was pulled up, showing off her rounded stomach while his hand was stark against the light pink cotton of her underwear. Tiny tufts of her hair peeked out from under the waistband as he massaged her mound gently.

She unzipped his pants, spilling his erection out. He couldn't move as she took him into her warm hands.

His body on fire, he slid his hand down through the moist curls at the juncture of her thighs so that he could touch her intimately while she stroked him.

She was so wet already, her nether lips swollen, begging for more. Her hands massaged him, causing him to harden to the point of pain.

He slid his fingers over her cleft, delighting in the sound of her murmured pleasure.

He dipped his head to her breast, to toy with her nipple. He sucked and teased, taking his time tasting her.

Wanting more of her, he went to slide his fingers into her, only to touch something that stunned him. Something that hadn't been there in the dream.

He went cold.

Pulling back, he frowned as he felt her hymen under his probing fingers. "You're a virgin?"

"Yes."

He cursed and moved away from her.

"You're a virgin," he repeated. "How the hell can you be a virgin?"

"Easy. I've never slept with a man before."

"But my dreams . . ."

"Those were dreams, Zarek. That wasn't really my body."

His vision turned dark. Unwarranted jealousy gnawed at him. His little nymph had found one hell of a loophole. "So how many men have you fucked in their sleep?"

"You bastard!" she snapped, rising up into a sitting position on the floor. "If I could find your face, I would slap you for that!"

Angry, she straightened her clothes and moved away from him. Her cheeks were flushed, her hands trembling, as she continued to curse both of them under her breath.

It was then he knew.

She wouldn't be this angry at them if she were guilty of what he'd said.

She'd never been with another man.

Only him.

That knowledge floored him.

He couldn't begin to understand why she would offer him something she hadn't offered to anyone else.

It didn't make sense in his world.

"Why do you want to be with me?"

She paused as she dressed and glared in his direction. "I have no idea. You are surly. Rude. Obnoxious. I have never in my life seen anyone more ill-mannered and . . . and . . . aggravating. You have no respect for anyone, not even yourself. All you can do is pick, pick, pick. You don't even know how to be happy."

Astrid opened her mouth to continue, then stopped as she became aware of the tone of Zarek's voice when he had posed his question to her.

It had been gently searching. Not accusatory.

Most of all, it had come from deep inside him.

And so she answered it from her heart. "You want to know the truth, Zarek? I want to be with you because there's something about you that makes me hot and shivery. Whenever I feel you near me, I want to reach out and touch you. To slide you into me so that I can hold you close and tell you that everything is all right. That I'm not going to let anyone else hurt you."

"I'm not a child," he said angrily.

Astrid reached out through the darkness and found his hand on the floor in front of her. She took it into hers and held it tight. "No, you're not a child. You never were. Children are supposed to be protected and cared for. You had no one to hold you when you cried. No one ever soothed you. They never told you stories or made you laugh when you were sad."

The tragedy of his life reached out to her then, penetrating her heart, making her want to weep for all the injustice that had been dealt him.

Things she had taken for granted as a child had been denied him. Friendship, happiness, family, treats. And most of all, love.

His life had been so unfair.

She trailed her hand up his muscular arm, to bury it in his hair so that she could stroke his scalp. "Make love to me, Zarek. I can't take away your past, but I can hold you now. I want to share my body with you, even if it's only for a little while."

He pulled her forcefully against him and kissed her heatedly. She moaned, arching her back as he laid her back down on the floor.

Astrid kicked her shoes off, then removed her pants and panties. She pulled her shirt off and unsnapped her bra.

She should be embarrassed—she'd never stripped in front of anyone before. Never been naked while they were clothed.

Yet she was not ashamed.

She felt powerful with him. Womanly. She knew he wanted her and she desired only to please him.

She lay back against his icy floor.

Mesmerized, Zarek couldn't move as Astrid bent her knees up and opened her legs in invitation.

Her nipples were puckered from the cold and her desire. Her hair was loose, spilling over her shoulders, and her hands rested on her stomach.

But it was her core that he stared at. She was already wet for him, her body swollen with need just as his was.

"I'm cold, Zarek," she whispered. "Will you warm me?"

He should get up and leave her there like that.

He couldn't.

No one had ever offered him such a precious gift.

No one but Astrid.

He grabbed the blankets from his pallet and covered her with them. He stripped his own clothes off, then joined her. Spreading her thighs wider, he took a moment to stare at the most private part of her body.

She was beautiful.

He ran his fingers down her rigid cleft, making her shiver even more under the warmth of his furs. Using his thumbs, he spread her open, then dipped down to take her into his mouth.

Astrid gasped at the sensation of Zarek's tongue sweeping against her. He licked and teased her, his breath warming her bottom.

His hot hands cupped her hips, pulling her closer to his mouth and to the prickly skin of his face.

He moaned as if the taste of her were heavenly. Licking her lips, she reached down to cup his face while he pleasured her.

Her heart pounded at the feeling of his jaw flexing under her hands.

In her dreams his touch had been incredible, but in reality it was far more intense.

Far more satisfying.

Her head swirled as her heart raced. Unbridled ecstasy danced through her and left her calling his name as she pressed herself closer to his lips.

And when she came, she screamed out, holding his head to her while her body disintegrated into a thousand sparks of pleasure.

Still he licked and teased her until she was whimpering from the bliss.

Zarek pulled back to see her panting on his floor. The top part of her was covered by his furs and blankets, but her lower half was bare, glistening in the low light of the lantern from the combination of her juices and him.

Her face was flushed, her eyes bright.

He'd never had a woman in his place before. Most especially not a naked one.

He pulled his covers away from her. She gasped as they scraped against her swollen, sensitive breasts. Zarek moved away from her only long enough to remove his clothes.

She reached out for him as he laid his body down over hers and let her heat warm him.

Zarek growled as her hard nipples rubbed against his chest. The tip of his shaft pressed against the damp hairs between her legs.

Astrid covered them with the blankets again and cradled him with her body.

Gods, how good she felt under him like this. Face to face. Her legs wrapped around his waist. Her hands stroking his naked back.

He lowered his head and kissed her, probing her mouth with his tongue.

But it wasn't her mouth he wanted to penetrate . . .

He trailed his hand down her arm until he could lace his fingers with hers. Holding her hand above their heads, he deepened his kiss.

Astrid swallowed as she felt Zarek shift his weight, bringing his entire lush, rippling male body flush with hers.

He pressed the tip of his shaft against her core. She arched her back, waiting for him to fill her.

He deepened his kiss and, with one thrust, slid himself deep inside.

Astrid cringed and whimpered at the sudden pain that overrode her pleasure.

Zarek pulled out immediately. "Oh, God, Astrid, did I hurt you? I'm sorry. I didn't know it was going to hurt."

His contrition was so immediate and heartfelt that it stunned her more than the pain had.

Apologies and Zarek were two things that went together like porcupines and balloons.

Obviously, he didn't know what she did.

"It's okay," she said, kissing him until he relaxed. "It's supposed to hurt the first time."

"It didn't hurt the first time I did it. Believe me."

She laughed at that. "It's a woman thing, Prince Charming. It's okay, really."

She reached down his body and found him still hard and throbbing. He groaned deep in his throat as she stroked him.

Biting her lip, she guided him back toward her.

He tensed, refusing to let her carry him home. "I don't want to hurt you."

Joy filled her. "You won't, Zarek. I want you inside me."

He hesitated a few minutes more before he slowly slid himself into her again.

They both moaned.

Astrid arched her back at the incredible feel of him deep and hard inside her. He was so full. So commanding.

She ran her hands up and over his muscular back and shoulders.

The only thing more perfect would be to be able to look into his eyes as he loved her. That was the only part she missed from having him in her dreams. Even though the sensation of him was so much richer now, she wished she could watch him again.

Moaning her name, he buried his lips against her throat, scraping her skin with his fangs as he rode her slowly, forcefully.

Zarek's heart raced as he savored the warm, wet feel of her. He allowed the softness of her body to soothe him.

There was heaven in her touch. Heaven in the sound of his name on her lips.

Not once had he dreamed that taking a woman like this could feel the way she did.

She cupped his face in her hands.

"What are you doing?" he whispered.

"I want to see you."

He placed his hand over hers and then turned his face so that he could kiss her open palm.

Astrid melted at the tenderness of his actions as he moved slow and hard against her. His whiskers pricked at her hands, but his lips were soft, gentle.

He was like a tamed panther. One that was still wild at heart but that might come up and nuzzle your hand so long as you took care of him and didn't move too fast.

He leaned forward over her and buried his lips against her neck. She shivered as she ran her hands over his strong back, down to his hips.

How she loved the feel of him there. The feel of his hips thrusting against hers.

She brought her hands around to the front of him and slid them between their bodies. His hairs gently scraped her skin as she encircled his wet shaft with her hands so that she could feel him sliding in and out of her.

Zarek held his breath as she touched him while he rode her. Oh, the sweetness of her hands on him . . .

He kissed her as she explored where they were joined, and when she gently squeezed his sac he growled as he came dangerously close to orgasm.

"Easy, princess," he breathed, pulling her hands away from him. "I don't want to come yet. I want to feel you for a little while longer."

Astrid smiled at his hoarse words. He held her arms above her head and dipped his head down to gently nip her breast.

How she loved this man.

Faults and irritability and all.

"I'm all yours, baby," she whispered. "Take your time."

And he did. He kissed every inch of her he could reach while still inside her.

The effect of every tender caress was heightened because she knew the rarity of the gesture. This wasn't a man who cuddled up to just anyone. He didn't go willingly to any woman who smiled at him.

He was her fox who only left his den when he heard *her* footsteps.

She alone had tamed him.

He would never belong to anyone the way he did to her.

Astrid came again calling out his name.

Zarek quickened his strokes and joined her in bliss, his head spinning.

He lay on top of her panting and weak, listening to her heart pound against his chest.

There was no place he'd rather be than with her, letting the smell of her sweet, sweaty skin lull and soothe him.

He'd never been so warm. So sated.

So happy.

All he wanted was to lie here naked with her and forget all about the rest of the world.

Unfortunately, it was the one thing he couldn't do.

Kissing her gently, he pulled back. "We should get dressed. I don't know if Thanatos will come here, but my money says he will."

She nodded.

Zarek hesitated as he saw the blood on her thighs from where he had breached her hymen.

Clenching his teeth, he turned away, ashamed of the fact that he had taken her on the floor like an animal after all. She didn't deserve this.

She didn't deserve him.

What had he done?

He had ruined her.

She sat up and touched his shoulder. The sensation of it tore through him. It was familiar.

It was sublime.

Why then did it make his stomach ache?

"Zarek? Is something wrong?"

"No," he lied, unable to tell her what he thought. She should never have lain with something like him. He was so far beneath her that he didn't deserve her kindness.

He deserved nothing.

And yet she reached out and touched him. It didn't make sense to him.

She leaned her cheek against his back and encircled his waist with her arm. He could barely breathe as she ran her hand over his chest in a comforting gesture.

"I have no regrets, Zarek. I hope you feel the same way."

He leaned back against her and tried not to let his aching heart overshadow what they had shared.

"How could I regret the best night of my life?" He laughed

bitterly as he remembered everything that had happened since
Jess had shaken him awake. "Well, except for the Terminator
who's after us and the goddess who wants me dead and—"

"I get the picture," she said with a laugh. She nuzzled
his neck, sending chills over him. "It does seem hopeless,
doesn't it?"

He thought about that. " 'Hopeless' implies that at one
time there was hope. And that's another word I don't understand. Hope only exists for people who have choices."

"And you don't?"

He toyed with a strand of her blond hair. "I'm a slave,
Astrid. I've never known hope. I just do what I'm told."

"Yet you never have."

That wasn't exactly true. As a human, he had never dared
open his mouth to protest anything. He had taken beating after
beating, degradation after degradation, and done nothing.

It was only as a Dark-Hunter that he had learned to fight.

"Do you think Sasha's okay?"

Her sudden change of topic surprised him. "I do. Jess is a
whiz with animals. Even Katagaria."

She chuckled at that. "Why, Zarek, I do believe you are
learning to comfort someone after all. I half-expected you to
say you were hoping he'd be lying dead in a ditch somewhere."

He looked down at her small hand on his skin, resting just
above his heart. It was true. She was taming him.

Changing him.

And it scared him more than the monster that was out to
kill them.

Thanatos he could deal with, but these emotions . . .

He was helpless before her.

"Yeah, well, with any luck he'll be beyond all help."

She laughed at that, then kissed him lightly on the back.
She pulled away to dress.

Zarek watched her, his heart pounding. What was it about

her that made him want to be something more than what he was?

For her, he actually wanted to be decent. Kind.

Humane.

Things he'd never been.

Forcing himself up, he tossed his old clothes into the trash can and pulled new ones out of his wardrobe. At least he no longer had the hole in the back of his coat. He took a couple of minutes to button her into one of his old parkas.

"What's this?" she asked as he draped it over her shoulders.

"It'll keep you warmer than your coat."

She put her arms through the much-too-long sleeves while he gathered up gloves, hats, and scarves for them.

"Where are we going? Won't it be dawn soon?"

"Yes and you'll see. Sort of."

Once he had her dressed properly and had pulled on his insulated boots, he moved the wood-burning stove aside so that he could reach the trapdoor underneath it.

He helped Astrid down the hole, then climbed down after her and closed the trapdoor. Using his telekinesis, he moved the stove back into place.

"Where are we?"

"The tunnels."

Zarek turned his flashlight on. It was darker than a tomb down here and colder than hell. But they would be safe. For a little while, at least.

If Thanatos came back during daylight, he wouldn't know about this place. No one did.

"What are the tunnels?"

"In short, my boredom. After I had carved up my cabin, I started digging under it. I figured it would give me more room to move about during the summer, and it's not quite so hot down here in summer or so cold in winter. Not to mention I was always paranoid Acheron would come to kill me one day. I wanted an escape route he didn't know about."

"But the ground is frozen solid. How did you manage?"

"I'm stronger than a human and I had nine hundred years to work on it. Being trapped and bored tends to make people do insane things."

"Like try to dig a tunnel to China?"

"Exactly."

He led her down the narrow corridor to a small room where he had weapons stored.

"Are we staying here for the day?"

"Since I don't want to spontaneously burst into flames from the sun, I think it's the safest thing to do, don't you?"

She nodded.

Once he had as much firepower as he could carry, he took her to the end of the longest tunnel. The trapdoor above them opened into the dense forest that surrounded his cabin. It would be a safe place to leave from after dark.

"Why don't you go ahead and get some sleep?" he said.

Without thinking, he pulled his musk-ox parka off and made her a small pallet on the floor.

Astrid started to protest, then stopped herself. Acts of kindness were alien to Zarek. She wasn't about to complain over his good deed.

Instead, she lay down on his coat.

But he made no move to join her. He walked around the limited space and seemed to be waiting for her to go to sleep.

Curious as to what he had planned, she closed her eyes and feigned slumber.

Zarek waited several minutes before he picked up the cell phone Spawn had given him. He climbed up the stairs and opened the trapdoor to the forest so that he could get some reception for the phone.

He made sure not to let the predawn light in.

Zarek didn't know if this would work or not, but he had to try.

He dialed Ash's number and pressed SEND.

"Come on, Acheron," he said under his breath. "Answer the damn phone."

Astrid lay quietly, knowing the cell phone would never ring where Ash was. Artemis wouldn't allow it.

But then, Artemis didn't control everything.

Using her limited powers, Astrid "helped" the signal.

Ash jerked awake the instant his phone rang. Out of habit, he rolled over in bed to reach for his backpack, only to remember where he was and that he wasn't allowed to answer his phone while in Artemis's temple.

Come to think of it, his phone shouldn't be ringing at all. It wasn't as if there was a cell tower on Olympus to carry the signal.

Which meant it had to be coming from Astrid . . .

But if Artemis caught him talking to the nymph, she'd go ballistic on him and recant their deal. Not that he cared what she did to him, but he wasn't about to unleash Artemis's temper on Astrid.

Grinding his teeth, he pulled his phone out and let his voice mail answer it while he listened to the message.

What he heard made his eyesight dim.

It wasn't Astrid. It was Zarek.

"Dammit, Acheron, where are you?" Zarek growled, then a few seconds of silence followed. "I . . . I need your help."

Ash's stomach tightened as he heard the four words he'd never expected Zarek to utter.

It must be bad for the ex-slave to ever admit he needed anything from anyone. Especially him.

"Look Acheron, I know I'm a dead man and I don't care. I'm not sure how much you know about my situation, but there's someone with me. Her name is Astrid and she says she's a justice nymph. This thing, Thanatos, is after me and he's already killed one Dark-Hunter tonight. I know if he gets his hands on Astrid he'll kill her, too. You have to protect her for me, Acheron . . . please. I need you to come get her and keep her safe while I fight Thanatos. If you won't do it for me, then do it for her. She doesn't deserve to die because she tried to help me."

Ash sat up in bed. He held the phone so tight it bit fiercely into his hand.

He wanted to answer it. But didn't dare. Fury and pain surged through him.

How dare Artemis betray him yet again.

Damn her for it.

He should have known she wouldn't pen Thanatos up as she had promised. What was one more life extinguished to her?

Nothing. Nothing mattered to her except what *she* wanted.

But he cared. He cared in a way Artemis would never comprehend.

"I'm at my cabin with Spawn's phone. Call me. We need to get her out of here as soon as possible."

The phone went dead.

Ash threw back the blankets and willed his clothes onto his body. Furious, he shoved the phone into his backpack and threw open the bedroom doors with a clatter.

Artemis sat on her throne with her twin brother, Apollo, standing in front of her.

They both jumped as he entered.

No wonder Artemis had told him he needed to rest.

She knew better than to let him and Apollo be in the same room together. They got along even "better" than Artemis and Simi did.

Apollo charged him.

Ash threw out his hand and knocked the god back. "Stay away from me, Sunshine-boy. I'm in no mood for you today."

Ash headed for the door only to find Artemis blocking his way again. "What are you doing?"

"I'm leaving."

"You can't."

"Out of my way, Artemis. In the mood I'm in, I just might hurt you if you continue to stand there."

"You swore you would stay here for two weeks. If you leave Olympus, you will die. You cannot break your word, you know that."

Ash closed his eyes and cursed at the one tiny thing he'd forgotten in his anger. Unlike those of the Olympian gods, his oath was binding. Once he uttered an oath, he was bound by it no matter how much he willed it otherwise.

"What is he doing here?" Apollo growled. "You told me he didn't come here anymore."

"Shut up, Apollo," he and Artemis said in unison.

Ash glared at Artemis as she took a step back. "Why did you lie to me about Thanatos? You told me he had been penned again."

"I didn't lie."

"No? Then why was he loose in Alaska last night, killing my Dark-Hunters, after you told me you had him penned again?"

"He killed Zarek?"

He curled his lip. "Wipe that hopeful look off your face. Zarek is alive, but someone else was killed."

Her face fell. "Who?"

"How would I know? I'm stuck up here with you."

She stiffened at the way he said that. "I told the Oracles to pen him after Dion had freed him. I assumed they had done so."

"Then who let him out this time?"

They both turned to look at Apollo.

"I didn't do it," Apollo snapped. "I don't even know where you house that creature."

"You better not have done it," Ash growled.

Apollo gave him a snide smirk. "You don't scare me, human. I killed you once, I can do it again."

Ash smiled slowly, coldly. That was then, this was now, and they played on a whole new field with a brand-new set of rules he would give just about anything to introduce to the god. "Please try."

Artemis stepped between them. "Apollo, leave."

"What about *him*?"

"He's not your concern."

Apollo looked as if they both repulsed him. "I can't believe you allow something like him into your temple."

Her face flushing, Artemis looked away, too embarrassed to say anything to her brother.

It was what Ash expected of her.

Ashamed of him and their relationship, Artemis had always tried to keep Ash away from the other Olympians as much as she could. For centuries now, the other gods knew he came to see her. Gossip abounded over what they did together and how long he stayed with her, but Artemis had never confirmed a relationship between them. Had never deigned to touch him in the presence of any other person.

Odd how even after eleven thousand years it still bothered him that he was her dirty little secret. That after everything they had shared and done, she could hardly stand to look at him whenever others were around.

And yet she bound him to her and refused to let him go.

Their relationship was sick and well he knew it.

Unfortunately, he had no choice in the matter.

But if he could ever break free of her, he would run as fast as he could. She knew it as well as he did.

It was why she held on to him so tightly.

Apollo raked him with a grimace. *"Tsoulus."*

Ash stiffened at the ancient Greek insult. It wasn't the

first time he'd been called that. As a human being, he had answered to it defiantly, with a sick kind of glee.

The only thing that really hurt was the knowledge that eleven thousand years later, it was every bit as applicable to him as it had been then.

Only now he didn't revel in the title.

Now it cut him soul deep.

Artemis grabbed her brother by the ear and pulled him toward the door. "Get out," she snarled as she shoved him outside and slammed the door.

She turned back to face Acheron.

Ash hadn't moved. The insult still smoldered deep inside him.

"He's an idiot."

Ash didn't bother to contradict her. He agreed completely.

"Simi, take human form."

Simi floated out of his sleeve to manifest beside him. "Yes, *akri*?"

"Protect Zarek and Astrid."

"No!" Artemis snapped. "You can't let it go, it might tell Zarek everything that happened."

"Then let her. It's time he understood."

"Understood what? Do you want him to know the truth about you?"

Ash felt a wave go through him and he knew his eyes flashed from silver to red. Artemis stepped back, further proving they had.

"It was the truth about *you* that I kept from him," Ash said between clenched teeth.

"Was it, Acheron? Was it truly about me or did you erase his memories of that night because you were afraid of what he'd think about *you*?"

The wave deepened.

Ash held his hand up to silence Artemis before it was

too late and his powers took control of him. It had been too long since he had last fed and he was too volatile to control himself.

If they continued to fight, there was no telling what he might do.

He looked to Simi who waited beside him. "Simi, don't speak to Zarek but make sure Thanatos doesn't kill either one of them."

"Tell it not to kill Thanatos, too."

Ash started to argue, then stopped. They didn't have time, nor did he have a tight enough grip on himself. If Thanatos killed Zarek and Astrid, life would be a lot more complicated for everyone.

"Don't kill Thanatos, Simi. Now, go."

"Okay, *akri,* I'll protect them." Simi vanished.

Artemis narrowed her green eyes at him. "I can't believe you sent it out on its own. It's worse than Zarek and Thanatos combined."

"I have no choice, Artie. Have you given any thought as to what will happen if Astrid dies? How do you think her sisters will react?"

"She can't die unless *they* will it."

"That's not true and you know it. There are some things that not even the Fates have control over. And I assure you that if your mad pet destroys their beloved baby sister, they will demand *your* head for it."

Ash didn't have to say anything more than that. Because if Artemis lost her head, then the world as all knew it would change into something truly frightening.

"I'll go talk to the Oracles."

"Yeah, you do that, Artie, and while you're at it, you better think about going after Thanatos yourself and bringing him home."

She curled her lip. "I'm a goddess, not a servant. I fetch for no one."

Ash moved to stand so close to her that barely a hand-breadth separated them. The air between them rippled with their warring powers, with the ferocity of their raw emotions. "Sooner or later, we all have to do things that are beneath us. Remember that, Artemis."

He moved away from her and turned his back.

"Just because you sold yourself so cheaply, Acheron, it doesn't mean I have to."

He froze, his back still to her, as her words ripped through him. They were cruel and harsh. It was on the tip of his tongue to curse her for that.

He didn't and she was damned lucky for his control.

Instead, he spoke calmly, and chose each deliberate word with care. "If I were you, Artie, I would pray that I never get what I truly deserve. But if Thanatos kills Astrid, not even *I* will be able to save you."

Chapter 12

Zarek tossed the phone down and stared at Astrid sleeping on his coat. He needed to rest too, but couldn't quite manage it. He was too wound up to sleep.

After closing the trapdoor, he moved toward her pallet.

Memories surged through him.

He saw himself on a rampage. Saw faces and flames. Felt the rage of his anger sizzling through him. He had killed the very people he was supposed to protect.

Had killed . . .

Evil laughter echoed in his head. A flash of lightning filled the room.

And Ash . . .

Zarek struggled to remember. Why couldn't he remember what had happened in New Orleans?

What had happened in his village?

It was all fragmented and nothing made sense. It was like thousands of puzzle pieces that had been tossed on the floor and he couldn't figure out what went where.

He paced the tight quarters, doing his best to recall the past.

Hours went by slowly as he listened for any telltale sounds of Thanatos approaching. Sometime around noon exhaustion overtook him and he lay down beside Astrid.

Against his will, he found himself gathering her into his arms and inhaling the sweet, fragrant scent of her hair.

He snuggled against her, closed his eyes and prayed for a kind dream . . .

Zarek stumbled as he was jerked forward and secured to the whipping post in the old Roman courtyard. His tattered, threadbare peplos was ripped from him, leaving his entire body bare to the three people gathered there to punish him.

He was eleven years old.

His brothers Marius and Marcus stood in front of him with bored looks on their faces while their father uncoiled the leather whip.

Zarek was already tense, knowing all too well the sting ing pain he was about to receive.

"I don't care how many lashes you give him, Father," Marius said. "I'm not sorry for insulting Maximillius and I intend to do it again the next time I see him."

Their father stopped moving. "What if I told you this pitiful slave was your brother? Would you care then?"

The two boys burst out laughing. "This wretch? There is no Roman blood in him."

His father moved forward. He buried his hand in Zarek's hair and pulled his head up so that his brothers could see his scarred face. "Are you sure he's not related?"

They stopped laughing.

Zarek held himself completely still, unable to breathe. He'd always known of his parentage. He was reminded of it every day when the other slaves spat in his food and threw things at him or hit him because they dared not take their anger and hatred out on the rest of his family.

"What are you saying, Father?" Marius asked.

His father shoved Zarek's head against the post, then let

go of him. "I sired him on your uncle's favorite whore. Why do you think he was sent to me as an infant?"

Marius curled his lip. "He is no brother of mine. Better I should claim Valerius than this scab."

Marius approached Zarek. He bent down, trying to make Zarek meet his gaze.

With no other recourse, Zarek closed his eyes. He'd learned a long time ago that to look his brothers in the face would mean an even harsher beating.

"What say you, slave? Have you any Roman blood in you?"

Zarek shook his head no.

"Are you my brother?"

Again he shook his head.

"Are you calling my noble father a liar then?"

Zarek froze as he realized he'd been tricked by them again. Panicking, he tried to pull away from the post. He wanted to run away from what would come over this.

"Are you?" Marius demanded.

He shook his head.

But it was too late. The whip cut through the air with a frightening hiss and bit into his back, slicing through his bared flesh.

Zarek came awake shaking. He struggled to breathe as he scrambled to sit up and look about wildly, half-expecting one of his brothers to be here.

"Zarek?"

He felt the warmth of a tender hand on his back.

"Are you all right?"

He couldn't speak as old memories flared inside him. From the moment Marius and Marcus had learned the truth until the day Zarek's father had bribed a slaver to take him, his brothers had gone out of their way to make Zarek pay for the fact they were related.

He had never known a single day of peace.

Beggar, peasant, or noble, they were all better than him.

And he was nothing but a pathetic whipping boy for them all.

Astrid sat up and wrapped her arms around his waist. "You're shaking. Are you cold?"

Still he didn't answer. He knew he should shove her away from him, but right then he wanted her comfort. He wanted someone to tell him he wasn't worthless.

Someone to tell him that they weren't ashamed of him.

Closing his eyes, he drew her to him and laid his head on her shoulder.

Astrid was stunned by his uncharacteristic actions. She stroked his hair and rocked him slowly in her arms. Just holding him.

"Will you tell me what's wrong?" she asked quietly.

"Why? It won't change anything."

"Because I care, Zarek. I want to make it better. If you'll let me."

His tone was so low that she had to struggle to hear what he said. "There is some pain that nothing heals."

She laid her hand against his stubbled cheek. "Such as?"

He hesitated for several heartbeats before he spoke again. "Do you know how I died?"

"No."

"On my hands and knees, like an animal on the ground, begging for mercy."

She flinched at his words. She hurt so much for him that she could barely breathe from the tightness in her chest.

"Why?"

He stiffened and swallowed. At first she thought he would pull away, but he didn't move. He remained there, letting her hold him.

"You saw how my father got rid of me? How he paid for the slaver to take me?"

"Yes."

"I lived with that slaver for five years."

His arms tightened around her as if he could barely stand to admit that to her. "You can't imagine how they treated me. What I was forced to clean up.

"Every day when I woke up, I cursed to find myself still alive. Every night I prayed to die while I slept. I never had a single dream of escaping that life. The idea of running away doesn't occur to you when you're born a slave. The thought that I didn't deserve what they did to me never entered my mind. It was what I was. All I knew. And I had no hope of anyone ever buying me to get me away from there. Every time a customer came in and saw me, I heard their sharp intakes of breath. Saw the blurry shadows of their horrified sneers."

Astrid's eyes teared up at his words. He was such a handsome man any woman would kill to have him, and yet his looks had been brutally ruined. For no reason other than cruelty.

No one should be maimed and degraded the way he had been.

No one.

She pressed her lips to his forehead, brushing his hair back from his face as he continued to confide in her what she was sure he had never confided to another living soul.

There was no emotion in his voice. Her only clue to the pain he felt was the tenseness of his body.

The fact that he had yet to let her go.

"One day a beautiful lady came in," he whispered. "She had a Roman soldier as her escort. She stood in the doorway wearing a dark blue peplos. Her hair was as black as the midnight sky, her skin smooth and unblemished. I couldn't see her very clearly, but I heard the other slaves whispering about her and they only did that when a woman was truly exceptional."

A stab of jealousy went through Astrid.

Had Zarek loved her?

"Who was she?" she asked.

"Just another noblewoman, wanting a slave."

Zarek's breath fell against her neck as he toyed with a strand of her hair between his callused fingers. The tenderness of that gesture wasn't lost on her.

"She neared the cell where I was cleaning out the chamber pots," he said. "I dared not look at her and then I heard her say, 'I want that one.' I assumed she meant one of the other men. But when they came for me, I was dumbstruck."

Astrid smiled sadly. "She recognized a good thing when she saw it."

"No," he said sharply. "She wanted a servant to warn her and her lover whenever her husband came home unexpectedly. She wanted a slave who would be loyal to her. One who would owe her everything. I was the most wretched creature there and she never failed to remind me of that. One word and she would have sent me right back to my hell."

He pulled away from her then.

She reached out to find him sitting just beside her. "Did she?"

"No. She kept me even though her husband was livid at my presence. He couldn't stand the sight of me. I was so repugnant. Crippled. Half-blind. I was scarred so badly that children used to cry whenever they saw me. Women would gasp and avert their eyes, then shuffle out of my way as if afraid my condition might rub off on them."

Astrid winced at what he described. "How long did you serve her?"

"Six years. I was completely loyal to her. I would have done anything she asked of me."

"She was kind to you?"

"No. Not really. She was merely *kinder* to me. She didn't want to look at me any more than anyone else did. So she kept me hidden in a small cell, and only brought me out whenever her lover came to visit. I would stand by the gate and listen for the guards to greet her lord. Whenever he returned while they were together, I would run to her room and rap on the door to warn them."

That explained a lot to her about his death. "Is that how you died? Did her lord catch you warning them?"

"No. On that day, I went to the door to warn her, but when I got there I heard her crying out in pain, telling her lover to stop hurting her. I rushed inside to find him beating her. I tried to pull him off. But he turned on me. He finally heard her husband outside and he left. She told me to leave too and I did."

Zarek fell silent as the memory of that day tore through him anew. He could still see the small cell that was his room. Smell the stench of it and his wounded body. Feel the sting of his face and neck where Arkus had punched him repeatedly as he tried to pull the soldier off Carlia.

The soldier had given him a beating so severe that he'd expected it to kill him. He'd been so sore and broken afterward that he could hardly move, hardly breathe, as he limped back to the hole where Carlia kept him.

Zarek had been sitting on the floor, staring at the wall, wishing for his body to stop hurting.

Then the door had crashed open.

He'd looked up to see the blurry image of Carlia's husband, Theodosius, glaring at him with raw fury contorting the old man's face.

At first Zarek had innocently assumed the senator had found out about his wife's infidelity and his own part in warning her whenever he came home.

It hadn't been.

"How dare you!" Theodosius had pulled him up by his hair and slung him from the cell. The man had beaten and kicked him across the villa's courtyard all the way back to Carlia's rooms.

Zarek had spilled into her bedroom, just a few feet away

from her. He lay on the floor, beaten and bloody and shaking, with no idea why he had been attacked this time.

Helpless, he waited for her to say something.

Her bruised face ashen, she had stood there like a tattered queen, clutching her torn and bloodied gown to her ravaged body.

"Is this the one who raped you?" Theodosius asked his wife.

Zarek's mouth had gone instantly dry at the question. No—he couldn't have heard that correctly.

She wept uncontrollably as her female attendant tried to comfort her. "Yes. He did this to me."

Zarek dared to look up at Carlia, unable to believe her lie. After all he had done for her . . .

After the beating he'd received from her lover to protect her. How could she do this to him?

"My lady—"

Theodosius had viciously kicked him in the head, cutting off the rest of his words. "Silence, you worthless dog." He turned on his wife then. "I told you you should have left him in the cesspit. See you what happens when you feel sorry for creatures such as this?"

Then Theodosius had called for his guards.

Zarek had been summarily pulled from the room, and taken to the authorities. He'd tried to protest his innocence, but Roman justice followed one basic principle: guilty until proven innocent.

His word as a slave was nothing compared to Carlia's.

Over the course of a week, his Roman judges managed to torture a full confession from him.

He would have said anything to get them to stop their painful torture.

He'd never known more pain than he did that week. Not even his father's cruelty could match the instruments of the Roman government.

And so he'd been convicted. He, a virgin who had never touched a woman's flesh in any way, was going to be executed for raping his owner.

"They dragged me from my cell and led me through town where everyone was gathered to spit on me," he whispered woodenly to Astrid. "They jeered and tossed rotten food, calling me every name you can imagine. The soldiers untied me from the wagon and dragged me to the center of the crowd. They tried to stand me up, but both my legs were broken. Ultimately, they left me there on my hands and knees so that the crowd could stone me. You know, I can still feel the rocks raining against my body. Hear them telling me to die."

Astrid struggled to breathe as he finished his tale.

"I'm so sorry, Zarek," she whispered, aching for him.

"Don't patronize me," he growled.

She leaned against him and pressed her lips to his cheek. "Believe me, I'm not. I would never patronize anyone with your strength."

He tried to pull away from her, but she held him fast. "I'm not strong."

"Yes you are. I don't know how you stood the pain of your life. I've always felt alone, but not the way you have."

He relaxed a degree as she leaned against his side. She wished she could see him now. See the emotions in his dark eyes.

"You know, I'm not really crazy."

She smiled. "I know you're not."

He let out a long, tired sigh. "Why didn't you go off with Jess when you had the chance? You could be safe now."

"If I leave you before the judgment is complete, the Fates will kill you."

"So what?"

"I don't want you to die, Zarek."

"You keep saying that and I still don't know why."

Because I love you. The words lodged in her throat. She

wanted desperately to have the courage to say them out loud to him, but she knew he wouldn't accept it.

Not her Prince Charming.

He would growl and push her away because in his mind such a thing didn't exist.

He didn't understand it.

She didn't know if he ever would.

Astrid wanted to hold him. To comfort him.

But most of all, she wanted to love him. In a way that made her ache and soar at the same time.

Would Zarek ever allow her or anyone else to love him?

"What can I say to you so you'll believe?" she asked back. "You'd laugh if I said I cared for you. You'd walk off angry if I said I loved you. So you tell me why I don't want you to die."

She felt the muscles of his jaw working underneath her hand. "I wish I could get you out of here, princess. You don't need to be with me."

"No, Zarek, I don't. But I *want* to be with you."

Zarek winced as she spoke the most beautiful words he'd ever heard in his life.

She amazed him. There were no walls between them now. No secrets. She knew him in a way no one ever had.

And she wasn't repulsed by him.

He didn't understand her. "I don't even want to be with me most of the time. Why do you?"

She gave him a shove. "I swear, you're like a three-year-old. Why? Why? Why? Why is the sky blue? Why are we here? Why does my dog have fur? Some things just are, Zarek. They don't have to make sense. Accept them."

"And if I can't?"

"Then you have worse problems than Thanatos wanting you dead."

He thought about that for a little while. Could he accept what she offered him?

Did he dare?

He didn't know how to be a friend. He didn't know how to laugh from pleasure or be nice.

For a man who was over two thousand years old, he really knew very little about life.

"Tell me, princess. Honestly. How are you going to judge me?"

She didn't hesitate to respond. "I'm going to acquit you if I can."

He laughed bitterly at that. "I was condemned for something I didn't do and acquitted for what I did. There's something not right about that."

"Zarek—"

"And will they accept your judgment now?" he asked, interrupting her. "You're not exactly impartial, are you?"

"I . . ." Astrid paused as she considered that. "They will accept it. We just have to find a way to prove to them that you are safe to be with other people."

"You don't sound too sure about that, princess."

She wasn't. Not once in all eternity had she breached the impartiality oath.

With Zarek she had.

"Lie down, Zarek," she said, pulling at his shoulder. "We both need to rest."

Zarek did as she said. To his chagrin and delight, she laid her head down on his chest and snuggled close.

He'd never held a woman like this and he found himself running his hand through her long blond hair. Spreading it out over his chest. He tilted his head so that he could look down at her.

She had her eyes closed as she idly traced circles on his chest, around his nipple, which was hard and swollen underneath his black jersey shirt.

He felt a closeness to her that was indescribable. If he knew how, he would wish they could stay like this forever.

But dreams and hopes were as alien to him as love and kindness.

Unlike her, he didn't see a future.

He only saw his death clearly in his mind.

Even if Thanatos didn't kill him, there was no use wishing he could stay with Astrid.

She was a goddess.

He was a slave.

He had no place in her world any more than he had a place in the realm of mortals.

Alone. He was always alone. And he would remain that way.

It didn't matter if he survived Thanatos. He was living only to see her safe.

Sighing, he closed his eyes and forced himself to go to sleep again.

Astrid listened to Zarek as he slept. His hand was buried in her hair, and even while unconscious, he held on to her as if afraid to let her go.

She wished she could get inside his head again. Wished for a moment where she could stare into his midnight-black eyes and see the beauty of her dark warrior.

But it wasn't his face and body that made her burn for him.

It was the man he was inside his battered and bruised heart. The one who was able to create poetry and art. The one who hid his vulnerability behind barbs and stinging retorts.

And she loved him. Even when he was mean and nasty. Even when he was angry.

But then, she understood that part of him.

How could anyone bear so much pain and not be scarred by it?

And what would become of him now?

Even if she did get her judgment to stand she doubted Artemis would ever let him leave Alaska.

He would be trapped here forever.

She shuddered at the thought of his isolation.

And what of her?

How could she go back to her life without him? She actually liked being with him. He was amusing in a very salty sort of way.

"Astrid?"

She lifted her head, amazed at the sound of her name on his lips. It was the first time he'd used it outside of his dreams. She hadn't even realized he was awake.

"Yes?"

"Make love to me."

She closed her eyes and savored those words as much as she had savored her name.

Impishly, she arched a brow at him. "Why?"

"Because I need to be inside you right now. I want to feel connected to you."

Her throat constricted at his words. How could she ever deny him so simple a request?

Astrid rose up on her knees, and straddled his hips. He cupped her face in his hands and pulled her down for a scorching kiss.

She'd never imagined a man could be like this. So tough, and yet so tender.

She nipped his lips and chin with her teeth. "You should be resting."

"I don't want to rest. I seldom sleep anyway."

She knew it was true. The only time he had slept more than a couple of hours at a stretch was when she had drugged him. Judging by what she'd seen of his dreams and what M'Adoc had said, she well understood why.

And in her heart she wanted to soothe him.

She pulled her shirt off over her head.

Zarek swallowed at the sight of her bare breasts and skin. He swelled underneath her. It had only been a few hours since they had screwed.

No, she didn't screw him.

That was why he needed to feel her now. He desperately craved her hands on his flesh. Her naked body against his.

Because they didn't screw each other. What they shared was so much more than that. It was basic and primal and it was sublime.

What had she done to him?

But then he knew.

She had done the impossible. She had slid herself inside his dead heart.

Astrid alone made him ache. Made him want.

Made him human.

In her arms, he had discovered his humanity. Even his missing soul.

She meant something to him and he could at least pretend he meant something to her.

He reached down slowly to unzip her pants so that he could slide his hand into her pink cotton panties and sink his fingers down into her moist heat. It still amazed him that she would let him touch her like this.

Granted, women had been much more receptive to him as a Dark-Hunter than they had been when he was a human, but it hadn't changed him. He'd avoided them, knowing the only reason they were drawn to him now was because Acheron had repaired his body. So he'd snarled at the ones who offered themselves to him and he had only taken a handful of them when he had gotten tired of jerking himself off.

But in the end, they had meant nothing to him. He couldn't even remember any of their faces.

Astrid moaned as he stroked her.

"Zarek," she whispered, her breath falling lightly against his cheek. "I love the way your hands feel on my body."

"Even though I'm a slave and you're a goddess?"

"I'm no more a goddess than you are a slave."

He started to contradict her, then stopped. He didn't want anything to spoil this moment. This could very well be the last moment he had with her.

Thanatos could come crashing through the door at any moment to kill him, and if he had to die, he wanted one moment of happiness.

And she made him happy. In a way he'd never thought possible.

When he was with her, it seemed like something inside him wanted to fly. To laugh.

He was warm through and through.

"You know," she whispered. "I think I was wrong earlier. I think you have made me a nympho."

Zarek smiled at that and pulled his hand away from her so that he could open his fly and free himself from his pants. He shoved them down his legs, to his knees, but didn't want to dislodge her to remove them completely.

He raised her up and then set her down on him.

They moaned in unison.

It was so erotic to watch her naked above him while he was still mostly dressed. He lifted his hips from the floor, thrusting himself deep inside her warmth while he ran his hands over her bare breasts.

Astrid gasped at Zarek's hardness inside her. She'd pushed his shirt up so that his hard, muscled stomach was bare, but he was still fully clothed. His leather pants brushed against her thighs with every move he made.

His hands left her.

A few seconds later, she felt his soft fur parka against her bare skin as he draped it around her.

"I don't want you to get cold," he explained quietly.

She smiled at him, touched by his thoughtfulness. "How could I ever be cold with you inside me?"

He rose up then and wrapped his arms around her. His lips possessed hers with a fiery passion that left her breathless and weak.

Astrid cried out as she came in his arms.

Zarek waited until he'd wrung the last tremor of her orgasm from her before he sat up, still inside her and leaned her back against the floor.

Kissing her again, he quickened his thrusts, seeking his own peace.

And when he found it, he didn't close his eyes. He stared down at the woman who had given it to him.

She lay beneath him, breathing raggedly, her eyes unseeing, her touch enchanting.

He knew then there was nothing he wouldn't do for her. If she asked, he would walk through the fires of hell just to make her smile.

He cursed at the knowledge.

"Zarek?"

He ground his teeth as he pulled away from her. "What?"

She took his chin in her hand and turned his face toward hers, then she kissed him fiercely. "Don't you dare turn away from me."

He couldn't breathe as he felt her with every fiber of his being. Her bare bottom was wet against his groin, her skin cool against his.

But it was the warmth of her lips and breath that heated him.

The fire of her undaunted will. It burned through him, tearing away centuries of loneliness and pain.

" 'You know—my flower,' " he breathed. " 'I am responsible for her.' " He kissed her gently. " 'She doesn't even have four thorns to protect herself from harm.' "

Astrid listened as he quoted from *The Little Prince*. "Why do you love that book so?" she asked.

"Because I want to hear the bells when I look up at the sky. I want to laugh, but I don't know how."

Her lips quivered in sadness. That was the lesson of the book. It was to remind people that it was okay to care and that once you let someone into your heart, you were never really alone. Even the most simple thing such as looking up at the sky could bring comfort to you, even when the one you loved was far away. "And if I taught you to laugh?"

"I would be tamed."

"Would you? Or would you be the sheep who has a muzzle with no strap and who eats the rose when he's not supposed to? I somehow think that even tamed, you would be beyond control."

Astrid felt the most remarkable thing then. Zarek's lips curled up beneath her hand.

"Are you smiling?"

"I'm smiling, princess. But not broadly. No teeth."

"Or fangs?"

"Or fangs."

She leaned forward and kissed him again. "I'll bet you're gorgeous when you smile."

He grunted at that, then helped her dress.

Astrid snuggled up to him once more so that she could hear the rhythm of his heart. She loved the sound of it, the feel of his strength beneath her.

Even though their lives were in danger, she felt oddly safe here.

With him.

Or so she thought.

In the stillness, she heard a strange scratching sound above them.

Zarek jerked up.

"What is it?" she whispered.

"Someone's upstairs in my cabin."

Horror consumed her. "You think it's Thanatos?"

"Yes."

He moved her gently off him and stood her against the wall. Terrified, she remained perfectly still as she listened to his movements and to those above.

Zarek grabbed a grenade, then reconsidered. The last thing he wanted was to trap them underground. He pulled on his spare set of silver claws that covered every finger of his left hand, and moved down the hallway back toward the trapdoor that was underneath his stove.

He heard light footsteps above him.

Then a curse.

Suddenly, there was silence again.

Zarek strained, desperate to hear who was up there and what they were doing.

A strange shiver went down his spine as the air behind him stirred.

He turned expecting to see Astrid.

It wasn't her.

Chapter 13

Standing behind him was an odd demonic woman with long blond hair, pointed ears, and large, batlike wings. She was cute in a very strange sort of way.

She stared at him without moving.

Zarek attacked.

Instead of fighting, she turned with a squeak and ran for the back of the cave.

Zarek followed her, intending to stop her before she reached Astrid, but he couldn't.

The demon ran straight for her and to his astonishment she rushed behind Astrid and put her between them. The demon's wings constricted and folded in around her body as if to protect her.

The demon placed a hand on Astrid's shoulder as she eyed him cautiously. "Tell him to leave me alone, Astrid. Else I'll have to barbecue him and make *akri* angry at me. I don't want to make *akri* angry."

Astrid covered the demon's hand with hers. "Simi? Is that you?"

"Yes. *C'est moi*. The little demon with hornays."

Zarek lowered his claws. "You two know each other?"

Astrid frowned as she faced him again. "Don't you know her?"

"She's a demon. Why would I know her?"

"Because she's Acheron's companion."

Completely stunned, Zarek gaped at the small creature who did have odd eyes much like Acheron's. They were pale and glowing, but hers were rimmed with red. "Ash has a companion?"

The demon snorted. She stood up and whispered loudly in Astrid's ear. "Dark-Hunters are cute, but very stupid."

He gave her a peeved glare as Astrid choked back a laugh.

"What are you doing here, Simi?" Astrid asked.

The demon looked around the tunnel and pouted in a way that reminded him of a small child. "Feeling peckish. Is there any food? Something not too heavy. Maybe a cow or two?"

"No, Simi," Astrid said. "No food."

The demon made a rude noise as she stepped away from Astrid. " 'No, Simi. No food,' " she mocked. "You sound like *akri*. 'Don't eat that, Simi, you'll cause an ecological disaster.' What is an ecological disaster, that's what I want to know? *Akri* says it's me on hunger binge, but I don't think that's quite right, but that's all hc'll say about it."

Disregarding both of them, the demon began searching through his weapons.

She grabbed a grenade and tried to bite into it.

Zarek snatched it away from her. "That's not food."

The demon opened her mouth as if to speak, then snapped it shut. "Why are you in a dark hole, Astrid? Did you fall?"

"We're hiding, Simi."

"Hiding?" She snorted again. "From what?"

"Thanatos."

"Pffft . . ." The demon rolled her eyes and waved her

hand dismissively. "Why you hiding from that loser? He wouldn't even make good barbecue. Barely take the edge off my peckishness. Hmmm . . . How come there's no food here?" She looked speculatively at Astrid.

Zarek stepped between them.

The demon stuck her tongue out at him and returned to searching his supplies.

"Why are you here?" Zarek asked.

The demon ignored him. "Where's Sasha, Astrid? He'd make good barbecue. Something about that wolf meat. Very tasty once you get all that hair off. Barbecued hair not particularly tasty, but it'll do in a pinch."

"He's not here, thankfully. But why are you here without Acheron?"

"*Akri* told me to come."

"Who is *akri*?" Zarek asked.

Simi ignored him.

"Acheron," Astrid explained. "*Akri* is an Atlantean term for 'lord and master.' "

He scoffed at that. "Well, la-di-da. No wonder he has such a big head, with a pet demon following him around, calling him 'lord and master.' "

Astrid gave him an agitated look. "He's not like that, Zarek, and you'd best not insult him around the Simi. She tends to take such things personally, and without Acheron here to call her off she's deadlier than a nuclear bomb."

He looked over at the small demon with new respect. "Really?"

Astrid nodded. "Her race once held dominion over the entire earth. Even the Olympian gods were terrified of the Charontes, and only the Atlanteans were ever able to defeat and harness them."

Simi looked up and gave him a wide, toothy grin that revealed her fangs evilly. She licked her lips as if savoring some tasty morsel. "I would like to barbecue those Olympian gods. They are very tasty. One day, I'm going to eat that redheaded goddess, too."

"She doesn't like Artemis," Astrid explained.

So he gathered.

"The Simi hates her, but *akri* says, 'No, Simi, you can't kill Artemis. Behave, Simi, don't shoot fire at her, don't make her bald, Simi.' No, no, no. It's all I hear."

She glared at Zarek meaningfully. "I don't like that word. 'No.' It even sounds evil. The Simi tends to barbecue anyone dumb enough to say it to her. But not *akri*. He's allowed to say no to me; I just don't like it when he does."

Zarek frowned as he watched Simi hop along from box to box like a butterfly. She exclaimed giddily when she found his store of gold and jewels that Artemis paid him with every month.

"Look!" Simi said, scooping up a handful of diamonds. "You got sparklies like *akri*. He gives all of his to me." She held an emerald necklace up to her throat. "He say I look beautiful in sparklies, 'specially them red ones that match my eyes. Here, Astrid," she said, bringing another necklace over to them and fastening it around Astrid's neck.

"I know you can't see it, Astrid, but it is very lovely, like you. You need to wear that and then you have sparklies, too." She looked up at Astrid's head. "But still no hornays. We need to fix you up with hornays one day so you can be a demon, too. It's fun being a demon—except when people try to exercise you . . . Wait, that's not the right word. I forget, but you know what I mean."

There was something strangely charismatic about her, but she didn't seem to be quite right . . . in more ways than one.

"Is she okay?" he asked Astrid. "I mean, no offense, she sounds more mental than I do."

Astrid laughed. "You have to remember that Acheron, shall we say, indulges her *a lot* and Simi's not fully grown."

"Yes I am," Simi said in a tone that reminded him of a five-year-old child. She had a peculiar singsongy accent unlike anything he'd ever heard before.

"The Simi has needs," she continued idly. "Lots of needs. I need *akri*'s plastic card, for one thing. It very nice. People give me lots of stuff when I hand it to them. Ooo, I really like the new plastic card he gave me with my own name on it. It blue and all sparkly and it says Simi Parthenopaeus."

She looked up like a giddy child. "Doesn't that have a nice ring to it? I have to say it again. Simi Parthenopaeus. I like that a lot. It even has my picture in the corner and I am a very attractive demon if I do say so myself. *Akri* says it, too. 'Simi, you are beautiful.' I like it when he tells me that."

"Does she always ramble on like this?" Zarek whispered under his breath in Astrid's ear.

She nodded. "Trust me, it's wise to let her ramble, too. She gets rather upset if you tell her to be quiet. She once ate a lesser god who did that."

Simi cocked her head as if another thought came to her addled mind. "And I particularly like men all of a sudden." She looked over at Zarek who involuntarily cringed. "But not that one. He's too dark. I like them blue-eyed people 'cause they remind me of my card. People like that Calvin Klein model Travis Fimmel who was on this big billboard in New York the last time *akri* took me there. He mighty fine and makes me want to do things to him other than flame-broil him. He makes me all warm and tingly."

"Okay, Simi. Warm and tingly. I think we need to switch topics," Astrid said.

Zarek wasn't sure if he should feel relieved or insulted by her comments about him. But he definitely agreed a change in topic would be nice.

Astrid turned to where she thought Simi might be, but Simi had already moved.

Again.

The demon seemed to have an aversion to sitting still.

"Simi, why did Acheron send you here?"

Simi pulled a sheathed dagger out of a box and examined it with a skill that made Zarek arch his brow. Childlike she might appear, but there was nothing childish in the way Simi handled his weapons.

She tested the balance of the blade like a pro. "To protect you from Thanatos so that your sisters don't get all freaky and destroy the world. Or something like that. I don't know why all of you fear the end of the world. It's not so bad, really. At least then *akri*'s mama be free. Then she wouldn't be so cranky at the Simi all the time."

Zarek started at her words. "Ash's mother is still alive?"

She covered her mouth with her hand and dropped the dagger. "Oh, *akri* get mad whenever I tell that. Bad Simi. I not talk anymore. I need food."

Zarek rubbed his head as Simi went back to opening boxes. Oh, this was great. He had a nymph to protect, a psycho something out to kill them, and now a mental demon to contend with.

Oh, yeah, this got better and better.

He looked over at Astrid, who had her brow furrowed as if thinking over Simi's disclosures.

"Just who are your sisters, Astrid, that they can destroy the world?" Zarek asked.

Astrid cringed a tiny bit and shifted uneasily.

This was about to get worse.

He knew it.

Cringing even more, she whispered, "The Fates."

Zarek went cold. Oh, yeah, his life, as bad as it was, just went careening down to Shitsville and there was no off ramp in sight.

"Your sisters are the Fates," he repeated, saying each word slowly and enunciating it clearly so that there could be no misunderstanding.

SHERRILYN KENYON

She nodded.

Anger enveloped him. "I see. Your sisters are the Moirae, the three Fates who are in charge of everything. Women who are known to have no mercy or pity on anyone. Women who the gods themselves fear."

She bit her lip. "They're really not so bad. They can be almost nice, if you catch them in the right moods."

"Oh, jeez." Zarek raked his hands through his hair as he struggled to keep his temper from exploding. No wonder Ash had sent Simi. If anything happened to Astrid, there was no telling what could happen. "Please tell me there was a family argument and you and your sisters don't speak to each other. That they can't stand the mention of your name."

"No, no, we're extremely friendly. I'm the baby of the family and they are more like three mothers to me."

Zarek actually whimpered at that. "So you're telling me that right now I'm responsible for Acheron's beloved pet and the favorite sister of the Fates?"

Simi widened her eyes. "Tell Fang-boy I'm not a pet. If he doesn't take a nicer tone to me, he's going to be really sorry."

Astrid ignored Simi's comment. "It's not all bad."

"No? Then by all means tell me something good, Astrid."

"They'll probably side with me when I judge you innocent."

"Probably?"

She nodded lamely.

Zarek growled at that. Leave it to him. Whenever he got screwed by something it was never in a little way.

Astrid turned back to the demon. "Simi, why aren't you talking to Zarek?"

"Because *akri* said not to. He didn't say I couldn't talk to you, though."

"Do you do everything he tells you to?" Zarek asked her.

Simi ignored him.

"Yes, she does," Astrid answered. "But the good news is, Simi can't lie, either. Can you, Simi?"

"Well, why would I? Lies are too confusing."

Oh, yeah, like she wasn't. He'd never seen anyone or anything more confusing than this demon.

"Why did Acheron tell you not to talk to Zarek?"

"I don't know. That redheaded bitch-goddess got all angry when he told me to come protect you. It went like this . . ."

The demon flashed from her form into that of Acheron. "Protect Zarek and Astrid. Now."

She transformed into Artemis. "No!" she snapped. "You can't let her go, she'll tell Zarek everything."

Simi, looking like Artemis, put her hand against her cheek and whispered loudly to Astrid. "This the part where the redheaded goddess went on and on about what happened in Zarek's village and *akri* got all upset at her. Don't know why he won't let me kill her and get it over with, but finally he say . . ."

She flashed into Ash's body once more. "Simi, don't speak to Zarek but make sure Thanatos doesn't kill either one of them."

Simi returned to her small, slight demonic self. "So I said okay and here I am not talking to Zarek."

"Wow," Zarek said as she stopped her one-demon show. "She's a camcorder, too. How convenient."

She leveled a murderous glare at him, but directed her words at Astrid. "I miss the days when the Simi could pick off Dark-Hunters and no one noticed."

Astrid moved forward to find Simi who took her hand and faced her with a benign, sweet look. It was obvious the demon liked her.

"What happened in his village that Artemis doesn't want Zarek to know about?"

Simi shrugged. "I don't know. She's all paranoid all the time anyway. Afraid *akri* is going to leave and not come back, which I keep telling him to do. But does he listen? No." Her next comment came out in Ash's voice. "She's not your concern, Simi. You don't understand, Simi."

She made another rude noise. "I understand, all right. I understand the bitch-goddess needs the Simi to barbecue her until she learns to be nice to people. I think she'd be rather attractive on fire. I could make her look like that old sea hag or something."

"Simi!" Astrid stressed her name and took her by her arms as if trying to keep the demon on the topic. "Please tell me what happened in Zarek's village."

"Oh, that. Well, the Thanatos thing, not the one after you now, but the one who came before him, went all wild and killed everybody. Them poor people didn't stand a chance. *Akri* was so mad he wanted the bitch-goddess's heart for it, only I say she don't have no heart to take."

Zarek felt as if someone had just slugged him. "What are you saying? You mean I didn't kill them?"

Astrid's mind whirled with what Simi was revealing. If Zarek were innocent of destroying his village, then why had he been banished?

"Zarek didn't kill them?" she asked Simi.

"Of course not. No Dark-Hunter would kill their charges. *Akri* would eat them if they did. Zarek killed them Apollites—which made everybody mad."

Zarek frowned. He didn't remember anything about Apollites. There had never been any around his village. "What Apollites?"

Astrid repeated his question.

Simi spoke slowly and carefully as if they were the ones who had trouble sticking with the conversation. "The ones that Thanatos gathered to use for cannon fodder. Jeez, don't you people know nothing about the Daimons and Apollites? Thanatos can summon them up and make them do things for him. He can do it with people too sometimes.

"He was sent by Artemis to kill some Dark-Hunter up in Scotland, then after he did that, he went after all the other Dark-Hunters so that he could destroy them and all the Apollites could live in peace and feed off the humans without worrying about any of you guys."

Astrid shivered at Simi's words as she remembered where she had been nine hundred years ago. "Thanatos is the one who killed Miles in Scotland?"

"Yes," Simi confirmed.

"Then he went after Zarek?"

Simi made an agitated noise. "He's a Dark-Hunter, isn't he? Are you two having some sort of strange human thing that you can't follow what I'm saying?"

Astrid patted Simi's hand hopefully to calm her a bit. "I'm sorry, Simi. You're just telling us some things we knew nothing about."

Simi cocked her head and looked at Zarek. "Oh, I guess that's okay then. Still . . . you should know something about Thanatos. Him being able to kill you and all."

Astrid sensed Zarek was about to speak. She gave him the kill signal while she continued to question Simi.

"Simi, why doesn't Zarek remember the first Thanatos coming after him?"

" 'Cause he's not supposed to. *Akri* had to kill Thanatos in front of him and he made it so that Zarek wouldn't remember anything about all that mess."

Zarek let out a slow breath as her words seeped in. Ash had made it so he wouldn't remember.

"Acheron scrambled my brains?"

Astrid's face filled with relief. "You're innocent, Zarek."

Rage tore through him. "So I was banished to this god-forsaken hellhole because Acheron killed Thanatos? What kind of bullshit is that?" He paced the floor angrily. "I'll kill that bastard."

Simi shifted instantly into the shape of a "small" dragon.

One that was wedged into their tunnel. Her eyes blazed angrily as she hissed at him. "Did you insult my *akri*?"

Ready for battle, Zarek opened his mouth to tell her yes and found Astrid shielding him. She stood between them and held him behind her.

"No, Simi. Zarek has a right to be angry. He's been exiled for something he didn't do."

Simi shifted back into her humanoid form. "No he wasn't. He was banished because he killed the Apollites."

Simi took on the form of Artemis. "See, I told you, Acheron, he's insane. He knew better than to kill them."

She became Acheron. "What was he supposed to do? They were throwing themselves at him, trying to kill him. It was self-defense."

"It was murder."

"I swear, Artemis, you kill Zarek over this and I will walk out of that door and never come back."

She transformed back into herself. "See. That's why he was banished. The bitch-goddess didn't want *akri* to leave her so she agreed to let Zarek live here just so long as other people weren't around him."

Simi looked around the dismal tunnel. "Honestly, I think I'd rather be dead myself. This place more boring than Katoteros and I didn't know it could get more boring than Katoteros. I stand corrected. The next time *akri* tell me it not so bad at home, I might believe him. You don't even have decent food here. No TV, neither."

Zarek stepped back and stared blankly at the wall as he tried to remember the past while Simi rattled on without pausing.

He could still hear screams from the villagers, but now he wondered . . .

Whose screams did he really hear?

Astrid felt her way toward him. The warmth of her

presence seeped into him. She touched his arm, making him burn reflexively. Something about her touch always rocked him and made him want to turn into her.

Made him want to touch her.

"Are you all right?" she asked.

"No, not really. I want to know what happened to me that night."

She nodded as if she understood. "Simi, is there anything that can undo what Acheron did to Zarek's memory?"

"Nope. *Akri* infallible. Well, except for a couple of things, and we don't talk about those 'cause it makes *akri* cranky. I like that word 'infallible.' It just like me. Infallible."

"Then it's hopeless," Zarek said under his breath. "I have no proof that I'm innocent and I'll never know what happened there."

"I'm not so sure," Astrid said, smiling at him. "Don't give up on me yet, Zarek. If we get proof of what she says, then my decision will stand. You're innocent. No one will be able to argue against it. My sisters won't let you be judged wrongfully."

He scoffed. "I was innocent when I was stoned to death, too, princess. Excuse me if I don't have a lot of faith in justice or your sisters."

Astrid swallowed. It was true, the innocent often suffered, too. Her mother and sisters dismissed that fact as the way of the universe, even though her mother did strive to give justice to everyone.

Sometimes unfair things did happen. There was no way around that.

Zarek was a perfect example.

Still, he needed to know the truth about what had happened to him. He deserved that much.

"Simi? Is there any way you can show Zarek what happened that night?"

Simi tapped her forefinger against her cheek as she thought that over. "I suppose so. *Akri* didn't say I couldn't 'show' him anything, he only said I couldn't talk to him."

Astrid smiled. Simi had always been extremely literal in her interpretation of everything Acheron ordered her to do.

"Will you? Please?"

Simi walked over to Zarek and took his chin in her hand.

Zarek started to protest, but something seemed to seep into him from her hand. It held him paralyzed.

Simi angled his face until he could stare into her now red and yellow eyes and there he saw the past.

Everything faded from around him and all he could focus on was Simi's eyes. The images flickered across her pupils, then straight into his mind. He didn't remember any of it having happened. It was like watching a movie of his own life.

He saw the fires of his village burning to the ground. The bodies scattered. Things that had haunted him for centuries. But that wasn't all he saw this time.

There was more . . .

Forgotten images that had been taken from him.

He saw himself stumbling upon the village. Bewildered. Angry. The damage had already been done; he wasn't responsible.

Someone else had come to the village before him.

He saw the old crone, whom he took into his arms as he always did. Only this time she said more than her usual accusation. "Death came looking for you. He killed everyone because he wanted us to tell him where you lived. We didn't know and it made him angry." Her old eyes had burned with hatred and condemnation. "Why didn't you come? It's all your fault. You were supposed to protect us and it was you who killed us. You killed my daughter."

He saw the old woman's face. Felt his fury again as he saw what the Daimons had done . . .

Zarek's heart pounded as he realized the truth.

He was innocent of killing his charges.

None of it had been his fault. He'd been making his normal rounds when he had spotted the fire and he'd rushed to them, but by then it had been too late.

Thanatos had come to the village during the daylight and destroyed it. There hadn't been any way for him to save them.

As he watched her eyes, Simi took him through his forgotten five-night trek to the Apollite village where he'd gone to seek those responsible for the deaths at Taberleigh.

He had fought the Spathi Daimons every step of the way, and one of them had told him of the Dayslayer who would unite their people and destroy the Dark-Hunters. The Spathi had laughed as he died, telling Zarek that the reign of the Dark-Hunters was over.

The Dayslayer would take back the human world and then they would take down the Olympians.

As each night passed and the Spathis increased in number, Zarek realized exactly what the world was facing. Every human village he passed was destroyed. The people dead. Slaughtered. Consumed by the Daimons who didn't want to die.

He'd never seen such devastation. Such waste.

Had he possessed a Squire, he would have sent him on to warn the other Dark-Hunters or to find Acheron and bring him here to help fight. As it was, there was only him and he wanted to stop the destruction before anyone else suffered.

Cold and hungry, Zarek had fought his way to the Apollite village that protected the mysterious entity who had slain his people.

Zarek had arrived only an hour after sundown. As was typical, the Apollites had made their homes underground. The catacombs had been dark and frigid and completely devoid of any souls. Back then, the Apollites had often made their homes near the dead so that they could take the bodi-less souls if they needed a quick pick-me-up. In addition, it provided them with a shield. Since Dark-Hunters were com-prised of soulless bodies, those souls who needed bodies had a nasty tendency to want to possess them. So catacombs and crypts made the best hiding places for Apollites and Daimons.

Since all the souls had been stripped before his arrival, Zarek had easily found his way through the catacombs.

As he searched the corridors and rooms of the under-ground lair, he discovered there weren't any Apollite or Daimon families present, only evidence of them having left in a hurry.

In one room, he found a woman with an infant who was weeping.

She looked up at him with a gasp.

"I won't hurt you," he said.

She started screaming for help.

Zarek had backed out of her home and shut the door.

His thoughts had been focused on only one person.

Thanatos.

The thing the Spathi had told him had been sent by Artemis to kill all the Dark-Hunters. She who was their cre-ator had betrayed them and created an invincible monster.

Unless he stopped it first. He had hated Artemis then. Hated her not only for creating Thanatos, but for unleashing something like this on the world without warning anyone.

As he moved through the catacombs, Daimons and Apol-lites attacked him. He fought them off, killing anyone who came at him with a sword. No, he hadn't cared if they were Daimon or Apollite. It hadn't mattered.

Only his vengeance had.

He'd found Thanatos down one of the longer corridors. He'd been with a dozen of his people in a chamber where the Apollites stored textiles.

Zarek had counted five Apollites there and eight Daimons.

But what had given him pause was the lone Apollite woman who had been standing beside Thanatos. She was dressed like the Spathis and stood ready to fight.

Thanatos had smiled evilly at him.

"See," he had said to the Apollites and Daimons gathered. "He is but one while we are many. The Dark-Hunters are not so fierce. They can't combine their numbers without it weakening them. We can kill them as easily as they kill us. Pierce his mark and he dies just like the rest of you."

They had rushed him then.

Zarek had tried to fight his way through them. But they had fought with more strength than he'd ever encountered before. It was as if they were drawing power from Thanatos.

They had overtaken him and thrown him to the ground while they ripped at his clothes trying to find his mark.

He'd already been wounded by previous fights. Weakened by his hunger.

It didn't stop him from fighting with everything he had.

"He doesn't bear the mark of Artemis!" one of them had cried out.

"Of course he does." Thanatos had come forward to see.

Zarek had taken the opportunity to get loose. He had gone for Thanatos's head with his sword.

Thanatos had stepped back and shoved the woman in front of him to protect himself.

With no time to react, Zarek stood there helplessly as she was impaled on his sword.

When she didn't explode, he realized she wasn't a Daimon after all. She was an Apollite.

Horrified, he had met her gaze and saw the tears in her eyes. He'd wanted to help her. To soothe her.

The last thing he had ever wanted was to see her hurt.

Never had he harmed a woman before . . . not even the woman who had accused him of raping her.

He'd hated himself then even more than he hated Artemis, hated the fact he hadn't been quicker. That he hadn't killed Thanatos instead.

One of the Apollites cried out.

A man. He rushed forward to take the woman and cradle her as she died.

The man looked up at him with hatred and rage.

It was the face of the new Thanatos.

Zarek tried to break away from Simi as he saw that. But she held him fast.

Forced him to watch his past play out.

Thanatos had grabbed him by his throat and shoved him against the wall. "Mark or no mark, you can still die if I dismember you."

Guilt-ridden over the woman, Zarek hadn't even bothered to fight. He'd just wanted it to end.

But as Thanatos went for him, Acheron had appeared out of nowhere.

"Let him go."

The remaining Daimons and Apollites had scattered in fear. Only the one man holding his now dead wife had remained.

Thanatos had turned slowly to face Ash. "And if I don't?"

Ash shot a blast from his hand into Thanatos, who instantly let go of Zarek. Zarek fell to the floor gasping for air through his swollen esophagus.

"It wasn't a choice," Ash said.

Thanatos had rushed to attack.

Ash's eyes had turned a deep, dark red. Darker than blood, they were filled with a swirling fire.

At the point where Thanatos would have attacked him, the invincible assassin disintegrated into dust.

No one had touched him.

Ash had stood there without moving, without flinching.

The lone Apollite had charged him then. Ash had whirled him around and trapped the man in his arms with his back to Ash's front. The Apollite had struggled for release, but Ash had held him effortlessly.

"Shh, Callyx," he'd breathed in the Apollite's ear. "Sleep . . ."

The Apollite collapsed.

Ash lowered him to the floor.

Shocked, Zarek didn't move as Ash approached him. He didn't know how Ash had known the Apollite's name or how he'd killed Thanatos so easily.

None of it made sense.

Ash didn't try to touch him. He squatted down beside him and cocked his head. "Are you all right?"

Zarek had ignored his question. "Why does Artemis want us dead?"

Ash had frowned at him. "What are you talking about?"

"The Spathis told me. She's creating an army to kill us. I was—"

Ash held his hand up. It felt as if something had paralyzed Zarek's vocal cords.

Indecision played across Ash's face as he stared at him. He swore he could feel the Atlantean in his mind, searching for something.

Finally Acheron sighed. "You've seen too much. Look at me, Zarek."

He had no choice but to obey.

Ash's eyes were once again their strange, swirling silver color. Everything became hazy then, dark. Zarek struggled against the oppressive heat.

The last thing he heard was Ash's voice. "Take him home, Simi. He needs to rest."

Simi released Zarek then.

He stood there motionless as her replay of the events that night filled in the sketchy details of his memory.

He was stunned by what he'd seen. What he'd learned.

"How did you show me all that?" he asked her.

The demon shrugged.

This was getting annoying. Damn Ash for giving her the order not to speak to him. "Astrid, please ask her my question."

Astrid did.

Simi looked at him as if he were dense. "Nothing ever goes away in the human mind. It just get misplaced, silly." She said to Astrid as she walked her fingers through his hair, "I just pulled the pieces out so I could see them and then he saw them too when he looked at me. Easy."

Numb from all he'd discovered, Zarek looked over to Astrid who was waiting patiently for them to finish.

"What is Acheron?" he asked her.

"I don't know," Astrid said.

Zarek stepped away, his mind whirling as he tried to remember New Orleans. "He did something with my mind again in New Orleans, didn't he?"

Simi whistled and looked around the room.

"Simi, did he?" Astrid asked.

"*Akri* only does it when he has to. There were some things in New Orleans that were bad. Things them Dark-Hunters and Olympian gods don't need to know about."

Zarek clenched his teeth. "Such as?"

Astrid repeated his question.

"I said none of you don't need to know."

He wanted to choke the demon, but after what he had just seen Ash do, he thought better of it. "Why does Acheron hide?"

Simi hissed at him and in her anger forgot Ash's order. "*Akri* hides from no one. He don't need to. Anyone hurt my *akri,* I eat them."

Zarek ignored her. "Is he human?" he asked Astrid.

Astrid let out a long breath. "I honestly don't know.

Whenever I have mentioned his name to my sisters, they become evasive and quiet. He alone seems to frighten them. I've always wondered why, but no one on Olympus will talk about him much. It's really very odd."

Her expression speculative, Astrid turned in the demon's direction. "Simi, tell me about Acheron."

"He's great and wonderful, and he treat me like a goddess. Goddess Simi. That's me."

Astrid winced a bit at that. "I mean, tell me about his birth."

"Oh, that. Acheron was born in 9548 B.C. on the Greek isle of Didymos."

"Who was he born to?"

"King Icarion and Queen Aara of Didymos and Lygos."

Zarek could tell that the answer surprised Astrid, but it didn't surprise him. He'd always suspected Ash was nobility. There was something inherently regal about him. Something that said, "I am the master, you the servant. Bow down and kiss my ass." It was why Zarek had never cared for him.

"Ash isn't a demigod?" Astrid asked.

Simi laughed uproariously at her question. "*Akri* a demigod? Puh-lease."

Zarek frowned as he realized what Simi had revealed. "Wait, I thought Ash was Atlantean?"

Astrid shook her head. "From the extremely rare rumors I've heard, they say he was born in Greece but raised in Atlantis. Rumor has it he's one of Zeus's sons. But like I said, most people are unwilling to say much of anything about him."

Simi laughed again. "Does he look like old thunder-butt? No. Son of Zeus? How many insults can my *akri* have?"

Zarek considered that for a minute, and then something else occurred to him. "Can Simi communicate with Ash right now?"

"Yes."

"Then tell him he'd better get his ass here and protect you."

Simi's eyes glared. Her wings flapped.

"Simi," Astrid said quickly. "He didn't mean it like that. Can Ash come here?"

She settled down a bit. "No. He promised the evil heifer goddess that he would stay on Olympus for two weeks. He can't break his oath."

"Then how do I kill Thanatos? I'm going to go out on a limb here and say Ash is the only one of us capable of just looking at him and making him go 'poof.' "

"Simi can kill him."

"No, I can't. *Akri* said so."

"Then how do we stop him?" Astrid asked.

Simi shrugged. "If *akri* would let me, I could barbecue him, but since you don't breathe fire it might be kind of hard for you to do that."

"I have a flamethrower."

Astrid snapped her head toward him. "You have a what?" she asked incredulously.

It was his turn to shrug. "It pays to be prepared."

"Well," Simi said. "Those are nice for toasting marshmallows, but they'll only make Thanatos mad. Regular fire won't hurt him. I have this really neat gelatinous goo that comes out with my fire and it squirts my victims so that it don't come off. Wanna see it?"

"No!" they said in unison.

Simi stiffened. "No? I don't like that word."

"We love you, Simi," Astrid said quickly. "We're just scared of your goo."

Astrid hit Zarek in the stomach as he started to correct her about loving Simi.

"Oh," Simi said, "that I understand. Okay, you can live."

After ascertaining that there really was no food there, Simi sat cross-legged on the floor. She hummed to herself as she twirled a strand of hair around her little finger. "So, you got QVC?"

"Afraid not, sweetie," Astrid said.

"You got Soap Net?"

Zarek shook his head.

"You got any TV?" Simi continued in a voice that sounded like a petulant toddler's.

"Sorry."

"Are you kidding?" Simi rested her chin in her hand and looked up at him. "You boring people. A demon needs her cable. *Akri* done tricked me. He didn't tell me I'd have to go without cable. Don't you even have one of those itty-bitty TVs that has batteries?"

Yeah and on that note, he pulled Astrid away from Simi.

"It won't work," she whispered.

"What?"

"Pulling me away so she won't hear. She hears everything."

He stopped. "Well, then, she's in for an earful."

Zarek stood there looking at Astrid. Memorizing every line of her face, every curve of her body.

He didn't know what to do to protect her. Jess couldn't come get her in the daylight and he didn't trust the Squires to get her to safety, either.

Not to mention the idea of letting them know of his hideout while they were out to kill him themselves didn't seem like a brilliant move either.

There was no one to trust and the only way he knew to protect Astrid was to call Thanatos out and finish this.

Tonight, he would find Thanatos and one of them would die.

It was something he didn't want to tell Astrid. She wouldn't let him go if she knew.

"Look, we'll need food tonight. I'm going to leave you and Simi here where it's safe and I'll go scout supplies."

"Why not send Simi? Nothing can hurt her."

Zarek slid his glance over to the demon, who was playing This Little Piggy on her bare toes.

"Yes, but I don't think she should be let out on her own, do you?"

Astrid hesitated. "You may be right."

Zarek sank to the floor and pulled her down with him. He checked his watch to see that it was less than two hours to sundown.

Less than two hours to be with the woman who had come to mean so much to him.

Lying down, he closed his eyes as she laid her head on his chest and traced circles over him.

"Tell me something good, princess. Tell me what you'll do when this is over."

Astrid stopped moving her hand in circles as she thought about that. What she wanted was to stay with Zarek. But how?

Artemis would have to let him go and she knew her cousin well enough to know Artemis didn't share her toys.

"I'll miss you, Prince Charming."

She felt him tense at that. "Will you really?"

"Yes, I will. What about you?"

"I'll survive. I always do."

Yes, he did. In ways that astounded her.

Astrid traced the line of his jaw. "You should be resting."

"I don't want to rest. I just want to feel you for a little while."

She smiled at that.

"Are you two going to kiss?" Simi asked. "Maybe I should go upstairs or something."

Astrid laughed. "It's okay, Simi. We won't kiss in front of you."

"Does she sleep?" Zarek asked.

"I don't know. Simi, do you sleep?"

"Yes, I do. I have a lovely bed, too. It got dragons carved on it and this big old ivory-colored canopy over the top. *Akri* had it special made for me long time ago and it has a windup dancer on the headboard. When I was a baby demon, *akri* would wind it up after he tucked me into bed and I used to watch it until I went to sleep. Sometimes he would sing lullabies to me, too. *Akri* a good daddy. He takes good care of his Simi."

"What about you, princess?" Zarek asked. "Did your mother tuck you in as a child?"

"Every night, unless she was judging someone and then my sister Atty would."

Astrid didn't ask Zarek who tucked him in. She already knew the answer to that.

No one.

She snuggled closer to him.

Zarek stared up at the jagged top of the tunnel. Funny how more than fifty years ago he'd dug this part of it never knowing that one day he would lie here with a lover by his side.

Astrid.

He had no business being with her. No right to touch her.

She was as close to heaven as a man like him was ever going to get.

And yet he didn't want to give her up. Not now.

Not ever.

She was the one person in all of history he would die for.

No doubt tonight he would.

Chapter 14

Thanatos lay on a warm, comfortable bed in the house of a Spathi warrior. The Spathi, like the Spathi's family members (both Daimons and Apollites), were all asleep in their bedrooms, waiting for sundown when it would be safe to go out.

After he had lost Zarek's trail last night, Thanatos had searched until exhaustion overtook him.

The Daimons had brought him back here to rest, and though he was still tired, he couldn't sleep anymore. Not while his nightmares racked him.

He could feel the call of the Oracles trying to summon him back to his cage in Tartarus.

He refused to heel.

For nine hundred years he'd been waiting for this. Waiting for his vengeance.

The day Artemis had created him, she had promised him that he would be able to kill Zarek of Moesia. Then for some unknown reason, she had changed their bargain.

Nothing had gone the way she had said.

Instead of living in wealth and comfort, he had been confined to a tiny cell, forgotten and alone.

"No one can ever know you're alive," she'd told him. "At least not until I need you."

And so he had waited. Year after year, century after century, screaming at the goddess to either let him out or kill him.

She'd never answered.

And he'd learned that there were some things worse than the short life span that terrified his Apollite kin.

Immortality in a dark hole was far worse.

He would not go back. No one would ever cage him again. He would tear down the whole of Olympus first.

Artemis had been so afraid of her Dark-Hunters running amok that she hadn't thought ahead. There was no one who could stop *him*.

Something flickered through his mind. A fragment of a memory.

He saw himself as an Apollite . . . saw . . .

The image changed to that of Zarek killing his wife.

Thanatos roared with anger.

No, killing Zarek was too easy.

He wanted the man to suffer just the way he had.

Suffer.

Pain . . .

For the first time in nine hundred years, he smiled. Yes. Zarek had protected a woman last night. He had cradled her against him on the snowmachine.

His woman.

Thanatos rose to his feet and shrugged his coat on. Even though he was exhausted, he wouldn't try to sleep any longer. He dressed quickly, quietly.

He would find the Dark-Hunter. Find his woman.

She would die, but Zarek . . . he would live. Just as Thanatos had. In eternal pain, aching for his love who was lost.

Zarek paused as he looked down at Astrid, who had fallen asleep while they'd been talking.

Talking.

He'd never thought to really do that with anyone. But then, he'd done a lot of things with her that he had never thought to experience.

Even asleep she looked tired. Her sweet eyes had circles underneath them.

He placed a kiss on her lips, and moved away so as not to disturb her.

The demon lay on the floor where she had been sitting. She was also sound asleep. One arm was curled under her head while the other hand was tucked under her chin. She reminded him of a little girl. No wonder Ash liked her.

He glanced back at Astrid. His strength.

His weakness.

Simi was Ash's.

And he had responsibility for both of them.

Feeling the full weight of that burden, Zarek grabbed an extra blanket and covered the demon.

She smiled in her sleep and said very softly, "Thank you, *akri*."

Zarek looked longingly at his coat, which was still underneath Astrid.

He took another blanket over to her and covered her, too. Reaching into his pocket, he pulled out the small items he'd collected when he'd ventured into his cabin a few minutes before to get food for Simi.

He set them beside Astrid and placed her hand over them so that she could "see" what they were when she awoke.

He let his hand linger on her face.

"I'll miss you," he breathed, knowing that even after he became a Shade she would torment him.

After all, he needed her more than he needed food or air.

She was his life.

Taking a deep breath, he ran his fingers through her hair,

letting it warm him. He imagined her fiery and soft in his arms. The way she looked when she came for him.

The way her voice sounded whenever she said his name.

Yes, he would definitely miss her.

It was why he had to keep her safe.

Forcing himself away from the comfort she offered, he left the two women.

He went to the end of the tunnel that led out into the woods.

Armed with as much firepower as he could carry, he opened the trapdoor, shivered as the cold air rushed over him, and left to find Thanatos.

Astrid jerked awake when a strange sound invaded her sleep.

"I like that Zarek. He quality people!"

She blinked her eyes open as she recognized Simi's voice. Astrid started to move until she felt something underneath her hand.

Some of Zarek's figurines lay there, and as she traced the lines of them with her fingers, she realized what they were.

Each one was a character from *The Little Prince*. There were six of them in all: the little prince himself, the sheep, the elephant, the rose, the fox, and the snake.

They were exquisite pieces that had been given even more attention to detail than the others she'd "seen."

"He even gave me a can opener so I don't have to use my fangs. I like that. Metal is hard on the teeth." Simi smacked her lips. "Pork and beans popsicle. Yummy! My favorite."

"Simi?" Astrid said, sitting up. "Where is Zarek?"

"I don't know. I woke up a few minutes ago and found this yummy food he left for me."

"Zarek?" Astrid called.

He didn't answer.

Of course, for him, that was typical.

"Simi, is he in the cabin?"

"I don't know."

"Would you please go see?"

"Zarek!" Simi shouted.

"Simi, I could have done that."

The demon gave a heavy, irritated sigh. "Okay, but don't let my beans thaw out." She paused, then added, "*Akri* said to protect you, Astrid, not to fetch for you. Zarek a big Dark-Hunter and he can walk about on his own."

Astrid felt the demon vanish.

After a few minutes she came back. "Nope, he not there, neither."

Astrid's heart pounded.

Maybe he had just gone for more food.

"Did he leave a note, Simi?"

"Nope."

Zarek kicked open the door to the first Apollite house he reached. The small community of Apollites had been here for several decades now on the outskirts of Fairbanks, but he'd left them alone.

Dark-Hunter Code forbade any Hunter from harming an Apollite until they turned into Daimons who fed off humans. So long as they kept to themselves and didn't harm humans and lived out their lives until they died at twenty-seven, they were afforded the same protection as any human being.

It was why, at least according to Simi, Zarek had been banished. To Artemis and the gods, killing an Apollite was as serious a crime as killing a human.

But at the moment, Zarek would gladly break that law and any other to keep Astrid safe.

As soon as the door crashed open, the female occupants of the house screamed and ran for cover while the men rushed him.

Zarek used his telekinesis to pin them to the walls.

"Don't even try it," he snarled at them. "I'm in no mood to deal with you. I'm here for Thanatos."

"He's not here," one of the men said.

"I figured as much. But then, I also figure you can get word to him. Can you?"

"No."

"He's going to kill us," a child's voice cried out from the rear of the house.

The fear in the child's tone calmed him, but only a bit.

Zarek released the Apollites he had pinned. "Tell Thanatos that if he wants me, I'll be waiting for him outside of town in Bear's Hollow. If he's not there in an hour, I'm coming back here and cleaning out the Daimons I can feel."

He turned and walked out the door.

Zarek paused a short distance away from them.

They bolted the door behind him and whispered among themselves until they had decided who should go fetch Thanatos.

Satisfied they would deliver his message, Zarek smirked and headed toward his snowmachine.

Getting on, he drove to the rendezvous and sat back to wait.

He pulled out Spawn's cell phone and called Jess.

The Cowboy answered on the third ring. "Hey, Eskimo, is that you?"

"Yeah, it's me. Listen, I left Astrid at my cabin."

"You did what? Are you—"

"Yes, I am insane, but they're safe where they are. I want you to wait for about three hours and then go get her. That should give me enough time."

"Enough time for what?"

"Don't worry about it. Enter my cabin and tell Astrid who you are. She'll be coming out of hiding with another woman. Be kind to the little one, she belongs to Ash."

"What little one?"

"You'll see."

"In three hours?" Jess repeated.

"Yeah."

Jess paused for a few seconds. "What about you, Eskimo?"

"What about me?"

"You're not doing something stupid, are you?"

"No. I'm doing something smart." Zarek hung up.

He tossed the phone into his backpack and pulled out his cigarettes and lighter. He lit up a cigarette while he waited and sat in the frigid cold missing his coat.

But as he thought of the coat, his thoughts turned to Astrid and he warmed up considerably.

How he wished he could have made love to her one more time.

Felt her skin on his. Her breath on his face. Her hands running over his flesh.

He'd never known anything or anyone like her, but then, she was a nymph after all. Wholly unlike anyone else in all the universe.

He still couldn't believe the way he felt about her.

How was she able to soothe the pain in him that he had thought would never cease.

Strange how she took his thoughts away from the past. Away from everything.

No wonder Talon had been willing to die for Sunshine.

It made total sense to him now.

But Zarek didn't want to die for Astrid. He wanted to live for her. He wanted to spend the rest of his immortality by her side.

He couldn't.

Looking up at the mountains around him, he thought of Olympus. Astrid's home.

Mortals couldn't live there and gods didn't live on earth.

It was hopeless between them.

And he was pragmatic enough to know it. There was no starry-eyed side of him to think for one minute anything could unite them. Any optimism he'd ever felt had been kicked out of him before he was old enough to shave.

Still, he couldn't stop the part of him that ached with loss. The part of him that screamed out soul deep for Astrid to stay with him.

"Damn you, Fates. Damn all of you."

But then, they had. Long, long ago.

He heard the rumble of a snowmachine's engine approaching.

Zarek didn't move until it drew near and stopped. He sat sideways on his seat with his legs stretched out before him, his ankles crossed. His arms folded over his chest, he waited patiently for the rider to dismount.

Thanatos pulled his helmet off and eyed him as if he couldn't believe what he was seeing. "You really are here."

Zarek inclined his head and offered the creature a cold, sinister smirk. "Hair of the dog, baby. Sooner or later, we all dance with the devil. Tonight, it's your turn."

Thanatos narrowed his eyes. "You are an arrogant bastard."

Zarek dropped his cigarette to the ground and crushed it out underneath his boot heel. He laughed bitterly as he pushed himself away from his snowmachine.

"No, not an arrogant bastard. I'm nothing but a piece of shit who touched a star." He pulled both Glocks out from his shoulder holsters. "Now I'm the son of a bitch who's going to put you out of your misery."

Zarek opened fire.

He didn't expect it to work and he was right.

It did nothing more than make Thanatos stumble back. And make Zarek feel a little better.

He ejected the clips into the snow, reloaded and fired again.

Thanatos laughed. "You can't kill me with a gun."

"I know, but it's fun as hell just shooting you." And with any luck, it might weaken Thanatos enough to where Zarek could stand some chance of killing him.

It was all he had.

When he'd spent his last round, he threw his weapons at Thanatos and followed it up with two grenades.

None of it worked.

It barely made Thanatos pause.

Growling, Zarek rushed him.

They fell to the ground fighting. Zarek kicked and punched with everything he had.

Thanatos was getting bloodier, but then, so was he.

"You can't kill me, Dark-Hunter."

"If you bleed, you can die."

Thanatos shook his head. "That's only a myth humans tell each other to feel better."

Zarek kicked him back and unsheathed his retractable sword. He pressed the button in the hilt, extending it out to its full five-foot length. "Dark-Hunters are myths too but if you cut our heads off, we die. What about you? Can you reattach your head?"

He saw panic flicker in the Daimon's eyes.

"I didn't think so." Zarek arced the blade up.

Thanatos ducked and twirled away from him. He pulled a large, ornamental dagger from his belt.

Zarek's sword skills were a bit rusty, but as they fought, his memory came back to him.

Oh, yeah, he remembered well how to skewer things.

He cut Thanatos across the chest. The Daimon hissed and stumbled back.

"You look afraid, Thanatos."

He curled his lips. "I fear nothing, least of all you."

Thanatos attacked him before he could pull back. He

caught Zarek's sword arm and twisted it. Zarek hissed as pain sliced through him.

But that was nothing compared to the stab wound Thanatos delivered to his left arm.

He cursed.

His arm numb, Zarek couldn't hold on to the sword.

Thanatos knocked him to the ground.

He put his knee on Zarek's spine and pulled his hair until his neck was exposed.

Zarek tried to buck him off, but there was nothing he could do except wait for Thanatos to cut his head off.

The dagger's blade cut into his neck.

Zarek held his breath, afraid to move lest he help the blade slice his throat.

Just as the blade cut into his neck, a blast of light flared across the snow, hitting Thanatos and knocking him back.

Zarek collapsed facedown in the snow.

"No, no, no," Simi said as she appeared in human form beside Zarek. "*Akri* said you can't kill Zarek. Bad Thanatos."

His body aching beyond belief, Zarek rolled over onto his back as Thanatos rose to his feet.

"What the hell are you?" Thanatos asked.

"Never you mind," she said, kneeling beside Zarek. She touched the cut on his brow and looked at his bleeding arm and neck. "Oh, no, you hurt bad, Dark-Hunter. Simi very sorry. We thought you'd come back but then Astrid got worried and made me come seek you. You don't look very good, though. You were much more attractive earlier."

Thanatos stalked toward them.

Zarek forced himself up and helped her to her feet. "Simi, go before you get hurt."

She snorted like a horse. "He can't hurt me. No one can."

Thanatos attacked with the dagger.

"See, watch." Simi turned around and let Thanatos stab her in the chest.

He sank the dagger in up to the hilt, then jerked it free.

The demon's eyes widened as she gasped in pain.

At first Zarek thought she might be playing until she staggered back. Tears were in her eyes as she looked up at Zarek in agonized disbelief.

"It's not supposed to hurt," she cried like a small child. "I'm invincible. *Akri* said so."

His heart pounded.

Blood trickled from her lips.

Zarek kicked Thanatos back and picked Simi up in his arms. Even though his injured arm trembled from the agony of it, he ran with Simi toward his snowmachine.

Thanatos stood back, waiting.

He watched them leave and smiled. "That's it, Zarek. Run back to your woman. Show me where you have her hidden."

Artemis felt the shock wave go through her temple like an earthquake. Something let out an angry, baleful roar.

Her attendants looked up, their faces white.

Artemis sat up on her throne. If she didn't know better she would think . . .

The door to her private chambers disintegrated. Pieces of it flew through the room as if propelled by a violent tornado.

Her women screamed and ran for the door that led outside, seeking shelter from the unexpected maelstrom. Artemis wanted to run, too, but her fear held her immobile.

It was extremely rare that she saw this side of Acheron.

She was too terrified of him to ever push him this far.

He floated out of her bedroom with his long black hair whipping around him. His eyes were blood-red, swirling like fire as his unnatural powers surged. His fangs were over-grown and large.

He was the very thing she feared most in the universe. In this state, he could kill her with nothing more than a passing thought.

She panicked. If she didn't get him calmed down the other gods would feel his presence and there would be hell to pay for everyone.

Most of all for her.

She used her powers to mask his, hoping to disguise his abilities as her own. With any luck, the other gods would assume she was having her own tantrum.

"Acheron?"

He cursed at her in Atlantean and held her back with an invisible wall. She felt his agony. He was in excruciating pain, but she didn't know why.

Everything in her temple whirled in the vortex of his powers and rage. The only thing still grounded were the two of them.

"Artemis? I have a problem."

She flinched as she heard Astrid's voice in her head. "Not now, Astrid. I have a situation here."

"Let me guess, Acheron is angry?"

"I am past anger, Astrid." His voice was low, deep, and evil sounding. Acheron's bloody gaze pierced Artemis. "How is it Simi is wounded?"

Artemis's fear tripled. "The demon's hurt?"

"Simi's dying." Astrid and Acheron spoke simultaneously.

Artemis covered her mouth. She felt suddenly ill. Sick. Horrified and scared beyond belief.

If anything happened to his demon . . .

He would kill her.

Acheron used his powers to pull her roughly to him. "Where did Thanatos get one of my daggers, Artemis?"

A tremor of guilt went through her with that question. When she had created the first Thanatos seven thousand years ago, she had granted him weapons to slay the Dark-Hunters. At the time she had thought it divine justice that he use one of Acheron's Atlantean daggers to kill them.

As soon as Acheron had realized a dagger was missing, he had gathered all his weapons together and destroyed them.

Now she understood why.

He'd done it to protect his demon.

"I didn't know your dagger would hurt it."

"Damn you, Artemis. You have taken everything from me. Everything!"

She felt his pain, his sorrow. She hated him for that. If she died tomorrow he wouldn't care at all.

But for the demon, he wept.

Why wouldn't he love and protect her like this?

"I'll go get it for you, Acheron."

Acheron stopped her from leaving his side. "Don't you do anything, Artemis. I know you. You're not to help or try to heal her in any way. You just pick her up and bring her right back here to me. Swear it on the River Styx."

"I swear."

He released her.

Artemis shimmered from her temple to where Astrid, Simi, and Zarek were hiding underground. The demon lay on the floor with Zarek and Astrid kneeling beside it.

"I want *akri!*" Simi sobbed. She was screaming and crying hysterically.

"Shh," Zarek said, soothing her. He held a tourniquet over her wound. Both the tourniquet and his hand were covered in blood. "You have to calm down, Simi. You're making it worse."

"I want my daddy! Take me home, Astrid. I need to go home now."

"I can't, Simi. That power is taken from me until I deliver a verdict to my mother."

"I want *akri,*" she wailed again. "I don't want to die without him. I'm scared. Please, please take me home. I just want my daddy."

Zarek looked up as a shadow fell over them.

It was a face he hadn't seen since the day he'd become a Dark-Hunter.

Artemis.

Her long auburn hair curled around her lithe, beautiful body. She wore a long, white dress and her green eyes glittered ominously in the dim light of the tunnel.

He held his breath, half-expecting her to kill him. No Dark-Hunter was ever allowed to be in the presence of a god.

Simi saw her and let out a terrible shriek. "Not her! The heifer goddess is going to kill me!"

"Shut up," Artemis snapped. "Believe me, I'd love to see you dead but if you die, I'll never hear the end of it."

Artemis picked her up in spite of her struggles.

She looked at Astrid and Zarek. "Have you judged him yet?"

Before Astrid could answer, the trapdoor behind them burst open.

Zarek cursed as he saw Thanatos coming through it.

He turned to order Artemis to take Astrid with Simi, but she'd already vanished.

He, alone, had to protect her.

Damn Artemis for this!

"Run!" he shouted at Astrid. He urged her toward the trapdoor that led into his cabin.

"What's happening?"

"Thanatos is here so unless you've got some god power that can kill him, run!"

"Where's Artemis?"

"She vaporized."

Astrid gave a disgusted look, then did as he said.

As Zarek helped her up, Thanatos reached them.

Zarek kicked him back.

"You're not going to escape me, Dark-Hunter. But then, it's not really you I'm after."

His blood running cold at those words, Zarek glanced down to see Thanatos's gaze locked on Astrid.

Thanatos licked his lips. "Vengeance is a dish best served cold."

Once Astrid was clear of the basement, Zarek dropped back down the ladder and began to pummel Thanatos. "We're in Alaska, dickhead. Here everything is cold."

Zarek slammed him back into the wall, then made a dash for the trapdoor.

Once he was in the cabin, he shut and locked the trapdoor. Zarek slid the wood-burning stove over it, then reached inside to remove the mink and her kits. The mother bit the crap out of him, but he didn't flinch.

As gently as he could, he put them in his backpack and rushed from the cabin.

Astrid was just outside his door.

"Zarek, is that you?"

He kissed her.

"That better be you."

He snorted at that.

With no time to waste, he raced over to Thanatos's snow-machine and ripped a hose from it. He led Astrid to his vehicle. "You have to get out of here, princess. My powers can't contain him for long."

"I can't see to drive this thing."

Zarek stared at her, memorizing her face. Memorizing the way she looked up under the moonlight that was spilling through the clouds.

She was beautiful, his star.

Unlike any in all the universe.

He heard Thanatos breaking free.

Then he did something he had never done before. It was a power Ash had shown him centuries before, but one he'd never had a use for.

Tonight he did.

He kissed her passionately.

Astrid felt the warmth of Zarek's lips. As his tongue danced with hers, her eyes started to burn.

She pulled back from him, hissing, only to realize that she could see everything around her.

Her heart stopped.

Zarek stood in front of her, his eyes the pale, pale blue hers were whenever she lost her vision. His lips were swollen and bruised, one of his eyes was black and blue.

Dried blood was crusted around his nose and ear. His clothes were also torn and bloodied.

He had been beaten to a pulp and had never uttered a word to her about it.

She choked as she saw the blood that was still pouring down his arm from where Thanatos had stabbed him.

He handed her his backpack, then fumbled with the snowmachine until he had it started.

"Go, Astrid. Fairbanks is straight that way." He pointed down a pathway through the woods. "Don't stop until you get there."

"What about you?"

"Don't worry about me."

"Zarek!" she snapped. "I won't leave you here to die."

He offered her a sad smile as he cupped her face in his hands. "It's okay, princess. I don't mind dying for you."

He kissed her lightly on the lips.

Thanatos burst through the cabin door.

"Get on the snowmachine, Zarek. Now!"

He shook his head. "It's better this way, Astrid. If I'm dead he won't have a reason to hurt you."

Her heart shattered at his words. At the sacrifice he was willing to make for her.

She started to protest, but the snowmachine took off. She tried to brake it, but Zarek must have been using his powers to keep the gas on.

The last thing she saw was a blind Zarek turning around to face Thanatos.

Ash grabbed Simi from Artemis the instant she materialized in front of him.

He cradled his "baby" gently in his arms as he took her to Artemis's bed.

"Akri!" Simi wailed, nuzzling against his chest. "The Simi is hurt. You told me I couldn't get hurt."

"I know, Sim, I know." He held her close, half-afraid to pull back her makeshift bandage and see the damage done to her.

Her tears fell down her cheeks, making his own eyes well up. Out of habit, he started singing to her, an ancient Atlantean lullaby he used to sing to her when she was barely more than a hatchling.

She calmed a bit.

Ash wiped the tears from her cold cheeks, then pulled the cloth away.

His dagger had sliced through her, narrowly missing her heart, but the wound was clean and the blood flow had slowed. Thanks to Zarek, no doubt.

He owed the man more than he could ever repay.

Summoning his powers, Ash laid his hand over her wound and healed her injury.

Simi glanced around, then she looked at him. "Simi better?"

He nodded and smiled. "Simi all better."

Simi looked at her chest. She pulled her shirt up and

looked underneath it, too, as if to verify to herself that she was okay.

Laughing, she threw herself into his arms.

Ash held her, grateful beyond measure that she hadn't died.

He held her close until she whined for him to let her go.

Kissing her brow, he released her. "Return to me, Simi."

For once, she didn't argue. In dragon form, she placed herself over his heart.

It was where she belonged.

Turning slowly, Ash faced Artemis.

In a pique, she stood with her hands on her hips and her body tensed. "Oh, come on, you're not still mad. I did the right thing. I brought it back to you."

"Her!" he barked, making her jump. "Simi isn't an it, Artemis. She's a *her* and I want for once to hear you say *her* name."

She stuck her chin out defiantly. Narrowing her green eyes, she forced herself to say, "Simi."

He inclined his head in approval. "As for the right thing . . . no, Artie. The right thing would have been to not steal from me. The right thing would have been to listen to me when I told you not to create another Thanatos. What you did today was the smart thing. Because of that, I'm not going to do the wrong thing and kill you. But Thanatos is another matter."

"You can't leave here to kill him."

"I don't have to leave here to kill him."

"You bastard!" Thanatos roared as he knocked Zarek aside.

Zarek tried to push himself to his feet, but his body no longer responded.

There was no part of him that didn't hurt. Didn't ache.

He was still using his powers to keep the snowmachine going in the right direction.

Depleted, he had nothing left to fight with. Not to mention the fact that he couldn't see Thanatos anyway.

The blows seemed to come at him from every direction.

Just as they had when he'd been human.

Zarek laughed.

"What is so funny?"

Zarek lay in the snow, freezing and bleeding but continuing to laugh. "You. Me. Life in general, and the fact that I'm freezing my ass off as usual."

Thanatos viciously kicked his side. "You are psychotic."

Yes, he was. But most of all he was weary. Too tired to get up and move. Too tired to fight anymore.

He thought of Astrid.

Fight for her . . .

For once in his life, he had something to live for. A reason to pick his blind ass up and fight.

Squeezing his eyes shut he tried to summon up some of his faltering powers to use against the creature.

Zarek heard the sound of a dagger leaving its sheath.

"Zarek . . ." Ash's voice whispered in his mind.

Zarek flinched as his eyesight came back unexpectedly. "What the hell?"

Five shining claws appeared on his left hand.

Zarek smiled at the sight of them as he balled his hand into a fist and felt the sharp ends of his finger caps biting into his palm.

Ash had always known him just a little too well.

"There's a crescent moon between Thanatos's shoulder blades," Ash's voice whispered. *"Stab it and he's dead. Artemis never creates anything without an off switch."*

Zarek flipped himself up to stand.

Thanatos arched a surprised brow. "So you do have more fight in you."

"Looks like the devil just hiked his ass up to Alaska to see the snow. C'mon, punk, let's dance."

Zarek hit him, and Thanatos flew back.

It appeared Ash had given him more than his claws. Strength and power surged through him unlike anything he'd ever experienced before.

Zarek took a deep breath as all the pain he felt vanished.

Thanatos struck him across the face.

Zarek laughed as the pain came and went. It didn't even faze him.

Thanatos paled.

"Yeah, you should be scared." He knocked him back. "It sucks when you're not the baddest thing out here, huh?"

Zarek picked him up and tossed him.

Thanatos rolled in the snow. He tried to get up and fell back.

Zarek stalked him.

It was time to put an end to this.

He placed his foot on Thanatos's back to hold him down and ripped open his coat and shirt to reveal the crescent sign.

So Ash hadn't lied.

"You can kill me, Dark-Hunter, but it won't take away the fact you should die for killing Dirce. She was innocent and you slaughtered her."

Zarek hesitated. "Dirce?"

"Do you not even remember her?" Thanatos tensed in rage as he twisted to look up at him accusingly. "She was only twenty years old when you cut her down."

Zarek's thoughts flashed to what Simi had shown him in her eyes . . .

The blond woman Thanatos had impaled on his sword.

"She was yours?"

"My wife, you bastard."

Zarek stared at Thanatos's mark.

He should kill him.

But he couldn't.

Both of them had been screwed by the same person. Artemis.

And it wasn't fair that he should kill Thanatos for wanting revenge.

Vengeance was something he understood all too well. Hell, he'd sold his own soul for it. How could he fault Thanatos for doing the same?

Zarek heard the sound of a snowmachine headed back toward him.

He knew without looking that it was Astrid. No doubt she'd turned around the instant he'd been distracted by the fight.

He used the powers Ash had given him to bind Thanatos to the ground.

The Daimon screamed for release.

He screamed for death.

Zarek knew the sound of both. Many nights he'd lain awake doing the same thing.

If he were merciful, he would kill him. But that wasn't his job.

He was a Dark-Hunter, and Thanatos . . .

Zarek would leave him for Acheron to deal with.

Astrid parked the snowmachine and came running up to him.

Her eyes were a deeper blue now that she could see.

"Is he contained?"

He nodded.

She threw herself into his arms. Zarek stumbled backward.

"Easy, princess. The only reason I'm standing and not sitting is mere strength of will."

Astrid looked past Zarek and saw Thanatos on the ground, cursing both of them. "Why didn't you kill him?"

"Not my place. Besides, I'm through being Artemis's lapdog. It's time I told the 'heifer goddess' to get lost."

Astrid went pale. "You can't just leave, Zarek. She'll kill you."

He smiled grimly. "Let her try. I'm in the mood to fight." He snorted at that. "Then again, I'm always in the mood to fight."

Astrid held her breath at his words. They gave her hope. "What about us?" she asked.

For the first time she could see the anguish on his face as he looked at her, see the pain in his midnight eyes. "There is no us, princess. There never was."

Astrid opened her mouth to argue, but before she could, her mother appeared with Sasha, who was in his human form.

Astrid gave her a droll look. "You're a little late, Mom."

"Blame your sisters. Atty told me to stay put. I came as soon as she would let me."

Sasha curled his lip at Zarek who glared back at him.

"Sorry, Scooby, I'm all out of LivaSnaps."

Sasha curled his lips. "I really hate you."

Zarek gave him a matching sneer. "Feeling's entirely mutual."

Themis ignored the men as she addressed Astrid. "Have you judged him, daughter?"

"He's innocent." She pointed to Thanatos, who was still cursing them. "There's the proof of his mercy and humanity."

An ear-piercing shriek sounded. It was followed by total silence.

"What the hell was that?" Zarek asked.

"Artemis," Astrid said in unison with her mother and Sasha.

Themis sighed. "I wouldn't want to be in Acheron's place tonight."

"Why?" Zarek asked.

It was Sasha who answered. "Never piss off a goddess. There's no telling what she'll do to him for getting you off the hook."

Zarek felt ill as he remembered some of the things Acheron had said to him in the past that hinted at the fact Artemis took her anger out on him. "She doesn't really punish him?"

The looks on their faces gave him the truth.

Zarek winced as he remembered all the times Ash had asked him to make it easy on him. All the times he had told Ash to burn in hell.

Sasha made his way to Thanatos.

"What's to become of him?" Zarek asked.

Themis shrugged. "It's up to Artemis. He belongs to her."

Zarek sighed at that. "Maybe I should have killed him after all."

Astrid used her sleeve to blot at the blood on his face.

"No," her mother said. "What you did for Simi and my daughter along with the mercy you showed Thanatos is why I'm allowing her verdict to stand even though she violated her impartiality oath."

Astrid smiled up at him, but he didn't feel happy with the way things had turned out.

"Come, Astrid," her mother said. "We need to go home."

Zarek couldn't take his eyes off her as those words wedged into his heart like a knife.

Let her go . . .

He had to.

And yet every molecule of his body was screaming at him to keep her. To reach out and take her hand in his.

"Have you anything to say about that, Dark-Hunter?" her mother asked.

He did, but the words wouldn't come.

Zarek had been strong all his life. He would be strong tonight. He would never bind her to him. It wouldn't be right.

"Sometimes stars do fall to earth."

He heard Acheron's words in his mind. It was true. They

did and then they became commonplace like the rest of the dirt on the planet.

His star was one of a kind.

He would never allow her to be like any other. Never allow her to become common or sullied.

No, her place was in the sky. With her family.

With her stinking pet wolf.

Never with him.

"Have a nice life, princess."

Astrid's lips trembled. Her eyes were filled with unshed tears. "You too, Prince Charming."

Her mother took her hand while Sasha collected Thanatos. In the blink of an eye they vanished.

Everything was the way it had been before she came.

And yet nothing was the same.

Zarek stood in the middle of his yard alone. There was no wind. Everything was motionless.

Still.

Calm.

Everything except for his heart, which was breaking.

Astrid was gone.

It was for her own good.

So why did he feel so brokenhearted?

As Zarek hung his head, he noticed the blood that was dripping from his arm.

He'd best tend the wound before any bears or wolves caught its scent. Sighing, he went into his empty cabin, shut the door and bolted it. He crossed the room to his cupboard and opened it.

There was really no way to tend the wound here. Since his generator had never been delivered, the water had frozen in the cold and there was no heat to thaw anything out.

Even his peroxide was frozen solid.

Zarek cursed and put the peroxide back in his pantry,

then grabbed a bottle of vodka instead. It was slushy and thick, but still liquid.

He heard a faint ringing coming from outside. Going back out into his yard, he retrieved his backpack that Astrid had left. The mink and her kits were still inside and still cranky.

Ignoring them, Zarek pulled his phone out. "Yeah?" he said, answering it.

"It's Jess. I just got a call from Acheron telling me and Andy to go home. I wanted to check in with you first, make sure you were still alive."

Zarek took the mink and her kits into his house and set them back inside the safety of his stove. "Since I answered the phone, my guess is yes, I'm still living."

"Smart-ass. You still need me to come get Astrid?"

"No, she's . . ." He choked on the word. Clearing his throat, he forced it out. "She's gone."

"I'm sorry."

"For what?"

Silence hung between them.

After a few seconds, Jess spoke again. "By the way, did anyone ever tell you about Sharon? In all the commotion, I didn't have time."

Zarek paused, his hand on the stove. "What about her?"

"Thanatos hurt her trying to find you, but she'll be okay. Otto is going to stay up here for a few more days to make sure she gets a new house and has someone to take care of her when she comes home from the hospital. I just thought you'd want to know. I . . . uh . . . I sent her some flowers from you."

He let out a slow breath. It pained him that she'd been hurt and he hadn't even known. He ruined everything he touched. "Thanks, Jess. It was a kind thing you did for me. I appreciate it."

Something struck the phone's receiver. Hard. It caused Zarek's ear to ring.

"Excuse me?" Jess asked in disbelief. "This is Frozen Zarek I'm talking to, right? Not some weird pod person?"

He shook his head at Jess's joking. "It's me, dickless."

"Hey, now, that's way too personal. I don't need to know that much about you."

Zarek gave a halfhearted smile. "Shut up."

"All right, then. I'm going to head out and let Mike take my ass out of here while I still got some of it left unfrozen . . . Oh, hey, by the way, Spawn headed out a while back. Said to tell you not to worry about returning his phone. You know, he's not half-bad for an Apollite and he's not that far from here. Maybe you ought to call him sometime."

"You playing matchmaker?"

"Um, no. Definitely not, and again you're freaking me out with that entire train of thought. I've heard enough stories about you Greeks and all that. In fact, tell you what, forget I said anything at all about Spawn. I'm out of here. You take care, Z. I'll see you online."

Zarek hung up the phone and turned it off. Might as well. Jess was the only person who ever called him anyway.

He stood in the center of his cabin, aching so much that he could barely breathe.

Alone now, he needed Astrid in a way that defied his ability to comprehend. He wanted something of hers.

No, he *needed* something.

Sliding the stove aside, he went back to his tunnel where he could remember holding her. Down here in the darkness, he could pretend she was still with him.

If he closed his eyes, he could even pretend she was in his dreams.

But it wasn't her. Not really.

Zarek let out a ragged breath and picked his coat up from the ground. As he started to pull it on, he caught a whiff of roses.

Astrid.

He clutched the coat to his skin, burying his face deep in the fur so that he could capture her scent.

He held it in trembling hands as emotions and memories crashed through him, racking him.

He needed her.

Oh, gods, he loved her. He loved her more than he'd ever imagined possible. He remembered every touch she'd given him. Every laugh she'd had around him.

The way she'd made him human.

And he didn't want to live without her. Not for one moment. Not a single one.

Zarek fell to his knees, unable to deal with the thought of never seeing her again.

Holding his coat that smelled of her, he wept.

Ash pulled away from Zarek, giving him privacy to grieve.

Artemis was outside in the temple courtyard, having one of her screaming tantrums over the verdict while he was alone in her throne room with Simi safe on his chest.

"What fools these mortals be," he breathed.

But then he too had been a fool for love. Love made fools of everyone. Gods and man alike.

Still, he couldn't believe Zarek had let Astrid go any more than he could believe Astrid had left.

Och mensch!

Artemis materialized before him. "How is this possible?" she railed. "Never in the entire history of her life has she judged a man innocent!"

He looked at her calmly. "Only because she's never before judged an innocent man."

"I hate you!"

He laughed bitterly at that. "Oh, please don't get my hopes up. You almost gave me a hard-on with that thought. At least tell me this time your hatred will last more than five minutes."

She tried to slap him, but he caught her hand. So instead she kissed him, then tore away from his lips shrieking.

Ash shook his head as she vanished again.

She would calm down in time. She always did.

But he had other things to worry about at the moment.

Closing his eyes, he breached the distance between Olympus and the human world.

There he found what he was looking for.

Zarek jerked his head up to find himself in the middle of a white and gold room. It was huge, with a gold-domed ceiling embossed with wildlife scenes. The room was encircled with white marble columns and in the center sat a large ivory settee.

What surprised him most was to see Acheron standing in front of the settee, staring at him with those strange swirling silver eyes.

The Atlantean had long, golden-blond hair and looked strangely vulnerable—which for Acheron was an impossibility. He was dressed in a pair of tight black leather pants and wore a long-sleeved black silk shirt that had been left unbuttoned.

"Thank you for Simi," Acheron said, inclining his head toward him. "I appreciate what you did for her when she was wounded."

Zarek cleared his throat, rose to his feet, and aimed an angry glare at Acheron. "Why did you fuck with my head?"

"I had to. There are some things people are better off not knowing."

"You let me think I had killed my own people."

"Would the truth have been any easier on you? Instead of the old crone's face, you would have been haunted by the face of a young woman and her husband. Not to mention you would have had the knowledge to kill any Dark-Hunter who got in your way, including Valerius, and had you done that, I wouldn't have been able to save you. Ever."

Zarek flinched at the mention of his brother. As much as he hated to admit it, Ash was right. He might very well have used his knowledge to kill Valerius. "You have no right to play with people's minds."

Acheron's agreement stunned him. "No, I don't. And believe it or not, I seldom do. But that's not why you're really mad, now is it?"

Zarek tensed. "I don't know what you mean."

"Yes you do, Z." He closed his eyes and cocked his head as if listening to something. "I know every thought inside you. Just as I did that night you slaughtered the Apollites and Daimons after Taberleigh. I tried to give you peace of mind by eliminating your memories, but you wouldn't take it. I couldn't stop your dreams and M'Adoc wouldn't help. For that I apologize. But right now you have a much bigger problem than what I did to you when I tried to help."

"Yeah? What's that?"

Acheron held his hand up and projected an image from his palm.

Zarek's breath caught as he saw Astrid weeping. She sat in a small atrium with three other women who were holding her as she cried.

He walked toward the image, only to remember he couldn't really touch it.

"It hurts so much," she sobbed.

"Atty, do something!" a blond woman said, looking at the redheaded woman who appeared to be the eldest. "Go kill him for hurting her."

"No," Astrid wailed. "Don't you dare. I'll never forgive you if you hurt him."

"Who are those women with her?" Zarek asked.

"The three Fates. Atty, or Atropos, is the one with red hair. Clotho is the one with blond hair holding Astrid, and the dark-headed one is Lachesis, or Lacy."

Zarek stared at them, his heart breaking at the pain he'd caused Astrid. The last thing he had ever wanted was to hurt her. "Why are you showing me this?"

Acheron answered his question with one of his own. "Do you remember what I said to you in New Orleans?"

Zarek looked at him wryly. "You said a lot of shit to me then."

So Acheron repeated it. "'The past is dead, Z. Tomorrow will become whatever decision you make.'"

Acheron's gaze burned into him. "With Dionysus's help you blew it that night in New Orleans when you attacked the cops, but you bought yourself another chance when you saved Sunshine." Ash indicated Astrid. "You have another crucial choice here, Z. What will you decide?"

Acheron closed his hand and the image of Astrid and her sisters vanished. "Everyone deserves to be loved, Zarek. Even you."

"Shut up!" he snarled. "You don't know what you're talking about, *Your Highness*." Zarek spat the title out. He was so sick of people lecturing him when they were ignorant of what he'd been through.

It was easy for someone like Acheron to tell him about love. What did a prince know about people hating him? Despising him?

When had anyone ever spat on the Atlantean?

But Acheron didn't speak.

At least not with words.

Instead, an image came into Zarek's mind. One of a blond teenager in chains in the middle of an ancient Greek home. The boy was bloody while being beaten.

He was begging those around him for mercy.

Zarek's breath caught as he recognized the youth . . .

"I understand you in a way no one else can," Acheron said quietly. "You have a rare chance, Z. Don't fuck it up."

For the first time ever, he listened to Acheron. And he looked on him with a newfound respect.

They were far more alike than he could have guessed and he wondered how Acheron had found the humanity that had abandoned Zarek so long ago.

"What if I hurt her?" Zarek asked.

"Do you plan on hurting her?"

"No, but I can't live here and she—"

"Why don't you ask her, Z?"

"What about her mother?"

"What about her? You were willing to fight Artemis for Thanatos. Isn't Astrid worth just as much?"

"More." He met Ash's gaze with fired determination. "Where is she?"

Before Zarek could blink, he found himself in the atrium Acheron had shown him.

Atty looked up with a hiss. "No man is allowed here!"

The one Acheron had called Clotho started to attack him. But she pulled up sharply as Acheron appeared beside him.

Zarek ignored them as he concentrated on Astrid who sat there with tears in her eyes, staring at him as if he were an apparition.

His heart pounding, he walked over to her and knelt down before her chair.

"Stars aren't supposed to cry," he whispered so that only she could hear him. "They're supposed to laugh."

"How can I laugh when I have no heart?"

He took her hand into his and kissed the tip of every finger. "You have a heart." He placed her hand over his. "One that only beats for you, princess."

She offered him a trembling smile. "Why are you here, Zarek?"

He brushed the tears from her cheeks. "I'm here to collect my rose, if she'll come home with me."

"Don't even go there," Atty cried. "Astrid, please don't tell me you're going to listen to that drivel?"

"He's a man, baby sister," Lacy chimed in. "If his lips are moving, he's lying."

"Why don't the three of you stay out of this?" Acheron said.

Atty stiffened. "Excuse me? We're the Fates and—"

A sideways glare from Acheron cut her off midstream.

"Why don't we leave them alone?" Atty said to her sisters. The three of them hurried off while Acheron watched Zarek and Astrid with his arms folded over his chest.

Zarek still hadn't taken his gaze off Astrid. "You going to be a voyeur, Ash?"

"Depends. You going to give me something to look at?"

"If you keep standing there, I am." He looked over his shoulder then.

Acheron inclined his head to him and turned around to leave. As he did so, the breeze caught a portion of his shirt and blew it back, showing a flash of one shoulder.

Zarek started at the red welts it revealed. Welts he knew from experience came from a whip.

"Wait!" Astrid said, stopping Acheron. "What about Zarek's soul?"

Acheron stiffened ever so slightly before he called out, "Artemis?"

She shimmered in beside him.

"What?" she snarled back.

He nodded toward them. "Astrid wants Zarek's soul."

"Oh, like I care, and what is *he* doing here anyway?" She narrowed her eyes at Astrid. "You should know better than to bring him here."

Ash cleared his throat. "I brought Zarek here."

"Oh." Artemis calmed instantly. "Why did you do that?"

"Because they belong together." He smiled ironically. "It's *fated*."

Artemis rolled her eyes. "Don't even go there."

Astrid came to her feet. "I want Zarek's soul, Artemis. Return it to him."

"I don't have it."

They were all stunned by her words.

"What do you mean you don't have it?" Acheron asked, his tone sharp and angry. "Don't tell me you lost it."

"Of course not." She looked over at Zarek and Astrid, and if Zarek didn't know better, he'd say she looked embarrassed. "I never really took it."

All three of them stared at her in disbelief.

"Come again?" Ash asked.

Artemis curled her lip as she looked at Zarek. "I couldn't take it. That would have involved my touching him and he was disgusting back then." She shuddered. "There was no way I would have put my hand on him. He smelled."

Open-mouthed, Acheron looked at Zarek. "You lucky bastard." Then he turned back to Artemis. "If you didn't touch him, how has he been an immortal Dark-Hunter all this time?"

Artemis gave him a haughty sneer. "You don't know everything after all, now do you, Acheron?"

He took a step toward her and she squeaked, putting more distance between them.

"I injected him with ichor," she said quickly.

Zarek was stunned. Ichor was a mineral found in the blood of the gods that was said to make them immortal.

"What about his Dark-Hunter powers?" Acheron asked.

"Those I gave to him separately, along with the fangs and such so that you wouldn't realize he wasn't like the others."

Acheron gave her a tired, repugnant stare. "Oh, I know I'm going to hate the answer for this one. But I have to know. What about the sunshine, Artemis? Since he has his soul my guess is he was never banished from daylight, was he?"

The look on her face confirmed it.

"You bitch!" Zarek snarled, rushing toward her.

To his surprise, it was Acheron who stopped him from reaching her.

"Let me go. I want to rip her throat out!"

Astrid pulled him back. "Leave her alone, Zarek. She has her own problems."

Zarek hissed at Artemis, baring his fangs.

Fangs that instantly vanished.

Zarek ran his tongue over his human teeth.

"A gift," Acheron said.

Zarek calmed a degree and then even more when he realized Astrid had her arms wrapped around his waist. Her front was tight against his back so that he could feel her breasts against his spine.

Closing his eyes, he savored the feel of her.

"You are free of Artemis, Zarek," Astrid said in his ear. "You've been judged innocent and you're immortal. Tell me, what do you want to do with the rest of eternity?"

"I want to go lie on the beach someplace warm."

Astrid's heart caught at his words. She'd foolishly thought he would say something about her.

"I see."

"But most of all," he said, turning in her arms to face her, "I want to piss off everyone."

"Everyone?" she asked, her heart breaking even more.

"Yeah," he said, granting her a rare smile. "The way I figure it, if I leave you, only me and you are unhappy. If I take you with me, everyone but us is pissed, especially that mangy thing you call a wolf. That has serious appeal for me."

She arched a brow at that. "If you're trying to woo me with that one, Prince Charming, you've—"

He stopped her words with a kiss so supreme that her toes curled. Her heart pounded.

Zarek nipped her lips, then pulled back to stare down at her. "Come away with me, Astrid."

"Why should I?"

His gaze burned into hers. "Because I love you, and even if I'm lying on the sun itself I'll be freezing there without you. I need my star so that I can hear laughter."

Laughing with excitement, she gave him an "Eskimo" kiss. "Bora Bora, here we come."

Zarek finished her words off with a real kiss.

A really *l-o-n-g* one.

Chapter 15

Ash opened the door to the small, cramped cell where Thanatos was kept.

Part of him wanted the man's blood for Bjorn's life, which Thanatos had taken, and for the people he had hurt. Most of all, he wanted his blood for Simi and her newfound fear.

But part of him understood why Thanatos had gone mad.

He too possessed a degree of insanity. It was what had kept him alive these last eleven thousand years.

Thanatos looked up as he entered, his face pale and tormented. "Who are you?"

Ash stepped aside so that the light from outside could illuminate the poor man on the floor. "Just call me the final fate. I've come to you to grant you peace, little brother."

"You're going to kill me?"

Ash shook his head as he reached down and pulled his dagger from the sheath at Thanatos's waist. He held it up and looked at the ancient etchings that covered the blade. Like all Atlantean daggers, this one was wavy from the hilt to the point. The cross hilt was solid gold and held a large ruby at its center.

It was the dagger of a long dead people who were more myth than real. Such a treasure as this was beyond value.

In the hands of the wrong person this weapon could do more than just hurt Simi. It could destroy the very world.

A surge of rage tore through him. At times, it was next to impossible not to kill Artemis.

But that wasn't his place. Like it or not, he was here to protect her, even from her own stupidity.

Ash summoned his Atlantean powers and used them to dissolve the dagger into nothingness.

No one would ever hurt his Simi again.

And no one would destroy the world. Not while he was here to guard it.

He extended his hand to Thanatos. "Stand up, Callyx. I have a choice for you."

"How do you know my name?"

Ash waited until he had taken his hand before he pulled him to his feet and answered his question. "I know everything about you and I'm very sorry for what you lost. I'm even sorrier that I couldn't stop it."

"It was the Thanatos powers, wasn't it?" he said quietly. "The other Thanatos killed my wife, not Zarek."

Ash nodded. He had tried to erase Callyx's memory all those centuries before, but Artemis had returned the memory to the Apollite so that she could turn him into her servant.

"The humans have an old saying. Absolute power destroys absolutely."

"No," Callyx whispered. "Absolute vengeance does that."

Ash was glad to see some clarity had come to the Apollite while he'd been banished to this nether hell.

"You said you had a choice for me?" Callyx asked hesitantly.

"I have worked a bargain so that you can either be set loose in the Elysian Fields for your eternal rest or I can place you alive at your current age in Cincinnati, Ohio."

Callyx frowned. "What is Cincinnati, Ohio?"

"It's a nice city in a country called America."

"Why would I want to go there?"

"Because there's a sophomore student at Ohio State University who's majoring in dance that I think you might want to meet." Ash opened his hand and showed him a picture of the girl. She was lovely, with long blond hair and big blue eyes, and stood in a circle of friends after class.

"Dirce," Callyx breathed, his voice breaking on her name.

"Actually, she's now Allison Grant. A human woman."

Callyx's eyes were tortured as he met Ash's gaze. "But I would be an Apollite, damned to die in just a few years."

He shook his head slightly. "If you choose to be with her, you'll be human, too. You won't remember anything about being Callyx or Thanatos. In your world there won't be any such thing as Daimons or Apollites. No Dark-Hunters or ancient gods. You'll be completely ignorant of all this."

"Then how will I find her if I don't remember who I am?"

Ash closed his hand so that Dirce was no longer visible. "I will make sure you find her. I swear it. You'll be a student there yourself."

"And family?"

"You'll be an orphan whose rich uncle Ash died and made you the sole heir to his estate. Neither one of you will ever want for anything as long as you live."

Callyx's lips trembled. "You would do that for me even though I killed one of your men?"

Ash's jaw flexed at the mention of Bjorn. "Forgiveness is the better part of valor."

"I always thought it was 'discretion.' "

Ash shook his head. "Discretion is easy. It's finding the courage to forgive yourself and others that is hard."

Callyx thought about that in silence for several minutes. "You're a wise man."

Ash gave a half-laugh at that. "Not really. So, have you decided?"

Callyx's gaze burned into his before he spoke the answer Ash knew he would. "There's no choice. How can I know paradise without Dirce? I want to go to Cincinnati."

"I thought you might feel that way."

Stepping back, Ash granted Callyx his wish.

Alone in Thanatos's cell, Ash glanced around the dark, dank walls and fought down his own demons. Artemis had had no right to condemn him to this.

One day she was going to get her comeuppance.

But first there was the matter of Dionysus to attend to. The next time the god of wine wanted to let loose one of Artemis's pets on Ash's men, he would think twice.

He also had a few other people to take care of. There was still the small matter of deleting from Jess, Syra, and the Squires the information about the bow-and-arrow mark.

No doubt he should delete it from Zarek as well, but he'd done enough damage to him.

Zarek wouldn't tell anyone and he had more important things to occupy himself with.

Besides, if everything turned out the way Ash knew it would, Zarek would learn a lot more interesting things about him and the Dark-Hunters than just the secret of their mark.

Artemis sat alone on her throne, toying with her pillows. Acheron had been gone a long time now and she was beginning to worry.

He couldn't leave Olympus, but he could do other things . . .

Things that could get her into a great deal of trouble if Zeus ever learned of them.

Maybe she had been foolish to let him have an afternoon of freedom on her mountain.

Just as she was ready to go find him, the doors of her temple opened.

She smiled at the sight of Acheron striding through them.

Her Acheron was gorgeous.

His long blond hair flowed around his shoulders and the black leather pants hugged a body that had been created for seduction. A body made to please others.

The doors closed behind him.

Her body warm, she pushed herself up in sweet expectation. She recognized the feral look in his eyes.

The raw, unadulterated hunger.

Desire flowed thick and heavy through her veins as she felt the moisture suddenly pooling between her legs.

This was the Acheron she loved best.

The predator. The one who took what he wanted and didn't negotiate.

His clothes dissolved from his body as he neared her.

So did her own

She shivered at the magnitude of his powers. Powers that made a mockery of hers.

He'd gone too long without feeding. They both knew it. Whenever he reached a certain point, his compassion died and he became amoral and unfeeling.

He'd reached that point.

She moaned as he grabbed her and pulled her close to his hard, muscular body. His erection burned against her hip.

"What do you want, Acheron?" she asked, but her breathlessness betrayed her affected nonchalance.

His hot gaze swept her naked body, making her burn even more. "You know what I want," he said hoarsely in Atlantean. "After all I'm the top of the Food Chain and you . . . you're the Food."

His eyes flashed to red as he parted her thighs.

Artemis groaned and came as soon as he masterfully entered her. Her head swimming, she held him close, running her hands over his smooth, muscled back as he thrust himself deep inside her over and over again in a pounding rhythm that made her dizzy.

Yes, this was what she wanted. This was the Acheron she had fallen in love with. The man she would defy even the very gods to keep.

The man for whom she had broken every rule so that she could bind him to her forever.

He made love to her furiously, his hunger building and firing her own.

Artemis leaned her head to the side waiting for what she knew was coming.

Acheron's eyes swirled like red fire an instant before he lowered himself and sank his teeth into her neck so that he could feed from her.

Artemis cried out as they came in unison. As his powers coursed through her, blinding her to everything except the powerful feel of him inside her.

She could pretend to rule him all she wanted to, but at the end of the day she knew the truth.

He ruled her.

And she hated him for that.

Epilogue

BORA BORA

Zarek lay on the beach letting the sun and hot wind sear his skin. Oh, the feel of it!

They had been here for close to a month now and still he couldn't get enough of being on the beach.

Of being with Astrid, night and day.

He felt something cold fall on his chest.

Opening his eyes, he saw Astrid above him, smiling down as she watched him. She held a small bowl in one hand and a glass in the other.

"Careful, princess, you know I hate it whenever something cold touches me."

She knelt down beside him, and set the bowl aside before wiping the drop of water off his chest, her touch more searing than the sun.

Her gaze traveled over his body, down to his swim shorts that now had a rather large bump in them.

She smiled wickedly at that. "You know, I remember watching a movie once . . ."

He was suspicious of the gleam in her eye. "Yeah?"

She pulled an ice cube from her glass and placed it in her mouth.

Zarek watched, transfixed by the sight of her licking it.

She pulled it out, then placed it on his skin.

"Astrid . . ."

"Shh," she said, circling his nipple until it was hard and firm. She blew her hot breath across it, causing him to swell even more. "You know what the best part is about being cold, don't you?"

"What?"

"Thawing you out."

Zarek moaned as she lowered her mouth to him and flicked her tongue back and forth over his nipple.

When she pulled back, he whimpered a small protest.

She ignored it and dodged his hands.

"Before I forget—" she said, playfully pushing his hands aside, "and if I keep doing this, I will forget—I have something for you."

Zarek leaned up on his elbows. "Please don't tell me Scooby's coming to visit."

She rolled her eyes at him. "No. Sasha is staying at Sanctuary in New Orleans for the time being. Since we've been staying at the beach he refuses to come 'see your naked ass' lest he go blind from it."

Zarek looked less than amused. "So what is it then?"

She handed him her bowl.

Zarek looked at the contents, which reminded him a bit of lemon Jell-O. "What is that?"

"Ambrosia. One bite of it and I can take you home with me to Olympus. Otherwise I have to leave you here in three days and go home alone."

"Why?"

She smoothed the frown from his forehead with her fingertips. "You know I can't live here on earth. I can only stay for a brief time. If you want to, you can stay and I'll come back when I can, but—"

He stopped her words with a kiss.

Zarek pulled back. "What will the others say when you show up with a slave by your side?"

"You're not a slave, Zarek, and I don't care what they say. Do you?"

He snorted at that. "Not at all."

She held the ambrosia up to his lips.

Zarek gave her a quick kiss, then ate the ambrosia and drank her nectar. He expected it to hurt or burn, but it went down just like the cotton candy she once gave him. The sweet, sugary taste dissolved instantly in his mouth.

"Is that it?" he asked suspiciously.

She nodded. "That's it. What? Were you expecting fireworks or something?"

"No, I only expect those when I make love to you."

"Aww," she breathed, rubbing her nose against his. "I love it when you talk nice to me."

Zarek kissed her hand, then started laughing as he thought over everything that had happened since he met her.

"What's so funny?" Astrid asked.

"I'm just thinking, here I am a slave who touched a star who then made him a demigod. I have to be the luckiest bastard who ever lived."

Her blue eyes burned into his. "Yes, you are, Prince Charming, and don't you ever forget it."

"Believe me, princess. I won't."